My Place

This edition has been adapted
for younger readers from the original text,
My Place (1987)

My Place

Sally Morgan

FREMANTLE PRESS

Some of the personal names included in this book
have been changed, or only first names included,
to protect the privacy of those concerned.

This edition first published 2020 by
FREMANTLE PRESS
25 Quarry Street, Fremantle WA 6160
www.fremantlepress.com.au

Original text first published by Fremantle Arts Centre Press, 1987.

Adaptation editor: Lu Sierra

Cover image: Sally Morgan *Women of the Earth* 1989
screenprint, printed in coloured inks, from multiple stencils;
printed image 40.6 (h) x 50.6 (w) cm; National Gallery of Australia, Canberra;
Gordon Darling Australasian Print Fund 1990; © Sally Morgan

Cover designer: Rebecca Mills

Printer: McPherson's Printing Group, Victoria, Australia

My Place
ISBN 9781925816761 (paperback)

 A catalogue record for this
book is available from the
National Library of Australia

Fremantle Press is supported by the State Government through the
Department of Local Government, Sport and Cultural Industries.

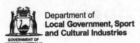

To My Family

How deprived we would have been if we
had been willing to let things stay as they were.
We would have survived, but not as a whole people.
We would never have known our place.

The hospital

The hospital again, and the echo of my reluctant feet through the long, empty corridors. I hated hospitals and hospital smells. I hated the bare boards that gleamed with newly applied polish, the dust-free window-sills, and the flashes of shiny chrome that snatched my distorted shape as we hurried past. I was a grubby five-year-old in an alien environment.

Sometimes I hated Dad for being sick and Mum for making me visit him. Mum only occasionally brought my younger sister and brother, Jill and Billy; my presence ensured no arguments. Mum was sick of arguments, sick and tired.

I sighed as we reached the end of the final corridor. The Doors were waiting for me again. Big, chunky doors with thick glass insets in the top. They swung on heavy brass hinges, and were covered in green linoleum. The linoleum had a swirl of white and the pattern reminded me of one of Mum's special rainbow cakes. She made them a cream colour with a swirl of pink and chocolate. I thought they were magic. There was no magic in The Doors, I knew what was behind them.

Sometimes, I pretended Dad wasn't really sick. I imagined that I'd walk through The Doors and he'd be smiling at me. 'Of course I'm not sick,' he'd say. 'Come and sit on my lap and talk to me.' And Mum would be there, laughing, and all of us would be happy.

Our entry into the ward never failed to be a major event. The men there had few visitors.

'Well, *look* who's here,' they called.

'I think she's gotten taller, what do ya reckon, Tom?'

'Fancy seeing you again, little girl.' I knew they weren't really surprised to see me; it was just a game they played.

After such an enthusiastic welcome, Mum would try and prompt me to talk. 'Say hello, darling,' she encouraged, as she gave me a quick dig in the back. My silences were embarrassing to Mum. She usually covered up for me by saying I was shy.

The men on the ward didn't give up easily. 'Come on, sweetie, come over here and talk to me,' one old man coaxed as he held out a Fantail toffee. My feet were glued to the floor. This man reminded me of a ghost. His close-cropped hair stood straight up, like short, white strands of toothbrush nylon. His right leg was missing below the knee, and his loose skin reminded me of a plucked chicken.

Mum had confided that all these men were Old Soldiers. They all had missing arms or legs. Dad was the only one who was all there.

Dad was standing in his usual spot, by the side of his bed. He never came forward to greet us or called out like the other men did, and yet we belonged to him. His dressing-gown hung so loosely around his lanky body that he reminded me of the wire coat-hangers Mum had hanging in the hall cupboard. Just a frame, that was Dad. The heart had gone out of him years ago.

Once Mum finished having a little talk and joke with the

men, we moved over to Dad's bed and then out onto the hospital verandah. The verandahs were the nicest place to sit; there were tables and chairs and you could look over the garden.

As Mum and Dad talked, I sniffed the air. It was a clear, blue spring day. I could smell the damp grass and feel the coolness of the breeze. It was such an optimistically beautiful day I felt like crying. Spring was always an emotional experience for me. It was for Nan, too. Only yesterday, she'd awakened me early to view her latest discovery.

'Sally ... wake up ...' Even as I dreamt, I wondered where that voice was coming from. It was faint, yet persistent, like the glow of a torch on a misty night. I didn't want to wake up. I burrowed deeper under the mound of coats and blankets piled on top of me. I wrapped my hands around my feet in an attempt to warm them.

Every night I'd call out, '*Mum ... I'm freezing!!*'

'Sally, you can't possibly be.' It was often her third trip to my bedside. She'd lift up the coat I'd pulled over my head and say, 'If I put any more on you, you'll suffocate. The others don't want all these coats on them.' I shared a bed with my brother Billy and my sister Jill. They never felt the cold.

Nan had only to add, 'It's a terrible thing to be cold, Glad,' for Mum to acquiesce and pull out more coats hanging in the hall cupboard.

Now, sitting on the hospital verandah, I smiled as I remembered the way Nan had rocked my sleepy body back and forth in an attempt to wake me up. It took a few minutes, but I finally came up for air and murmured dopily, 'Nan, do ya have to wake me so early?'

'Shhh, be quiet, you'll wake the others. Don't you remember? I said I'd wake you early so you could hear the bullfrog again, and the bird.'

The bullfrog and the bird — how could I have forgotten? For the whole week Dad had been in hospital, she'd talked of nothing else.

Nan encouraged me out by peeling back the layers on top of me. With sudden decision, I leapt from my bed and shivered my body into an old red jumper. Then, barefoot, I followed Nan out onto the back verandah.

'Sit still on the steps,' she told me. 'And be very quiet.' I was used to such warnings. I knew you never heard anything special unless you were very quiet.

The early morning was Nan's favourite time of the day, when she always made some new discovery in the garden. A fat bobtail goanna, snake tracks, crickets with unusual feelers, myriads of creatures who had, for their own unique reasons, chosen our particular yard to reside in.

I'd heard the bullfrog yesterday; it was one of Nan's favourite creatures. She dug up a smaller, motley brown frog as well, and, after I inspected it, she buried it back safe in the earth. I expected the bullfrog to be out again this morning; he'll come out any minute, I thought.

I felt excited, but it wasn't the thought of the bullfrog that excited me. This morning, I was waiting for the bird call. Nan called it her special bird; nobody had heard it but her. This morning, I was going to hear it, too.

'Broak, Broak!' The noise startled me. I smiled. That was the old bullfrog telling us he was broke again. I looked up at the sky; it was a cool, hazy blue with the promise of coming warmth.

Still no bird. I squirmed impatiently. Nan poked her stick in the dirt and said, 'It'll be here soon.' She spoke with certainty.

Suddenly, the yard filled with a high trilling sound. My eyes searched the trees. I couldn't see that bird, but his call was there. The music stopped as abruptly as it had begun.

Nan smiled at me, 'Did you hear him? Did you hear the bird call?'

'I heard him, Nan,' I whispered in awe.

What a magical moment it had been. I sighed. I was with Dad now, and there was no room for magic in hospitals. I peered back at Mum and Dad. They both seemed nervous. I wondered how long I'd been day-dreaming. Mum reached over and patted Dad's arm.

'How are you feeling, dear?'

'How do ya bloody well think!' It was a stupid question; he never got any better.

Dad's fingers began to curl and uncurl around the arms of his chair. He had slim hands for a man. I remembered someone saying once, 'Your father's a clever lad.' Was that where I got my ability to draw from? I'd never seen Dad draw or paint, but I'd seen a letter he'd written once; it was beautiful. I knew he'd have trouble writing anything now — his hands never stopped shaking. Sometimes, I even had to light his cigarettes for him.

My gaze moved from his hands, up the long length of his arms, to his face. It dawned on me then that he'd lost more weight. Dad caught my gaze; he was paler and the hollows under his cheekbones were more defined. Only the familiar hazel eyes were the same: confused, wet, and watching me.

'I'm making you something,' he said nervously. 'I'll go and get it.' He disappeared into the ward and returned a few minutes later with a small, blue leather shoulderbag. There was maroon thonging all the way around, except for the last part of the strap, which wasn't quite finished. As he laid it gently in my lap, Mum said brightly, 'Isn't Daddy clever to make that for you?' I stared at the bag. Mum interrupted my thoughts with, 'Don't you like it?'

I was trapped. I mumbled a reluctant yes, and let my gaze slip from the bag to the large expanse of green grass nearby. I wanted to run and fling myself on the grass. I wanted to shout, *'No!* I don't think Daddy's clever. *Anyone* could have made this bag. *He* doesn't think it's clever either!'

By the time I turned back, Mum and Dad were both looking off into the distance.

The visitors' bell rang unexpectedly. I wanted to leap up. Instead, I forced myself to sit still. I knew Mum wouldn't like it if I appeared too eager. Finally, Mum rose, and while she gave Dad a cheery goodbye, I slowly prised myself from my chair.

As we walked into the ward, the men called out.

'What? Leaving already?'

'You weren't here for long, little girl.'

They all made a great show of waving goodbye, and just as we passed through The Doors and into the empty corridor, a voice called, 'We'll be waiting for you next time, little girl.'

Strong, cool air blew through the window all the way home in the bus. I kept thinking, can a person be wrinkled inside? I had never heard adults talk about such a thing, but that's how I felt, as though my insides needed ironing. I pushed my face into the wind and felt it roar up my nostrils and down into my throat. I closed my eyes, relaxed and breathed out. And then, in a flash, I saw Dad's face. Those sad, silent eyes. I hadn't fooled him. He'd known what I'd been thinking.

Dad came home for a while a couple of weeks after that, and then, in the following January, 1957, Mum turned up on the doorstep with another baby. Her fourth. I was really cross with her. She showed me the white bundle and said, 'Isn't that a wonderful birthday present, Sally, to have your own little brother born on the same day as you?' I was disgusted. Fancy getting that for your birthday. And I couldn't understand Dad's attitude at all. He actually seemed pleased David had arrived!

The factory

Mum chattered cheerfully as she led me down the bitumen path, through the main entrance to the grey weatherboard and asbestos buildings. One look and I was convinced that, like The Hospital, it was a place dedicated to taking the spirit out of life.

After touring the toilets, we sat down on the bottom step of the verandah. I was certain Mum would never leave me in such a dreadful place, so I sat patiently, waiting for her to take me home.

'Have you got your sandwich and toiletbag?' she asked nervously when she realised I was staring at her.

'Yeah.'

Then, looking off into the distance, Mum said brightly, 'I'm sure you're going to love it here.'

Alarm bells. I knew that tone of voice. It was the one she always used whenever she spoke about Dad getting better. I knew there was no hope.

'You're gunna leave me here, aren't ya?'

Mum smiled guiltily. 'You'll love it here. Look at all the kids the same age as you. You'll make friends. All children have to go to school someday. You're growing up.'

'So what?'

'So, when you turn six, you have to go to school, that's the law. I couldn't keep you home, even if I wanted to. Now don't be silly, Sally. I'll stay with you till the bell goes.'

'What bell?'

'Oh … they ring a bell when it's time for you to line up to go into your class. And later on, they ring a bell when it's time for you to leave.'

'So I'm gunna spend all day listenin' for bells?'

'Sally,' Mum reasoned in an exasperated kind of way, 'don't be like that. You'll learn here, and they'll teach you how to add up. You love stories, don't you? They'll tell you stories.'

Just then, a tall, middle-aged lady, with hair the colour and shape of macaroni, emerged from the first classroom in the block.

'May I have your attention please?' she said loudly. Everyone immediately stopped talking. 'My name is Miss Glazberg. The bell will be going shortly,' the tall lady informed the mothers, 'and when that happens I want you to instruct your children to line up in a straight line on the playground. I hope you heard that too, children, I will be checking to see who is the straightest. And I would appreciate it if the mothers would all move off quickly and quietly after the children have lined up. That way, I will have plenty of time to settle them down and get to know them.'

I glared at Mum. 'I'll come with you to the line,' she whispered.

The bell rang suddenly, loudly, terrifyingly. I clutched Mum's arm.

Slowly, she led me to where the other children were beginning to gather. She removed my hands from her arm but I grabbed onto the skirt of her dress. Some of the other mothers began moving off as instructed, waving as they went. One little boy in front of me started to cry. Suddenly, I wanted to cry, too.

'Come now, we can't have this,' said Miss Glazberg as she freed Mum's dress from my clutches. I kept my eyes down and grabbed onto another part of Mum.

'I have to go now, dear,' Mum said desperately.

Miss Glazberg wrenched my fingers from around Mum's thigh and said, 'Say goodbye to your mother.' It was too late; Mum had turned and fled to the safety of the verandah.

'*Mum!*' I screamed as she hobbled off. '*Come back!*'

Despite the urgings of Miss Glazberg to follow the rest of the children inside, I stood firmly rooted to the playground, screaming and clutching for security my plastic toiletbag and a Vegemite sandwich.

By the beginning of second term at school, I had learnt to read, and was the best reader in my class. Reading opened up new horizons for me, but it also created a hunger that school couldn't satisfy. Miss Glazberg could see no reason for me to have a new book when the rest of the children in my class were still struggling with the old one. Every day I endured the same old adventures of Nip and Fluff, and every day I found my eyes drawn to the back of the class where a small library was kept.

I pestered Mum so much about my reading that she finally dug up the courage to ask my teacher if I could have a new book. It was very brave of her. I felt quite proud, as I knew she hated approaching my teacher about anything.

'I'm sorry, darling,' Mum told me that night. 'Your teacher said you'll be getting a new book in Grade Two.'

There weren't many books at our house, but there were plenty of old newspapers, and I started trying to read those. One day, I found Dad's plumbing manuals in a box in the laundry. I could work out some of the pictures, but the words were too difficult.

Towards the end of second term, Miss Glazberg told us there was going to be a night when all the parents came to school and looked at our work. Then, instead of our usual sheets of butcher's paper, she passed out clean, white rectangles that were flat on one side and shiny on the other. I gazed in awe at my paper; it was beautiful and crying out for a beautiful picture.

'Now children, I want you all to do your very best. It has to be a picture of your mother and father, and only the very best ones will be chosen for display on Parents' Night.'

There was no doubt in my mind that mine would be one of the chosen few. With great concentration and determination, I pored over my page, crayoning and detailing my parents. Suddenly, a hand tapped my shoulder and Miss Glazberg said, 'Let me see yours, Sally.' I sat back in my chair.

'Ooh, goodness me!' she muttered as she patted her heart. 'Oh no, dear, not like that. Definitely not like that!'

Before I could stop her, she picked up my page and walked quickly to her desk. I watched in dismay as my big-bosomed, large-nippled mother and well-equipped father disappeared with a scrunch into her personal bin. I was hurt and embarrassed. The children around me snickered. It hadn't occurred to me you were meant to draw your parents with their clothes on.

By the beginning of third term, I had developed an active

dislike of school. I was bored and lonely. Even though the other children talked to me, I found it difficult to respond.

I was allowed certain privileges now I was at school. The best one was being allowed to stay up later than the others and share Dad's tea. He loved seafood. He had a drinking mate with a boat, and if there was a good catch, crayfish came our way. Fleshy, white crayfish and tomato dipped in vinegar was Dad's favourite meal.

I knew some of Dad's tastes were a legacy of the war. That particular one was from the time Italian partisans had sheltered him from the Germans. Dad had told me about his friends Guiseppe and Maria, and their daughter Edema. He'd taught me to sing the Communist anthem in Italian. I thought I was very clever being able to sing in another language.

We had some good times, then. Some nights, Dad would hide chocolates in the deep pockets of his overalls and we were allowed to fish them out. Sometimes, he'd laugh and joke, and when he swore, we knew he didn't really mean it.

Dad slipped in and out of our lives. He was often in hospital for periods of a few days to a month or so, and the longest he was at home at one time was about three months; usually it was a lot less. When he first came home from hospital, he would be so doped up with drugs he wasn't able to communicate much. Then, he would seem to be all right for a while, but would rapidly deteriorate. He stayed in his room, drinking heavily, and didn't mix with us at all. And soon, he was back in hospital again.

Dad was a plumber by trade, but, when he was at home, he

was often out of work. Every time he returned from hospital, he had to try to find another job. Mum provided the only steady income from various part-time jobs, mostly cleaning.

When Dad was happy, I wanted him to be like that forever, but there was always the war. Just when things seemed to be looking up, it would intrude and overwhelm us. The war had never ended for Dad. He lived with it day and night. There were things in his head that wouldn't go away.

Part of the reason I was so unhappy at school was probably because I was worrying about what was happening at home. Sometimes, I was so tired I just wanted to lay my head on my desk and sleep. I only slept well at night when Dad was in hospital; there were no arguments then.

I kept a vigil when Mum and Dad argued; so did Nan. I made a secret pact with myself. Awake, I was my parents' guardian angel; asleep, my power was gone. I was worried that, one night, something terrible might happen and I wouldn't be awake to stop it.

Some nights I'd try and understand what they were arguing about; but, after a while, their voices became indistinguishable from one another, merging into angry abandon. It was then I resorted to my pillow. I pulled it down tightly over my head and tried to drown out the noise.

I was grateful Dad didn't belt Mum. Although, one night, he did push her and she fell. I squatted on the kitchen floor and peered around the door jamb to see what had happened. Mum just lay in a crumpled heap. I peered up at Dad; he was so tall he seemed to go on forever. He ran his hand back through his hair, looked down on me, and groaned. Swearing under his breath, he pushed roughly past Nan and staggered out to his room on the back verandah. I felt sorry for Dad — he hated himself.

Nan hurried into the hall and hovered over Mum, making sympathetic noises. Not words, just noises. I guess that's how I remember Nan all those early years — hovering, waiting for something to happen.

I'm in the army now

The following year, I was pleased Jill was starting school. I felt sure I would not be so lonely with her there.

As we walked to school that morning, I watched Jill curiously. She seemed neither excited nor daunted by the prospect of being away from home. I put her calmness down to ignorance, and felt sure that, once our walk led us within sight of school, Jill would break down.

Mum deposited me at the door of my new class, then, taking Jill's hand, she said, 'Come on, I'll show you the toilets.'

I watched as, a few minutes later, Jill emerged from her tour of the toilets.

'What do I do now?' she asked as she trotted up the verandah to me.

'Aah, ya have to wait for the bell. That's your class down there. Go and sit with Mum on the step. She'll stay with you till the bell goes, but she won't be here all day.'

'Okay.' I scanned her face. Poor kid, I thought, it hasn't sunk in yet.

Within a few minutes, the bell was ringing loudly. Mum waved and began moving off. I was shocked when Jill calmly took her place in the queue that was forming at the front of her class.

'Mum's going now!' I called out, but she was too busy chatting to the boy in front of her to reply.

I watched with a mixture of envy and surprise as she continued talking to the other children. They were all strangers to her, and yet she seemed to fit in, somehow. I knew then that, when it came to school, Jill and I would never agree.

My daydreaming was suddenly interrupted by a deep, grumbly voice calling, 'You girl, you with the long plaits, pay attention.' I'd been so busy watching Jill that I'd failed to notice my classmates had also formed a line.

My new teacher began slowly walking down the line, carefully inspecting each of her forty charges. 'Don't slouch. Stomach in, chest out, chin up!' She tapped my chin lightly with her wooden ruler.

We moved quietly into class and the presence of each one of us was duly recorded in the roll book. When that was finished, our teacher drew herself up to her full flat-chested height of five foot eleven inches and said, 'I … am Miss Roberts.' Apart from her pause after the word 'I', she spoke quickly and very, very clearly.

'Now children, I … am going to hand out some reading books. You will all remain as quiet as mice while *I*'m doing this.'

I smiled to myself. It wasn't going to be so terrible after all — my new book was on its way.

By the time she finally reached my desk, I was practically brimming over with excitement. She placed my book on my desk, and I couldn't help groaning out loud. It seemed that Dick, Dora, Nip and Fluff had somehow managed to graduate with me to Grade Two. I resigned myself to another year of boredom.

Towards the end of first term, I had an encounter with Miss Roberts that wiped out any confidence I might have had for the rest of the year.

Our school seats comprised a heavy metal frame with jarrah slats spaced across the seat and back. This proved unfortunate for me because, one day, after what seemed hours of holding my arm in the air trying to attract Miss Roberts' attention, I was unable to avoid wetting myself.

Miss Roberts had been intent on marking our latest tests and had failed to notice my desperately flailing arm. But one of the clean, shiny-haired, no-cavity girls next to me began to chant quietly, 'You've wet ya pa-ants, you've wet ya pa-ants!'

'I have not,' I denied hotly. 'It's just water under my chair.'

'Oh yeah, well then, how come you've dumped all those hankies on it?' She had me there.

By this time, most of the surrounding children were starting to giggle.

Miss Roberts raised her horn-rimmed eyes and said firmly, '*Quiet*, please!' She stared at us a few seconds longer, obviously waiting for her eagle-like gaze to have its usual effect. When the last giggle was giggled, she pushed back her solid wooden chair, breathed deeply and said, 'I … have an announcement to make.'

We were very impressed with Miss Roberts' use of the word 'I'. For the whole term, I had been convinced Miss Roberts was even more important than the headmistress.

'I … have finished marking your test papers.' We all waited anxiously to hear who had missed the mark this time.

'I … must commend you all on your efforts. All, except Rrrodney.' You'd think he was her favourite with the amount of attention she gave him. In fact, the opposite was true: Rodney could do nothing right.

'Rrrodney,' she continued, 'how many times have I told you bottom is spelt b-o-t-t-o-m *not* b-u-m!'

Rodney grinned, and we all snickered, but were instantly checked by Miss Roberts' look of disgust.

'Now,' she said, in a way that made us all straighten up and give full attention, 'where is Sally, hmmmn?' She peered around the class in an attempt to locate my nondescript brown face amongst a sea of forty knowing smiles. 'Oh, there you are, dear.' I had been cowering behind the girl in front of me, with my hands stuffed between my legs in an attempt to prevent further trickles.

'Sally has, for the *first* time this year, managed to complete her test correctly. In fact, this week she is the only one to have done so.' Pausing, she allowed time for the greatness of my achievement to sink in. Everyone knew what was coming next, and, mistaking the smothered raspberries and giggles for eagerness, she said, 'Well, come on Sally. Come out to the front and hold up your book. I ... can tell the class is anxious to see your work.'

Miss Roberts waited as I rose carefully to my feet. I hurriedly twisted the wet part of my dress around as far as I could, holding it tightly bunched in my left hand. With my knees locked together, and my left elbow jutting out at an unusual angle behind my back, I jerked spasmodically forward. Fortunately, Miss Roberts was gazing in amazement at my test book, and so was not confronted with the sight of my contorted body.

'I ... want you to hold it up to the class so they can all see it. Look how eager they are to see a test that has scored one hundred per cent!'

Clutching my book in my right hand, I leant as far from Miss Roberts as possible, lest she smell my condition.

My misshapen body must have alerted her to the fact that something was wrong, because she snapped impatiently, 'Hold the book with two hands! And put your dress down — we are not interested in seeing your pants!'

A wave of giggling swept over the class. As I patted down the full skirt of my blue cotton dress, Miss Roberts' large nostrils flared violently, and she snorted in disgust.

Grasping me by the elbow, she hauled me back to my desk and, pointing to the offending puddle, demanded, 'And *where* have all those handkerchiefs come from?' Flinging back the lid of my desk, she shrieked, 'Oh no! There are more in here!' I felt so embarrassed. It was obvious she didn't know what to attack first — my pile of dirty handkerchiefs nestled near my overflowing jar of pencil shavings, my collection of hardened orange peel, or my old apple core turned brown and on the brink of mould.

Shaking her head in disbelief, she muttered, 'You dirty, dirty girl.'

She dragged me back to the front of the class and shoved me out the door. 'Out you go. You are not to enter this class again. You sit out there and dry off!'

I sat alone and wet on the hard jarrah bench.

After that incident, my attitude towards school took an even more rapid downhill turn. I felt different from the other children in my class. They were the spick-and-span brigade, and I was the grubby offender.

Drinking men

Things at home weren't getting any better, either. Dad was drinking more than he was eating, and he was very thin.

He had stopped even trying to get work, and was in hospital more than he was at home. Gone were the days when he couldn't go past a pet shop window without buying half-a-dozen little chickens for us. He still lived in his favourite blue overalls, but he never hid tiny Nestle milk chocolates deep in his pockets any more. He only hid himself, now. When he was home, he never came out of his room. The only thing he seemed interested in was the pub.

Our local pub was called the Raffles. It was on the banks of the Swan River and had a Mediterranean outlook. There was a huge group of returned soldiers who drank there. It was like a club. Give Dad a few beers down the Raffles with his mates and he was soon in another world. He forgot about us and Mum, and became one of the boys.

We kids often went to the pub with Dad. While he enjoyed himself in the bar, we sat, bored and forgotten, in the car.

Summer was the worst. Dad always wound the windows up and locked what doors were lockable in case anyone should try to steal us. He forbade us ever to get out of the car. These precautions meant that on hot summer's nights we nearly suffocated.

One summer's evening, I could stand it no longer. Dad had been gone for ages, and I'd given up all hope of him returning with some bags of potato chips. Somehow, the sweet, clean smell of the Swan River managed to penetrate our glass and metal confines, beckoning me to come.

'Let's go play down the river,' I said suddenly. 'He won't notice we've gone.'

'We're supposed to stay in the car,' Jill said as she eyed me doubtfully. Two terms at school and she was a real stickler for convention.

'Look, Jill, he's forgotten about us again. I'm going whether you come or not.'

The thought of a paddle was too much for Billy, who leapt out with me. Jill followed, reluctantly. We wound our way quickly through the crowded carpark and down to the sandy foreshore. We splashed and laughed and built sandcastles decorated with bits of seaweed and stick.

Just as we were constructing an elaborate moat, a tall figure loomed above the beach.

'What the bloody hell are you kids doing down here? I told you to stay in the car.' Dad advanced menacingly, and we froze.

Suddenly, I yelled, 'Well what did ya expect us to do, sit in the car all night? You've been gone for ages *and* ya didn't give us any chips!' I stopped abruptly — where had my sudden bravery come from?

Fortunately, Dad was as surprised as me. He stopped and stood looking down at us. His gaze took in three haphazard sandcastles, and the beginning of an elaborate irrigation system.

Without another word, he ushered us quietly to the car and took us home.

My father's brothers were big drinkers too, and proud of it. The only one who seemed different was Uncle John; he was a lot younger than Dad, and we kids quite liked him. He always had a joke with us and never drank as much as the others.

Even apart from our relations, we seemed surrounded by drinking men. There wasn't one of Dad's mates who was a teetotaller. In fact, drinking seemed to be the main hobby of everyone we mixed with.

I suppose it's not surprising that I developed a keen interest in drinking and smoking at a young age. I was adept at rolling Dad's cigarettes and then passing them to him to light. I could pour a glass of beer with no head on it in a few seconds. Fortunately, it wasn't long before the taste of beer sickened me. I thought it tasted just the way I imagined urine to taste. And the fact that I'd heard some of Dad's mates refer to it as 'The Piss' only deepened my impression. I decided that that was one tradition I wasn't going to maintain.

Dad's family often came to our place for Christmas lunch. In the two days before Christmas, Mum and Nan cooked cakes and puddings, gave the house a real good clean, and prepared the stuffing for the chickens. I was really excited because we only ate chicken once a year, and I loved it.

On the twenty-fourth of December, Dad would stride to the chook shed armed with an axe. He always looked really determined, and I would sit and think that maybe this year he'd do it. About ten minutes would pass, and then he'd stride back again, with a clean axe and no chooks. He'd walk past me and hand the axe to Nan, who'd be patiently waiting on the back verandah. 'Jeez, I can't do it, Dais. You'll have to.'

It wasn't a task Nan relished. She had a special relationship with the birds and chooks we kept, but she knew we were too poor to be able to consider her finer feelings. Within a few minutes, she'd be back with two limp chooks and a bloody axe. 'Come on Sal, time to gut.'

She'd spread newspaper over an old table we had on the back verandah, and we'd set to work. I liked pulling out the feathers, because I was keen to collect them. Sometimes, to scare Jill, I'd thrust a bloodied arm in her direction, and she'd scream and run inside to Mum.

The day Uncle Frank entered our lives, I felt I'd found a kindred spirit. He just blew in out of nowhere one day and Dad was very pleased to see him.

'Oh, God,' Mum groaned as she eyed the brown paper bag tucked snugly under Frank's muscly arm. 'That's all Bill needs, more grog.'

I could tell by the gleam in Dad's eyes that, contrary to Mum's opinion, he thought it was exactly what he needed. Mum gave them both The Silent Treatment. She was sick of us mixing with drinking men.

'You kids go out the back and play,' she commanded as Dad and Frank plonked themselves on the front porch. 'He's got the most dreadful language,' Mum whispered to Nan, 'I don't want the children hearing talk like that.'

I sighed as I nipped down the back verandah steps, but then

ran around to the front of the house, where I happily joined the drinking men on the porch.

Within a few minutes, Frank had me totally fascinated. He used so many words I'd never heard before, and they all sounded exciting. I'd have given anything to be able to talk like Frank.

'Young lady,' said Frank as he drained his glass, 'do ya know this bastard saved my life during the war?'

'Give it a rest, Frank,' Dad groaned. I leaned forward eagerly in the hope that Frank would continue.

'Aah, yes, your father doesn't like me telling this story. I'm gunna tell ya!' Frank pointed his brown, calloused finger towards me.

'We were both poor bastards stuck on a POW transport bound for the camps, Italian job she was, when *Boom!* a bloody Pommy sub got us right up the Mediterranean! Jesus bloody Christ, I'll never forget that one. Anyhow, we stayed afloat and beached on the Greek coast. I couldn't move. I was wounded in the chest. I thought I'd cashed in me chips. Then ya know what happened?'

'No, what?' I whispered.

'This son-of-a-bitch,' he jerked his thumb towards Dad, 'heaved me over his shoulder, dragged me up to the top deck and got me to shore. Christ-All-Bloody-Mighty. I was no lightweight then, either. I made bloody sure I got a look at his face before I passed out. I wasn't going to forget a bastard like that in a hurry.' Frank threw back his tight, curly head and roared laughing.

'Jeez, Frank,' Dad said, 'you were so bloody I thought you were dead already!'

That made them both laugh. I thought they were very tough.

Why was I cursed with being a girl?

Frank visited regularly after that. I loved to hear him talk about all the crazy things that happened down on the Fremantle docks. He was always bringing us around something that had happened to drop out of a crate. I decided all his muscles must be due to all the crates he lifted. He had the biggest, brownest belly I'd ever seen. It was as tight as a drum.

I grew quite fond of Uncle Frank, but I never demonstrated my affection. Kissing Uncle Frank would have been like kissing a barnacle — he had a lot of rough edges.

Pretending

Nineteen fifty-nine, and another Milroy began school. Billy's initial reaction was similar to mine: he hated it. Every morning when we set off for school, Billy lagged behind, sobbing. Some days, he began his sobbing ritual so early that by the time we left, his face was red and puffy, and his nose snotty and snorting. These occasions were generally too much for Mum, who only let him get as far as our letterbox before calling him back.

Billy's unhappiness at school never spilled over into recess and lunchtime. He was the kind of boy other boys looked up to, so he was never short of a pal. Billy was the image of Dad and, when it came to mateship, exactly like him.

Nan had a soft spot for Billy, too. 'Let him have the day off, Glad,' she pleaded when Billy began his crying routine. 'The child's not well.'

To Billy's credit, he didn't look well. I attempted to copy his mournful look several times, but to no avail. I had to resort to more deceitful means.

I found that a light spattering of talcum powder, rubbed first into my hands and then patted lightly over my face, worked wonderfully well.

'I feel really sick in the stomach, Nan,' I groaned as she

gazed at my pale face. 'I think I'm gunna vomit.' Nan grabbed an empty saucepan and bent me over it. After emitting a few strangled noises, I straightened up and said, 'It's no use, it's gone down again.'

'Go and lie down,' Nan instructed. 'I'll send your mother in.'

Within a few minutes, Mum was standing by my bedside, looking extremely sceptical. 'Sally ... are you *really* sick?'

'I'm not puttin' it on, Mum, honest. I feel real crook.'

'All right,' Mum relented, 'you can stay home, but don't eat anything and stay in bed.'

Once Jill and Billy had left for school, and Mum had left for her part-time job in Boans' Floral Department, I called out to Nan, 'I'm feelin' a bit better, Nan. Do ya think I could eat something?'

Nan pottered in and said, 'Oooh, you still look white, Sally. I don't think you eat enough. You stay there and I'll bring in some toast and a hot cup of tea.'

After six or so rounds of toast and jam and a couple of mugs of tea, I said to Nan, 'Gee, it's stuffy in here, Nan.'

'Yes, it is. Go and sit outside. There's nothin' like a bit of fresh air when you're sick in the stomach.'

Nan only spoke to me after that to tell me when lunch was ready. I spent the rest of the day outdoors, playing all my usual games and climbing trees.

I was sitting on the back verandah step, inspecting the cache of small rocks I'd collected, when Mum returned home from her day at work. 'How's Sally?'

'Hmmph, she's all right,' Nan grumbled. And then, with a giggle, she added, 'Been sittin' in that tree all day.'

Mum wandered out. 'Another miraculous recovery, eh Sal?'

Apart from learning different ways to feign illness, there wasn't much to school that year. All my lessons seemed unrelated to real life. I often wondered how my teacher could be so interested in the sums I got wrong, and so uninterested in the games I played outside school, and whether Dad was home from hospital or not.

The best thing about school was that Grades Two and Three shared the same room, so this meant I saw more of Jill and we sat near one another.

It was early in Grade Three that I developed my infallible Look At The Lunch method for telling which part of Manning my classmates came from. I knew I came from the rough-and-tumble part, where there were teenage gangs called Bodgies and Widgies, and where hardly anyone looked after their garden. There was another part of Manning that, before I'd started school, I had been unaware of. The residents there preferred to call it Como. The houses were similar, only in better condition. The gardens were neat and tidy, and, I'd heard, there was carpet on the floors.

Children from Como always had totally different lunches to children from Manning. They had pieces of salad, chopped up and sealed in plastic containers. Their cake was wrapped neatly in grease-proof paper, and they had real cordial in a proper flask. There was a kid in our class whose parents were so wealthy that they gave him bacon sandwiches for lunch.

By contrast, kids from Manning drank from the water fountain and carried sticky jam sandwiches in brown paper bags.

In April that year, my youngest sister, Helen, was born. I found myself taking an interest in her because at least she had the good sense not to be born on my birthday. There were five of us now. I wondered how many more kids Mum was going to try and squeeze into the house.

Each year, our house seemed to get smaller. In my room, we had two single beds lashed together with a bit of rope and a big, double kapok mattress plonked on top. Jill, Billy and I slept in there, sometimes David too, and, more often than not, Nan as well. I loved that mattress. Whenever I lay on it, I imagined I was sinking into a bed of feathers, just like a fairy princess.

The kids at school were amazed to hear that I shared a bed with my brother and sister. I never told them about the times we'd squeezed five in that bed. All my classmates had their own beds; some of them even had their own rooms. I considered them disadvantaged. I couldn't explain the happy feeling of warm security I felt when we all snuggled in together.

Also, I found some of their attitudes to their brothers and sisters hard to understand. They didn't seem to really like one another, and you never caught them together at school. We were just the opposite. Billy, Jill and I always spoke in the playground and we often walked home together, too. We felt our family was the most important thing in the world. One of the girls in my class said accusingly one day, 'Aah, you lot stick like glue.' You're right, I thought, we do.

The kids at school had also begun asking us what country we came from. This puzzled me because, up until then, I'd thought we were the same as them. If we insisted that we came from Australia, they'd reply, 'Yeah, but what about ya parents? Bet they didn't come from Australia.'

One day, I tackled Mum about it as she washed the dishes.

'The kids at school want to know what country we come from. They reckon we're not Aussies. Are we Aussies, Mum?'

Mum was silent. Nan grunted in a cross sort of way, then got up from the table and walked outside.

'Come on, Mum, what are we?'

'What do the kids at school say?'

'Anything. Italian, Greek, Indian.'

'Tell them you're Indian.'

I got really excited, then. 'Are we really? Indian!' It sounded so exotic. 'When did we come here?' I added.

'A long time ago,' Mum replied. 'Now, no more questions. You just tell them you're Indian.'

It was good to finally have an answer, and it satisfied our playmates. They could quite believe we were Indian; they just didn't want us pretending we were Aussies when we weren't.

Only a dream

By the time I was eight-and-a-half, an ambulance parked out the front of our house was a neighbourhood tradition. It would come belting down our street with the siren blaring on and off and halt abruptly at our front gate. The ambulance officers knew just how to manage Dad; they were very firm, but gentle. Usually, Dad teetered out awkwardly by himself, with the officers on either side offering only token support. Other times, as when his left lung collapsed, he went out on a grey-blanketed stretcher.

Jill, Billy and I accepted his comings and goings with the innocent selfishness of children. We never doubted he'd be back.

Dad hated being in hospital; he reckoned the head shrinkers didn't have a clue. He got sick of being sedated. It was supposed to help him, but it never did.

I heard him telling Mum about how he'd woken up in hospital one night, screaming. He thought he'd been captured again. There was dirt in his mouth and a rifle butt in his back. He tried to get up, but he couldn't move. Next thing he knew, the night sister was flicking a torch in his eyes and saying, 'All tangled up again are we, Mr Milroy? It's only a dream. No need to upset yourself.'

Only a dream, I thought. I was just a kid, and I knew it wasn't a dream.

When Dad got really bad, and Mum and Nan feared the worst, our only way out was a midnight flit to Aunty Grace's house. Aunty Grace was a civilian widow who lived at the back of us. Nan had knocked out six pickets in the back fence so we could easily run from our yard to hers.

It often puzzled me that we only needed a sanctuary at night. I associated Dad's bad fits with the darkness and never realised that, by dusk, he'd be so tanked up with booze and drugs as to be just about completely irrational.

Many times, we were quietly woken in the dark and bundled off to Grace's house. 'Sally … wake up. Get out of bed, but be very quiet.'

'Aw, not again, Nan.' It had been a bad two weeks.

I walked quickly through the kitchen, scuttled across the verandah and into the shadows, where Mum was standing with the babies. She was rocking Helen to stop her from crying and David was leaning against her legs, half asleep. Nan shuffled down the steps with Billy and Jill, and we were on our way.

We followed the line of shadows to the rear of our yard. Just as we neared the gap in the back picket fence, Dad flung open the door of his sleep out and staggered onto the verandah, yelling abuse.

Oh no, I thought, he knows we're leaving. He's gunna come and get us! We all crouched down and hid behind some bushes. 'Stay low and be very quiet,' Mum whispered. I prayed Helen wouldn't cry. My heart was pounding.

For some reason, Dad stopped yelling and swearing. He

peered out into the darkness of the yard, and then he turned and shuffled back to his room.

'Now, kids!' Mum said. We didn't need to be told twice. With unusual speed, Billy, Jill and I darted through the gap in the fence. Within seconds, we were all grouped around Grace's wood stove, cooking toast and waiting for our cup of tea. I felt safe now.

We never stayed at Aunty Grace's long, just until Dad was back on an even keel. Prior to our return, I would be sent to negotiate with him. 'He'll listen to you,' they said. I don't think he ever did.

After my mother had bedded my brothers and sisters down on the floor of Grace's lounge, Nan walked me to the gap in the picket fence. After that, I was on my own. One night, I told Nan I didn't want to go, but she replied, 'You must, there's no one else.'

My father's room was the sleep out, and his light burnt all hours. I think he disliked the dark as much as I did.

I took up my usual position on the end of his bed and dangled my feet back and forth. The grey blanket I sat on was rough, and I plucked at it nervously. Dad sat with his shoulders hunched on his hard, narrow bed, surrounded by empties. His greased hair curled forward, one persistent lock dropping over his brow and partly obscuring three deep parallel wrinkles. When Dad smiled, his eyes crinkled at the corners. It was nice. He wasn't smiling now, though.

'Dad, we'll all come back if you'll be good,' I stated matter-of-factly.

He responded with his usual brief, wry smile, and then gave me his usual answer, 'I'll let you all come back as long as your grandmother doesn't.' He had a thing about Nan.

'You know we won't come back without her, Dad,' I said firmly. We both knew Mum would never agree. How would she cope with him on her own? And anyway, where would Nan go?

Dad ran his hand through his hair. He was thinking. Reaching behind his back and down the side of his bed, he pulled out three unopened packets of potato chips. Slowly, he placed them one by one in my lap. Suddenly my mouth was full of water.

'You can have them all,' he said quietly, 'if … you stay with me.'

Dad looked at me and I looked at the chips. They were a rare treat. I swallowed the water in my mouth and reluctantly handed them back. We both understood it was a bribe.

Deep down, he understood my decision. Reaching up, he opened the door and I walked out onto the verandah. Click! went the lock and I was alone.

I walked towards the outside door and stopped. Maybe if I waited for a while, he would call me back. Maybe he would say, 'Here, Sally, have some chips, anyway.' There was no harm in waiting. I squatted on the bare verandah. Time seemed to pass so slowly. I shuddered; the air was getting cooler and damper.

His bedroom door suddenly opened and light streamed out, illuminating my small hunched figure. Towering over me, Dad yelled, 'What the bloody hell do you think you're doing here? GET GOING!' and he pointed in the direction of Aunty Grace's house.

I shot down the three back steps and sped along the track that cut through our grass. I leapt through the gap in the back picket fence and, in no time at all, arrived panting at the door of Aunty Grace's laundry.

Mum and Nan always questioned me in detail about what Dad had said. They'd nod their heads seriously, as though everything I said was of great importance. Eventually, I'd go to bed, and the following day, we generally returned home. I guess Dad had slept it off.

A change

It was halfway through the second term of my fourth year at school that I suddenly discovered a friend. Our teacher began reading stories about Winnie the Pooh every Wednesday. From then on, I was never sick on Wednesdays.

In a way, discovering Pooh was my salvation. He made me feel more normal. I saw something of myself in him. Pooh lived in a world of his own and he believed in magic, the same as me. He wasn't particularly good at anything, but everyone loved him anyway. I was fascinated by the way he could make an adventure out of anything, even tracks in the snow. And while Pooh was obsessed with honey, I was obsessed with drawing.

When I couldn't find any paper or pencils, I would fish small pieces of charcoal from the fire, and tear strips off the paperbark tree in our yard and draw on that. I drew in the sand, on the footpath, the road, even on the walls when Mum wasn't looking. One day, a neighbour gave me a batch of oil paints left over from a stint in prison. I felt like a real artist.

My drawings were very personal. I hated anyone watching me draw. I didn't even like people seeing my drawings when they were finished. I drew for myself, not anyone else. One day, Mum asked me why I always drew sad things. I hadn't realised until then that my drawings were sad. I was shocked to see my feelings glaring up at me from the page. I became even more secretive about anything I drew after that.

Dad never took any interest in my drawings; he was completely enveloped in his own world. He never went to the pub now; we were too poor to be able to afford the petrol. There was never any money for toys, clothes, furniture, barely enough for food, but always enough for Dad's beer. Everything valuable had been hocked.

One day, Dad was so desperate that he raided our money-boxes. I'll never forget our dismay when Jill and I found our little tin moneyboxes had been opened with a can-opener and all our hard-won threepenny bits removed. What was even more upsetting was that he'd opened them at the bottom, and then placed them back on the shelf as though they'd never been tampered with. We kept putting our money in and he kept taking it out. I felt really hurt. If Dad had asked me, I'd have given him the contents willingly.

Dad hated being poor, and I could forgive him for that because I hated it myself. He loved the luxuries working-class people couldn't afford. If he had been able to, he would have given us anything. Instead, his craving for beer and his illness left us with nothing. I knew that Mum and Dad had had dreams once. It wasn't supposed to have turned out like this.

That year, Dad's love of luxuries really broke our budget, but it also gave us the status of being the first family in our street to have television.

We all rushed at him excitedly as he carried in an awkward-looking square on four pointy legs. 'Get out the bloody way, you kids,' he yelled, as he staggered into the hall and set the hallowed object down in the lounge room.

We lined up in awe behind Dad, waiting for our first glimpse of this modern-day miracle. We were disappointed. All we saw were white flecks darting across a grey screen, and all we heard was a buzzing noise. It was only after Mum and Dad had both banged the set several times that Dad realised the rental people had forgotten to leave the aerial.

We all went racing out the front, hoping the ute that had delivered our television set was still parked in the drive. 'Jesus Bloody Christ!' Dad swore as he gazed up the long length of empty road.

The aerial arrived the following day, but it never made the difference I imagined it would. Grey, human-like figures became discernible and their conversations with one another audible, but they didn't impress me. I had the feeling they weren't quite sure of whatever it was they were supposed to be doing.

In July, we had a surprise visit. We were all playing happily outside when Mum called us in. There was an urgency in her voice. What's going on? I thought. I peeped into Dad's room. He was lying down, reading an old paper.

When we reached the hall, I stopped dead in my tracks. Mum grinned at me and said, 'Well, say hello. These are your cousins.' As usual, my mouth had difficulty working. The small group of dark children stared at me. They seemed shy, too.

Just then, a very tall, dark man walked down and patted me on the head. He had the biggest smile I'd ever seen. 'This is Arthur,' Mum said proudly, 'he's Nanna's brother.' I stared at him in shock. I didn't know she had a brother.

Arthur returned to the lounge room and us kids all sat on the floor, giggling behind our hands and staring at one another. Mum slipped into the kitchen to make a cup of tea. I glimpsed her going into Dad's room. Then she returned, finished off the tea and dug out some biscuits. I helped pass them around.

Mum said very brightly to Arthur, 'He's asleep. Perhaps he'll wake up before you leave.' I knew she was lying, but I didn't understand why.

After a while, they all left. I was surprised to hear Arthur speak English. I thought maybe he could speak English and Indian, whereas the kids probably spoke only Indian.

I don't remember ever seeing them again while I was a child, but the image of their smiling faces lodged deep in my memory. I often wondered about them. I never said anything to Mum. I knew, instinctively, that if I asked about them, she wouldn't tell me anything.

Dad seemed to be getting sicker and sicker. By the time September came around, he had been in hospital more than he'd been home. At least he managed to return for Jill's birthday towards the end of September.

One morning a few weeks later, Dad emerged from his room early as we were just finishing breakfast. All the previous week, he'd been in hospital, so we were surprised by the cheery look on his face. Nan hovered near the table, intent on hurrying us along. She knew we'd seize on any pretext to miss school.

'Aw, let then stay home, Dais,' Dad said. 'I'll look after them.' Had I heard right? It wasn't like Dad to interfere with anything to do with us. I'd heard him call Nan 'Dais' before. It was his way of charming her.

Nan was as surprised as me. She flicked her dirty tea towel towards us and muttered in her grumpiest voice, 'They have to go to school, Bill, they can't stay home.'

'Well, let little Billy stay then, Dais,' Dad coaxed. He'd called her Dais again. How could she resist?

'All right,' Nan relented, 'just Billy. Now, off you girls go!'

Billy waved at us smugly. Jill and I grumbled as we dressed.

By lunchtime, we'd forgotten all about Billy. Jill and I had been taken off normal classwork to help paint curtains for the school's Parents' Night, which was held at the end of each year. We were halfway through drawing a black swan family when the headmaster came down and told us we could go home early. We were puzzled, but very pleased to be leaving before the other kids.

Nan wasn't happy when she saw us shuffling up the footpath. 'What are you kids doing here? They were supposed to keep you late at school.'

We just shrugged our shoulders. Neither Jill nor I had the faintest idea what she was talking about.

'Go outside and play,' Nan ordered grumpily.

Jill immediately raced out the back to play with Billy, but the familiar sound of an ambulance siren drew me to the front door. Nan stood impatiently on the porch with her hand over her mouth.

Two ambulance men hurried up the path. A stretcher case, I noted, as they walked briskly through. In a few minutes, they returned, and I watched as they carried Dad carefully, but quickly, down our faded red footpath. This time, I couldn't see his face.

Billy, Jill and David pushed up behind me, followed by Mrs Mainwaring, our neighbour. Before I knew it, she'd ushered us into the lounge room and told us all to sit down. It was then that I noticed Mum squashed in the old cane chair in the corner of the room. Nan hovered beside her, stuffing men's handkerchiefs into Mum's hand. I tried to reassure her by saying confidently, 'He always comes back,' at which she broke down completely and hid her face in a striped grey handkerchief.

'Please sit down, Sally,' said Mrs Mainwaring. 'I have something to tell you all.' I obeyed instantly. She was a nice middle-aged lady and we were a little in awe of her. Her home was very neat.

'Now …' she continued, 'I have some bad news for you all.' She paused and took a deep breath.

'He's dead, isn't he?' I was sure I said it out loud, but I couldn't have, because everyone ignored me. My heart was pounding. Mrs Mainwaring's lips were moving, but I couldn't hear a word. He was dead. I knew it. Dad was gone.

'Now children, I want you all to go to your rooms.' Somehow, this sentence managed to penetrate my numb brain. I looked around. No one was moving. I craned my neck to look at Mum, but she was avoiding my gaze.

Mrs Mainwaring finally pulled each one of us up and ushered us out. As I closed the bedroom door, Jill said, 'What are we s'posed to do?'

I was shocked, it wasn't like her not to know what the right thing was. With the superior confidence of a nine-year-old, I flung myself stomach-down on the bed and said, 'I s'pose we'd better cry.'

We cried for what seemed a long time, then our bedroom door slowly opened and the freckled face of Billy peered around.

'I'm going outside. Who wants to come and play?'

'You horrible boy,' I growled. 'Don't you know Dad's dead?!'

Billy vanished. 'He doesn't understand,' Jill defended him as usual.

We lay on our beds a few moments longer. I began to count the fly specks on the ceiling.

'Sally ... do ya think ... we could ... go outside and play now?' Jill asked hesitantly.

'Oh, come on then,' I relented. And leaping up, we joined Billy in the yard.

Family and friends

A couple of weeks after Dad died, Mum informed us all that Billy was now the man of the house. This came as a great surprise to me, because Billy was only six years old. It was an old-fashioned thought: Billy was the eldest son. I think Mum meant to reassure us with her statements, but she only confused us. We wondered if Billy had special powers we didn't know about.

A few months after Dad's death, Mum found out the contents of the Coroner's Report. The verdict was suicide. Mum was very upset. She had told us all that the war had killed Dad.

But the coroner did our family a favour, as he attributed Dad's suicide to the after-effects of war, and that meant there were no problems with Mum obtaining a war pension. It was regular money at a time when we needed it.

Fear had suddenly vanished from our lives. There were no more midnight flits to Aunty Grace's house, no more hospitals, no more ambulances. We were on our own, but peace had returned.

Dad's death crystallised many things for me. I decided that, when I grew up, I would never drink or marry a man who drank. The smell of alcohol, especially beer, had the power to make me sick. I also decided that I would never be poor. It wasn't that I was ashamed of the way we lived, it was just that there were things I longed for that I knew only money could buy. Like art paper and paints, piano lessons, a pink nylon dress and bacon sandwiches.

It had also made me very choosy about different men who seemed keen to befriend our family. There was one local chap who was always keen to take us on outings, but I knew he was only interested in Mum, not us.

Mum growled at me several times for being so rude to him. This made me really mad, because I felt she couldn't see through him and I could. I decided a secret meeting was necessary.

We all agreed that he had to go. And go he did. We told Mum, quite bluntly, that if this chap kept coming round, we would run away. I made her promise faithfully never to marry again. She agreed to this quite happily and it certainly was a weight off our minds.

We saw very little of Dad's brothers during those early months. One uncle gave Mum what he thought was good advice. 'Glad,' he said, 'a good-looking woman like you in your position, there's only one thing ya can do. Find a bloke and live with him. If ya lucky, he might take the kids as well.' Another uncle turned up a few weeks later and drove off in our only asset, the 1948 Ford van. He reasoned that as Mum didn't have her driver's licence, she wouldn't be needing it.

Mum was pretty down after that. 'Men,' she told us cynically, 'they're useless. No good for anything!'

If it hadn't been for Uncle Frank, we probably would have

gone along with Mum's theory. Mind you, she wasn't too pleased when he showed up. She was sick of drinking men.

'G'day, Glad,' he said when she answered the front door, 'just brought this around for ya.' He grinned as we appeared behind Mum in the doorway. 'Well, better get goin'. See ya later, kids. We'll have to go out one day. Bye, Glad.' Mum smiled and closed the door.

'What you got there?' Nan said as she poked in the box. 'Chicken, eh? And vegetables.'

I couldn't believe it was real chicken. Such a luxury. I don't think Mum could believe it, either. Frank, of all people — she'd thought he was just another boozer.

To our surprise, Frank came around the following weeks with the same thing. Then, Mum found out that the Raffles Hotel was holding a weekly lottery. The prize was always a box of fruit and vegetables and a fresh chicken, and the winner was always Uncle Frank. His lucky run was to continue for over twelve months.

Frank gave us more than just a helping hand. He introduced his wife to Mum and they became good friends. Aunty Lorna had a little car and she took us for picnics in the bush. She always packed a delicious lunch.

Frank encouraged Mum to have driving lessons. He was a bit of a mechanic in his spare time. He said he'd fix the van up for Mum. My uncle had returned it after other blokes had made comments to him about it.

Pretty soon Mum got her licence, then she and Lorna took it in turns to drive to the hills. We were still poor, but Nan was good at making a little bit go a long way. And, as far as us kids were concerned, it was more than we'd ever had.

Now that Mum had her driver's licence, she also began to make regular visits to Grandma and Grandpa's house. I think she was hoping they'd take an interest in us kids, but it didn't really work out like that. The only one they were really keen on was Billy, and that was only because he was the image of Dad. Grandpa always liked to have Billy close to him, but the rest of us were relegated to the backyard. Our cousins were allowed inside, but we had to stay outside.

It wasn't that our grandparents disliked us. In fact, they always treated us kindly, in their own way. After all, half of us belonged to Dad. It was the other half they were worried about.

It took only a few months for our regular visits to cease. Sometimes, we bumped into Grandpa in town. He would cry when he saw Billy. I remember once he actually tried to apologise to Mum for Grandma's attitude. 'What can I do, Glad? Ya know what she's like.' Mum just shrugged her shoulders. When we said goodbye, Grandpa would mop his eyes in a resigned kind of way. He always spoke nicely to us, but Grandma ruled the roost.

Fortunately, Mum managed to hang onto the television after Dad died. There were many other things we needed in our house far more desperately, but the TV did more for us than warm clothes or extra beds ever could. It gave us a way out.

We got into the habit of making up rough beds on the floor of the lounge room. Mum stoked up the fire, and we snuggled beneath our coats and rugs. We became enraptured by movies of the twenties, thirties and forties.

When television finished for the evening, Mum made us all hot cups of sweet tea and toast with jam or Vegemite. We stoked up the fire again and swapped yarns and stories until the early hours of the morning. Sometimes, we had a singalong — those went on for hours. We only stopped when we were asleep or too hoarse to sing any more.

I'll never forget those evenings: the open fire, Mum and Nan, all of us laughing and joking. I felt very secure, then. I knew it was us against the world, but I also knew that, as long as I had my family, I'd make it.

I had little idea of how hard that first year was for Mum and Nan. Mum was thirty-one when Dad died, and she had five of us to rear. I was nine years old, while Helen, the youngest, was only eighteen months old.

Mum didn't like leaving us, but she knew that if we were ever to get ahead, she would have to work. That was one thing you could say about Mum: she wasn't afraid to work. In all the years Dad was sick, she had always kept some money coming with some part-time work, but now she increased her load and took on whatever jobs were going. It was difficult to find full-time employment, so she accepted numerous part-time positions, most of which only lasted a few weeks.

Mum had an old friend, Lois, who helped out financially. Lois was an older lady who we didn't see much of, but she had befriended Mum in Mum's teenage years and, having no children of her own, considered her a daughter. She'd never liked Dad, but wasn't one to bear a grudge.

I remember, at one stage, we were really desperate. Mum

and Nan decided to write a letter to Alice Drake-Brockman in Sydney to see if her family could lend us some money. They were really disappointed when the reply came; it said that they were broke, too, and couldn't lend us anything. Nan was very bitter. She said she didn't care that they were bankrupt, they owed her. I didn't know what she was talking about.

Besides good old Uncle Frank and Lois, the other saviour of our family at this time was Legacy. All fatherless families of returned soldiers were assigned a Legatee. Legatees were generally gentlemen of good community standing who had a soft spot for children, and, while the system was only as good as the particular Legatee you got, we were very fortunate. Ours proved to be a kindly, older man with only one child of his own. His name was Mr Wilson, but we affectionately shortened it to Mr Willie.

Mr Willie got into the habit of taking us to the beach, and on picnics and barbecues. He had what we considered a really flashy car, and we always felt very special when we rode in it.

Mr Willie told us he would be taking us to all the Legacy outings, and that we would all have to take part in the Anzac Day march once a year.

'Why do we have to march?' I asked him one day.

'Because your father was a soldier. All children who belong to soldiers have to march. People need to be reminded of the legacy the war has left. And anyway, your father was a brave man; you should march to honour him.'

I wasn't keen to remind people of the war, but I couldn't fault his argument about Dad.

Wildlife

In no time at all, our house became inundated with pets. Cats, dogs, budgies, rabbits and, of course, the chickens — any stray creature found a home with us. When our cat population hit thirteen, Mum decided it was too much and found other homes for half of them. Then, my white rabbit escaped, one of the dogs was run over, and another cat went wild.

The dog we lost had been an old and treasured member of the family. I decided we needed another dog to replace him, so I persuaded Mum to look around some local pet shops.

'We won't buy one, Mum,' I confided, 'we'll just look.'

'No more animals, Sally.'

'I know, Mum, I know, but can't we look?'

'All right. It'll be an outing for you kids.'

A pet shop nearby had six kelpie-cross pups, all of them adorable. We all huddled around their cage in awe as they licked our fingers and looked at us appealingly.

'That one,' I said to Mum, as I eyed the largest pup. 'We'll take that one, Mum.'

'I'm not buying a dog, Sally. I've hardly got enough money to feed what we've got without adding to it.'

'That one's older than the others,' interrupted the shopkeeper.

'No one seems to want him.' It was the best thing he could have said.

'You see, Mum, no one wants him. What'll become of him if we don't buy him?'

'I'm not buying him.'

'Can I take him out of the cage and hold him, Mum? It might be the only cuddle he ever gets.'

'Good idea, little lady,' said the storekeeper enthusiastically as he opened the cage.

I lifted the pup out. He was gangly and awkward. 'Isn't he beautiful?' I held him up to Mum.

'Oh my God, look at the size of his paws, they're huge. He'll be a big boy when he's fully grown.'

'But Mum, we've never had a big dog.'

'Please, Mum,' pleaded my brothers and sisters.

'We-ll,' Mum sighed as the pup gave her a lick.

'I'll let you have him for half price,' coaxed the storekeeper.

'Oh, all right,' Mum groaned, 'we'll take him.'

We named the pup Blackie, because he was mostly black. A few weeks later, we renamed him Widdles, because of a tendency he had that we didn't seem to be able to train him out of.

The only pets we weren't allowed to keep were wild ones. Goannas, tadpoles, frogs, gilgies and insects all had to be returned alive and well to their natural habitat. Nan influenced us greatly when it came to our attitudes to the wildlife around us.

Our lives revolved around her, now that she kept the home fires burning while Mum worked three part-time jobs — two with a florist and one cleaning. Nan did the cooking, the cleaning, the washing, the ironing and the mending, as well as chopping all our wood and looking after the garden. The kitchen had become her personal domain, and she disliked us kids intruding. 'You kids get out of my kitchen,' she'd yell as she flicked a tea towel towards us. Even when we offered to help, she scolded us and sent us outside to play.

The highlight of 1961 occurred when I was walking home late one afternoon and happened to hear an urgent call coming from the bush nearby, a frantic *Cheep! Cheep!* I trod carefully into the bush until I came to a small clearing. There, at the base of a tall, white gum tree was a tiny baby mudlark. I stepped back and looked up at the branches high above me. Amongst the moving leaves, I could just glimpse the dark outline of a small nest. I knew there was no chance of returning him up there; it was far too high, and, even if I did, the mother might smell human on her baby and kick him out. There was only one thing I could do: take him home.

When Mum saw the bulge in the pocket of my dress, she sighed, 'Oh no, what have you got in there?'

I showed her the bird. 'I'm going to call him Muddy,' I said optimistically.

'I told you, Sally, no more pets. You kids bring them home and I'm the one that ends up feeding them.'

'But he's only a baby. I promise I'll look after him.'

'Oh, all right, but you have to look after it … You know, Sally, there might be something wrong with that bird. I've heard of mothers getting rid of babies for that reason. He might not live, he's very small.'

'Hmmph, he'll be all right,' said Nan, entering the fray. 'Bit of food, make sure he's warm at night, that's all he needs.'

I devised my own method of feeding Muddy. I simply placed a small piece of meat on the end of my finger and then stuck my finger down his throat. The technique seemed to suit him, because in no time at all he'd grown into a fine, healthy bird. He was my pal, and while our greatest adventure together was no more than running errands to the corner shop, in my mind, we experienced far more exciting escapades. About that time, I was into reading Famous Five books, and Muddy fulfilled the role of Timmy, George's dog.

At night, Mud slept on a chair in my room. 'Night, Mud,' I'd whisper. He'd stare back, his eyes and beak intense. That night, I dreamt of all the tricks I would teach him. What a show that would be — Mud and me, stars!

The next morning, I awoke to silence. I yawned and stretched. Normally, Muddy's shrill, hungry calls disturbed my sleep; this morning, there were none. I glanced at his chair. Mud was hanging upside down. What's he doing? I thought. Must be a new trick.

Mud was hanging stiffly upside down, not because he was concentrating, but because rigor mortis had set in.

He joined a host of past pets buried under the fig tree in the far corner of our yard. I felt that some of my own personal status died with him. Now, when I ran errands to the corner shop, no one commented on the wild mudlark perched precariously on my shoulder. There was just me: a scrawny, pigtailed kid wearing grubby clothes and a sulky look. Adventures, even in your imagination, were no fun on your own.

The swamp behind our place had become an important place for me. It was now part of me, part of what I was as a person. When I was in the swamp, I lost all track of time. I wallowed in the small, muddish-brown creek that meandered through on its way to join the Canning River. I caught gilgies by hanging over an old stormwater drain and wriggling my fingers in the water. As soon as the gilgies latched on, it required only a quick flick of the wrist to land them, gasping, on the bank.

I loved to think of the swamp as a very wild place. Every summer, our neighbours caught at least three or four large dugites and tiger snakes. It was strange, because, in all my forays into the bush, I never encountered any. Of course, I sensed they were about, but as long as I stayed out of their way, they seemed happy to stay out of mine.

Jill and I had many fun times down there. And we were always carting home some new find to show Nan. Once she'd inspected our prizes and we'd discussed what they were and how they lived, she'd make us return them to the swamp.

But there was no need to visit the swamp during winter, because our backyard invariably flooded with water teeming with tadpoles and small fish. Normally, the water rose to just above our ankles, but after a really good rain, it would get as high as halfway up our lower legs. Such days were greeted with squeals of delight as we splashed boisterously about, squeezing our toes into the muddy bottom and flicking up sand at one another.

'We don't need a swimming pool, do we, Mum?' I laughed as I splashed towards her.

'No, not only have we got water, but fish as well!'

Nan had a less optimistic nature, especially during winter. Her view of the physical world was a deeply personal one. And when she wasn't outside chopping wood or raking leaves, she was observing the weather. Her concern with atmospheric conditions was based on a rather pessimistic view of the frequency of natural disasters. Even though she avidly listened to weather reports on the radio, she never put her complete faith in any meteorologist's opinion. Nan knew their predictions weren't as reliable as her own.

Daily, she checked the sky, the clouds, the wind, and, on particularly still days, the reactions of our animals. Sometimes, she would sit up half the night checking on the movement of a particular star, or pondering the meaning of a new colour she'd seen in the sky at sunset.

On rare occasions, Mum was called in for consultation. It always amused me to see them standing at the end of our footpath, arms raised upwards, as if in supplication — Nan pointing out various dubious cumulus formations, and Mum nodding and muttering, 'Yes, yes. I see what you mean.'

Cure-alls

Mum had always been quite religious in her own way, but it only became really obvious to us after Dad died. She had occasionally gone to a church meeting when I was younger, but Dad was not very positive towards such things. Religion and the spiritual were private and personal for Mum.

She supplemented her prayers by taking us to every religious meeting imaginable. She wasn't biased when it came to religion. We attended the Roman Catholic, Baptist, Anglican, Church of Christ and Seventh Day Adventist churches.

Every evening before we went to bed, Mum liked us to recite the Lord's Prayer. Jill had a wonderful memory. She could read a large page of writing and then recite it word for word. We all thought she was very clever. After Mum listened to Jill's prayer, she came and sat on the end of my bed to coax me to say mine.

Usually, I hid my head under the covers and pretended I was asleep, but she would pull back the rugs and say, 'It's your turn now, Sally.'

'I can't see the point, Mum.'

Mum sighed and said, 'Well, perhaps you'll feel like saying it tomorrow night.' Then, she tucked me in and turned out the light. The bathroom was just near our room and the light there burned all night. I was too scared to sleep in total darkness.

When Mum wasn't praying for the benefit of my health and wellbeing, she was taking me to the doctor. I used to feel very frustrated with my weak body. If I could have, I would have disowned it.

Almost a year to the day after Dad died, I contracted rheumatic fever. Many times on the way to school, I had to stop and hold my chest until the pain had passed. Mum rushed me to the local doctor twice, but he maintained that I was merely suffering from growing pains. I had no idea that getting taller could be such agony.

Night-times were the worst. I curled myself up into a tight little ball and willed the pain to go away. I hurt too much to cry. Nan tried to help me as much as she could. I could tell by the look on her face and the sympathetic noises she made that she was worried about me.

She spent hours wrapping wet towels and torn-off strips of sheeting around my limbs, all the time reassuring me that the pain would soon disappear. I remember a couple of nights, when I was particularly bad, she just ran her hands slowly down the full length of my body, not touching me, but saying, 'You'll be all right. I won't let anything happen to you.'

As soon as the bandages and towels had dried, she slowly unwound them and then wet them again. 'You're very hot, Sally,' she said. 'It's not good for a child to be that hot.' By the time I finally fell asleep, I felt as stiff as a cardboard doll. When I awoke the following morning, the pain had generally gone, but not for long. I learnt a valuable lesson from being that sick: I learnt I was strong inside. I had to be to survive. My illness eventually subsided without any medical treatment.

Nan had many beliefs to do with health that she passed on to us. For one thing, she was obsessed with healthy bowels. Both Mum and Nan convinced us that a lot of illness was caused by constipation. We were quite happy to go along with their views in theory, but when their obsession began to extend to us in the form of regular doses of castor oil, Laxettes and what we crudely termed 'glycerine sticks', we balked. Our co-operation became more and more difficult to obtain, and Mum finally decided that the hassle in first discovering our separate hiding places and then literally dragging us from them wasn't worth the satisfaction she got when we all lined up for the toilet.

It was Nan who first brought out the sceptic in me. I was especially suspicious of those in authority. Nan convinced me that most people were untrustworthy, doctors in particular. For years, she had been talking about the Old Cures, the ones they used in the early days. I knew the Old Cures were the best.

One of Nan's great cure-alls was pepper. Any gashes were stuffed full with pepper and then tightly bound with strips torn from an old, white sheet. She also believed that eating a tin of beetroot would replace the blood you lost. While we exhibited various higgledy-piggledy scars on our arms and legs, the result of wounds stitched at Hollywood Repatriation Hospital, Nan had none. Her skin always healed soft and whole.

Nan's interest in health was not restricted to the human population.

One hot Saturday afternoon, as I was stretched out on an itchy blue towel soaking up the sun, it slowly dawned on my numbed senses that Nan's restless movements around the yard had ceased. Curiosity overcame lethargy, and, peering under my sweaty armpit, I took a quick glance around to see where she was.

I observed her, standing very still, close to the smallest gum tree in our backyard. Using the back of her knuckles, she tapped on the trunk twice, and then once with her stick. Then, she inclined her head towards the trunk as though listening for something. After a lengthy pause, she seemed satisfied, and, giving the earth a quick prod with her stick, she moved on to the paperbark further down.

'Nan,' I called out, 'what on earth are you doing?'

She started in surprise. I had been quiet for so long it was obvious she'd forgotten I was there. She waved her stick at me in a threatening manner and said crossly, 'You can't be trusted any more, Sally. I can't walk round my own backyard without one of you kids spying on me.'

'I wasn't spying. I just happened to see, that's all. Now, are you going to tell me what you were doing or not?'

She could see I wasn't going to give up without a fight, so she said, ' I was just checking on them to make sure they were all right, that's all. Now, no more questions, I got work to do!'

'Okay,' I sighed as I burrowed my head down into my towel once again.

I hadn't comprehended her answer at all. What on earth did she mean, making sure they were all right? I puzzled over her words for a few seconds and then dismissed them. There was so much about Nan I didn't understand.

Getting ahead

Mum was offered a job as a cleaner at our school at the beginning of the year I started Grade Six. The hours were perfect because they fitted in with the two other part-time jobs she was doing. But she didn't accept the job straightaway. First, she got us all together and asked if we would mind her taking it.

'What are you talking about, Mum?' I said.

'Well, I don't want to take the job if you children would mind. I thought you might worry about what your friends would think.'

Without hesitation I replied, 'We wouldn't mind, Mum. We'd really like it because we'd see more of you.'

Mum smiled at me. She knew how naive I was, that I didn't realise being a school cleaner carried with it very little status.

We helped her after school, wiping down the boards, emptying the bins and sweeping the floors. I enjoyed the boards the most, mainly because it gave me access to the chalk. Before wiping them down, I would scrawl rude comments about school across the whole length of the board. It gave me a great sense of power.

With more money coming in, Mum took to indulging us whenever she could. This indulgence took the form of unlimited lollies and fruit, rather than new clothes, toys or books. She'd managed to take us all to the Royal Show the year before, and this year she told us that, because of her new job, we would really do it in style.

We bought show bags crammed with Smarties, Cherry Ripes, Samboy potato chips and Violet Crumble bars — we weren't interested in the educational ones. One of our show bags had a large packet of marshmallows in it and Mum came up with the super idea of toasting them at home over the fire. Just like the Famous Five.

For Nan, Mum's extra job meant she had more work to do around the house, but it also meant a twice-yearly bottle of brandy and a reasonable amount to bet on the TAB. Sometimes, Nan let us pick a horse, too, and she would get the lady next door to put a bet on for us as well.

Besides the TAB, Nan loved lottery tickets. Both she and Mum were convinced that, one day, our family would come into a lot of money. It was a poor-man's dream, but we believed it.

Having more money also meant that Nan could really indulge in chain-smoking. In fact, she took to smoking so consistently that the front of her hair changed colour. While the rest of her frizzy mop was a light grey, the front was nicotine yellow. When we pointed it out to her, she was quite pleased. 'It's better than hair dye,' she chuckled as she looked in the mirror.

We came to consider Nan's cigarettes as an extension of her anatomy. She had mastered the skill of being able to talk and smoke at the same time. It seemed it didn't matter what Nan did, her cigarette would remain glued to the corner of her mouth as securely as that part of her lip. While smoking, and the cough she was developing with it, were now an integral part of her personality, there was one important occasion when she didn't smoke.

It was during summer when the dry bush surrounding the swamp would ignite into a raging bushfire. She never smoked while the fire was still burning. She felt it added to the heat.

Bushfires were a real threat to our house in those days. As billowing clouds of black smoke engulfed the neighbourhood, the firemen came knocking at each door with the message, 'Look luv, if the wind doesn't change soon, you'll have to evacuate.'

Nan always responded with, 'We're not leavin'. This is the only home we got.' If the men tried to argue with her, she pointed to her garden hose and said, 'You're not the only ones with water, you know.'

Their usual response to that was to explain to Nan how easily the flames could leap from roof to roof. Nan countered this by giving them a tour of our yard just to show them how many hoses she had. For some reason, six strategically placed garden hoses meant little to the firemen. 'Listen, luv,' they reasoned, 'if that wind doesn't change, the flames'll be in next door's and then they'll be in your place and you'll all go up in smoke. You got five kids here, too — can't someone have them for the day?'

'We got no one,' Nan would reply grumpily. 'Anyway, they're all right, I've wet them down.' It was true: we were dripping wet. Any hint of a fire in the swamp and Nan would line us all up and squirt us down with the hose. Then it was the chooks', cats', dogs' and budgies' turn.

Nan kept great stores of men's handkerchiefs in case of fire. She would wet them and then plaster them over our heads and faces. It made it easier to breathe when the ash rained down.

Fortunately for us, the wind did always change, and somehow we survived the heat and the ash and the billowing smoke. It was only when the fire in the swamp was completely out that Nan would relax and light up another cigarette.

That Christmas, Mum's old friend Lois gave her a dog. It was a tiny pedigree terrier.

Jill loved our new dog and her affection was returned. Tiger, as she named him, soon answered only to her. Tiger used to yap viciously from our bedroom windowsill every morning at anything that moved. I complained to Mum one morning that she never let him outside; it wasn't a healthy way for a dog to live. Mum said she was afraid he might get run over or bite someone.

But, because of my complaint and the fact that Tiger spent his time tearing around the house destroying anything he could sink his fangs into, Mum relented. Tiger was given his freedom and then proceeded to attack the cat next door. By the time Mum managed to catch him, she was worn to a frazzle. I got The Silent Treatment.

We were certainly glad that Widdles wasn't fierce. He'd grown into a beautiful big dog and could have really hurt someone if that was his nature. With absolutely no encouragement on our part, he'd trained himself to do many helpful things around the house, like bringing in the paper, and generally tidying up the place. He shared his food and bed with our black-and-white cat and had never been in trouble in his life.

Tiger decided that he liked his freedom, so as soon as Mum opened the front door early in the morning, he darted swiftly between her legs and tore onto the oval opposite. There was a large group of neighbourhood dogs who were in the habit of taking an early morning stroll, and Tiger loved to nip behind each one and sink his sharp little fangs into their back legs. Within minutes, the pack would be in a frenzy and Mum would dispatch faithful old Widdles to the rescue. He would bark his authority over the pack and then pick Tiger up by the scruff of the neck and carry him home.

It was a wonderful partnership, but one destined for an early end.

One afternoon, Mum broke the sad news to Jill that Tiger had passed on. Jill naturally assumed that one of the bigger dogs from the pack had finally got its revenge. Mum found it difficult to keep a straight face as she explained how Tiger had single-handedly attacked the number 37 bus. It was a fitting end.

With all the extra jobs Mum kept digging up, the money was really rolling in — at least, that's how it seemed to us. For one thing, we now had access to ridiculous quantities of food, especially during winter. We arrived home from school, soaked to the skin, dumped our bags in the hall and then made straight for the wood stove in the kitchen, where we set our smelly shoes and socks to dry on the open door of the oven.

'Eat! Eat!' Nan commanded as she placed huge chunks of jam tart and mince pie before us. 'You kids got to eat. I know what it's like to be hungry, it's a terrible thing.'

We never thought much about the way Nan carried on over food, much less considered the possibility that she might have known hard times. We had no conception of what it was like to have a really empty stomach. Even when Dad was alive, there'd always been something to fill up on; Nan had cooked rabbit a lot and she was good at making damper. Now we had food aplenty, and Nan was giving us the impression that going without food for any length of time wasn't normal. While she thought she was doing the right thing by squeezing in as many meals as possible in one day, it would lead to eating habits later in life that were difficult to break.

We learnt not only to eat in quantity, but quickly as well. The child who finished their dinner last often had part of their dessert pinched, or missed out on the extra baked potatoes browning in the oven.

Our conversations were never regulated either. When we spoke, we all spoke at once, and whoever had the loudest voice or the funniest story dominated the table.

There was nothing we loved better than huddling around the wood stove on cold afternoons, swapping stories. An open fire was always at the centre of our family gatherings. If it wasn't inside, it was out in the yard. And if it wasn't the wood stove in the kitchen, it was in the red-brick fireplace in the lounge room. There was something about an open fire that drew us all together.

Triumphs and failures

Grade Seven was a mixture of triumphs and failures. It was also the year my brother David began primary school.

David was a quiet, gentle little boy with lots of imagination. Unfortunately for him, he was landed with a teacher who was stern and unyielding. David was easily flustered, especially when he was trying to do the right thing. Consequently, he was continually in trouble over minor details like lost rubbers, books, drawings and pencils. It wasn't, of course, entirely David's fault; our home was so disorganised it was difficult to find even large items, let alone the small things he was supposed to keep in his school case.

At the beginning of third term, I won the coveted Dick Cleaver Award for Citizenship. The whole school voted, and, for some reason, I won. I wondered who Jill had bribed; she had a lot of influence in the lower grades.

My prize was a choice of any book available from the bookshops. When our headmaster, Mr Buddee, asked me what I had in mind, I replied, without hesitation, 'A book of fairytales, please.' I think he was rather taken aback, because he told me to go away and think about it for a few days.

I stuck to my choice, even though my class teacher tried to talk me into something 'more suitable'. My classmates thought I was potty, too. But I knew fairytales were the stuff dreams were made of.

It was during that final year at primary school that I noticed for the first time that whenever we brought our friends home to play after school, Nan would disappear.

'How come Nan nicks off when our friends are here?' I asked Jill one day.

'Dunno. She's been doin' it for years.'

One day, I walked into the kitchen with one of my friends and Nan was there, making a cup of tea. She was furious with me. After my friend had left, she said, 'You're not to keep bringin' people inside, Sally. You got no shame. We don't want them to see how we live.'

'Why not?'

'People talk, you know. We don't want people talkin' about us. You dunno what they might say!'

I didn't care what they said, but I went along with what Nan was saying.

'Okay, Nan,' I agreed. I wasn't pally with a lot of kids so it wasn't often I had friends after school.

Towards the end of the year, our class was given a batch of IQ tests. We were told that they were a sure way of measuring our intelligence, and would indicate at which level we would be placed the following year in high school.

There were only two streams in high school: the Professional stream, which generally included at least two maths and one science subject, and was aimed at entrance to university or other colleges of advanced education; and the Commercial stream, which meant you took shorthand and typing and left school at fifteen. On the basis of the tests, it was recommended that I be placed in the Commercial stream.

We had been given one test after another. There were pages of complicated drawings and numerous questions about farmers and their produce. When I wasn't day-dreaming, I simply marked each multiple choice question a,b,c simultaneously.

Mr Buddee took a personal interest in my case. He couldn't understand how I could do so well in school, despite all my illnesses, and yet so badly on the IQ tests.

One morning, he called Mum in for an interview and explained to her the difficulty he was having in getting me placed in the Professional stream. Mum had never heard of IQ tests before, and I think she thought they'd discovered I was mentally retarded.

That night, I pestered Mum to tell me what Mr Buddee had said. At first she refused, but, after some pestering, she finally explained what it all meant. I was deeply offended by the fact that I had been labelled dumb by the stupid, boring test. Yet, at the same time, I was excited by the prospect that I would be allowed to leave school at fifteen. Mum wasn't having a bar of it. She was determined that, by hook or by crook, I would go on to tertiary studies.

'But, Mum, the only place I want to study is at that famous art school in Paris. If I can't do that, I don't care what I do.'

Mum was aghast. She protested that she wasn't made of

money. 'Wouldn't you miss your family?' she added as an after-thought.

'Naah,' I retorted, 'I'd be too busy painting.'

Poor Mum. She had a heart like a sponge and the most flexible will in the neighbourhood. I gave her the run around for years. She deserved better.

Growing up

At school, we had been warned over and over about strangers, and the importance of refusing lifts from anyone we didn't know. What no one ever warned us about were friends or relations.

The summer vacation following my final year in primary school was spent with some elderly friends of Dad's. We called them Uncle and Aunty.

Aunty was a pleasant, white-haired old soul who wore the kind of glasses that glittered in the dark. Uncle wasn't so nice. I disliked him on sight. He was short, with corrugated hair, a beetroot-shaped nose and a ruddy face. He was a boozer and very friendly to Jill and me, often patting us on the head or shoulder.

One day, he told us about some beautiful jewellery that he kept in his toolshed, which was hidden behind some tall trees at the rear of the yard. It was a Blue Bird necklace and bracelet. That jewellery was all the rage then, so we were quite happy to go with him to the shed.

As promised, he showed us his treasure, but then he climbed up and tucked it away on a shelf too high for us to reach.

I tugged at Jill's arm. 'C'mon, let's go,' I whispered. It was obvious we weren't going to get anything out of him. Jill wouldn't move. Her eyes were glued to the shelf where he'd hidden the jewellery.

'Don't go yet, girls,' he coaxed, 'I've got other things to show.'

'Listen,' I said urgently, 'I can hear Mum calling us for lunch.' I grabbed Jill's arm and we both raced out of the shed and back towards the house. I hadn't liked the way he was looking at us.

He certainly was persistent. He took to following Jill and me around whenever Mum wasn't on the scene. I warned Jill never to go up to his shed again.

I was frightened for her, yet I couldn't explain what I was frightened of. She disregarded my warning. On two occasions, I caught her plodding along silently after Uncle. I caught up with her and distracted her with something else.

It was a reversal of roles for us. Jill had always been physically stronger than me and was always fighting my battles. Now, it was my turn to look out for her.

That summer signalled the start of my growing up. I was very self-conscious — none of my body seemed to be in proportion. I had long legs, long arms and the bit in between was flat and skinny.

I think what I disliked most about myself, though, was the lack of pigmentation in certain patches of skin around my neck and shoulders. I always buttoned my shirts right up to the collar.

Mum must have noticed how self-conscious I was, because she took me to see a skin specialist, who said there was nothing he could do and referred me to a cosmetician.

The cosmetician gave me different coloured batches of

make-up to mix together so I could conceal my patches.

After all the trouble Mum had gone to, I didn't have the courage to tell her I had no intention of ever using the make-up. At the first opportunity, I wrapped my make-up in newspaper and threw it in the bin. It was a symbolic gesture. I decided that, from then on, I would bare that part of my body, and if people were repulsed, that was their problem, not mine. It was the first time my lower neck had seen the light of days for years.

Apart from my appearance, over those holidays my main worry was high school. I kept wishing it didn't exist. For a time, I had very romantic notions about running away to join a circus. But the circus never came and, in February 1962, I started high school.

I felt terribly old-fashioned. I still had two long plaits dangling down my back. All the other girls had short hair, and they were much more mature than me. There were about twelve hundred students at our school. I felt lost and intimidated.

As we all waited silently in line that first day, I kept wondering what stream they were going to put me in, Commercial or Professional. We'd been told there were going to be four Professional classes, denoted by the letters A to D. Only the exceptionally brainy students were permitted in the A class; everyone else was slotted into the other classes according to their varying degrees of intelligence. I sat glumly as the teachers read through first the A list, the B and C. By the time they got to the bottom of the D list, my name was called out. I didn't know whether I wanted to laugh or cry. I hated school, yet, at the same time, I didn't want people thinking I didn't have a brain in my head.

Mum was ecstatic when I arrived home. Apparently, Mr

Buddee had rung her and told her he'd fixed things up. She greeted me excitedly with, 'Maybe you'll become a vet.' That was the next best thing to being a doctor.

'I've gone off animals, Mum,' I replied sarcastically.

'A doctor, then?' Mum said hopefully.

'Don't like 'em.'

'Well, anything, Sally, anything. You've got too much talent to waste.'

Mum was rather deflated. I think she expected me to be as excited as she was. I found myself feeling a little sorry for her. She had five kids and she seemed to be pinning her hopes on me, the worst one. Jill would be the one to achieve something, not me. I consoled myself with the thought that there were four kids in our family younger than me, and at least one of them must have a good chance of becoming a doctor, especially if Mum kept pushing. I didn't like to think of all of us ending up as failures.

Early in the school year, I made friends with a girl called Steph. She lived seven blocks away from us, in the part they called Como, so we took to visiting each other on weekends. I loved Steph's bedroom; it was decorated mainly in lilac and it reminded me of something straight off a Hollywood filmset. Surprisingly, Steph was equally fascinated by my home. She loved the free-and-easy atmosphere, and the tall stories and jokes.

But I think my intense admiration for Steph's room caused me to become somewhat dissatisfied. I suddenly realised there was a whole world beyond what I knew. Sometimes when

Steph's parents talked to me, my mind went blank. I always seemed to say the wrong thing, so, for fear of offending them, I began saying nothing at all, which was even worse.

By the time I turned fourteen and was in second year high school, I was becoming more and more aware that I was different to the other kids at school. I had little in common with the girls in my class. Even Steph was changing. She no longer raced me to the top of the tree in her yard and she thought my frequent absences from school were something to be ashamed of.

Jill was in high school now and, as I expected, was having no difficulty fitting in. Sometimes, I desperately wished I could be more like her. Everything seemed to be so hard for me. Even little Helen had taken to school like a duck to water. She began primary school that year.

'Maybe she'll be the doctor, then,' I said sarcastically.

'Yes, perhaps you're right,' Mum replied thoughtfully. 'I'm sure you'll all do well, once you set your minds to it. You could do anything, if you really wanted to.'

'But that's just it, Mum, I don't want to.'

When I looked at other people, I realised how abnormal I was, or at least, that's how I felt. None of my brothers and sisters seemed to be tormented by the things that tormented me. I really felt as though I just couldn't understand the world any more. It was horrible being a teenager.

Part of the reason why I hated school was the regimentation. I hated routine. I wanted to do something exciting and different all the time. I really couldn't see the point in learning about subjects I wasn't interested in. I had no long-term goals and my only short-term one was to leave school as soon as I could.

I found that the only way to cope was to truant as much as possible. I became an expert in ways to miss school. But then the school began enforcing stricter rules in an attempt to reduce the high rate of truancy among its students. Mum was threatened with the Truant Officer many times. To her, this was as bad as having a policeman call. So she began to try to make us stay at school all day.

She was in a difficult situation because, while she wanted us to have a good education and to get on in the world, she was also sympathetic to our claims of being bored, tired or unhappy. Also, I knew it wasn't the fact that we truanted so much that upset her, but that now and then we got caught. Getting caught inevitably brought us to the personal attention of the school staff, which also meant that, in some way, she lost face in their eyes. Like most people, I suppose, Mum liked others to think well of her.

She was particularly upset after one visit to our Head. He had shown her three different sets of handwriting, all purporting to be hers, and all excusing either Jill or me from a morning or afternoon at school. 'You've got to get yourselves organised,' she told us crossly. 'If you're going to forge notes from me, at least do it in the same style.'

The longer I stayed at school, the more difficult I became and the more reluctant Mum became to support my truanting. She was tired of the Head and the Guidance Officer ringing her up. I sympathised with her; I was sick of visiting the Guidance Officer myself. Mum was finally advised to allow me to leave school early and let me become a shop assistant.

Rather peculiar pets

Mum had slowly built up a collection of stuffed animals, reptiles and birds. Her favourites were two long snakeskins, one of which still had the head and fangs intact, though a trifle flattened. Then there were an Irish pheasant, an echidna, a turtle, an eagle, eight frogs playing different musical instruments and numerous crocodiles of varying shapes and sizes.

As Mum seemed to like owning peculiar things, none of us was surprised when, one day, she turned up with a stray dog that she had rescued from being run over on a busy city street. To everyone else he looked like a shaggy, black mongrel, but in Mum's eyes, Curly, as she had named him, had a fine pedigree.

I tried to point out to her how close set his little black eyes were, and how his only pursuits were of the basest nature. But nothing would dampen Mum's enthusiasm; to her, he was still a gem of a dog.

One of his most embarrassing habits was to greet newcomers to our home with a unique ritual of his own. He simply focused his zealous, close-set, black eyes on his intended victim and, in a flash, rammed his wet, black nose into their crotch, sniffing deeply. Mum's initial reaction to this extraordinary behaviour was one of wanton laughter, but then, she'd never been attacked.

She rationalised his actions by pointing out that since Curly had been with us, the number of Mormons, Jehovah's Witnesses and Avon ladies knocking on our door had decreased.

One evening, Mr Willie came round to visit and to inform us that he would soon be moving to Victoria. He was sorry he was leaving, but would make sure we got a nice Legatee in his place.

We were all rude to Mr Willie that night, and, after he left, Mum told us she was ashamed of our behaviour. She didn't understand that we felt abandoned. He'd called us his second family.

It wasn't long before our new Legatee rang to say he'd be popping around in an hour or so to visit us. Anxious to make a good impression, Mum rapidly tidied up the house. This was done in her usual manner of shoving all the clothes and junk scattered over the floor into the wardrobes and under the beds. Anything she couldn't find a spot for was simply screened from view by closing the door.

Our new Legatee arrived promptly at six p.m. and knocked loudly on the door. Curly, who had just finished his dinner, pricked up his furry, flea-bitten ears and darted to the door.

'Sally, grab him,' Mum yelled as she hurled an old dishcloth in a futile attempt to halt his frenzied exit. I grabbed him by the scruff of the neck and dragged him down the hall and into Mum's bedroom.

I managed to pull the door shut just as Mum said to our guest, 'Hello, please come in. Sorry to keep you waiting.'

'That's quite all right, Mrs Milroy,' responded our visitor politely.

'Come and meet the family,' Mum said as she grasped his arm

and led the way into our lounge room, where we were waiting quietly. Suddenly Mum shrieked, 'Oh my God!'

Somehow, Curly had freed himself, and, with unparalleled speed, zapped out of the bedroom, down the hall and up between our guest's half-open legs. Our visitor, who was only a short man, leapt to his tiptoes and clutched the wall behind him. Mum, her fingers desperately digging into Curly's matted fur, yelled, 'Down Curly, down!' All to no avail. He was abnormally strong for a small dog.

'Hey, hey, hey,' our victim spluttered as he leapt repeatedly in the air in response to Curly's probing nose.

'You disgusting dog!' Mum scolded as, with one final heave, she tore him away and tucked him firmly under her arm. 'I don't know what's got into him,' she added unconvincingly. 'He's normally such a good dog. I'm so terribly sorry.' Still apologising, Mum lugged Curly out through the kitchen and onto the back verandah.

Much to Curly's disappointment, the gentleman never returned. A few weeks later, we were informed that we had been appointed another Legatee. Whether he heard about Curly from his predecessor I don't know, but he rarely visited, preferring instead to communicate by telephone or letter.

A black grandmother

Apart from Art and English, I failed nearly everything else in the second term of my third year in high school. And Mum was appalled with my seven per cent for Geometry and Trigonometry.

'You've got your Junior, soon. How on earth do you expect to pass that?'

'I don't care whether I pass or not. Why don't you let me leave school?'

'You'll leave school over my dead body!'

'What's the point in all this education if I'm going to spend the rest of my life drawing and painting?'

Mum gave up arguing and I retreated to my room.

The following weekend, my Aunty Judy came to lunch. She was a friend of Mum's. Her family, the Drake-Brockmans, and ours had known each other for years. 'Sally, I want to have a talk with you about your future,' she said quietly, after we'd finished dessert.

I glared at Mum.

'You know you can't be an artist. They don't get anywhere in this world. You shouldn't worry your mother like that. She wants you to stay at school and finish your Leaving.'

I was absolutely furious. Not because of anything Aunty Judy had said, but because Mum had the nerve to get someone from outside the family to speak to me. Mum walked around looking guilty for the rest of the afternoon.

It wasn't only Mum and Aunty Judy, it was my Art teacher at school as well. He held up one of my drawings in front of the class one day and pointed out everything wrong with it. There was no perspective, I was the only one with no horizon line, my people were flat and floating ... on and on he went. By the end of ten minutes, the whole class was laughing and I felt very small. I always believed that drawing was my only talent, but now I knew I was no good at that, either.

That evening, when I was alone in my room, I suddenly felt tears rushing to my eyes and spilling down my cheeks. I decided then to give up drawing. I was sick of banging my head against a brick wall. I got together my collection of drawings and paintings, sneaked down to the back of the yard, and burnt them.

When Mum and Nan found out what I'd done, they were horrified. 'All those beautiful pictures,' Nan moaned, 'gone for ever.' Mum just glared at me. I knew she felt she couldn't say too much; after all, she was partly responsible for driving me to it.

It took about a month for Mum and me to make up. She insisted that if I did my Junior, she wouldn't necessarily make me go on to my Leaving. I, like a fool, believed her.

Towards the end of the school year, I arrived home early one day to find Nan sitting at the kitchen table, crying. I froze in the doorway; I'd never seen her cry before.

'Nan ... what's wrong?'

She lifted up her arm and thumped her clenched fist hard on the kitchen table. 'You bloody kids don't want me. You want a bloody white grandmother, and I'm black. Do you hear? Black, black, black!' With that, Nan pushed back her chair and hurried out to her room. I continued to stand in the doorway, too stunned to move.

For the first time in my fifteen years, I was conscious of Nan's colouring. She was right, she wasn't white. Well, I thought logically, if she wasn't white, then neither were we. What did that make us? I had never thought of myself as being black before.

That night, as Jill and I were lying quietly on our beds, looking at a poster of John, Paul, George and Ringo, I said, 'Jill ... did you know Nan was black?'

'Course I did.'

'I didn't. I just found out.'

'I know you didn't. You're really dumb, sometimes ... You know we're not Indian, don't you?'

'Mum said we're Indian.'

'Look at Nan, does she look Indian?'

'I've never really thought about how she looks. Maybe she comes from some Indian tribe we don't know about.'

'Ha! That'll be the day! You know what we are, don't you? We're boongs!' I could see Jill was unhappy with the idea.

It took a few minutes before I summoned up enough courage to say, 'What's a boong?'

'A boong. You know, Aboriginal. God, of all things, we're Aboriginal!'

'Oh.' I suddenly understood. There was a great deal of social stigma attached to being Aboriginal at our school.

'Haven't you ever listened to the kids at school? If they want to run you down, they say, "Aah, ya just a boong." Honestly, Sally, you live the whole of your life in a daze!'

Jill was right, I did live in a world of my own.

'You know, Jill,' I said after a while, 'if we are boongs — and I don't know if we are or not — but if we are, there's nothing we can do about it, so we might as well just accept it.'

'Accept it? Can you tell me one good thing about being an Abo?'

'Well, I don't know much about them,' I answered. 'But don't Abos feel close to the earth and all that stuff?'

'God, I don't know. All I know is none of my friends like them. You know, I've been trying to convince Lee for two years that we're Indian.' Lee was Jill's best friend and her opinions were very important. Lee loved Nan, so I didn't see that it mattered.

'You know Susan?' Jill said, interrupting my thoughts. 'Her mother said she doesn't want her mixing with you because you're a bad influence. She reckons all Abos are a bad influence.'

'Aaah, I don't care about Susan. Never liked her much anyway.'

'You still don't understand, do you,' Jill groaned in disbelief. 'It's a terrible thing to be Aboriginal. Nobody wants to know you, not just Susan. You can be Indian, Dutch, Italian, anything, but not Aboriginal! I suppose it's all right for someone like you. You don't care what people think, but I do!' Jill pulled her rugs over her head and pretended she'd gone to sleep. I think she was crying, but I had too much new information to think about to try and comfort her.

Nan's outburst over her colouring and Jill's assertion that we were Aboriginal heralded a new phase in my relationship with my mother. I began to pester her incessantly about our background. Mum was a hard nut to crack and consistently denied Jill's assertion. She even told me that Nan had come out on a boat from India in the early days.

When I wasn't pestering Mum, I was busy pestering Nan. Whenever I attempted to question her, though, she either lost her temper and began to accuse me of all sorts of things, or she locked herself in her room and wouldn't emerge until it was time for Mum to come home from work.

One night, Mum came into my room and sat on the end of my bed. She had her This Is Serious look on her face. With an unusual amount of firmness in her voice, she said quietly, 'Sally, I want to talk to you.'

I lowered my *Archie* comic. 'What is it?'

'You're not to bother Nan any more. She's not as young as she used to be and your questions are making her sick. She never knows when you're going to try and trick her. There's no point in digging up the past. Some things are better left buried. Do you understand what I'm saying? You're to leave her alone.'

'Okay Mum,' I replied glibly, 'but on one condition.'

'What's that?'

'You answer one question for me. Are we Aboriginal?'

Mum snorted in anger and stormed out. Jill chuckled from her bed. 'I don't know why you keep it up. I think it's better not to know for sure, that way you don't have to face up to it.'

'I keep pestering them because I want to know the truth, and I want to hear it from Mum's own lips.'

'It's a lost cause. They'll never tell you.'

I settled back into my mattress and began to think about the past. Were we Aboriginal? I sighed and closed my eyes. A mental picture flashed vividly before me.

I was a little girl again, and Nan and I were squatting in the sand near the back steps.

'This is a track, Sally. See how they go.' I watched, entranced, as she made the pattern of a kangaroo. 'Now, this is a goanna and here are emu tracks. You see, they all different. You got to know all of them if you want to catch tucker.'

'That's real good, Nan.'

'You want me to draw you a picture, Sal?' she said as she picked up a stick.

'Okay.'

'These are men, you see. Three men. They are very quiet; they're hunting. Here are kangaroos. They're listening, waiting. They'll take off if they know you're coming.' Nan wiped the sand picture out with her hand. 'It's your turn now,' she said, 'you draw something.' I grasped the stick eagerly.

'This is Jill and this is me. We're going down the swamp.' I drew some trees and bushes.

I opened my eyes, and, just as suddenly, the picture vanished. Had I remembered something important? I didn't know. That was the trouble, I knew nothing about Aboriginal people. I was clutching at straws.

It wasn't long before I was too caught up in my preparation for my Junior examinations to bother too much about where we'd come from. At that time, the Junior exam was the first major one in high school, and, to a large extent, it determined your future. If you failed, you automatically left school and looked for a job. If you passed, it was generally accepted that you would do another two years' study and aim at entrance to university.

Mum was keen on me doing well, so I decided that, for her, I'd make the effort and try and pass subjects I'd previously failed. For the first time in my school life, I actually sat up late, studying my textbooks. It was hard work, but Mum encouraged me by bringing in cups of tea and cake or toast and jam.

Much to the surprise of the whole family, I passed every subject, even scoring close to the distinction mark in English and Art. Mum was elated.

'Now, aren't you pleased? I knew you could do it. Mr Buddee was right about you.'

Good old Mr Buddee. I didn't know whether to curse or thank him. Now that I had passed my Junior, I sensed that there was no hope of Mum allowing me to leave school. I should have deliberately failed, I thought. Then she wouldn't have had any choice. Actually, I had considered doing just that, but, for some reason, I couldn't bring myself to do it. I guess it was my pride again.

What people are we?

Fourth year high school was different to third year. It was a transitional year, where we were treated more like adults and less like difficult teenagers. Even our classes were structured to mimic the kind of organisation we might find later in tertiary institutions. I was a year older, but I was still the same person with the same problems. However, some deep and important things did happen to me that year.

One day I happened to bump into a girl whom I'd been friendly with in my Sunday School days. She invited me to a youth meeting to be held at a nearby church hall.

'It's got nothing to do with religion,' she said confidently. 'Just some Chinese food and a bit of a get-together, that's all.'

'Okay, I'll come. I know some other kids who like Chinese food. I might bring them, too.'

'Great. See you there.'

I arrived at the meeting with seven girls from around our neighbourhood and two from school. The food was quite good, and, even though everyone else there ignored us, we enjoyed ourselves.

When everyone had finished stuffing themselves, a chap stood up and said, 'We have a Mr McClean here to give us a little talk. I'd like you all to be quiet while we listen to what he has to say.'

Uh-oh, I thought. Here it comes. I looked towards the back of the hall, the door was closed and there were two elderly gentlemen standing in front of it. I was trapped. I could feel my insides twisting themselves into a knot. If Mr McClean turned out to be half as boring as some of the teachers I'd had in Sunday School, my friends would never forgive me.

Mr McClean stood up and smiled nicely at us all. 'I'm here to talk to all you young people about your future,' he said. 'Your eternal future.'

I'd heard it all before. It was going to be a long night.

As he continued, I thought of other things. But, suddenly, there was someone talking to me. I knew it wasn't Mr McClean. I looked around in a furtive kind of way, trying to see who it was. All eyes were fixed on the speaker, and there was no one new in the room.

'Who are you?' I asked mentally.

With a sudden dreadful insight, I knew it was God.

'What are you doing here?' I asked. I don't know why I was surprised. It was a church hall, after all.

It had to be Him because the voice seemed to come from without not within. I couldn't see my surroundings any more. I was having an audience with Him, whom I dreaded. The mental images that I had built up of Him so far in my life began to dissolve, and in their place came a new image. A person with overwhelming love, acceptance and humour. What Nan'd call real class. In an instant, I became what others refer to as a believer.

I joined the local youth group after that. I was full of ideas for making the meetings and outings we went on more interesting, but it was difficult to change the pattern that had been set in motion so many years before.

I think Mum was relieved that I was finally channelling my energies into what she saw as something creative. She hoped that, with the encouragement of people at church, I would begin to lead a more productive and less rebellious life. She was wrong.

One night, one of the deacons of the church asked if he could talk to me. I was friendly with his daughter and he seemed like a nice man, so I agreed.

'You and Mary are having quite a lot to do with one another, aren't you?' he asked.

'I suppose so.'

'Well, Sally,' he smiled, 'I want to ask a favour of you.'

'Sure, anything.'

'I'd like you to stop mixing with Mary.' He smiled his charming smile again.

'Why?' I was genuinely puzzled.

'I think you know why. You're a bad influence — you must realise that.' Believe it or not, that was one part of my character I was unaware of.

'What do you mean?' I wanted him to spell it out.

'This is Mary's Leaving year, the same as yours. I don't want her mixing with you in case she picks up any of your bad habits.'

Aaah, I thought. He's heard about my truancy.

'What about after Leaving?' I asked meekly. I sensed there was more to this than just that.

'No. I don't think so. Really, it'd be better if you broke off your friendship entirely. You do understand, don't you?' he said in an incredibly charming way.

'Oh, I understand,' I replied.

'Good girl, I knew you would.' He was relieved. 'Oh, by the way. I can count on you not to say anything to Mary, can't I? You'll find a way of breaking things off between you, won't you?'

I nodded my head, and he walked off.

I was hurt and disappointed. He was a deacon, and I'd looked up to him. I was lucky I had my pride, as it came to my rescue yet again. I didn't need people like him, I decided.

It was about that time that I began to analyse my own attitudes and feelings more closely. I looked at Mum and Nan and I realised that part of my inability to deal constructively with people in authority had come from them. They were completely baffled by the workings of government or its bureaucracies. Whenever there were difficulties, rather than tackle the system directly, they'd taught us it was much more effective to circumvent or forestall it. And if that didn't work, you could always ignore it.

That summer, the State Housing decided to paint the exterior of all the houses in our street. This really panicked Nan. She made sure the front and back doors were kept locked so they couldn't come inside, and she spent most of the day peeping out at them from behind the curtains. For her, they were here to check on us, and the possibility of eviction was always there, hanging over our heads like some invisible guillotine.

I thought back to all the years she had spent buttering up

the rent men. Each rent day, Nan would go through the same routine. She rose early and spent all morning cleaning the house. Then she washed and dried our best cup and saucer and arranged a plate of biscuits in tempting display. Her final touch was to plump up the cushion we had sitting on the chair on the front porch. She wanted him to be comfortable.

And the whole time Nan was preparing morning tea, she'd grumble under her breath, 'That bloody rent man! Who does he think he is, taking up my time like this?' Of course, once he arrived, it was a different story.

'You're here at last,' she'd smile. 'Sit down, you must be tired. They shouldn't make you walk so far.'

Why did she do it? I asked myself. Why was she afraid? I decided I'd try to explain how things worked.

After Nan had given the painters a slap-up morning tea, I cornered her out the back, where she was raking up leaves. 'Nan,' I said suspiciously, 'I think I've just realised why you've been treating the rent man like royalty all these years. You've been bribing them, haven't you?'

'I don't know what you're talking about, Sally.'

'Nan,' I said, in a reasonable tone of voice, 'I don't think you understand about the house we rent. You only get evicted if you don't look after the place. For example, if we were to smash a wall or break all the windows, they might think about throwing us all out, but otherwise, as long as we pay the rent, they let you stay.'

'Hmmph, you think you know everything, don't you?' she replied bitterly. 'You don't know nothin', girl. You don't know what it's like for people like us. We're like those Jews. We got to look out for ourselves.'

'What do you mean people like us?'

'In this world, there's no justice. People like us'd all be dead and gone now if it was up to this country.' Her eyes looked tired and wet.

'Nan,' I said carefully. 'What people are we?'

She looked sharply at me with the look of a rabbit sensing danger. 'You're tryin' to trick me again. Aaah, you can't be trusted. I'm not stupid, you know. I'm not saying nothing. Nothing, do you hear?'

I suddenly felt terribly sad. The barriers were up again.

I sighed and walked back to the house. Inside, I felt all churned up, but I didn't know why. I had accepted by now that Nan was dark, and that our heritage was not that shared by most Australians, but I hadn't accepted that we were Aboriginal. I was too ignorant, and I found myself coming back to the same old question: if Nan was Aboriginal, why didn't she and Mum just say so? The fact that both made consistent denials made me think I was barking up the wrong tree. I could see no reason why they would pretend to be something they weren't. And Nan's remark about the Jews had confused me even more. I knew a lot about the Jews because of the war and Dad. In my mind, there was no possible comparison between us and them.

Make something of yourself

Mum was always a hard worker and had plenty of drive, but, in a small way, she was also proving to be quite a successful business woman. She had been doing so well for many years working as a florist that, in 1967, with the help of a loan from her old friend Lois, she was able to buy her own florist's business. Things were now really looking up, financially.

But Mum would have been more contented if she could have seen greater evidence that some of her own drive and ambition was rubbing off on her children. 'You want to make something of yourself,' Mum urged repeatedlty.

How could I tell her it was me, and her and Nan. The sum total of all the things that I didn't understand about them or myself. The feeling that a very vital part of me was missing and that I'd never belong anywhere. Never resolve anything.

I suppose it wasn't surprising that I returned to my final year in high school with a rather depressed attitude. This naturally led to a great deal of initial truanting, which both helped and hindered the inner search I seemed to have unwittingly begun on.

At the end of first term, our Physics teacher gave the class a little talk.

'It's interesting,' he said, 'only two more terms to go and I can already tell which of you will pass or fail. And I'm not just talking about Physics. In this class, most of you will pass. Then there are a few who are borderline, and one who will definitely fail.' He looked with pity at me. 'I don't know why you bother to turn up at all. You might as well throw in the towel now.'

Everyone laughed. I was really mad. Up until then, I hadn't cared whether I passed or failed. I'll prove you wrong, you crumb, I thought.

During second term, I made sporadic attempts at study. Once the August holidays were over, I began in earnest. I knew it wasn't going to be an easy task. I lacked the photographic memory of my two sisters, and I was way behind in my work. As usual, Mum tried to encourage me by bringing every snack imaginable.

By the end of my exams, I knew I'd passed English, History and Economics. I was doubtful about Chemistry and I was almost certain that I had failed Physics, Maths 1 and Maths 2.

I confided none of my fears to Mum. I figured she'd be disappointed soon enough. I needed five subjects to score my Leaving Certificate and I was confident of only three. It seemed all my hard work had been for nothing.

Mum gave me what she considered good advice for every teenager.

'Now that you've finished your exams, you want to go out and let your hair down a bit.' I knew she thought it wasn't normal for a girl my age to be spending so many nights at home.

'Look, Mum, will you give it a rest?' I yelled. 'I just want to sit here and be left in peace!'

Poor Mum, she now had within her family two extremes. On the one hand, there was me attending prayer meetings, and on the other, there were Jill and Bill who, like normal teenagers, spent their weekends raging about Perth. Bill had just completed his Junior Certificate exams.

I was becoming very worried about my soon-to-be-published Leaving results. The results were printed every year in the *West Australian* and I thought this was terrible because it meant your shame was made public. I could cope with the public exposure myself, but what about Mum? She'd always boasted to the neighbours about how bright all her children were. It would be a real slap in the face if they should see her eldest daughter's name in print with a string of fails after it.

'Please, God,' I prayed, 'Mum deserves some success in life.'

My prayer was answered, because the day the results came out, Mum extolled my superior intelligence and patted me on the back for passing five subjects. She had now convinced herself that I'd go to university and become a doctor.

You can imagine how disappointed she was, then, in my decision to never study again. I told her I was sick of people telling me what to do with my life. I wanted to work and earn some money. I wanted to be independent.

'But Sally,' she protested, 'you're the first one in our family to have gone this far. Why can't you go to university?'

'Mum,' I groaned. ' I just don't want to do any more study.'

'So you've come all this way for nothing? You're too stubborn for your own good. You'll regret it one day, you mark my words.'

'Oh, stop complaining. You're lucky I lasted this long. Aren't you pleased you'll be having a bit of extra money coming in?'

'I never worried about the money. All that work …' Mum bemoaned.

The working life

Towards the end of summer, in 1969, I managed to secure a job as a clerk in a government department. It was an incredibly boring job. I had nothing to do. I begged my superiors to give me more work, but they said there was none. I just had to master the art of looking busy, like they did. In desperation I took to hiding novels in government files; that way, I could sit at my desk and read without everyone telling me, 'Look busy, girl. Look busy!'

I lasted there about six months and then I resigned. And I thought school was boring. That was my first experience of being employed and I hadn't liked it one bit. It was an important experience for me, because it taught me something about myself that I had been unaware of. I wasn't going to be satisfied with just anything. And I wasn't lazy.

I had been unemployed about four months when I found a job as a laboratory assistant. For some reason, my new employer assumed that as I had studied physics and chemistry at school I must have known something about them. My job was to analyse mineral samples from different parts of Western Australia for tin, iron oxide, and so on.

I accidentally disposed of my first lot of samples, so, in desperation, I invented the results. My boss was quite excited.

'Hmmm,' he said as he looked over my recording sheet, 'these aren't bad. Good girl, good girl!'

I felt so guilty. I imagined that, on the basis of my analysis, they might begin drilling straightaway in the hope of a big strike. I took more care after that.

The women I worked with all had strong personalities. Our boss was hardly ever in so we took extended lunch hours and had long conversations about whatever came into our heads. I was very impressed with the whole group. They were the first females I'd met who actually had something to say.

One day I returned to the office from my lunch hour to find everyone abnormally subdued. Our office was going to be moved away from the city.

No one was keen on this, because it meant the whole company, instead of maintaining small branches here and there, would be under one roof. We would all have to knuckle under and behave. I decided to resign.

My boss offered me a rise in pay if I stayed. He said I was the best laboratory assistant they'd ever had. The decision was taken out of my hands when I suddenly developed industrial acne as a result of being allergic to the chemicals I was using.

By the time I left the laboratory job, I had developed an interest in psychology. I was more realistic about myself now. I realised that the chances of me finding a job I was really happy in were remote. I needed to do further study. I decided to enrol in university for the following year, along with Jill who, having now completed her Leaving, was keen to study Law.

Home improvements

Home improvements were a long time coming to our house. Now that I was getting older and had more experience of the world, I wanted our home to be more like everyone else's. Not that I wanted our lifestyle to change; rather, I was hoping that Mum might be persuaded to spend a bit of money and install some modern conveniences. There were some things I found increasingly difficult to live with — like the pink chip heater in the bathroom and the way Nan boiled up all our clothes in the copper.

The copper was good in that your clothes always came out clean, if a trifle shrunken. What was not good was the fact that numerous cigarette burns and holes gradually appeared in every item due to Nan's incessant smoking. Even Mum was becoming fed up.

One afternoon, Mum went out and bought a twin-tub washing machine and installed it in the laundry. 'From now on, the clothes are washed in this machine,' she told Nan crossly. 'I won't have any more holes in my dresses.'

Nan was reluctant to use the machine. It ran off electricity and she feared that, combined with the water, she'd get electrocuted. Mum finally gave her an ultimatum: use the machine or give up smoking while she washed. Now, giving up smoking for any length of time to Nan was like cutting off an arm or a leg. She agreed to have a go at the machine.

The pink chip heater in our bathroom had been a thorn in my side for years. Jill, Bill and I had all pleaded with Mum to have a new hot-water system installed, but Mum was adamant that she couldn't afford one. We knew this was just an excuse, because with Mum's florist business doing well, and the loan paid off, we were now better off than we'd ever been.

Great skill and ingenuity were required to maintain a consistent trickle of hot water from the shower, which was positioned over the bath. In fact, it was only possible by one of two methods. The first required teamwork. A leisurely soak could be enjoyed if someone else could be persuaded to man the heater and continually feed it with small woodchips and pieces of scrunched-up newspaper while you showered. The second method was more modest, but less convenient. Three buckets of woodchips were placed near the heater. As the water coming from the shower cooled, you leapt naked from the bath, taking care not to slip on the bare cement floor, threw a few handfuls of chips into the heater, and leapt back under again.

The issue finally came to a head one Saturday afternoon when a friend of mine asked if he could shower at our place before going out that evening. We assumed that everyone's bathroom was the same, and so we began to matter-of-factly explain the workings of our chip heater.

I watched as my friend's ready smile slowly changed to dismay, and then to a lopsided grin.

'Stop,' he cried. 'Stop having me on!'

The culture shock Jeff experienced when he saw our heater was enough to send Mum running to the nearest gas appliance centre in shame.

A new career

Mum was both surprised and pleased when I began an Arts degree in February.

I found university to my liking. I was amazed that none of the lecturers checked to see whether you turned up or not. Even missing tutorials wasn't a deadly sin. I spent many long afternoons in the library, reading books totally unrelated to my course. Then there were hours in the coffee shop discussing the meaning of life, and days stretched out in the sun under the giant palms that dotted the campus. Jill was more conscientious than me, and she was enjoying studying Law and making new friends.

I was studying on a Repatriation scholarship and while there was never any money left over, my needs were small. I'd never been one to indulge in following all the fashion trends, and, apart from my bus fares and lunches, I had few expenses.

I found travelling to university in winter terrible. I hated the cold. I had to catch two buses and they rarely connected in time for me to transfer immediately from one to the other. On really wet, stormy days, I stayed at home. I would sit in front of the fire all day, watch television, and read my latest book from the library. Nan always brought me in a huge lunch.

It amazed me that, after all those years, she was still trying to fatten me up. My brother David and I were her only failures.

By the time I'd been at university a term, I was finding it very difficult to study at home. Apart from the high noise level and general chaos, I had no desk to work at, and, being disorganised myself, I was always losing important notes and papers, which I had to replace by photocopying someone else's.

Then, when the August holidays came around, it suddenly dawned on me that if I was to pass anything, I would have to actually do some work. The trouble was I'd missed out on so much I didn't know where to begin.

My first attempts at a concentrated effort were rather futile because I had to keep interrupting my study to call out, 'Turn down that radio!' or, 'The TV's too loud!' or, 'Will you all shut up, I'm trying to study!'

After a week or so of constant yelling and arguing, I came to the realisation that it was impossible to change my environment. I decided to try and change myself instead. I found that if I tried really hard, I could work amidst the greatest mess and loudest noise level with no bother whatsoever. I just switched off and pretended I was the only one in the house.

This was no mean feat, because our house was always full of people. Many of my brother David's friends loved staying overnight and would just doss down on the lounge room floor. David had just begun high school that year. It never occurred to any of us to tell Mum there'd be someone extra for tea. We just assumed that she'd make what she had go a little bit further. I have to admit I was one of the worst offenders, but Mum never complained. She always told us, 'Your friends are welcome in this house.'

My technique for passing my exams that first year was simple: I crammed. The knowledge I gained was of little use to me afterwards, because as soon as my exams were over, I deleted it from my memory. I passed that year with a B and three C's. Mum was pleased, but she urged me to spend more time studying so I could score A's, like Jill.

My brother Bill also had important exams that year, his Leaving. Unfortunately, he was not successful. However, he was able to find employment fairly quickly as a clerk with the Public Service.

I decided that I would like to spend my second year at university living away from home. Mum was mortified by the idea. I would be the first to leave the family nest. She urged me to reconsider.

After weeks of tearful arguments, she relented and said that if the Repatriation Department agreed to pay my fees, I could go. Fortunately, they did agree, and I was soon ensconced in my own little room in Currie Hall, a co-educational boarding house just opposite the university.

Now for most of my teenage years, Mum had been concerned over my lack of interest in boys. I had had plenty of good friendships with the opposite sex, but never a real romance. She was worried I would end up an old maid, and she, an old lady with no grandchildren. But now that I was living in a co-ed college, she suddenly started worrying that I would develop an interest I couldn't control and join the permissive society.

It was difficult for Mum to let me grow up. She often visited me at Currie Hall, but she always left in tears. One night, we had a huge argument because I wouldn't kiss her goodbye. I thought she was expecting a bit much, wanting me to kiss her in front of ten male students gathered around the exit to my building — I had an image to maintain. Eventually, I asked Mum not to come and see me at all if she was going to break down. It was too exhausting.

I had great difficulty seeing through my second year. I had developed an intense dislike of the subject I was majoring in. At our first tutorial, I was dismayed when I discovered that a good deal of our laboratory work would involve training white rats. Rats were one of the few animals I disliked.

Apart from handling lab rats, I was sick of trying to master statistics. I had a mental block when it came to any form of mathematics. 'Rats and Stats,' I complained to a fellow student one day, 'I came here to learn about people.' I got to the stage where I was ready to pull out of university completely. However, I was going out with Paul, a schoolteacher, by then, and he persuaded me to stick it out.

I met Paul through his brother, with whom I had been friends for many years. In fact, Bruce had lived with our family for a while. He was like a brother to me and also a favourite of Nan's. Bruce was a lot like my brother Bill.

Nan never disappeared when Paul or Bruce were around. She actually seemed to enjoy their company. Paul commented once that Nan reminded him of many of the old people who had looked after him up North. I just nodded. It never occurred to me at the time to think about who those people were.

In a short period, Paul and I got to know each other well, spending a lot of time together. We discovered that we had a lot in common. I liked the artistic side of his nature and he seemed to find my wit amusing. Also, he fitted into our family well.

Paul had spent his childhood in the North-west, living mostly at Derby. His parents were missionaries, as were his grand-parents and many of his relatives. When Paul was thirteen his family moved to Perth, where his parents started a hostel for mission children who came to the city to attend high school. Paul found high school very difficult at first, because, apart from the normal adjustments all children have to make and the fact that he had come from such a vastly different environment, he had a language problem. He only spoke pidgin English.

By the end of the second term of my third year at university, we'd fallen in love and decided to get married. This came as a real shock to Mum, because I had always told her Paul was just another good friend. It kept her off my back.

I added to her trauma by telling her I'd decided to be married in our backyard. This immediately prompted her to worry about how she could manage to lock up all the chooks so they didn't molest my wedding guests. And, of course, there was the problem of Curly.

Mum pushed one panic button after another over the following weeks. The drive was too sandy, the grass too prickly and nearly dead, she didn't have enough chairs or glasses or plates. How much food would we need, where did she get it from, how many guests would be coming? I told her that there'd only be about one hundred people. I thought this would allay her fears, but it only served to heighten them. In the end, I said to her quite sternly,

'Pull yourself together. You're the mother of the bride. You've got to stop worrying and get organised. Think of it as a challenge!'

It was the best advice I could have given her. There was nothing Mum loved more than a challenge.

Our wedding date was set for two months hence, and, as the days passed, Mum swung into action like a real trooper. Every morning and night, she watered the grass in an attempt to coax back the green colour normally associated with lawn. However, as the big day drew closer, she became obsessed with the yard, specifically, the drive. For some reason, it became the focal point of all her worries.

One afternoon, a huge load of gravel was deposited on our verge. And three days later, a three-foot-high cement roller, weighing in the vicinity of a ton, arrived. In the meantime, Bill had agreed to help rake out the gravel over the drive, but when he arrived to see the cement roller, he looked at Mum in disgust and said, 'What the bloody hell is that?'

'It's to help flatten the gravel. You know, make it more like bitumen.'

Bill scratched his head and breathed out. 'Yeah ... and how are we going to pull it up and down?'

Mum was not to be put off. 'Look, it's got these two sticks poking out. I thought you boys could strap yourselves between them and pull it along.'

'Mother dear,' he said between clenched teeth, 'if you think I'm gunna strap myself to that bloody thing, you've got another thing coming. Sorry, Sal,' he said as he turned to me, 'not even for you.'

'That's okay, Bill, it was Mum's idea.'

When Mum approached David the following day, he was more sympathetic. After she pleaded with him, he promised to give it a go.

It was nearly a hundred degrees in the shade the day he strapped himself to the roller. Mum cheered him on with cold glasses of lemonade and comments like, 'You're the only one who does anything for me, David.' This kept him going for a couple of hours; however, as the temperature continued to rise, his strength sapped.

'I'm not doin' any more, Mum. Bill was right, it's a bloody stupid idea!'

Mum spent the following week working on me, telling me in detail how bad the drive was and hinting that Paul might like to take a turn.

The following Saturday, after lunch, we led him like a lamb to the slaughter. Anxious to get him started, Mum positioned herself between the straps and, with grunts and groans, indicated what was expected of him. Paul looked desperately at me. I looked at the roller.

'Please?' I pleaded.

'All right,' he relented. And, removing his shirt, he strapped himself to the roller and began pulling.

'Oh Paul, that's good,' Mum encouraged. 'You're much better than David.'

He laboured admirably for two hours. But finally, he staggered inside, dripping with sweat, and collapsed on the lounge.

'Listen, Sal,' he gasped. 'I don't care if people get their feet dirty or if their shoes stick in the gravel. They can break their bloody ankles for all I care. I'm not pulling that roller another inch.'

Just then, Mum entered with more lemonade. 'Drink this. You're a silly boy working in that heat.' Paul choked on the lemonade and then looked at Mum in amazement.

'That'll do for now, Paul,' Mum said kindly. 'It's too hot to work any more. Perhaps you could finish it off tomorrow?' Paul's stunned silence was enough to send Mum scurrying after Jill.

Owning up

My wedding day, the ninth of December 1972, dawned bright and sunny. I nicked into town early that morning to buy a wedding dress. I found an Indian caftan that I liked; it was cream with gold embroidery down the front. I was pleased because it was lovely and cool; it was becoming obvious that the day was going to be a stinker. By the time I got home, the temperature was over the hundred-degree mark.

My Aunty Vi arrived early to help. Aunty Vi had been a close friend of Mum's in her teenage years and they were both florists. Although they hadn't seen much of one another over the years, they still maintained a friendship on the basis of an occasional lunch date or phone call.

Our laundry was jammed with buckets of cut flowers. 'Mum,' I complained as I tried to fight my way through the buckets to the toilet, 'you won't need all these flowers. And what on earth are these for?' I called as I spied a huge carton of plastic roses.

'Never mind what they're for,' Mum said crossly. 'You just stay out of the way and mind your own business!'

I was suspicious by then. 'You're not up to anything silly, are you, Mum?'

'Of course she isn't,' Nan grumbled as she came to her rescue.

'Now you hurry up and get out of here. We've got work to do.'

'Well, listen Nan,' I said, 'whatever else you get up to, make sure you lock up the chooks. And I don't want Curly interfering with anyone.'

'Oh, the chooks are all right,' she replied. 'I'll pen them up before anyone comes. Curly's going to be in my room.'

Just then, Paul's parents arrived. I made the introductions, and then as I was about to head for the shower, Bill came in.

'Sal,' he said, 'There's something I'd like to say to you.'

'Sure, Bill, what is it?'

'I just wanted you to know this. If Paul doesn't ever do the right thing by you, you just let me know, and I'll fix things up.'

'I'll remember that, Bill,' I said, 'but Paul's a nice bloke. I don't think we'll have any problems.'

'Yeah, well, just thought I'd say that to you, okay?'

'Thanks, Bill.' Bill left, and I couldn't help thinking that Mum's prophecy after Dad died had finally come true. Bill really was the man of our house. I felt very lucky. I had a wonderful family.

When I emerged from the shower, cooler and cleaner, I found Paul's dad, Mr Morgan, busily stacking up glasses in the kitchen. Mrs Morgan had disappeared and so had everyone else. I wandered out the back and, to my surprise, saw Mum, Aunty Vi and Mrs Morgan squatting on their knees in the dirt. They were surrounded by buckets and buckets of cut flowers. 'That's right, Margaret,' Mum said coaxingly to my future mother-in-law, 'just stick them straight in like that. No one will know the difference.'

Just then, Nan joined them. 'I've put all those plastic roses in the front garden, Glad,' she said. 'They do look beautiful. You'd think they were real.'

Oh no, I thought. They can't be doing this! I raced back in through the house and out to the front. Garishly coloured flowers of all descriptions were stuck in what had previously been bare earth. They stood straight up, their faces towards the sun.

Mum appeared behind me. 'Oh Sally, what are you doing here?' she asked nervously.

'MUM! How could you??! Honestly, Mum, this is one of the stupidest things you've ever done!'

'But the garden looks lovely now, Sal. No one will know they're standing there with no roots.'

'It's a stinking hot day. They'll keel over in half an hour.'

'No, they won't. Nan's keeping the sprinkler on them right up till the guests start arriving.'

'Oh, Mum,' I wailed, 'you'll never change!'

Everything seemed to go smoothly after that. The wedding ceremony was brief and to the point.

After the ceremony was over, I went in search of Nan. I'd been concerned that, with the yard full of people she considered strangers, she might pull one of her disappearing acts. Mum had already explained to her that it was important she be seen as she was the grandmother of the bride. I finally found her behind our old garden shed, crying.

'Nan, what's wrong?'

'You kids don't need me any more,' she sobbed, 'you're all grown up now.'

'But we still need you,' I replied, trying to reassure her. She shook her head and continued to cry.

'Would you like me to get Mum?' I asked anxiously.

She nodded. So I patted her arm and went and got Mum. She persuaded Nan to go inside the house, where she settled her down with a cup of tea. I felt at a loss. It seemed it never mattered what I did, it was always the wrong thing.

The rest of the afternoon wasn't too traumatic. Little things like the chooks and dogs running wild and a few guests ending up drunk didn't seem to matter. Everyone enjoyed themselves immensely and quite a few people commented that it was the most unusual wedding they'd ever been to. Mum took this as a compliment.

It was close to midnight when the last guest finally left. No one had wanted to go home.

'I did all right, didn't I, Sally?' Mum asked smugly.

'Yeah,' I replied, 'maybe you should go into the catering business.'

'I was thinking that myself!'

I gaped at her in fear. We both laughed.

Shortly after my wedding, I found out that I had passed all my units at university, except Psychology. I wasn't surprised. I disliked the work I was doing so much that I hadn't bothered to study for my exams. I decided to change my major for the following year, but Paul talked me out of it. 'You'll have to repeat,' he said.

'Repeat?' I was disgusted at the thought. Another year with the rats was almost too much to bear. However, I'd heard that there was some human content in third-year Psychology, so I decided to persevere.

Towards the end of the summer vacation, Paul and I moved into a run-down old weatherboard house in South Perth. The toilet was miles down the back of the yard, only one gas burner worked on the stove, the hot-water system wasn't even as decent as the old chip heater we'd had at home, and the place was infested with tiny sandfleas. After living in there for a few weeks, we also discovered that there were rats residing underneath the floorboards. For some reason, none of this seemed to bother us. We thought the place had character and it was adventurous being on our own.

And I was learning new skills, like how to cook and make beds. Considering what a good cook Nan was, it might have been expected that I'd have more flair, but I was hopeless. Nan had never allowed us to cook as children, or even to wash up the dishes. She'd always shoo us away with the comment, 'You stay out of my kitchen.'

To Nan's credit, she had taught me how to light a fire, chop wood, gut chickens and look after sick animals. However, I found these were skills I rarely had to use now.

After a while, Jill moved in with us and then two other friends as well. We were a happy little group. Most of our evenings were filled with Bob Dylan music, poetry and long discussions about current world issues. It was a lovely time in my life.

The day the university year began, I had to force myself to attend. I was convinced I was going to fail again. Many times, I came near to giving up my course entirely, but Paul always talked me into continuing. He gave me the impression that some of my attitudes were very immature. That was quite a shock. I had never thought of myself as being immature before.

Now that Jill and I were once again living in the same house, we often had long talks about our childhood. And the subject of Nan's origins always came up.

'We'll never know for sure,' Jill said one night. 'Mum will never tell us.'

'Hmmn, I might start pestering her again. We're older now, we've got a right to know.'

'What does Paul think?'

'When I asked him whether he thought Nan was Aboriginal, he just laughed and said, "Isn't it obvious? Of course she is."' Paul, of course, had been brought up with Aboriginal people.

'I don't think we can really decide until we hear Mum admit it from her own lips.'

A few weeks later, Mum popped in her for usual visit, laden with fattening cakes and eager to tell me about the latest bargain she'd bought at auction. We settled down in the kitchen and had a cup of tea. Mum was soon in a relaxed and talkative mood.

Then, after a while, there was a lull in the conversation, so I said very casually, 'We're Aboriginal, aren't we, Mum?'

'Yes, dear,' she replied, without thinking.

'Do you realise what you just said?!' I grinned triumphantly.

Mum put her cake back onto her plate and looked as though she was going to be sick.

'Don't you back down!' I said quickly. 'There's been too many skeletons in our family closet. It's time things came out in the open.' After a few minutes' strained silence, Mum said, 'Why shouldn't you kids know now? You're old enough; besides, it's different now.'

'All those years, Mum,' I said, 'how could you have lied to us all those years?'

'It was only a little white lie,' she replied sadly.

I couldn't help laughing at her unintentional humour. In no time at all, we were both giggling uncontrollably. It was as if a wall that had been between us suddenly crumbled away. I felt closer to Mum then than I had for years.

A beginning

I was very excited by my new heritage. When I told Jill that evening what Mum had said, she replied, 'I don't know what you're making a fuss about. I told you years ago Nan was Aboriginal. The fact that Mum's owned up doesn't change anything.' Sometimes, Jill was so logical I wanted to hit her.

'Jill, it does mean something, to have admitted it. Now she might tell us more about the past. Don't you want to know?'

'Yeah, I guess so, but there's probably not much to tell.'

'But that's just it, we don't know. There could be tons we don't know. What other skeletons are lurking in the cupboard?'

'You always did have too much imagination!'

'I'm going to keep pestering her now till she tells us the whole story.'

'She won't tell you any more.'

'Maybe not,' I replied, 'but the way I look at it, it's a beginning. Before, we had nothing. At least now, we've got a beginning.'

'Mum's right about you, you should have gone on the stage.'

When Mum popped in a week later with a large sponge cake filled with chocolate custard, I was ecstatic. Not because of the cake, but because I had a bombshell to drop, and I was anxious to get on with it. I made coffee for a change and I waited until

Mum was halfway through a crumbling piece of sponge before I said, 'I've applied for an Aboriginal scholarship.'

'What?!' she choked as she slammed down her mug and spat out the sponge.

'There's an Aboriginal scholarship you can get, Mum. Anyone of Aboriginal descent is eligible to apply.'

'Oh Sally, you can't,' Mum giggled, as if speaking to a naughty child.

'Why can't I?' I demanded. 'Or are you going to tell me that Nan's really Indian after all?'

'Oh, Sally, you're awful,' Mum chuckled, and then she added thoughtfully, 'Well, why shouldn't you apply? Nan's had a hard life. Why shouldn't her grandchildren get something out of it?'

'Exactly,' I replied.

I don't think Mum realised how deep my feelings went. It wasn't the money I was after; I was still receiving the Repatriation scholarship. I desperately wanted to do something to identify with my new-found heritage, and that was the only thing I could think of.

When I was granted an interview for my scholarship application, Mum was amazed. I think she expected them to ignore me. She was very worried about what I was going to tell them. She had been inventing stories and making exaggerated claims since the day she was born. It was part of her personality. She found it difficult to imagine how anyone could get through life any other way, so, consequently, when I responded to her question about my interview with, 'I'm going to tell them the truth', she was flabbergasted.

I was successful in my scholarship application, but for the

next few months, I was the butt of many family jokes. We all felt shy and awkward about our new-found past. No one was sure what to do with it or about it, and none of the family could agree on whether I'd done the right thing or not. In keeping with my character, I had leapt in feet first. I'd wanted to do something positive. I'd wanted to say, 'My grandmother's Aboriginal and it's a part of me too.' I wasn't sure where my actions would lead, and the fact that Nan remained singularly unimpressed with my efforts added only confusion to my already tenuous sense of identity.

'Did Mum tell you I got the scholarship, Nan?' I asked one day.

'Yes. What did you tell them?'

'I told them that our family was Aboriginal but that we'd been brought up to believe differently.'

'What did you tell them about me?'

'Nothing. So relax.'

'You won't ever tell them about me, will you, Sally? I don't like strangers knowing our business, especially government people. You never know what they might do.'

'Why are you so suspicious, Nan?' I asked gently. She ignored my question and shuffled outside to do the garden.

Slowly, over that year, Mum and I began to notice a change in Nan. Not a miraculous change, but a change just the same. Her interests began to extend beyond who was in the telephone box opposite our house, to world affairs. Nan had always watched the news every night on each channel if she could, but now, instead of just noting world disasters, she began to take an interest in news about black people.

If the story was sad, she'd put her hand to her mouth and say, 'See, see what they do to black people.' On the other hand, if black people were doing well for themselves, she'd complain, 'Just look at them, showing off. Who do they think they are? They just black like me.'

About this time, Nan's favourite word became Nyoongah. She'd heard it used on a television report and had taken an instant liking to it. To Nan, anyone dark was now Nyoongah. Africans, Burmese, African Americans were all Nyoongahs. She identified with them. In a sense, they were her people, because they shared the common bond of blackness and the oppression that, for so long, that colour had brought. It was only a small change, but it was a beginning.

In a strange sort of way, my life had new purpose because of that. I wondered whether, because Jill and I had accepted that part of ourselves, perhaps Nan was coming to terms with it, too. I was anxious to learn as much as I could about the past. I made a habit of taking advantage of Mum's general good nature.

'Where was Nan born, Mum?' I asked her one day.

'Oh, I don't know. Up North somewhere. You know she won't talk about the past. She says she can't remember.'

'Mum, is there anyone who could tell me anything about Nan?'

'Only Judy. Nan worked for their family.'

'In what capacity?'

'Oh, you know, housework, that sort of thing.'

'You mean she was a servant?'

'Yes, I suppose so.'

'How long did she work for them?'

'Oh, I don't know, Sally. Why do you always bring this up? Can't we talk about something else?' Nearly all of our conversations ended like that.

Amazingly, I passed my Psychology unit at the end of that year. I even scored a B. I was looking forward to my final year because there was quite a large slice about people in the course and that, after all, was what I'd come to learn about.

By now, both Jill and I had many friends at university. All our lives, people had asked us what nationality we were. Most had assumed we were Greek or Italian, but we'd always replied, 'Indian.' Now when we were asked, we said, 'Aboriginal.'

We often swapped tales of what the latest comment was. A few of our acquaintances had said, 'Aaah, you're only on the scholarship because of the money.' At that time, the Aboriginal allowance exceeded the allowance most students got. We felt embarrassed when anyone said that, because we knew that that must be how it seemed. We had suddenly switched our allegiance from India to Aboriginal Australia and I guess, in their eyes, they could see no reason why we would do that except for the money.

Sometimes, people would say, 'But you're lucky, you'd never know you were that; you could pass for anything.' Many students reacted with an embarrassed silence. Perhaps that was the worst reaction of all. It was like we'd said a forbidden word.

Up until now, we'd both thought Australia was the least racist country in the world; now we knew better. I began to wonder what it was like for Aboriginal people with really dark skin and broad features. How did Australians react to them? How had white Australians reacted to my grandmother in the past? Was that the cause of her bitterness?

About halfway through that year, 1973, I received a brief note from the Commonwealth Department of Education, asking me to come in for an interview with a senior officer of the department. I was scared stiff.

'Mrs Morgan,' the senior officer said as I sat down in his office two days later. 'We'll get straight to the point. We have received information, from what appears to be a very reliable source, that you have obtained the Aboriginal scholarship under false pretences. This person, who is a close friend of you and your sister, has told us that you have been bragging all over the university campus about how easy it is to obtain the scholarship without even being Aboriginal. Apparently, you've been saying that anyone can get it.'

I was so amazed at the ridiculousness of the accusation that I burst out laughing. That was a great tactical error on my part.

'This is no laughing matter! This is a very serious offence. Have you lied to this department?'

I felt very angry. It was obvious I had been judged guilty already, and I knew why. It was because Jill and I were doing well. The department considered it more in keeping with Aboriginal students if we both failed consistently.

'Who made the complaint?'

'I can't tell you. We promised confidentiality.'

'It was no friend of ours. If they know us really well, they would have been to our home and met my grandmother and mother, in which case they'd never have made this complaint.'

'Is that all you have to say?'

'You've obviously already judged me guilty, so what else can I say?'

'You don't seem very keen to prove your innocence.'

I'd had it by then. 'Look,' I said angrily, 'when I applied for this scholarship, I told your people everything I knew about my family. It was their decision to grant me a scholarship, so if there's any blame to be laid, it's your fault, not mine. How do you expect me to prove anything? What would you like me to do, bring my grandmother and mother in and parade them up and down so you can all have a look? There's no way I'll do that, even if you tell me to. I'd rather lose the allowance. It's my word against whoever complained, so it's up to you to decide, isn't it?'

My heart was pounding fiercely. It was very difficult for me to stand up for myself. I wasn't used to dealing with authority figures so directly. No wonder Mum and Nan didn't like dealing with government people, I thought. They don't give you a chance.

The senior officer looked at me silently for a few minutes and then said, 'Well, Mrs Morgan. You are either telling the truth, or you're a very good actress!'

I was amazed. Still my innocence wasn't to be conceded.

'I'm telling the truth,' I said crossly.

'Very well, you may go.' I was dismissed with a nod of the head. I was unable to move.

'I'm not sure I want this scholarship any more,' I said. 'What if someone else makes a complaint? Will I be hauled in here for the same thing?'

The senior office thought for a moment, then said, 'No. If someone else complains, we'll ignore it.'

Satisfied, I left and walked quickly to the elevator. I felt sick.

It was just as well I'd lost my temper, I thought. Otherwise, I wouldn't have defended myself at all. It was the thought that somehow Mum and Nan might have to be involved that had angered me. It had seemed so demeaning.

Then I thought, maybe I'm doing the wrong thing. It hadn't been easy trying to identify with being Aboriginal. No one was sympathetic, so many people equated it with dollars and cents, no one understood why it was so important. I should chuck it all in, I thought. Paul was supporting me now; I could finish my studies without the scholarship. It wasn't worth it.

I wanted to cry. I hated myself when I got like that. I never cried, and yet, since all this had been going on, I'd wanted to cry often. It wasn't something I could control. Sometimes when I looked at Nan, I just wanted to cry. It was absurd. There was so much about myself I didn't understand.

The bus pulled in and I hopped on and paid my fare. My eyes were clouded with unshed tears. I turned my face to the window and stared out. Had I been dishonest with myself? What did it really mean to be Aboriginal? I'd never lived off the land and been a hunter and a gatherer. I'd never participated in corroborees or heard stories of the Dreamtime. I hardly knew any Aboriginal people. What did it mean for someone like me?

Halfway home on the bus, I felt so weighed down with all my questions that I decided to give it all up. I would telephone the department and tell them I wanted to go off the scholarship. And I'd do it as soon as possible.

Just then, for some reason, I could see Nan. She was standing in front of me, looking at me. Her eyes were sad. 'Oh Nan,' I sighed, 'why did you have to turn up now, of all times?' She vanished as quickly as she'd come. I knew then that, for some reason, it was very important I stayed on the scholarship. If I denied my tentative identification with the past now, I'd be denying her as well. I had to hold on to the fact that, some day, it might all mean something. And if that turned out to be the belief of a fool, then I would just have to live with it.

When I told Jill about my interview, she was amazed. 'I'm glad it was you and not me,' she said. 'I couldn't have said what you did. I can't stick up for myself like that.'

'I don't know how I did it, either,' I replied. 'But you know what, I'm really glad I did. From now on, I'm going to be more assertive. Who do you think dobbed me in?'

'Dunno. It makes you suspicious, though.'

For the next few weeks, we watched all our friends closely, searching for any small signs of guilt and betrayal. There were none.

'I give up,' I told Jill one lunchtime, 'if we keeping watching everyone, we'll never trust anyone again. Better to forget it.'

On the weekend, I told Mum what had happened. She was much more upset than I had anticipated. Nan took an interest in the proceedings as well. She wasn't angry, just very pessimistic. 'You shouldn't have done it, Sally,' she growled. 'You don't know what they'll do now. They might send someone to the house. Government people are like that. Best to say nothing, and just go along with them till you see which way the wind blows.'

'Oh don't be stupid, Nan,' Mum yelled. 'She did right to defend herself. No one's going to come snooping around. Times have changed.'

'You're stupid, Glad,' Nan grunted, and before Mum could reply, she shuffled out to her bedroom.

'She's frightened, you see,' Mum said. 'She's been frightened all her life. You can tell her things have changed, but she won't listen. She thinks it's still like the old days when people could do what they liked with you.'

'Could they, Mum?'

'Oh, I don't know. I don't want to talk now, Sally. Not now.'

However, my run-in with the Education Department did produce some unexpected results. Mum suddenly became more sympathetic to my desire to learn about the past. One day, she said to me, 'Of course, you know Nan was born on Corunna Downs Station, don't you?'

'I've heard her mention that station,' I replied. 'Remember when David got that map of the north and showed her on the map where Corunna Downs was? She was quite excited that it was on a map, wasn't she? Yet, she still won't talk.'

'I know. It really upsets me, sometimes.'

'Mum, who owned Corunna Downs?'

'Judy's father, Alfred Howden Drake-Brockman.'

'Fancy that. I suppose that's why Judy and Nan are so close. That and the fact that Nan used to work for the family.'

'Yes. Nan was Judy's nursemaid when she was little.'

'Tell me the other things she used to do then, Mum.'

'I remember she used to work very hard. Very, very hard … Oh, I don't want to talk any more. Maybe some other time.'

For once, I accepted her decision without complaint. I knew now there would be other times.

Even though I was married, I saw my family nearly every day. There were such strong bonds between us it was impossible for me not to want to see them. Just as well Paul was the uncomplaining sort.

One Saturday afternoon, I was over visiting Mum when she asked me to help her with Curly. 'He's in one of his cantankerous moods and won't come inside,' she said. 'See what you can do with him.'

I eyed Curly in disgust from my standpoint on the front porch. He was lying in the middle of the road as usual. All morning, cars had been tooting at him, all to no avail. Curly moved for no one.

'You'll get run over, Curl,' I called in my Let's Be Reasonable voice. Still no response.

'I think you'd better go inside, Mum,' I advised. 'He'll never listen to me with you standing there.' Mum disappeared and I called once again to the flat layer of black fur lying on the road.

'Listen, you bloody mongrel,' I yelled.

But before I could continue my tirade, Nan came up behind me and said, 'Don't say that, Sally, it hurts me here,' she patted her chest. 'Fancy, my own granddaughter sayin' that.'

'It's no use you going on, Nan,' I said without listening, 'he is a bloody mongrel!'

'Don't! Don't!' she said, as though I was inflicting some kind of pain on her.

'Nan,' I reasoned, 'someone has got to be firm with him or he'll get run over one day.'

'What are you talkin' about, Sally?'

'I'm talking about Curly,' I replied in exasperation, and then paused. 'Why, what are you talking about?'

Nan gazed towards the oval directly opposite our house. Just where the bitumen ended and the grass began sat a small Aboriginal boy. I recognised him as belonging to a house around the corner from us. He was intent on some sort of game.

'Nan!' I said in shock. 'You don't think I was calling that little fella a bloody mongrel, do you? Oh Nan, I'd never call a kid that. How could you think I'd do such a thing?'

'I've heard them called that. It's not right, they got feelings.'

'Nan, did you say you'd been called that?'

She put her hand over her mouth.

'Who was it, Nan? What rotten bugger called you that?'

'Don't want to talk about it, Sally,' she shook her head.

'You've been called that more than once, haven't you, Nan?' She ignored my question and turned to go inside. Halfway through the doorway, she stopped and said, 'Sal? Promise me you won't ever call them that? When you see a little bloke like that, think of your Nanna.'

I nodded my head. I was too close to tears to reply. I wished I could wipe memories like that from her mind. She looked so vulnerable, not like her usual complaining self. It was times like that I realised just how much I loved her.

A visitor

After I graduated from university, I continued postgraduate studies in Psychology at the Western Australian Institute of Technology.

My brother David was also successful in completing his Leaving exams that year, and now Helen was the only one of us still at school. She was in third year high school.

In 1975, I gave birth to a daughter, Ambelin Star. The family was very excited; it was our first grandchild. Mum cried when she saw her, and so did Nan. Now, instead of collecting antiques, Mum started buying up toys and children's books.

I passed my course at WAIT and decided to give up study for a while to concentrate on being a wife and mother.

I continued to prompt Nan about the past, but she dug her heels in further and further. In fact, she became so consistently cantankerous that she gradually drove us all away. Everyone in the family got to the stage where, if we could avoid seeing Nan, we would.

Paul and I also became fed-up with city life at this time, so we thought we'd try the country for a while. Paul's parents were now living in Albany on a small farmlet, so we moved down to Albany for twelve months.

Jill had now left university and was helping Mum run her florist shop. She had had enough of study for a while, although she did return later and complete an Arts degree.

My brothers were now working. Bill was up North with a mining company and David in the city with a firm of auctioneers. David was also working at night and in the evenings as a musician with a rock-and-roll band.

In 1976, Helen successfully completed her Tertiary Admittance Examination. The TAE had replaced the Leaving examination.

In 1977, lack of money and poor employment prospects drove us back to Perth, where Paul began his own cleaning business. He had resigned from teaching when we moved to Albany. I became pregnant with my second child that year and was very sick, spending a number of weeks in hospital.

Because of these various factors, my search for the past seemed to have reached a standstill from 1975 to 1978.

By the time I'd had my second child, Blaze Jake, in 1978, a change was beginning to take place in our family. Nan's brother, Arthur, began making regular visits. He was keen to see more of Nan now they were both getting older. And he was very fond of Mum.

'Who is he?' I asked, when I found him parked in front of the TV one day with a huge meal on his lap.

'Arthur, Nan's brother. When you were little, he visited us a couple of times, remember?'

I cast my mind back and suddenly I saw him as he had been so many years before. Tall and dark, with a big smile.

'Is he her only brother?' I asked. 'No other relatives hidden away in the closet?'

'No,' Mum laughed, 'he's the only one that I know of. He's a darling old bloke, a real character. I think Nan's jealous of him.'

'That'd be right! Great to think they're seeing each other after all these years.'

'It's wonderful,' Mum said with tears in her eyes. 'I've told him to come and stay whenever he likes.'

It took a while for me to get close to Arthur. He loved Mum, but he was wary of the rest of us. If he had known how insatiably curious we were about him and his past, he would probably have been scared off.

But on one of these early visits, he unexpectedly did provide us with a very vivid picture from the past. Some old photographs of Nan, taken in the 1920s. Nan had always refused to allow any of us to take her photograph, so it was exciting to be able to see her as a young woman. Nan, however, was not impressed.

It became obvious in a very short time that Nan and Arthur were brother and sister, because they fought like cat and dog. When Arthur was around, Nan behaved like a child. She was jealous because Mum loved him and enjoyed his company. She was also frightened of what he might tell us.

'Don't listen to him,' she told us one day when he was halfway through a story about the old times.'

'Is she goin' on again?' Arthur said to Mum. He loved pretending Nan wasn't there.

'Nobody's interested in your stories,' she grumbled. 'You're just a silly old blackfella.'

'Aah, you'll have to think of a better name than that to call me,' he smiled, 'I'm proud of bein' a blackfella. Anyway, you're a blackfella yourself, what do ya think of that?!'

Nan was incensed. She bent down to him and said, 'I may be a blackfella, but I'm not like you. I dress decent and I know the right way to do things.'

'I feel sorry for you,' Arthur replied sympathetically, 'you got my pity. You don't have a good word to say about anyone. I tell you, this is a warning, one day I'm gunna get a young wife. I'll bring her round here and then you won't dare to talk to me like that.'

'No one would have you,' she hooted. 'Young girls are smart these days, they see you comin' and they run like a willy-willy. Who'd want a silly old blackfella like you, you got no money.'

'You don't know what I got,' Arthur replied. 'I got all my land up in Mukinbudin, that's more than what most blackfellas got.'

'Your land, your land,' Nan mimicked him. 'I bet all the kangaroos eat your crops.'

That was the last straw as far as Arthur was concerned. He'd told her about a part of his land that he kept uncleared so the wildlife could prosper in peace; now she was using this confidence against him.

'I'm tellin' you nothin' no more,' he said. 'We'll ignore her. Tell her to go, Glad,' he added to Mum.

'Now, Nanna,' Mum said in her Let's Be Reasonable voice. 'Arthur is your only brother. Whenever he comes, you pick a fight with him. You're both getting old — it's time you made up. He doesn't want to listen to your complaints all the time.'

'And we don't want to hear his stories either,' Nan said forcefully. 'He goes over and over the same old thing. He wasn't the only one hard done by.'

'No, he wasn't,' Mum replied, 'but at least he'll talk about it. You won't tell us anything. Whenever we ask you about the past, you get nasty. We're your family; we've got a right to know.'

Nan opened her mouth to reply, but Arthur cut her off with, 'If you don't go, Daisy, I'll tell them your Aboriginal name.'

Nan was furious. 'You wouldn't!' she fumed.

'Too right I will,' said Arthur. Nan knew when she was beaten. She stormed off.

'What is it?' both Mum and I asked excitedly after she'd gone.

'No, I can't tell you,' he said. 'It's not as if I wouldn't like to, but Daisy should tell you herself. There's a lot she could tell you. She knows more about some of our people than I do.'

'But she won't talk, Arthur,' Mum replied. 'Sometimes, I think she thinks she's white. She's ashamed of her family.'

'Aah, she's bin with whitefellas too long. They make her feel 'shamed — that's what white people do to you. Why should we be 'shamed, we bin here longer than them. You don't see the black man diggin' up the land, scarrin' it. The white man got no sense.'

I sat and listened to many conversations between Mum and Arthur after that. Whenever he turned up for a visit, Mum would ring me at home and say, 'He's here!' and I would go rushing over.

On one such afternoon, I wandered out to the backyard to find Nan and Arthur under a gum tree, jabbering away in what sounded to me like a foreign language. I sat down very quietly on the steps and listened. I prayed they wouldn't see me.

After a few minutes, Nan said, 'My eyes aren't that bad, Sally. I can see you there, spyin' on us.'

'I'm not spying,' I defended myself. 'Keep talking, don't let me stop you.'

'We're not talkin' no more,' Nan said. 'You hear that, Arthur, no more!'

Just then, Mum came out with a tray full of afternoon tea. After she'd given them their tea and cake, I followed her inside.

'Mum,' I said excitedly, 'did you hear them? They were talking in their own language! And not just a few words — she was jabbering away like she always talked like that.'

'But it must be years since she used her own language. Fancy, her remembering it all this time.'

Over the following weeks, whenever I saw Nan, I'd bring up the topic of her language. She was very defensive at first and would lose her temper with me, but, after a while, she gradually came around. One day she said, 'Hey, Sally, you know what goombo is?'

'No, what?' I grinned.

'Wee-wee.'

Nan chuckled and walked off.

She told me many words after that, but I could never get her to say a sentence for me. It would be a long time before I would learn to be content with the little she was willing to give.

Where there's a will

'I'm going to write a book.' It was the beginning of 1979, a good time for resolutions.

Mum looked shocked. 'Another new scheme, eh?' she asked sarcastically.

'Not just a scheme this time, Mum,' I said determinedly. 'This time, I'm really going to do it.'

'Is it going to be a children's book?'

'Nope. A book about our family history.'

'You can't write a book about our family,' she spluttered, 'you don't know anything!'

'Aah, but I'm going to find out, aren't I? Where there's a will, there's a way, Mum,' I said light-heartedly. 'I've got plenty of will.'

'Oh Sally,' she groaned. 'You get everyone all fired up and then you don't carry through. Well, I'm not going to worry about you writing a book. You'll soon lose interest.'

'Wanna bet?'

Mum took me more seriously the following week when I brought a typewriter and started to type. As she watched my jerky two-finger effort she said, 'It'll take you a lifetime to do a page at that rate.'

'No, it won't. I'm going to teach myself how to type. I'll get quicker.'

'What are you typing, anyway?'

'I'm putting down what I know. It's not much, but it's a start. Then I'm going to try and fill in what I don't know, and I expect you to help me. You've spent all your life with Nan. You must be able to tell me something about her. What seems unimportant to you could be a really good lead for me. For example, how come Nan and Judy are so close?'

'I've already told you, Nan was Judy's nursemaid. Judy was quite sick as a child. I suppose that drew them closer together.'

'How come Nan was their nursemaid and not someone else?'

'Oh, I don't know. I told you Nan came from the station that Judy's father owned.'

'Yeah, that's right,' I said slowly. 'You know, I think I'll go and talk to Judy. I don't know why I didn't think of it before. There, you see, you've given me a lead already!'

'Judy won't tell you anything; her and Nan love secrets.'

'No harm in trying. I'll ask her about the station and why they chose Nan to come down to Perth. I'll ask her about Ivanhoe too.' Ivanhoe was a grand old house in Claremont situated on the banks of the Swan River, where Nan had spent much of her working life.

'I went to Battye Library the other day, Mum. I wanted to read up about Aborigines.'

'Oh,' Mum said keenly, 'did you find out anything interesting?'

'I sure did. I found out there was a lot to be ashamed of.'

'You mean we should feel ashamed?'

'No, I mean Australia should.'

Mum sat down. 'Tell me what you read.'

'Well, when Nan was younger, Aborigines were considered sub-normal and not capable of being educated the way whites were. You know, the pastoral industry was built on the back of slave labour. Aboriginal people were forced to work; if they didn't, the station owners called the police in. I always thought Australia was different to America, Mum, but we had slavery here, too. The people might not have been sold on the blocks like the American Negroes were, but they were owned, just the same.'

'I know,' Mum said. There were tears in her eyes. 'They were treated just awful. I know Nan ...' She stopped. 'I better get going, Sal, I've got to go to work early tomorrow.'

'What were you going to say?'

'It's nothing, Sally, nothing. I don't want to talk about it now. Maybe later. If you want my help, you'll have to give me time.' I could see Mum was quite upset.

'Okay, I'll give you all the time you want, as long as you help me. Hey, I meant to tell you: I got a copy of your birth certificate the other day.'

'How did you do that? I didn't know you could do that.'

'It's easy. You just apply to the Registrar General's Office. I said I wanted it for the purposes of family history. I tried to get Nan's and Arthur's, but they didn't have one. Hardly any Aboriginal people had birth certificates in those days.'

'Sally ...' Mum said tentatively, 'who did they say my father was? Was that on the certificate?'

'There was just a blank there, Mum. I'm sorry.'

'Just a blank?' Mum muttered slowly. 'That's awful, like nobody owns me.'

I hadn't anticipated Mum being so cut up about it. I felt awful. 'I'm really sorry, Mum,' I said gently. 'I got your certificate because I thought it might give me some leads, but it didn't. You've asked Nan who your father was, haven't you?'

'Yes.'

'Maybe Judy would know.'

'She probably does,' Mum sighed, 'but she won't tell. I asked her once and she just kept saying, "It's in the blood", whatever that means.'

A few days later, I rang Aunty Judy. I explained that I was writing a book about Nan and Arthur and I thought she might be able to help me. We agreed that I would come down for lunch and she said she could tell me who Nan's father was. I was surprised. I had expected to encounter opposition. I felt really excited after our talk on the telephone. Would I really discover who my great-grandfather was? If I was lucky, I might even find out about my grandfather as well. I was so filled with optimism I leapt up and down three times and gave God the thumbs-up sign.

My day for lunch at Aunty Judy's dawned, and Mum had agreed to drop me in Cottesloe, where Judy was now living, and mind the children while we had our talk.

During lunch, Aunty Judy suddenly said, 'You know, I think I have some old photos of your mother you might be interested in. I'll dig them out.'

'Oh great! I'd really appreciate that.'

After lunch, we retired to the more comfortable chairs in the lounge room.

'Now, dear,' Aunty Judy said, 'what would you like to know?'

'Well, first of all, I'd like to know who Nan's father was and also a bit about what her life was like when she was at Ivanhoe.'

'Well, that's no problem. My mother told me that Nan's father was a mystery man. He was a chap they called Maltese Sam and he used to be cook on Corunna Downs. He was supposed to have come from a wealthy Maltese family; I think he could have been the younger son, a ne'er-do-well. My mother said that he always used to tell them that, one day, he was going back to Malta to claim his inheritance. The trouble was he was a drinker. He'd save money for the trip and then he'd go on a binge and have to start all over again. He used to talk to my father, Howden, a lot. He was proud Nanna was his little girl.'

'Did he ever come and visit Nan when she was at Ivanhoe?'

'Yes, I think he did, once. But he was drunk, apparently, and wanted to take Nanna away with him. My mother said to him, you go back to Malta and put things right. When you've claimed your inheritance, you can have Daisy. We never saw him again. I don't know what happened to him. Nan didn't want to go with him; we were her family by then.'

'Did you meet Maltese Sam?'

'Oh, goodness, no. I was only a child. My mother told me the story.'

'How old was Nan when she came down to Perth? And what were her duties at Ivanhoe?'

'She was about fifteen or sixteen when she arrived. She looked after us children.'

'Aunty Judy, do you know who Mum's father is?'

'Your mother knows who her father is.'

'No, she doesn't. She wants to know and Nan won't tell her.'

'Well, I'm not sure I should tell you. You never know about these things.'

'Mum wanted me to ask you.'

Aunty Judy paused and looked at me silently for a few seconds. Then she said slowly, 'All right. Everybody knows who her father was — it was Jack Grime. Everyone always said that Gladdie's the image of him.'

'Jack Grime? And Mum takes after him, does she?'

'Like two peas in a pod.'

'Who was Jack Grime?'

'He was an Englishman, an engineer, very, very clever. He lived with us at Ivanhoe; he was a friend of my father's. He was very fond of your mother. When she was working as a florist, he'd call in and see her. We could always tell when he'd been to see Gladdie; he'd have a certain look on his face. He'd say, "I've been to see Gladdie" and we'd just nod.'

'Did he ever marry and have other children?'

'No. He was a very handsome man, but he never married and, as far as I know, there were no other children. He spent the rest of his life living in Sydney. He was about eighty-six when he died.'

'Eighty-six? Well, that couldn't have been that long ago, then? If he was so fond of Mum, you'd think he'd have left her something in his will. Not necessarily money, just a token to say he owned her. After all, she was his only child.'

'No, there was nothing. He wasn't a wealthy man; there was

no money to leave. You know Roberta?'

'Yes, Mum's been out to dinner with her a few times.'

'Well, she's the daughter of Jack's brother, Robert. She's Gladdie's first cousin.'

'Mum doesn't know that. Does Roberta?'

'Yes, she knows. She asked me a year ago whether she should say something to your mother, but I said it'd be better to leave it.'

'Perhaps Mum could talk to her. Can you tell me anything about Nan's mother?'

'Not a lot. Her name was Annie. She was a magnificent-looking woman. She was a good dressmaker. My father had taught her how to sew. She could design anything.'

Our conversation continued for another half an hour or so. I kept thinking, had Mum lied? Did she really know who her father was? Was she really against me digging up the past, just like Nan? I had one last question.

'Aunty Judy, I was talking to Arthur, Nan's brother, the other day and he said that his father was the same as yours, Alfred Howden Drake-Brockman. Isn't it possible he could have been Nan's as well.'

'No. That's not what everyone said. I've told you who Nan's father is. I'm certain Arthur's father wasn't Howden. I don't know who his father was.'

'Arthur also told me about his half-brother, Albert. He said Howden was his father, too.'

'Well, he went by the name of Brockman so I suppose it might be possible, but certainly not the other two.'

'Well, thanks a lot, Aunty Judy. I suppose I'd better be going.

Mum will be here any minute. She's picking me up.'

'You know who you should talk to, don't you? Mum-mum. She's still alive and better than she's been for a long time.' Mum-mum was a pet name for Aunty Judy's mother, Alice.

'She must be in her nineties by now,' I said. 'Do you think she'd mind talking to me?'

'No. I don't think so, but you'd have to go interstate. She's in a nursing home in Wollongong. You could probably stay with June.' June was Judy's younger sister. Nan had been her nursemaid too.

'I'll think about it, Aunty Judy. Thanks a lot.'

'That's all right, dear.'

I walked out to the front gate and, just as I opened it, Mum pulled up in the car.

'How did you go?' she said eagerly.

'All right,' I replied. 'Mum, are you sure you don't know who your father is?'

'Of course I don't know who my father is, Sally. Didn't you find out, after all?' She was disappointed. I felt ashamed of myself for doubting her.

'No Mum, I found out. It was Jack Grime, and Roberta is your first cousin.'

'Oh, God. I can't believe it!' She was stunned.

'Can you remember anything about him, Mum? You're supposed to look a lot like him.'

'No, I can't remember much, except he used to wear a big gold watch that chimed.'

'Judy said he used to visit you when you were working as a florist. Can you recall any times when he did?'

'Well, yes, he popped in now and then, but then a lot of people did. I was a friendly sort of girl. Sometimes, after Nan had left there, I would go and have lunch with him at Ivanhoe. To think I was lunching with my own father!'

An overwhelming sadness struck me. My mother was fifty-five years of age and she'd only just discovered who her father was. It didn't seem fair.

'Mum, does Nan know I've been to see Judy?'

'Yes, she knew you were going. She's been in a bad mood all week. Did you find out anything else?'

'Judy says Nan's father was a bloke called Maltese Sam. That he came from a wealthy family and wanted to take Nan away with him.'

'Maltese Sam? What an unusual name. I've never heard anyone talk about him. Arthur's coming tomorrow night, I'll ask him what he thinks. Of course, you know who he says is Nan's father, don't you?'

'Yeah, I know. Judy doesn't agree with him.'

The following evening, Mum and I sat chatting to Arthur. After we'd finished tea, I said, 'I visited Judith Drake-Brockman the other day, Arthur. I thought she might be able to tell me something about Corunna Downs and something about Nan.'

'You wanna know about Corunna, you come to me. I knew all the people there.'

'I know you did.' I paused. 'Judy told me Nan's father was a chap by the name of Maltese Sam. Have you ever heard of him?'

'She said WHAT? Don't you listen to her,' he said. 'She never lived on the station, so how would she know?'

'Well, she got the story from her mother, Alice, who got the story from her husband, Howden, who said that Annie had confided in him.'

Arthur threw back his head and laughed. Then he thumped his fist on the arm of his chair and said, 'Now you listen to me: Daisy's father is the same as mine. Daisy is my only full sister. Albert, he's our half-brother. His father was Howden too, but by a different woman.'

'So you reckoned he fathered the both of you.'

'By jove, he did! Are you gunna take the word of white people against your own flesh and blood? I got no papers to prove what I'm sayin'. Nobody cared how many blackfellas were born in those days, nor how many died. I know because my mother, Annie, told me. She said Daisy and I belonged to one another. Don't you go takin' the word of white people against mine.'

Arthur had us both nearly completely convinced, except for one thing, he avoided our eyes. So I said again, 'You're sure about this, Arthur?'

'Too right! Now, about this Maltese Sam. Don't forget Alice was Howden's second wife and they had the Victorian way of thinking in those days. Before there were white women, our father owned us. We went by his name, but later, after he married his first wife, Nell, he changed our names. He didn't want to own us no more. They were real fuddy-duddies in those days. No white man wants to have black kids runnin' round the place with his name. And Howden's mother and father, they were real religious types. I bet they didn't know about no black kids that belonged to them.'

We all laughed then. Arthur was like Mum, it wasn't often he failed to see the funny side of things.

When we'd all finally calmed down, he said, 'You know, if only you could get Daisy to talk. She could tell you so much. I know she's got her secrets, but there are things she could tell you without tellin' those.'

'She won't talk, Arthur,' I sighed. 'You know a lot about Nan, can't you tell us?'

He was silent for a moment, thoughtful. Then he said, 'I'd like to. I really would, but it'd be breakin' a trust. Some things 'bout her I can't tell. It wouldn't be right. She could tell you everything you want to know. You see, Howden was a lonely man. One night at Ivanhoe, we both got drunk together and he told me all his troubles. He used to go down to Daisy's room at night and talk to her. I can't say no more. You'll have to ask her.'

After he left, Mum and I sat analysing everything for ages. We knew that the small pieces of information we now possessed weren't the complete truth.

'Sally,' Mum said, breaking into my thoughts, 'do you remember when Arthur first started visiting us and he said Albert was his full brother?'

'Yeah, but that was before he knew us well.'

'Yes, but remember how he almost whispered when he told us the truth about Albert? He didn't want to hurt the feelings of any of Albert's family and he loved him so much I suppose he thought it didn't matter.'

'Yeah, I know. You think there might be more to Nan's parentage?'

'It's possible.'

'There's another possibility: Howden may have been her

father. But there could be something else, some secret he wants to keep, that is somehow tied in with all of this. Perhaps that's why he didn't look us in the eye.'

'Yes, that's possible, too. And I can't see why he wouldn't tell us the truth, because he knows how much it means to us. I don't think we'll ever know the full story.'

'It makes me feel so sad to think no one wants to own our family.'

'I know, Mum, but look at it this way: just on a logical basis, it's possible he was her father. We know he was sleeping with Annie, and Arthur said that even after he married his first wife, he was still sleeping with Annie, so he could have sired her.'

'Yes, it's possible.'

'Well, that's all we can go on then: possibilities. Now, Judy said Jack Grime was your father, but maybe he wasn't. He was living at Ivanhoe at the time you were born, but that doesn't necessarily mean he fathered you, does it?'

'Oh God, Sally,' Mum laughed, 'let's not get in any deeper. I've had enough for one night.'

Part of our history

A few days later, I popped in to see Mum. Nan told me she'd just gone up the shops and would be back in a few minutes. I decided to wait. I wasn't intending to say anything to Nan about my trip to Judy's, as I wasn't in the mood for an argument. Uncharacteristically, she began following me around the house, making conversation about whatever came into her head. Finally, after half an hour of general chit-chat, she blurted out, 'Well, what did Judy tell you?'

We both went and sat down in the lounge room. After we'd made ourselves comfortable, I said, 'Well, she told me that you were the nursemaid at Ivanhoe.'

Nan grunted. 'Hmmph, that and everything else.'

'Judy also said your father was a bloke called Maltese Sam, and that he visited you at Ivanhoe and wanted to take you away with him. Do you remember anyone visiting you there?'

'Only Arthur, and that wasn't till I was older.'

'There was no one else?'

'I'd know if I had visitors, wouldn't I? I'm not stupid, Sally, despite what you kids might think.'

'We don't think you're stupid.'

Nan pressed her lips together and stared hard at the red-brick fireplace directly opposite where we were sitting.

'Nan,' I said gently, 'was your father Maltese Sam?'

She sighed, then murmured, 'Well, if Judy says he is, then I s'pose it's true.' I looked at her closely; there were tears in her eyes. I suddenly realised she was hurt, and I felt terrible, because I'd caused it. I decided to change the subject. I began to talk about my children and the latest naughty things they'd been up to. We had a chuckle, and then I said, 'Wouldn't you have liked to have had more children, Nan?' She shrugged her shoulders and looked away.

'Think I'll do some gardening now, Sal,' she said. 'Those leaves need raking up.'

Three evenings later, after they'd finished eating a big roast dinner, Mum said quietly, 'Don't go and watch television yet, Nan, I want to talk to you. Sit with me for a while.'

'I'm not talking about the past, Gladdie. It makes me sick to talk about the past.'

Mum persisted, in spite of this protest, and said, 'I'm only going to ask you one question, then you can do whatever you like, all right?' Nan sat still. 'Now, you know Sally's trying to write a book about the family?'

'Yes. I don't know why she wants to tell everyone our business.'

'Why shouldn't she write a book?' Mum said firmly. 'There's been nothing written about people like us, all the history's about the white man. There's nothing about Aboriginal people and what they've been through.'

'All right,' she muttered, 'what do you want to ask?'

'Well, you know when you write a book, it has to be the truth.

152

You can't put lies in a book. You know that, don't you Nan?'

'I know that, Glad,' Nan nodded.

'Good. Now, what I want to know is who you think your father was. I know Judy says it was Maltese Sam and Arthur says it was Howden. Well, I'm not interested in what they say. I want to know what you say. Can you tell me, Nan: who do you think he really was?'

Nan was quiet for a few seconds and then, pressing her lips together, she said very slowly, 'I … think … my father was … Howden Drake-Brockman.'

It was a small victory, but an important one. Not so much for the knowledge, but for the fact that Nan had finally found it possible to trust her family with a piece of information that was important to her.

Mum gave Nan a week to recover before tackling her about Jack Grime. She'd been trying to spend more time at home and, in a gentle way, talk about the past.

Finally one evening, she said, 'Nan, I know who my father was.' Nan was silent. 'It was Jack Grime, wasn't it, Nan?' Silence. 'Wasn't it, Nan?'

'Judy tell you that, did she?'

'Yes.'

'Well, if that's what she says.'

'But was he, Nan?'

'I did love Jack.'

'What happened then, Nan? Tell me what happened. Why didn't it work out?'

'How could it? He was well-off, high society. He mixed with all the wealthy white people; I was just a black servant.'

Nan ignored Mum's pleas to tell her more and disappeared into her room, leaving Mum to cry on her own.

When Mum and I talked about this later, Mum said, 'You know, he probably was my father, Nan obviously had a relationship with him. If he was, I feel very bitter towards him. There's never been any acknowledgment or feeling of love from him. Later, when he moved east with Judy's family, he never wrote, there were no goodbyes, and I never saw or heard from him again. All I can remember is that he used to tell wonderful stories. He was like a childhood uncle, but definitely not a father.'

We hoped that Nan would tell us more, especially about the people she had known on Corunna Downs. Mum was anxious to hear about her grandmother, Annie, and her great-grandmother, and I was keen to learn what life had been like for the people in those days. To our great disappointment, Nan would tell us nothing. She maintained that if we wanted to find out about the past, we had to do it without her help. 'I'm taking my secrets to the grave,' she told Mum and me dramatically, one day.

The next time I saw Arthur, he asked me to tell him about the book I was writing.

'I want to write the history of my own family,' I told him.

'What do you want to do that for?'

'Well, there's almost nothing written from a personal point of view about Aboriginal people. All our history is about the white man. No one knows what it was like for us. A lot of our history has been lost. People have been too frightened to say anything. There's a lot of our history we can't even get at, Arthur. There are all sorts of files about Aboriginals that go way back, and the government won't release them. You take the old police files. They're not even controlled by Battye Library — they're controlled by the police. And they don't like letting them out, because there are so many instances of police abusing their power when they were supposed to be Protectors of Aborigines! I mean, our own government had terrible policies for Aboriginal people. Thousands of families in Australia were destroyed by the government policy of taking children away. I just want to try to tell a little bit of the other side of the story.'

Arthur was silent for a few seconds, then he said thoughtfully, 'I tell you how I look at it: it's part of our history, like. Do you think you could put my story in that book of yours?'

'Oh Arthur, I'd love to!'

'Then we got a deal. You got that tape-recorder of yours? We'll use that. You just listen to what I got to say. If you want to ask questions, you stop me. Now, some things I might tell you, I don't want in the book, is that all right?'

'Yes, that's fine. I won't put anything in you don't want me to.'

'Before we start, there's something else. I don't want my story mixed up with the Drake-Brockmans'. If you're goin' to write their story as well, I'll have none of it. Let them write their own story.'

'Agreed.'

It took three months or more to record Arthur's story. We went over and over the same incidents and, each time, he added a little more detail. He had a fantastic memory. Sometimes when he spoke, it was like he was actually reliving what had happened. We became very close. There were times when I worried that I was working him too hard, but, if I slacked off, he'd say, 'We haven't finished yet, you know.' He was always worried about my cassette recorder. I had to check it each time to make sure it was working. 'You don't want to miss nothin',' he'd remind me. 'Those batteries get low.' Even if the batteries were new, I still had to check.

One night, after I'd spent a long session with Arthur, I fell into bed, exhausted. That night, I had a dream. I knew he was going to die.

'What's wrong?' Paul asked me the following morning when I burst into tears over my cornflakes.

'It's Arthur,' I sobbed, 'he's going to die.'

'Aw, Sal,' Paul said, 'what makes you think something like that.'

'I dreamt about it last night. I think he knows he's going — that's why he wants to get his story done.'

'Well, if he is, there's nothing you can do about it. The best thing is to finish his story, seeing it means so much to him.'

'Yeah, I know.'

So it was that I spent the next few weeks nonstop recording everything I could. When we finished, we were both pleased.

'We've done it,' Arthur laughed. 'We've done it! I got no more story to tell now.'

'I can't believe it,' I said. 'We've actually finished.'

'I got a good story, eh?'

'You sure have.'

'You think people will read that?'

'Of course they will, and they'll love it. If they don't, they've got no heart.'

'What you gunna do now? You gunna type that all up?'

'Yep. I'll finish typing all the cassettes. Then I'll put it all together, because we've got bits and pieces all over the place. You know I'm going to Sydney, don't you, to meet Alice Drake-Brockman? She's still alive, you know.'

'Say hello to her for me.'

'I will. I'm only going for a week. When I get back, we can talk some more.'

'Too right. 'Cause you know I'm going back to Mucka, don't you? I got a yearning for that place. My own home, my land. I been away too long. Can you understand that?'

'Yes.'

'Anyway, I told you my story. You'll look after it, won't you?'

'Yes, of course I will.' I couldn't say any more. I had a lump in my throat. I knew he wanted to die on his own land.

Links with the past

'Are you sure it's wise going to Sydney now, Sally? Why don't you want till after the baby's born?' It was now 1982 and I was six months pregnant with my third child.

'It's too important to wait, Mum. Alice is in her nineties — how do I know she'll be alive in three months' time? I'll be fine, Mum. Don't worry.'

The following week, I flew to Sydney and then caught the bus to Wollongong. Aunty June, Judy's sister, and her husband, Angus, met me at the bus station. I felt very nervous. The last time I'd seen them, I was a child; now I was a woman with a mission.

I could not have had two kinder hosts. They did everything to make me feel at home. We swapped many funny yarns and stories about home.

Alice Drake-Brockman was in a nearby nursing home. She was ninety-three and in the best of health. Aunty June took me to the home and explained who I was and why I was there.

'You look a lot like your mother,' Alice said. 'Now tell me, how is Daisy? It's been years since I've seen her.'

'She's fine, getting old, though. Her eyesight isn't too good.'

'So you want to know a bit about Corunna, eh?'

'Yes, would you mind if I asked you a few questions?'

'Not at all. Go ahead.'

'Can you tell me who Nan's father might have been, Alice?'

'Oh yes. Your great-grandfather was a Maltese. I think he came from a wealthy family, but was the younger son. He was always saying he must go back and right his affairs in the old country. He had good blood in him, but he never got past the nearest pub. One time, I think he managed to get as far as Carnarvon, but then he spent all his money and had to come back again.'

'Did you ever meet Nan's mother?'

'Oh yes! She was a born designer. I didn't get to know her well, because I left the station, and, when I left, I took Daisy with me. Annie had said to me shortly before, "Take her with you, mistress, I don't want my daughter to grow up and marry a native." It was at her request that I took Daisy. Of course, what I was doing was illegal, you weren't supposed to bring natives into Perth. The magistrate said, "I can't give you permission to take her, because that's against the law, but the captain can't refuse her passage." She was fourteen years of age when she came with me and terrified of the sea. She'd never even seen a boat, living inland all those years.'

'What was Corunna Downs Station like then?'

'Well, I can't tell you a lot about that, because I was only there once. After my husband sold Corunna, he bought Towera, which was about nine hundred miles away. When my husband was on Corunna, all the squatters were asked to send boys down to school. I suppose that was when Albert and Arthur went down. Albert came back to work at Corunna, but Arthur ran away. He had ambitions of his own. Corunna Downs was named by my husband. He was reading a book at the time with the natives, and in it was a poem about Corunna, I think it was in Spain, so he named the station after that. When I went to Corunna, there were about forty natives working for us. Every Sunday night, we'd roll the piano out and onto the verandah; it'd be cold, so we'd have a big log fire out in the open. The natives would sit around and we'd have a church service and a singsong. The natives just loved it. At nine o'clock, we'd stop. Then, they'd all be given cocoa and hot buns. That was their life. The natives never liked to work. You had to work with them if you wanted them to work. They always wanted to go walkabout. They couldn't stand the tedium of the same job. We used to change their jobs. Daisy always had that tendency. She'd get tired of one job, so I'd say, "Come on, let's chuck the housework", and we'd go shopping.'

'Did Nan ever see her mother again?'

'Yes. I sent her back for a holiday with Howden. I said, "Take her back for a holiday, let her see her mother." She went back by boat. She saw them and she was happy, but, by then, we'd become her family.'

'What were her duties at Ivanhoe?'

'Oh, housework, that sort of thing. She was always good with Granny. She'd come quietly and take her shoes off after lunch when it was time for her to have her afternoon sleep. She was simply devoted. No white trained nurse had better experience. She grew up loving us and we were her family; there were no servants. She couldn't read a clock, but she knew the time better than any of us. She knew everybody's handwriting that came to the place.'

'Why did she leave Ivanhoe?'

'Why? The police came and took Daisy from me. She was manpowered during the war. No one could have any home help. She was a wonderful cook. Later, she rented a little house near the Ocean Beach Hotel. I gave her quite a lot of furniture, brooms and things, that I could do without. That's how she supplied herself.'

'Can you tell me who my mother's father might have been?'

'No. I couldn't tell you. He must have been white, maybe a station hand. When Daisy was pregnant, I was absolutely ignorant. My husband said to me one night, "I think you'd better get up. Daisy seems to be in pain." She slept in a room just off ours; it was his dressing-room, which we turned into a room for Daisy. She was groaning and I said, "What's up, Daisy?" She said, "I don't know, mistress, but I think I'm going to have a baby." I hadn't any idea. She was wearing loose dresses. I called Betty, who was about sixteen at the time. I said, "Betty, had you any idea?" "Yes, of course I had, Mum," she said. Well, I was absolutely ignorant, so I rushed over in the car to the hospital, knowing that Nurse Hedges would be there. I told her and she said, "Look, don't wait to get permission. Go home and pack for her and get her to the midwifery hospital. They won't be able to refuse her." So I went and packed a suitcase and took her to the hospital. The baby was born a few hours later. But who the father was, we never found out. Gladys was always a beautiful girl. She went to Parkerville; we took her there. That was a home run by the Church of England sisters, a charity home for the ones that had no parents. Gladys grew up with just as nice manners as anybody could wish. Later, when she was grown up, I said to the florist in Claremont, "Will you take this girl on trial for me? I just can't bear to think of her becoming a servant somewhere." So they took her to please me, even though it was forbidden to take on a native, and they kept her as one of the family. She looked like a lovely Grecian girl. She never looked back. You see, she was so well brought up by those Church of England sisters. It was only through my being an old scholar that I was able to get her in. It was very hard to get her in.'

When Alice finished talking, I felt a little stunned. All my life, I'd been under the impression that Mum had lived with Nan at Ivanhoe. It was a shock for me to discover that she'd been placed in a children's home. Why hadn't she told us?

'Well, it's been very interesting talking to you,' I smiled. 'I've heard a lot about you over the years. Can I come and see you again some other time?'

'Any time you like, dear.'

I spoke with Alice again after that, and she told me a little more about Corunna and the early days. I was pleased I'd made the trip, even though I hadn't come up with a great deal of new information.

In talking to Alice, it dawned on me how different Australian society must have been in those days. There would have been a strong English tradition amongst the upper classes. I could understand the effects these attitudes could have had on someone like Nan. She must have felt terribly out of place. At the same time, I was aware that it would be unfair of me to judge Alice's attitudes from my standpoint in the nineteen eighties.

On my return from Sydney, Mum met me at the airport. On the

way home in the car, I described my trip in detail to Mum. I never mentioned her being in Parkerville Children's Home. I wasn't sure how to tackle her about that.

Several days later, I popped round to visit Jill. Jill was living in Subiaco, sharing a house with Helen, and was still working in Mum's florist shop. I was quietly sipping a cup of coffee when she suddenly said, 'Oh goodness, I forgot! It's Arthur,' she said. 'He's dead. He died a few days ago. He went home to Mukinbudin and, apparently, he just had a heart attack and died virtually straightaway.'

I wanted to cry, but I couldn't. I felt too shocked. I knew he wanted to go, but the reality of never being able to talk to him again was very painful. He was one of the few links I had with the past.

I saw Mum that afternoon. 'Did you see him before he went to Mucka?'

'Yes.'

'When?'

Mum looked a bit awkward. 'The night before you came home from Sydney. I think he came round to say goodbye. He knew he was going to die once he got to Mucka, and he wanted to see us all one last time. He really wanted to see you, Sally. I was supposed to take you around the night you got home.'

'Aw, Mum, why didn't you?'

'You looked so tired when you got off the plane, and I was worried about the baby. I knew if I did, you'd insist on going over there.'

'Oh, Mum, he might have wanted to tell me something.'

'I don't think so, dear. I'm sorry. He knew you cared about

him and you'd make sure people read his story. He knew that, so don't go upsetting yourself.'

'Yeah, I guess so. When's the funeral?'

'In a couple of days' time, you coming?'

'Yeah, I'll come. I hate funerals.'

I went with my brother Bill and Mum. I couldn't feel sad for him any more. I knew he was tired of his life, and I knew he was happy. When we got home, we described the funeral to Nan. She hadn't wanted to go. She hated people looking at her. Nan had a good cry, then she said, 'Well, I can't be too sad for him, he wanted to go. I got no brother now.' After that, she rarely mentioned him.

It was about a week after Arthur's funeral that I decided to ask Mum about Parkerville Children's Home. She had always led us to believe that she'd spent all her childhood at Ivanhoe. It wasn't that she'd actually lied about it; it was a sin of omission more than anything else.

I raised the issue over afternoon tea. But before she had time to gather her wits, I said, 'You deliberately misled us. Why on earth didn't you tell us the truth?' It was a tactical error; if Mum hadn't been on the defensive before, she certainly was now.

'I spent holidays at Ivanhoe. Anyway, there's nothing to tell,' she replied. 'Who told you I was brought up in Parkerville, anyway?'

'Alice told me. How did you think I felt, finding out like that. I was shocked.'

'You didn't say anything to June, did you?'

'Of course not, but it was all I could think about. You're

lucky I didn't ring you up and abuse you over the phone. You're supposed to be helping me with this book and here you are, hoarding your own little secrets. And you complain about Nan.'

'All right, all right! I'll tell you about it, one day, but only if you promise me you won't tell any of the others.'

'I'll only promise that if you'll promise to spill the beans one day. I mean soon, not in ten years' time. I could be dead by then.'

I spent the next few months transcribing Arthur's cassettes and putting his story together. It was very important to me to finish his story. I owed him a great debt. He'd told me so much about himself and his life, and, in doing so, he'd told me something about my own heritage.

When I had completed it all, I rang Mum.

'It's finished,' I said when she answered the phone. 'Arthur's story is finished.'

'Can I come and read it?'

'That's what I'm ringing you for.'

Arthur Corunna's Story

My name is Arthur Corunna. I can't tell you how old I am exactly, because I don't know. A few years ago, I wrote to Alice Drake-Brockman, my father's second wife, and asked her if she knew my age. She said that I could have been born around 1893–1894. Later, her daughter Judy wrote to me and said I could have been born before that. So I guess I have to settle for around there somewhere. Anyway, I'm old, and proud of it.

The early years of my life were spent on Corunna Downs Station in the Pilbara, in the north of Western Australia. We called the top half of the station, where I lived, Mool-nya-moonya. The lower half, the outstation, we called Boog-gi-gee-moonya. The land of my people was all round there, from the Condin River to Nullagine, right through the Kimberley.

After my people had worked for so long on the station, they were allowed to go walkabout. We would go for weeks at a time, from one station to another, visiting people that belonged to us. We always went to Hillside, that was Dr Gillespie's station. The eastern part of Western Australia, that's different. We call that Pukara. Our land was Yabara, the north.

My mother's name was Annie Padewani and my father was Alfred Howden Drake-Brockman, the white station-owner.

*We called him Good-da-goonya. He lived on Corunna Downs
nine years before marrying his first wife, Eleanor Boddington.
She had been a governess in the area. While on the station, he
shared my Aboriginal father's two wives, Annie and Ginnie.*

*Ginnie, or Binddiging as we called her, was a big-built
woman. She was older, argumentative. She bossed my mother
around. I used to cry for my mother when she was in a fight.
I'd run round and grab her skirts and try and protect her from
Ginnie. Ginnie only had one child by Howden, and that was my
half-brother Albert.*

*My mother was small and pretty. She was very young when she
had me. I was her first child. Then she had Lily by my Aboriginal
father. Later, there was Daisy. She is my only sister who shares
with me the same parents. I was a good deal older than her
when they took me away to the mission; she was only a babe in
arms, then. My mother was pregnant with other children, but
she lost them.*

*My Aboriginal father was one of the headmen of our tribe.
He was a leader. He got our people to work on the station
and, in return, he was given a rifle, tea, tobacco and sugar. He
was a well-known man, tall and powerful. Many people were
scared of him. Sometimes, he would go walkabout, right down
to Fremantle, then up through Leonora, Ethel Creek and back
to Corunna Downs. Men were frightened of him because he was
a boolyah man.*

*My uncle and grandfather were also boolyah men. For
centuries, the men in my family have been boolyah men. I
remember when my grandfather was dying, he called me to him.
I was only a kid. He said, 'You know I can't use my power to*

heal myself. I will pass my powers into you and then I want you to heal me.' He did this, and I ran away and played, even though he was calling me. I was only a kid, I didn't understand. My grandfather died. It wasn't until years later that I began to learn just what powers he had given me.

One day, my uncle said to my mother, 'Never worry about Jilly-yung (that was my Aboriginal name). I will look after him when I'm dead. I will always be close to him. He may not know I am there. I may be a bird in the tree or a lizard on the ground, but I will be close to him.' That was my Uncle Gibbya. He was married to Annie's sister.

My Uncle Gibbya was a powerful rainmaker. He didn't always live on Corunna Downs. One day when he was visiting our people, Howden said to him, 'You can work with me on the station as long as you can make it rain.' My Uncle Gibbya said, 'I will make it rain. Three o'clock this afternoon, it will rain.' Howden looked at the sky; it was blue and cloudless. He shook his head. Later that day, white clouds began to gather, like a mob of sheep slowly coming in. At three o'clock, it rained. My uncle got his job. He was the best rainmaker in the area.

On the station, I had my Aboriginal name, Jilly-yung, which meant silly young kid. When I was a child, I copied everything everyone said. Repeated it like a ninety-nine parrot. The people would say, 'Silly young kid! Jilly-yung!'

I loved my mother; she was my favourite. My mother was always good to me. When others were against me, she stood by me. She used to tell me a story about a big snake. A snake especially for me, with pretty eggs. 'One day,' she said, 'you will be able to go and get these eggs.' I belonged to the snake, *and I was anxious to see the pretty snake's eggs, but they took me away to the mission, and that finished that. It was a great mystery. If I had've stayed there, I would have gone through the Law, then I would've known.*

When we went on holidays, we called it going pink-eye, my Aboriginal father carried me on his shoulders when I was tired. I remember one time, it was at night and very dark, we were going through a gorge, when the feather foots, or ginnawandas, began to whistle. I was scared. The whistling means that they want you to talk. They began lighting fires all along the gorge. After we called out our names, my family was allowed through.

One day, I took a tomato from the vegetable garden. I'd been watching it for days. Watching it grow big and round and red. Then I picked it and Dudley saw me. He was Howden Drake-Brockman's brother and we called him Irrabindi. He gave orders for my Aboriginal father to beat me. Maybe he had his eye on that tomato too.

I was beaten with a stirrup strap. I spun round and round, crying and crying. I was only a kid in a shirt in those days. My Aboriginal father never hit me unless an order was given. Then he had to do it, boss's orders. He was good to me otherwise, so I never kept any bad feelings against him.

Dudley Drake-Brockman wasn't like Howden. They were brothers, but they were different. Dudley was a short little man. He couldn't ride. He was cruel and didn't like blackfellas. My people used to say about Dudley ngulloo-moolo, which means make him sick. We didn't want him there. In the end, he got sick and died.

I used to play with Pixie, Dudley's son. We used to fight, too, but I never beat him. I was afraid of his father. My mother used to say to me, 'Jilly-yung, never beat Pixie in a fight. When he wants to fight, you walk away.' She was a wise woman.

Howden was a good-looking man, well liked. He could ride all the horses there, even the buck jumpers. There was one big, black horse he named Corunna. He would always ride him when he went out baiting dingoes.

I remember Howden used to dance on his own in the dining room. He'd be doin' this foxtrot, kicking his leg around with no partner. I used to watch. There was a big dining room then, and a great, huge fan that we had to pull to cool people off who were eating there. They gave us a handful of raisins for doing that.

We had other jobs on the station besides pulling the fan. For every tin full of locusts we killed with a switch, we got one hard-boiled lolly. I remember once, I was a tar boy for the shearers. In those days, it was blade shearing, not like the machines they have now. The shed was stinking hot and the click, click, click of the shears made a rhythmic sound. I couldn't help goin' to sleep. Next thing I knew, I got a smack in the face. They were all singin' out 'TAR! TAR!' and I was asleep. When the girls brought down the dishes of cakes and buckets of tea, I made sure I was there. I wasn't going to sleep through that.

Archie McGregor was one of the few white men on the station. He worked on the windmills and the pumps. When the pumps went bung, Archie had to go down in the deep well and fix them. He was the one that taught Albert and me how to build windmills. Those windmills were a terrible height. They had to be to catch the wind. I thought he was teachin' us things so we could help run the station one day. I was wrong.

When Howden married Eleanor Boddington, he built another house. He didn't stay living with Dudley. He built it by himself too. He was a carpenter.

I spent a lot of my time on the station with my brother, Albert, and my sister, Lily. When we were kids, we'd run round finding lizards, sticking our fingers in the holes in the ground and wood. One time I did that, it was a snake. A snake won't chase you to bite and kill you. They just want to get away. You only get bitten if you tread on them; they're just protectin' themselves.

Albert lost two fingers because of me. I chopped them off in the tank machine. He stuck his fingers in to try and stop the cogs going round. I turned the handle and chopped them off. We were just messing around. I didn't know he had his fingers in there.

Albert was older than me and they started educatin' him early. Mrs McGregor, Archie's wife, was the teacher. She trained Albert to write on a slate with chalk. He had to speak English and learn the white man's ways and table manners. The other children weren't taught, only Albert and, later, me. She also gave us what you call religious instruction. We learnt all about the saints. She had a big roll of colour pictures that we used to look at.

I went with my mother everywhere until they rounded me up to be educated. When I heard they were after me, I ran away. They caught me in the end, put me with Albert and Mrs McGregor. I wasn't allowed to talk blackfella after that. If I did, Dudley beat me. I liked my language, but I got a good hiding if I spoke it. I had to talk English. When I was sleeping on the homestead verandah, I used to call to my mother in my own language, 'Save me meat.'

Of course, when they caught me, Albert could already talk English. When we were being educated, Albert and me slept on the homestead verandah. We had a bed side by side. Some nights, I'd wet my bed and jump into his. I'd dream someone was hitting me so I'd fight them in bed, I'd punch them and call out, then when I looked at my bed, I found it was wet.

Even though Albert was the older one, I took no notice of him. I was the mischievous one. He was too frightened to do anything. Sometimes he needed protecting.

I knew all the people on the station, they was a good mob. There was Chook Eye, Wongyung and Mingibung. They were house-girls. They used to take in cups of tea and look after the house. Then there was Tiger Minnie; she used to help Howden bait the dingoes. No one could bait like her. Then there was Sarah; she was a big woman, she helped look after the garden. She grew pumpkins and cabbages for the cook and shooed the birds away. She was half-caste, like me. When her own baby was born, it was nearly white. A white blackfella. We all reckoned those extra babies belonged to either Fred Stream or Sam Moody, the cook.

We used to call Sam Moody backwards, Moody Sam. He was a white man and a good cook. He'd cook bread, cut it in big slices and give it to the natives through the small kitchen window. We'd all get bread and slices of meat. We'd poke our billies through that little window and get tea too. If Moody Sam didn't cook, we'd get slices of mutton, make a fire outside and cook it ourselves. For extra meat, my people used to catch kangaroos and wild turkeys and fish from the creek. We'd go down to the creek and we'd stand with our legs bent and apart, then we'd catch them between our knees. We'd grab them with our hands and throw them on the bank.

Old Fred Stream, I think he was German. He used to take me on trips to Condin. Corunna Downs wool used to be stored there, ready to be loaded on the sailing ships bound for Fremantle.

On the way back to Corunna Downs, we camped at DeGrey Station. You should have seen all the pretty dresses come runnin' to meet our wagon. There was red, pink and green, all the colours of the rainbow. They was all runnin' to come and see me too. I was only a little fella, I wasn't much in those days.

Some of the people there had pet pigs. They sold two to Fred Stream. Before we reached Corunna Downs, he knocked one on the head and cooked it in the ashes. I reckoned he was cruel, to eat a little pig like that! I couldn't look at him and I couldn't eat it. I kept thinking, fancy killing such a little pig. He was only a baby. I take after my old grandfather, I'm tender-hearted.

I remember one time when I was very small, it must have been Christmas, because I was all dressed up in a shirt and pants that day, and there was so much food laid out on this big table on the verandah. I kept thinking to myself, I should eat more, I should eat more. I knew I wasn't goin' to see food like that again for a long time. I just kept thinkin' what a shame it was to go away and leave it. Even though my belly was already aching, I made myself eat more. A while later, I brought it all up. My belly was swollen and I just couldn't keep it in!

There were always corroborees at Corunna. You needed special permission to watch them. We used to go with Howden. I hadn't been put through the Law by then, because I was still too young. That happens when you are fourteen or fifteen. I didn't want to go through the Law. I used to say, 'Don't let them do that to me, Mum.' I didn't want to be cut this way and that. For the real black ones, it was compulsory. I was half-caste, so I could be exempted. The women were just marked on the chest. Just one mark, here in the middle. That was their ceremony.

There was some wonderful wildlife on Corunna Downs. There was one little bird, he was a jay or a squeaker, he'd sing out three times and then the rains would come. He was never wrong. While he was there, there was always a good feed, but when he was gone, drought! When the little frogs sang out, we knew it was going to rain. They were lovely colours, white and brown with black spots. They were all different, there wasn't one the same. Wonderful creatures. There were no insecticides then to kill the birds. That's why the blackfellas want their own land, with no white man messin' about destroyin' it.

All the people round there, we all belonged to each other. We were the tribe that made the station. The Drake-Brockmans didn't make it on their own. There were only a few white men there, ones that fixed the pumps and sank wells by contract. The blackfellas did the rest.

I remember seein' native people all chained up around the neck and hands, walkin' behind a policeman. They often passed the station that way. I used to think, what have they done to be treated like that. Made me want to cry, just watchin'. Sometimes, we'd hear about white men goin' shooting blackfellas for sport, just like we was some kind of animal. We'd all get scared then. We didn't want that to happen to us. Aah, things was hard for the blackfellas in those days.

One day, I'd like to go back to Corunna Downs, see what improvements there are. I believe it was used for a military base during the war. When I was there, Brockmans built a hump and stuck a flagpole in it. Whenever any visitors came, they raised the Union Jack.

Aah, I always wish I'd never left there. It was my home. Sometimes, I wish I'd been born black as the ace of spades, then they'd never have took me. They only took half-castes. They took Albert and they took me and Katie, our friend. She was put in Parkerville. She had a big doll with her when she went; Albert had me. Others went, too. I was about eleven or twelve.

When I left, Lily cried and cried. She was only little, but she ran away and hid; no one could find her. I was her favourite. She was full blood, real black, so they didn't want to take her. Daisy was only a baby, she didn't know what was goin' on.

They told my mother and the others we wouldn't be gone for long. People were callin', 'Bring us back a shirt, bring us this, bring us that.' They didn't realise they wouldn't be seein' us no more. I thought they wanted us educated so we could help run the station some day, but I was wrong.

When they came to get me, I clung to my mother and tried to sing* them. I wanted them to die. I was too young. I didn't know how to sing them properly. I cried and cried, calling to my mother, 'I don't want to go, I don't want to go! I want to stop with you!' She was my favourite. I loved her. I never saw her again.

***

When we left Corunna Downs to come to the Swan Native and Half-Caste Mission, we had to travel through Marble Bar and then to Port Hedland. We caught the ship, the Ballara; me, my brother Albert, Pixie and Dudley Drake-Brockman. Albert and I travelled steerage. Sometimes, I'd sneak out and head towards the front end of the boat to see what was going on. Dudley Drake-Brockman would always catch me and shout, 'Get back to where you belong!'

It was a fine day when we arrived in Fremantle. We were taken straight to the mission, which was situated near the banks of the Swan River in Guildford.

The first thing they did was christen us. We were christened Corunna; they didn't give us our father's name. That's when I got the name of Arthur. Albert had always been called Albert and he stayed that way.

For a long time, I was very worried about my mother. Albert didn't seem to mind so much. I think he was too frightened to mind anything. You see, we couldn't understand why they'd taken us away. The mission wasn't our family. They called us inmates then, all us kids, just like in a prison.

We soon found out that there were bullies at the mission. I suppose you get them everywhere. There was one that wanted to try us out. I was worried about Albert. I knew he couldn't fight his way out of a paper bag. He was bigger than me, older than me, yet I knew they could belt him up and tie him in knots. I'd tackle whoever was beating up Albert and finish them off. They never tackled me again and they learnt not to touch Albert, because he was my brother.

I was made different to Albert. I could fall off a horse, do anything and there was never nothing damaged or broken, even if I landed on a rock. I'm like rubber, you can bounce me anywhere. Albert wasn't like that. He used to get sick a lot. I cried for him when he was sick.

One man that worked on the mission, Mr Ferguson, he said about Albert and me, 'These boys have been well brought up. They say thank you for everything.' We even said thank you when they gave us a hiding.

They soon learnt I was reliable and that they could give me a job and I'd do it, no matter what. I had ten hurricane lamps to clean. I cleaned the glasses, then filled them with kero. I was the mailman and the milkman too. I delivered milk and eggs to Mr and Mrs Anderson in Guildford. Then I'd continue on to Thompson's place over the railway line; they bought our milk too. There were lots of people who bought things from the mission. I was the only one who was allowed to collect mail from the Midland post office. They sent me because I was the fastest walker.

If Matron needed any medicine, she sent me. She'd give me a letter to take to the chemist. One time while I was waiting in the chemist shop, a lady started talking to me, she was waiting too. She told me what she was there for, and she had so many things wrong with her I was amazed she was still alive. All this time she was talking, she was drinking lemonade. It was a real hot day. She told me all her troubles and I just sat there and listened and looked at her lemonade. She didn't even offer me one drop.

After Albert and me had been there a while, the mission was visited by a man called Governor Bedford. He was an Englishman, a *grey-headed thing. After his visit, the darker kids were separated from the lighter kids. He didn't like us being together.*

Before the Governor's visit, they built a building close to the bridge and near the brickyard. It looked like an ark to us, so we all called it Noah's Ark. We all thought that was fitting, because we was all in there together: white ones and black ones. We liked sharing that ark. Governor Bedford didn't like it one bit. He separated us all out. The light-coloured ones had to go where the girls were and the girls were moved to the west side of the mission.

Funny thing was, they put Freddy Lockyer in with the white kids. He had fair hair and fair skin, but really, he was a white blackfella. He didn't want to go; he wanted to stay with us blackies. He belonged to us, but they made him go. I said to him, 'You're not black enough to stay with us, you have to go.' I felt sorry for him. He was really one of us.

There was always a boundary between the girls and the boys. Apart from when we played, you had to stick to your side. When the girls were older, they were put into service as housegirls and maids for anyone who wanted one. Once the boys reached adolescence, they were completely separated from the girls and put in a nearby orphanage. I suppose they were worried we might chase them.

After a while, the bigger boys started running away to Moora. They were brought back, but if they ran away a second time, the mission people would try and find work for them with the farmers up there. They were all well taught by then. I was still there when nearly all the older boys from the orphanage had run away. The only one left was Pinjarra Frank.

Bob Coulson was another man who worked on the mission. He was a good man with a hammer. I used to watch him. If he saw any cats sneakin' around the chicken house, he'd corner them and hit them on the head with a hammer. A cat only had to look at him and he was a goner.

Coulson wasn't a big man, but he had a nose like a devil. He used to be a soldier and he often showed us his bayonet. He was full of bluff. I think he was afraid the blackfellas might tackle him one day; that's why he kept on showing us his bayonet.

Corunji was Coulson's dog. He was a nice old dog. One day, we were going into Guildford on deliveries and Corunji followed us. We had to cross the railway line, and when a train came, old Corunji started running and barking and chasing the engine. He must have slipped, because his foot went under the wheel and his leg was cut off. We were all crying. 'Corunji, Corunji. Poor old Corunji!' We ran all the way back to the mission to tell Coulson what had happened. He got on his bike and cycled back to the railway line. We all followed. Poor old Corunji was still lyin' there, just lookin' at us as if to say, 'Can't you help me?' Coulson got off his bike, walked over to Corunji, put his hand over his snout, pulled out his hammer and hit him over the head. Then, he got on his bike and cycled back to the mission. He just left him lyin' there. He did that to his own dog. I couldn't help thinking if he'd do that to his own dog, he might do that to me one day. I didn't trust him after that.

When I was in my fourth year at the mission, Coulson caught me and some other boys outside the mission boundaries. We were playing in a public picnic area near the river. It was a popular *spot and we were hoping to find some money that people might have dropped. When he found us, he was real mad. He ordered us back to our dormitory and said he was going to give us a beating. You can imagine how scared we all were.*

We didn't go back to the dormitory; we ran all the way to Midland, to the police station. You see, the police were called Protectors of Aborigines in those days, so we thought we might get some protection from them. We told the policeman what Coulson was going to do to us. He listened then he said, 'Get back to the mission! It's none of my business what happens to you!'

As we came out of the station, Coulson came riding down the road on his bike. He spotted us, rounded us up and walked us back to the mission.

By this time, he was just about boiling over. He shoved us all in a dormitory, locked the door and told us to strip off. Then, when we were naked, he raced around the dormitory like a madman, beating us with a long cane over the head and body. He didn't care where he hit us, he just beat us and beat us till we bled. There was bits of blood everywhere. We were all crying. Some of the boys were screaming, 'No more, no more, master!' He liked you to call him master.

I was the only one that didn't cry out. He came over and grabbed me and said, 'Arthur, I've never had to beat you before, but BY GOD I'm going to give it to you now!' He beat me and he beat me, but I wouldn't cry for him. He beat me harder and harder, my thighs were running with blood and I still wouldn't cry for him. He was very, very angry, but I wasn't going to give him the satisfaction of making me cry.

After that, I decided that when my wounds were better and I could walk again, I would run away. Albert could stay there if he wanted to, but I didn't want to be skinned and belted around. I'm real old now and I can still show you the scars from that beating. My wounds took a long time to heal. I was in a bad way.

I think Coulson felt guilty for beating me so hard because, later, he took me for a train ride to visit his sister and her husband. It made no difference to me. I was pleased that when I ran away, I'd be rid of him.

Pinjarra Frank and Tommy decided to come with me. I wanted Albert to come too, but he was too frightened. He thought that, if we ran away and we got caught, Coulson might beat him the way he'd beaten me.

We told all the mission kids we intended to head towards Geraldton. We didn't tell anyone we really planned to head towards the Goldfields. It was a good plan because, that way, if any of our friends were asked questions, they didn't have to lie.

We did run away. I must have been about fifteen or sixteen, then.

Coulson didn't stay at the mission long after that. He was sacked. I guess the Anglican mob that ran the mission began to realise that all the boys had been running away because of the way Coulson had been treating them. Maybe the other kids told them what Coulson had done to me.

I was sorry to leave Albert behind. After I left, he had no one to protect him and he got sick again. They sent him to hospital. Then Howden came down and took him back to Corunna Downs. Dudley was dead by then. As far as I know, Albert worked there until it was sold to Foulkes-Taylor. Then Albert went to Dr

Gillespie's station, Hillside. A lot of people went to Hillside. They knew that Foulkes-Taylor was a hard man.

I heard people was looking for me, I heard Howden was looking for me, but I was gone. I didn't want to be found. And I wasn't having anything more to do with school.

***

A lot of things happened to me after I left the mission. We walked for a long time after we crossed the railway line. We were very careful not to be seen. Finally, we got to Parkerville and camped in the bush there for a rest. Suddenly, a man appeared out of nowhere. 'What are you boys doing here?' he growled. We jumped up, scared out of our wits. We told him our story and showed him the scars on our legs. He felt sorry for us. 'Stay where you are, boys,' he said. 'I'll get you something to help you on your way.' He came back with some bread and dripping and a box of matches, so we could light a fire at night and keep warm.

After that, we kept walking until it was dark. Luckily, we came across an old abandoned house. It was falling down, but it was better than nothing. We got some old, dry gum leaves and sticks from the bush and lit a fire. Then we settled down for the night. There was an occupied house further down the hill, but we'd been careful to avoid it.

Early next morning, we made our way to the railway line. There was a goods train waiting there. I took my two boomerangs and walked up to the engineer. 'Please mister,' I said, 'will you swap two boomerangs for a ride on your train?'

'No!' he said.

When the train pulled out, we jumped on a wagon that was only half full. The train passed through Northam and we finally ended up at Kellerberrin. We didn't know where the train was headed, but riding on that wagon was a lot better than walking.

At Kellerberrin station, the stationmaster spotted us. He came running over and hauled us down. 'You're the boys wanted by the police, aren't you?' he said. He looked us over real good and then said, 'Right, boys, you see that building over there? That's the police station. I want you to go and present yourselves to the constable. He'll know what to do with you.'

We walked slowly down the track. We wasn't sure if he was watching us or not. When we got near some bush, we veered off and ran for our lives.

No one chased after us, so, after a while, we stopped. We were starving hungry by then. We found some mouldy bread and an old milk can. We ate the bread and scraped out what was left from inside of the can, then we set off again.

We kept following the railway line. Just as the sun was setting, we reached Hines Hill. We were dog tired by then. We sat down at the bottom of a hill to rest. Suddenly, we spotted a tall man coming slowly down the hill towards us. The sun was in our eyes, so we were frightened he was a policeman, but we were too tired to get up and run.

He walked right up and said, 'What are you boys doing here?' We told him our story. He looked at the scars on our legs and shook his head. He told us he was a farmer. We asked him if he could give us some flour to make damper and some tea and sugar. He went away and came back with some tucker.

He warned us to be careful; he said the police had been asking about us.

After he left, we built a fire in the bush. We still had a few matches left and we wanted to fill our bellies real quick.

Just as we were making damper, a man appeared from nowhere and shouted, 'What are you boys up to?' He said he was the stationmaster from Hines Hill and he'd spotted our smoke and tracked us down. We were scared, tired and starving — we didn't have the heart or the strength to run away. He walked up close to us and looked us up and down. 'Where'd you boys get those scars?' We told him our story and he took pity on us. 'Put out that fire, boys,' he said. 'I'll take you to a friend of mine. You'll eat better there.'

We followed him through the bush. We were too tired to care where he took us. We ended up at a small house. It was owned by a contractor with three daughters. He was a widower. They sat us down at a table inside the house. They took us inside, just like that. Wasn't that something? The girls giggled when they looked at us. They cooked us a big meal and we were allowed to eat as much as we liked. Can you believe that? They even let us sleep the night there.

The next morning, Tommy decided to strike off by himself. He was from the Goldfields and he wanted to get back home. He missed the people. Pinjarra Frank and me didn't know what to do. We thought we'd just keep on walking.

Then, the contractor came to us and said, 'Boys, how'd you like to stay with me for two weeks and help with some fencing? I can't pay you, but you'll have your tucker.' That was good enough for us. We didn't have anywhere else to go.

We helped with the fencing and whatever else he wanted doing. The two weeks turned into over a month and we were still there. The girls cooked us good meals. They were allowed to play with me, but not with Pinjarra Frank. He was real dark and he didn't work as hard as me.

One day, a man came by. He was a good-looking man with a big moustache. He came in a sulky, all dressed up. At first, when I saw him coming, I thought he was a policeman, and I nearly ran away. He pulled up at the house and said to the contractor, 'I'm after a boy who can ride. I hear you've got two boys. Can they ride? There's jobs going if they can.'

'I can ride,' I said. I prayed the horse wouldn't throw me as soon as I jumped on. The contractor said, 'Stay with us, we're fond of you. Let Pinjarra go.' He was a good man, that contractor, but his house was close to the railway line and, all the time I'd been there, I'd been lookin' over my shoulder, wonderin' when the police would catch up with me. I decided to go with the stranger. McQuarie was his name.

McQuarie climbed down from the sulky and unhitched two horses from the back. 'On you get,' he said. Pinjarra leapt on, but they had to give me a leg up — I was too small. I clung onto the reins and mane and prayed with all my heart I wouldn't fall off. For twenty-five miles McQuarie drove the sulky, and for twenty-five miles I bumped up and down, barely hanging in the saddle. My bottom and the insides of my legs were painful sore. We went through forest country they were clearing for a new settlement, then one more hill, then Nungarin. The sun had set by then. It was teatime. That was my first start in life.

The next day, McQuarie's son Ernie came to me and said,

'Come on, I'll show you the ropes. I hear you need some riding lessons.' That day, I learnt to canter so my body didn't jolt around so much. My legs and bottom were still sore, but I wasn't giving up that easy.

Ernie took me out to one of the runs and we stopped at a lake. He reined his horse in, climbed down and lay on the grass. I did the same. I thought he was going to tell me about the run. He said nothing. He pulled his hat down over his eyes, took out a plug of tobacco from his pouch and rolled a big, fat cigarette. Then he smoked it real slow. All the time, he was looking at the lake. When he finished, I sat up. I thought, now he's going to tell me about the run. He didn't even look at me, he just lay back, pulled a book out from his pocket, and started to read. He turned each page real slow and deliberate like. I sat looking at the lake. We stayed like that all day, not talking, just laying there. When it was dark, he said, 'Right, let's go.' They were the only words he said to me. We rode back to the station and had tucker.

I had tucker in the kitchen. The white workers sat at one table, the blacks at another. McQuarie and his family ate in the formal dining room. That night, I slept in the stripper. I lifted up the top and crawled inside. Later I got an old sheepskin for a mattress and, sometimes, I had a blanket too, if there was one to spare. Later on, they floored the barn ready for barn dances and I slept in there with the horses. I reckon I must have slept in that barn for well over two years.

The following day, Ernie took me to a different run. It was a long way out. By and by, he reined in his horse, climbed down and sat on the ground. He pulled out a plug of tobacco and *rolled another big, fat cigarette. We did the same thing we had the day before.*

The third day was the same, except in a different place. I soon learnt that Ernie was not only lazy, but greedy, too. He never shared anything. Not his tobacco, not his food, nothing. You could be starving and he wouldn't offer you anything. Later on, McQuarie built a store and Ernie would sneak in there and eat big tins of peaches when we were supposed to be boundary riding. He never offered me a drop. He'd open up a big tin of peaches and scoop them out with a spoon. He'd lean against the counter, look me straight in the eye and eat some more.

Eventually, Ernie ran the store and all the farmers who lived nearby bought on credit, payable after harvest. No one paid their debts, Ernie kept on eating and eating, and the store went bankrupt.

As for me, I decided never to worry about tucker. When I was out all day minding the cattle, they only gave me one piece of bread and a thin slice of pork. The meat was so thin that, if you held it up to the sun, you could see through it.

After I'd been there a while, McQuarie told me I was now a stockman. From then on I took my orders from him. He said my conditions were five bob a year, my horse and saddle, board and tucker. I never did get that five bob a year, but then, I wasn't worried about wages. I had a home.

In three years, I was head stockman and mustering cattle all over the district. It was pioneer days, then. They were just clearing Nungarin and the railway line wasn't even there, only the earthworks.

When there was no stock work to be done, I spent my time

grubbing boab tea-tree and clearing more and more land ready for cropping. Other times, I did errands for McQuarie, driving him and his friends here and there in the sulky.

All this time, I went under the name of Marble. I thought it might give me some protection from the police, who were still looking for me. McQuarie told me, 'Marble, if you ever see the police round here, you hide, and I'll tell them to take Pinjarra Frank instead. I'll send you word when they've gone.'

McQuarie didn't want Pinjarra — he was real black. They wanted me. Even though Pinjarra was older than me, I was his boss. Pinjarra was lazy and, in the end, McQuarie gave him the sack.

McQuarie was a good man; he never growled at me. I remember once, I was in the barn putting blinkers on a horse. I had to climb up onto the manger to do it. McQuarie came in and saw me and laughed, 'Hey, Marble,' he said, 'when are you going to grow?' I didn't say nothin'. I'm like a tree that never been watered. I just thought to myself, yeah, I don't get enough to eat.

Dick McQuarie, the other son, used to give me clothes. They were always too big, but I just rolled them up till I grew into them. They fitted me for years.

Sometimes, McQuarie would ask me to drive a visitor around or help someone with work they were doing. Everyone wanted me in those days.

I remember this fella Baird. They call the shop he owned in Perth Myers, these days. It used to be called Bairds. He came to Nungarin once to help build a house for his brother. I took him out with his tools and he got interested in me. One day he said,

'Would you like to come to Perth, Marble? I'll look after you, and give you a good schooling.' I thought about that hiding I got at the mission. That was supposed to be schooling. I thought, nobody's going to school me again. Seems funny, thinking about it all now. If I'd have taken his offer, I might have ended up as a shopwalker for Bairds.

I decided to stay with McQuarie. He never said, 'How long are you gunna be?' I was my own boss. He never gave me any money and I never worried about it. I was just growing up and there was nothing to spend money on.

One chap McQuarie had me drive round was a big squatter from Victoria by name of Syd Stock. I had to take him by buggy to his brothers in Nungarin. One night, we was sitting by the fire, when he said to me, 'Would you like to come back to Victoria with me, Marble? I've got stations there and horses and buggies, too. You can work on one of my stations.' I looked at him. He was a good man, the kind of man I liked. Then I said, 'No. I don't want to go far away from the North. I might never come back. This land is my home.'

Now, that could have been an opportunity missed. He was an old man and he trusted me. I was young then, with no ties, just a young, working man. He might have given me a station. I knew he was a good man because, whenever we went to the hotel, he never put me outside or cast me away like most white men. Where he went, I went. He kept me with him always. Treated me like his equal. That was a rare thing in those days. A thing to be treasured.

Everybody seemed to like me then. I couldn't make out why. I'd look in a mirror and what'd I see? Me. An ugly bloke like me. What did they see in me? But each time someone asked me to go with them, I said no.

One day, Dick said to me, 'Come on, Marble, we'll take you to the Northam Show.' They gave me new clothes and everything. They stayed in their Aunty's pub, the Shamrock Hotel, and I camped in the horses' manger nearby. I used to sit on the beer cases outside the hotel and eat my tucker.

I loved that Show. They had merry-go-rounds and all sorts of things I hadn't seen before.

When I went to the Show week races, it was the only time I hit the boss for some money. Dick said to the boss, 'Give me some money,' so I said, 'Me too, boss.' He gave me half a sovereign. When we got to the races, I gave it to a bloke to put on a winner for me. I never saw that half sovereign again.

As far as crops go, 1911 was a good harvest for nearly everyone. It was never as good after that. Dry conditions seemed to set in. Things got bad and we took three hundred head of cattle further north, trying to find better grazing and water.

It was July 1912. Miners were finding gold at Paynes Find then. There was traffic on the roads. When the bit of water we found finally dried up, we took the cattle back to Nungarin. In the end, we had to sell most of them.

We kept working McQuarie's station, but things got worse and worse. The first time McQuarie went broke was because everyone owed him money. All the farmers were in debt to him and none of them could pay their bills. The bailiff came to sell off the stock and the machinery. All the farmers got together and agreed not to bid against McQuarie. He used his sister's money and got everything back for ten shillings or a pound.

After that first time, McQuarie got the other farmers to help him clear a lot of land for extra cropping. He wasn't going to get nothin' out of that crop, just enough to pay his bills. Jackatee and me cleared even more land and put in more crops. We pulled out big boab trees, raked the roots together and burnt them. Then, we put the crop in. Jackatee was a good worker. He was real black. At night, we'd boil our billy in the bush and cook pancakes for tea on the forge. That was all the tucker we had. He was a good friend, old Jackatee.

Anyway, turned out the crop was better than before, but still not good enough to save McQuarie. A bad drought came and finished him off. There was no water, no feed for the animals. Dick and me had to shoot poor old Bess. She was a good horse, but there was nothin' for her to eat. What stock there was was in bad condition. Then we let them go. Poor buggers. There was no food. Some of them were too far gone to be helped.

I stopped with McQuarie till he was real broke. The farmers still owed him money and the bailiff was coming again. I finally left with Jackatee in 1913. There was no food for me then either.

We went into Nungarin, trying to find work. We'd do anything. One chap saw us in the street and asked us to help him load a truck. He gave us threepence. Threepence, for all that work! We bought some bread and ate it. We were starvin' hungry. A big load of sandalwood came in and the storekeeper came over and said, 'You boys want work loading that sandalwood?'

'Yes,' we said. We were desperate; we didn't ask the pay.

When we finished loading twelve ton of sandalwood, he gave us half a crown. Then, we gave it back to him in his store for *some sardines and biscuits, and that was the end of that. It seems like the whitefella doesn't want the blackfella to get a foot in this world.*

I had no money, no job. I was about twenty, twenty-one then. I could see I couldn't live in Nungarin. I decided to strike out for Goomalling. There were two friends of mine who wanted to go there, too: Billy One Moon and Hunting Maggie. Hunting Maggie was blind. Billy was her husband and he used to lead her along the road with a stick. I called them Aunty and Uncle. I wasn't in my home country and I thought if any other natives asked who I was, it would give me some protection.

By the time we were three or four miles out of Nungarin, McQuarie pulled up behind us in a buggy. 'Hey, Marble,' he said, 'I want you to drive me to Hines Hill, and the bailiff wants a boy to help round up stock.'

'Righto,' I said. I told my friends I would meet them later.

After I got back from Hines Hill, I rounded up the stock. They were no trouble. I had a bad time with my old pony. She wanted to stop with me. She didn't want to go in the corral with the others. I thought McQuarie might say, 'Take her, Marble, she's your horse,' but he didn't. I nearly cried when I saw her go.

After that, the bailiff said, 'You want another job?'

'Too right,' I said. 'I got no job.'

'Good,' he said. 'I want you to shepherd the sheep near the pub till we're ready to truck 'em.'

While I was minding the sheep, a man came up and spoke to me.

'When you finished working for that bailiff, how about coming and working for me? I'll give you ten bob a week plus board.'

'That's all right by me!' I said. It was the most I ever been offered.

After they trucked the sheep, the bailiff gave me thirty shillings. That was more than I expected. I picked up my swag and went over and saw Dick McQuarie.

'Dick,' I said, 'how much you want for that old bike of yours?'

'My old bike? Well, let me see, about thirty bob would do.'

I gave him my thirty bob and wheeled the bike across the railway line to Hancock's place. It had no tyres or tubes. I didn't mind. I had a bike and I was looking forward to my new job.

***

From 1913 to 1916, I worked for Hancock. In all that time I got no pay, only my tucker, and I worked damn hard. I never saw that ten bob a week he promised me. Most of the time I was there, I was freezing cold. We just lived in an old bough shed. There was no proper place to sleep and, in winter, the wind cut right through you. I used to get old gallon tins and fill them with hot water, tie bags around them, then strap them to my feet. My feet felt the cold the most. Like ice, they were. I never had shoes. The tins gave some relief. I tell you, it's hard to keep warm in an open bough shed.

Most of my working time was spent clearing the land, seeding and cropping. It was hard work, but I was used to it. In between times, I made mud bricks for a hut with a chimney and fireplace. I used to tread the mud with my bare feet, and when a stick tickled my foot, I'd pull it out. If I didn't, the brick would crack. The bricks started to mount up. We dug out a hole inside to throw out the heat. Winter came and we'd used all the bricks, so we slept in the cellar. It sure was warmer than that shed. I felt like a king that winter.

While I was at Hancock's, I managed to get tyres and tubes for my bike. I fixed that bike up real good, oiled it and kept it nice. In my spare time I'd ride around all over the countryside, looking at the land and the bush. It was what you'd call my entertainment. I met lots of different people when I was out. Most of them was friendly. 'Gidday,' they'd say, or 'Mornin'.' Course, you got some that weren't interested in talkin' to you, but I never let them worry me. I loved that bike. It made me feel real grand.

It was during my time at Hancock's that I met up with a Welshman named Davy Jones. He was working on the Trans Line, out on the Nullarbor Plain, and now and then he came to Nungarin to check on his land. It was at the time when Lord Kitchener had ordered all the States to be linked by railway line, in case of war. That way, they could help each other.

Davy couldn't write then, so he'd get Hancock to write letters for him. He didn't just talk to Hancock, he talked to me, as well. He seemed real friendly. More like a white blackfella, really. Towards the end of three years with Hancock, I could see I wasn't gettng anywhere. The hut was built by then, but I was still just getting me tucker, no money. 'Hancock,' I said to him one day, 'how about paying me that money you owe me?' He went real quiet and looked at me. The year was 1916, it was the middle of winter and there was a flood on. After a while, he said, 'Marble, you clear that forty acres of land I been wantin' cleared and I'll give you twelve pounds — no more, no less!'

Now he'd tried to get all sorts of people to clear that land. Nobody could do it. It was covered with big logs and stumps, and, with the flood on, the job was worth more like one hundred pounds, not twelve pounds! Trouble was, I knew he had me, and he knew too. Where could I go? I had no money, no home. 'Right,' I said, 'I'll clear the land for you, as long as you pay me. For three years, I been working for you, breaking my back and you never paid me yet. I got no choice: I got to stick with you or I got nothing.'

I don't think he believed I'd clear the land. He thought he'd have me there three more years, doing his work for him, building his house. He didn't know me. I worked from three hours before sunrise till sunset, clearing and burning. During that time, the flood got worse and the railway line was nearly washed away. Every day, I was soaking wet. My feet were like blocks of ice. Sometimes, the rain drove down so hard I couldn't see in front of me, but I kept going. I wasn't going to give up; it was my only way out. The job took me three weeks. I cleared that land by myself when no other man would, or could.

I showed Hancock the land, then asked him for my money. He couldn't believe I'd done it. He didn't give me the money right away, but he kept me waiting, waiting, hoping I'd forget about it. He knew I'd leave as soon as he gave me the money. I kept asking him for my pay. In the end, he went to Perth and got the money from the bank. Then, he took out fifteen shillings a week board for the three weeks it had taken me to clear the land.

Despite the flood, 1916 was a good year for most farmers. There'd been drought earlier on, and maize, lucerne and *crushed fodder had been imported from Argentina. There was none to be had around Northam. We couldn't get any from New South Wales either.*

When Micky Farrell heard I'd left Hancock, he offered me two weeks' work carting two hundred tons of chaff for twenty-five shillings a week. There were two wagons and a steam cutter and fifteen men on the job, but only me doing the carting. I wasn't afraid to work. After that, Mr Williams gave me a job harvesting. I got two pounds a week for that. When that job wound up, I met up with Davy Jones again. I hadn't seen him for quite a while. He told me he'd finished working on the Trans Line.

'Marble,' he said, 'why don't you come sharefarming with me? You buy the horses and harness, and come and work my land with me.'

'All right, Dave,' I said, 'that suits me fine.' I had nothing else to do.

He would've been stuck if he hadn't got me. He was a failure. He'd tried cropping his land before, but left it too late. He spent all his time putting in crops for Micky Farrell and Mr Lochlan to earn some money, but by the time he was free to put in his own crop, the season was just about at an end.

When I started with Davy, I put in two hundred acres with my team. They were a good team of hard-working animals. As hard as me. I bought their feed and watered them and looked after them real well. That year, we had the best crops in the district. One paddock gave ten bags to the acre; the other seven bags. The lowest yield we got was eighteen bushels to the acre. From then on, we never looked back. All our crops were bumpers, right through till 1923.

Davy Jones became Mr Davy Jones of the Nungarin district. He was independent now. He didn't have to work for no one. When he was working on the Trans Line, he had a tiny little purse he kept with him in camp. It had all his money in it. Now, he was banking with Lloyds of London. He had money in his pockets and I had money in mine, but not as much. It was his land, but I did all the work. The only thing I owned was the team. My share after harvest was one quarter; Davy got the rest.

I saved all my money, never spent a penny. Pretty soon, I had enough to buy a farm. I bought a nice little farm in Mukinbudin.

I'll never forget Mucka when I first saw it. There was nothing there. A few houses now and then, but nothing more. Later, I had the first truck there and I used to cart water for the townspeople from ten miles out. They didn't even have a pub till years later.

My name was good right through the district. Everyone knew I was a good worker. Later, I had six men working for me, clearing my land. I paid them out of a cheque book. I was the only farmer in the area to have a cheque book. All the other farmers were mortgaged to the bank. They were all jealous of me, a black man, doing better than what they were. When I first bought the farm, they all made fun of me. 'What would you know about farming?' they'd yell. They thought I knew nothin'. I proved them wrong.

Anyway, before long, I was working my own farm as well as share-farming with Davy. Things were going real well for me. One day, Davy came up to me and said, 'Listen, Marble, you've got your farm in Mucka now, what about if you just stick to that and I give Bill Bradley a go? You know, the bloke that's working for Hull's. I'd like to sharefarm with him.'

I didn't know what to say. Davy was my friend. It wasn't that I was thinking about the extra money, it just seemed that Davy didn't want me with him any more, after so long together. Davy was standing there and I kept looking at the ground. In the end, I said, 'All right, Dave, if that's what you want to do. I can pull out and go home.'

That year, I put in my last crop with Davy. Bill and Mrs Bradley moved in with Davy while the crop was still growing.

One Sunday night, the rain came, and the thunder and lightning, and the hail as well. The hail took the crop right off. There wasn't one head left — even the trees were stripped bare. They looked dead, standing there with no leaves on.

I think God must have been looking after me. Something told me to get insured that year. I came out with my quarter and Dave got nothing.

Davy's bad luck continued. The next year, he put his own crop in, but forgot to seed with super and it died off. The following year, Davy was in the same position he was in before he joined up with me. He still had no team and had not bothered to buy one, so this meant he had to take off Hull's crop and Micky Farrell's before he could have the use of their team to take off his own crop.

If Davy had've stuck with me, I'd have had his crop off early on and my own as well. No one could work a team the way I could. It was me that gave him his start. I did all the work; he just stood back and collected the money.

By the time the thirties came round and the Depression hit, he wanted me back. I was married by then. I had responsibilities.

Davy said, 'You can bring your wife too, Arthur.'

I was going by my real name, now. I left Marble behind when I left Davy. Now I was Arthur Corunna, farmer of Mukinbudin.

***

After I left Davy in the twenties, some important things happened to me. In 1925, I went down to Perth. I'd heard that my little sister Daisy was living at Ivanhoe. Ivanhoe was a big house in Claremont on the banks of the Swan River. Daisy was a servant there, living with our father, Howden Drake-Brockman, and his second wife, Alice.

I was keen to see Daisy again. She was my sister, my family. I wanted my little sister Daisy to know she had a brother who was getting on in the world.

I hardly recognised her when I saw her. When they took me from Corunna Downs, she was only a baby, with real white blonde hair; and now, here she was, a grown woman, with black frizzy hair. She was small and pretty, like our mother, Annie. I was sure glad to see her.

When I first called in at Ivanhoe, Mrs Drake-Brockman was out. Later that day, she came home to find me sitting in the kitchen doorway, talking to Daisy, my legs stretched out onto the verandah. You see, I'd finally started to grow, I was a big man. I wasn't small no more.

After seeing Daisy again, I took to visiting her as often as I could. One year, I hired a buggy and pair for two shillings and took her to the Show. We thought we were real grand, travelling along in that thing. I took her to the races and on picnics, every-

where. Daisy loved the horses. Nothing she liked better than seeing those wonderful animals go for their lives round the track. We both loved horses.

Helen Bunda, our cousin, used to come, as well. She was in service with another white family. She did the most beautiful needlework. She was a clever woman with her hands.

I made friends with a chap in Perth, Mr McKenzie. He was a real nice man. He'd lend me his car so I could pick up the girls and take them on outings. I always returned his car safe and sound. He knew he could trust me.

Judith, June and Dick Drake-Brockman were only little then. I used to give them horsey rides when I was at Ivanhoe and scare them by chasing them round the lawn. Daisy was their nursemaid.

On one of my visits to Ivanhoe, Alice Drake-Brockman gave me a little dog. She told me Foulkes-Taylor had given it to her when he bought Corunna Downs, but she didn't want it. I called him Pixie, after Dudley's son — that was his nickname. I took that little dog with me wherever I went. He was a good little dog. I've always had a tender spot for little creatures like that.

When I saw Daisy again in 1925, it was also the first time I'd seen Howden since I'd run away. I wondered what he'd say to me. Mrs Drake-Brockman said I could sleep with Daisy in her room. When Howden came home, he came straight to Daisy's room. He knocked on the door and came in and shook me by the hand real hard. He hadn't changed. He looked older, more tired, but apart from that, he was just the same. I was a grown man too, now. We were both men. 'I'm pleased to see you, Arthur,' he said. I didn't know what to say.

After that, whenever I stayed in Perth, I always slept in Daisy's room. At night, we had long talks, catching up on the news. I went and saw a lawyer and made a will, leaving all my earthly goods to Daisy. I wasn't married then. She was my only family.

Sometimes when I was in Perth, I'd ride on the electric trams. I went on the trains, too. In those days, you could go from Merredin to Perth for seventeen shillings. I loved riding on the trains. I felt like I was someone important, being able to get on, pay my fare and sit there like a king until I got off at the next stop.

***

In 1927 I got a letter from Howden. I hadn't seen Daisy for a while, as I'd been busy on the farm. The letter asked if I'd like to have Daisy with me. It said they didn't want her no more and they wondered if I could come and get her. Too right, I thought. Nothing I'd like better.

I went and talked to one of my neighbours. He was a white man but a good man, young and single. He was well off, too, and I knew he'd treat Daisy right. I asked him if he wanted a wife. I told him about Daisy and how pretty she was and how hard she worked and what a good wife she'd make. He said, 'Arthur, any sister of yours is all right by me.' I knew I had him then. I didn't want Daisy just marrying anyone. I wanted someone I could trust, someone who would treat her real nice. She was my family. My little sister.

I finished what I had to do on the farm and was all set to go get Daisy when another letter arrived. It said they'd changed their minds and I couldn't have her after all. I was disappointed, and so was the farmer next door.

In December 1927, I heard Daisy had had a baby girl. It was news to me. I wondered, then, if that was why they'd changed their minds. They must have found out she was pregnant. I'd have had her still. I wish she'd come to me, baby and all. I love kids.

Early in 1928, Howden died. He'd been a sick man for some time. Personally, I think he left his heart in Corunna. Howden saw Daisy's baby before he died. They called her Gladys. He held her in his arms and said, 'She's very beautiful.' She was one of the most beautiful babies I'd ever seen.

Shortly before his death, Howden mailed me a whole pile of photos that had been taken on Corunna Downs. I guess Howden figured no one else would want old pictures. That was why he sent them to me. It was the only thing he ever gave me.

***

Apart from Daisy, the other thing I discovered in the twenties was boxing. Actually, boxing and wrestling. I was good at both, but I didn't know it till then. I was a farmer and wasn't trained for fighting, but one punch from me and I could flatten them.

Whenever the Shows came round Nungarin, I'd put in for the boxing and wrestling. Sometimes, they were too scared to take me on. I remember one bloke took a long look at me and then said, 'I'm not taking you on, mate. I seen a bloke look like you once before. He gave me a terrible time.' I missed out that year.

One time, a bloke came up to me and pushed me on the shoulder. He was one of the trainers. 'You can't wrestle, mate,' he said. I just grabbed him, clothes and all. Lifted him up and dropped him. Pinned him to the dirt. 'What do you think of yourself now, mate!' I said. 'WHO can't wrestle??' He went for his life, dirt all over him. The men in the ring had seen what happened and they wouldn't take me on after that. I looked too tough.

There was a boxer I remember well, Jack Yakem. He was white and he fought everywhere. Everyone was scared of him. He was the same weight as me, and I thought, Arthur, have a go.

When they let me into the ring, the crowd was full round us, wanting to see me get beat. Jack didn't waste no time. He started pummelling me in the ribs with his fists.

After a few minutes, I thought, I've had enough of this. I hit him fair over the earhole and dropped him right there. He went flying, flat to the ground. The crowd roared.

Anyhow, he got up and I dropped him again. Eleven times I dropped him, quick with my fists. I'd drop him, then wait for him to get up, then drop him again!

I won that fight, but they never gave me any money. It was always the same. Later when I got home, I took my singlet off. I was black and blue all round my ribs where he'd pummelled me. I don't know what colour he was.

I was a hard nut to crack when I was young. My life was full of sport.

***

When I was young, I had girls runnin' after me all the time. I was a good catch and they all wanted me. Trouble is, I was like my old grandfather, tender-hearted. I wouldn't go with any girl, because if I got her into trouble, I'd have to marry her. Other blokes were different. They'd take a girl out, get her into trouble and then let her go. Have another one and let them go. Only my own, what I'm going to have — that's how I am.

In the old days, you were nobody unless you were somebody important. And when they announced your engagement, they took your photo and put it in the paper. I was worried about that. I thought to myself, when I get engaged, what can I say? Who could I say I was and who was my father? I decided I'd trick them all. If they ask me, I'd say, 'Well my father is Mr Corunna from Corunna Downs Station.' That's what I would put in the paper and no one would know any better. No one would know about Howden and Annie and how they wasn't married white man's way. You see, they were very particular about such things in those days.

There were times when I could have protected myself through the name of Brockman, but I never did. Howden never gave me nothin'. I've only got one good father and He's in heaven. No matter which way the wind's blowin', He's there with you.

Before I married my wife, Adeline, she came to me and said, 'Arthur, I've seen a fortune-teller and she told me I'm going to marry you. She also told me what your life will be like and that, one day, somebody will rob you of your farm.'

I said, 'Nobody's goin' to rob me. They'll get this fist if they try!' I was gettin' on in years, about thirty-five, and I'd been thinkin' I should marry, but when Adeline said that, I thought, better not get married or I'll be losin' my farm.

Still, I couldn't stay single for ever, so I thought the only fair way was to put all the girls' names in a hat. I figured the name that I picked out would be my wife. I thought, well, Helen Bunda's name could come out. She was my cousin and her name was in there. I wanted a small girl, not a big woman. Someone like my mother.

One of my mates held the hat up and I picked out a slip. On it was written Adeline Wilks!

'That can't be the one,' I said, 'she's plump. Let me have another go.'

We mixed the papers round real good, they held up the hat and I chose another one. Adeline Wilks again.

'Those papers ain't mixed up right,' I said. 'Give me one more go.' This time, we gave those papers a mixin' they'll never forget. They held up the hat once more.

I closed my eyes, put my hand in and pulled out a slip. Adeline Wilks! I gave up.

'Well, if she's the one I got to have, so be it,' I said. I think the spirit of her people must have chosen her for me.

We were married in the early thirties in Perth in St Marys Cathedral by Bishop Prindiville. She was a Catholic and I was an Anglican. I agreed to bring up the little ones as Catholics. It didn't seem important — all one God, after all.

Shortly after we were married, I was out in the paddock, diggin' roots. It was a hot day, the sweat was pourin' off me. Anyhow, I was diggin' away, when, suddenly, I was struck blind. I closed my eyes and opened them, but I couldn't see nothin'. I could feel my hand on my face, but I couldn't see it. I sat down and closed my eyes and stayed there for a while, real still like.

That's when I knew Annie was dead. My poor old mother who I hadn't seen since they took me away was dead. I stood up and opened my eyes. I could see again, but Annie was dead. I wish I'd seen her again, just one more time.

The first farm I had in Muckinbudin was hard work. My house was only a bit of tin. I had to cut great big sleepers on drums with a handsaw for the roof. No electricity or water. We had to go over the line if we wanted water.

Men teased me when I bought the farm; they didn't want a blackfella movin' in.

'Where you gunna get stock?' they said. I just ignored them. When I should have had sheep, they wouldn't give me any, because my colour wasn't right. Everybody else got them, not me.

I was on my own, a black man with no one to help him. I done all the fencing myself, bought everything, the dam too. Paid money for men to clear land. I chopped all the fence posts, dug out the holes and, when there was nothing else to do, helped clear the land. I made sure I owed no one. I didn't want no mortgage.

After I'd improved the farm, a bloke wanted to buy it. Jack Edwards was his name. He already had other farms and he wanted mine as well. You see, the white man gets greedy, and he wants to take everything.

With the Depression, the price of wheat fell to ten shillings *a bushel and then to five shillings. I had two boys, Arthur and Manfred, by then, and in 1934, my third son, Albert, was born. My crop yielded eight bags to the acre that year, but, at five bob a bushel, it didn't amount to much. All we got out of it was a pram for Albert.*

In 1936 my daughter, Norma, was born and life was real hard. I'd do anything to make a few bob then, anything to keep my wife and family. I picked roots at a shilling an acre, I cleared five hundred acres of mallees for seven pounds. I burnt mallees for charcoal to sell to gas producers. By gee, some men were mean then, they'd pinch my roots and my charcoal. I was doin' the work and they was gettin' the profits.

Later on during the Depression, the Agricultural Bank served a summons on me for owin' them one thousand three hundred pounds. I'd had to mortgage my farm with them to get by. They sold up everything, all my machinery, except my horses. I had nowhere to keep them, and they were strayin' everywhere. I had to round them up and I sold them for three pounds a head to be shot for pig feed. Can you tell me that was fair, for all my pioneering days, to be treated like that?

The Depression didn't do no favours for my neighbour who'd had four farms either. He had to sell up, and he left the district for good. I had to take my family and start again on new, uncleared land. It's hard for the black man to get ahead. Struggling under all disabilities, I went on in hardship on my new land.

My neighbours in Mucka were a mixed bag — some good, some very bad. There was a man that give me a lot of trouble; he was mean, and he didn't like blacks. He's dead and gone now. God finished him. That man used to shoot my horses and pigs.

One day, he was in town and he said to one of my neighbours, 'Have you managed to get Arthur off his farm, yet?' He went on and on, talkin' to my neighbour about how two white men can easily get rid of one black man. My neighbour said, 'You're talkin' to the wrong bloke. I don't want Arthur off his farm.'

You see, he thought he was going to turn this man against me, but this man was my friend. I'd helped him when things went wrong. When he was in hospital, I'd helped cut his hay and shear his sheep. He was my mate. Whenever I wanted a wagon or anything, he'd say, 'Take what you like, Arthur.' If I wanted hay, he'd give it to me. Later, he married and moved to Arthur River. He took all his cows, and his wife and family and moved on. His name was William Arthur Bird and he was a good man.

Now, you take the bloke that give me all the trouble. He was only livin' on what he could steal off me. He put a fence right round the lake so he could steal my sheep. Got his son to lift up the bottom fence at the bottom dam and mix my sheep with his. I lost a lot of sheep that way.

When the sheep came back to my land, he summonsed me. I had no earmark on my sheep, only a woolbrand. He put his own earmark on my sheep and then accused me of stealin' them. The police came out and saw my Corriedale sheep runnin' back to me.

I went down to Perth and saw a lawyer. When I told him what was going on, he rang the police.

'What's this I hear about Corunna being accused of stealing sheep?' he said.

I don't know what the policeman said, but my lawyer replied, 'You speak to me like that again, man, and I'll have you in gaol! Any further action on this has to go through me: I'm Corunna's lawyer. We're going to fight you on this!'

After that, they dropped the case against me. They knew I wasn't stealin' those sheep, they was just comin' home.

I never did nothin' mean to the men who robbed me. You got to leave God to do His own work.

No one could ever rightly accuse me of stealin', because everything I got I paid for. I didn't want no one sayin' to me, 'You in debt, we got to sell you up!' You see, they'll get you if they can — even the government. You got to be a blackfella to know what the pressure is from the government.

They never even treated the blackfellas right during the war. I heard of this native bloke, he went and fought for the country overseas. When he came back he still wasn't a citizen, and he wasn't even allowed to vote. That's the white man's justice for you. You see, the black man remembers these things. The black man's got a long memory.

They took a lot of natives away to Palm Flats, Moore River, during the war, old ones and all. Neville was still the Protector of Aborigines. Any blackfella that had dealings with Neville got no good word to say about him. He wasn't protectin' the Aborigines — he was destroyin' them!

These poor blackfellas they took away had to live in a compound with soldiers around them. The young girls would say to the soldiers, 'Why you worried about us for? We not your enemies; Australia's our country.' The soldiers couldn't do anything, it was their business to keep them there. So, in the end, the girls made love to the soldiers and got away.

Anyone who escaped, they sent trackers after them. They'd catch them, beat them up and put them back in gaol. Our own country and we not free. They didn't let no one out till the end of the war.

I don't know why they didn't lock me up too. Maybe they didn't think of me as a real blackfella. They seemed to go for the real dark ones, the ones out of work and battlin' for a livin'.

Aah, it seems funny, lookin' back now. Mucka was a good place to live in the old days. People were more friendly, they needed each other. The black man was workin' for the farmers, gettin' paid in tea, flour and sugar. Blackfellas cleared the land, put crops in, pulled sandalwood. I remember the lake country used to be full of dingoes; the blackfellas used to track them, hunt them down. Aah yes, no one can say the blackfella didn't do his share of work in Mucka. They helped make it what it is today. I hope they won't be forgotten.

***

Well, I'd like to finish my story there. That's the important part. I been livin' in Mucka for years now. I got my children all growed up and my farm is comin' along real nice. I still put a crop in and I got my pigs and there's plenty of the wildlife on my place. The wildlife always got a home with me.

I wish I could give advice for the young blackfellas of today, but I can't. Each man has to find his own way. You see, the trouble is that colonialism isn't over yet. We still have a White

Australia policy against the Aborigines. Aah, it's always been the same. They say there's been no difference between black and white, we all Australian, that's a lie. I tell you, the black man has nothin', the government's been robbin' him blind for years.

There's so much the whitefellas don't understand. They want us to be assimilated into the white, but we don't want to be. They complain about our land rights, but they don't understand the way we want to live. They say we shouldn't get the land, but the white man's had land rights since this country was invaded — our land rights. Most of the land the Aborigine wants, no white man would touch. The government is like a big dog with a bone with no meat on it. They don't want to live on that land themselves, but they don't want the black man to get it either. Yet, you find somethin' valuable on the land the Aborigine has got and whites are all there with their hands out.

Those Aborigines in the desert, they don't want to live like the white man, owin' this and owin' that. They just want to live their life free. They don't need the white man's law, they got their own. If they want water in the Gibson Desert, they do a rainsong and fill up the places they want. If it's cold, they can bring the warm weather like the wind. They don't need the white man to put them in gaol; they can do their own punishment. They don't have to hunt too hard — the spirits can bring birds to them. Say they want a wild turkey; that turkey will come along, go past them and they can spear it. Kangaroo, too. They don't kill unless they hungry. The white man's the one who kills for sport. Aah, there's so much they don't understand.

Now, if I had been born a white man, my life would have been different. I'd have had an education the proper way, without the whipping. As it is, I got to take my papers to someone who's educated to get me through. Some things aren't understandable to me. Now I got some of my grandchildren educated; they help me. If I'd have been a wealthy farmer, I'd have given all my kids a real good education.

I'm a great-grandfather now and proud of it. Only thing is, Daisy's got more great-grandchildren than me. I got to catch up with her. Daisy's family and my family, we special. I got healing powers, but Daisy's got them stronger than me. You see, the spirit is strong in our family. When I die, someone will get my powers. I don't know who. They have to have a good heart, and live a simple life. Your power comes from above. You can't cure yourself. You got to use that power to help others.

I'm at the end of my story now. To live to ninety, that's an achievement. I haven't really felt the effect of old age, though — of course, the visibility's gone away a bit, but me mind is not so bad. I've had everything a man could want, really. A little bit of sport and a little bit of music. I'm an entertainer. You take me anywhere and I'll join in — could be playing the mouth organ or anything, I'll give it a go. Everybody liked me, even some of the men I worked for.

Now my life is nearly over, I'm lookin' forward to heaven. I'll have a better time up there. I'll be a little angel, flyin' around, lookin' after stars and planets, doin' the spring cleaning. God is the best mate a man could have. You don't have Him, you don't have no friend at all. You look away from God, you go to ruin.

Take the white people in Australia, they brought the religion here with them and the commandment, Thou Shalt Not Steal, and yet they stole this country. They took it from the innocent. You see, they twisted the religion. That's not the way it's supposed to be.

I look back on my life and think how lucky I am. I'm an old fella now and I got one of my granddaughters lookin' after me. And I got Daisy's grand-daughter writin' my story. I been tryin' to get someone to write it for years, now I'm glad I didn't. It should be someone in the family, like. It's fittin'.

I got no desires for myself any more. I want to get my land fixed up so my children can get it and I want my story finished. I want everyone to read it. Arthur Corunna's story! I might be famous. You see, it's important, because then maybe they'll understand how hard it's been for the blackfella to live the way he wants. I'm part of history, that's how I look on it. Some people read history, don't they?

Where to next?

'It's a wonderful story.' Mum had tears in her eyes when she finished reading Arthur's story.

Like me, Mum now felt that at last we had something from the past to hang on to. And, for Mum in particular, there was something to be proud of.

However, in an odd way, we also experienced a sense of loss. We were suddenly much more aware of how little we knew about Nan and about the history and experience of our own family. We were now desperate to learn more, but there appeared to be few obvious leads left.

After much thought, I decided that our best course was to return to Nan and Arthur's birthplace, Corunna Downs.

Paul thought this was a wonderful idea. He loved the North and he also could see no other way forward for us. He hoped we could persuade Nan to go with us.

When I approached Nan about the idea of going up North, she was disgusted. 'You're like your mother, you like to throw money away. All you'll be lookin' at is dirt. Dirt and scrub.'

I ignored her and said, 'Why don't you come with me? You might meet some of your old mates up there.'

'Haa!' she laughed and shook her head in disbelief. 'I'm too old to go bush now. You think I got young legs? Look at them!'

Just then, Mum entered the fray. All this time, she'd been quietly observing Nan's reaction.

'Nan's right, Sally,' she said, much to Nan's surprise. 'You shouldn't spend that money just to look at dirt. What will it achieve? There's no one up there we know. What are you going to do, anyway, walk up to strangers in the street and ask them if they knew Daisy or Arthur Corunna?'

'Yep,' I replied. 'I'll take my tape-recorder — who knows what we will find out?'

'You're really determined to do this, aren't you?' she said in a rather hoarse voice.

'You know me, Mum.'

'You know,' Mum said wistfully, 'I've always had a hankering to go North.'

'Who said anything about taking you? I don't want to be dragging a reluctant mother around,' I said. 'No, it wouldn't work. You stay here with Nan. I'll go with Paul and the kids.'

'I'm coming and that's that!' she said.

Nan suddenly interrupted. 'You two, you're both nuts! You, Glad, you're like the wind. You blow here and you blow there. You got no mind of your own!'

Over the following few weeks, I made arrangements for our trip. We decided to go in the May school holidays, that way the children could come and Paul, who was a teacher, could do most of the driving. As the weeks passed, Mum became more and more excited.

'What are you hoping to find at Corunna?'

'Oh, I don't know.' I felt awkward talking about why I wanted to see Corunna, even with Mum. 'I guess I want to see if there are any of the old buildings left. Buildings that might have been there in Nan's day. And I want to look at the land. I want to walk on it. I know that sounds silly, but I want to be there, and imagine what it was like for the people then.'

Mum nodded, there were tears in her eyes. We'd both been very emotional lately.

As the time for us to leave drew near, Nan became more and more outspoken in her opposition. Apart from threatening us with cyclones, flooded rivers and crocodiles, she tried to convince us that, while we were away, something terrible would happen to her.

'There'll be no one to look after me.'

'Now, Nan, don't be silly,' Mum coaxed. 'You'll have Beryl here.' Beryl was a friend of Mum's and had looked after Nan before.

'You know my heart's not too good, Gladdie. You'll be sorry if you go away and I die.'

'You've been dying ever since I've known you,' Mum said firmly. Nan, sensing that, for once, Mum was not going to be moved, shuffled off with her hand over her supposedly weak heart.

True to form, Nan began developing aches and pains the following week, along with other vague symptoms. One morning, she stayed in bed.

'I think it's genuine, this time,' Mum told me despairingly the following evening. 'I think she really has got something wrong with her.'

'You can't make a proper diagnosis without calling the doctor. If she's faking, she'll recover quick smart, and if she's really sick, she should have a doctor look at her.'

'But she always gets so upset when I talk about getting the doctor in.'

'Look, Mum, how many years has Nan been having these convenient illnesses? If she's really sick this time, then, of course, you can't leave her. But do you want to miss out on going North just because of a fake illness?'

When Mum returned home that night, she told Nan that, if she wasn't better in the morning, she was going to call the doctor. Nan was silent.

'If the doctor says it's serious, then I'll stay here and look after you. I just hope they won't put you in hospital, that's all.'

'I'm sure I only need rest.'

'You might need medicine, antibiotics or something like that. It's the only way. Now, you snuggle down and I'll bring you in a cup of tea.'

Nan's recovery had begun.

Over the next week, we organised the last details of our trip. We obtained a video camera to film the trip so that we could show Nan and my brothers and sisters when we returned.

Amber and Blaze were terribly excited. Zeke was only six weeks old. The children were convinced that going North was as adventurous as exploring deepest, darkest Africa.

By five o'clock on the morning of our departure, we were on our way.

Return to Corunna

By the time we arrived in Port Hedland, we were eager to begin our investigations. We'd been told to look up an older gentleman by the name of Jack, as he knew a lot of people in the area and might be able to help us.

As soon as we saw Jack, we liked him. He was very friendly. We were amazed when he told us that Albert Brockman had been his good friend and that they'd worked together for many years.

'Jiggawarra, that's his Aboriginal name, that's what we all call him up here. Now, he had a brother and a sister that were taken away. They never came back. I think the brother was called Arthur.'

'That's right!' I added excitedly, 'and the sister was called Daisy, that's my grandmother.'

'Well, I'll be,' he said, with tears in his eyes. 'Fancy, you comin' back after all these years.'

'Are we related to you, then?'

'Well now, which way do you go by: the blackfella's way or the white man's way?'

'The blackfella's way.'

'Then I'm your grandfather,' he said, 'and your mother would be my nuba — that means I can marry her.'

Mum laughed. We felt excited at discovering even that.

Jack went on to explain that he was, in fact, Nanna's cousin and that his mother's sister had been on Corunna in the very early days and had married one of the people from Corunna.

'I could have been there myself as a young baby,' he added, 'but that's too far back to remember. I was born in 1903 and worked on Corunna from 1924 onwards. Foulkes-Taylor owned it then. They was a real good mob, that Corunna lot, but, slowly, they started drifting away. They didn't like the boss.'

'What about Lily?' Mum asked. 'Did you know her?' Lily was Nan and Arthur's half-sister.

'Lily? I'd forgotten about her. Oh yes, I knew Lily, she was a good mate of mine. So was her bloke, Big Eadie. He was a Corunna man too. Aah, we used to have a lot of corroborees in those days. I can't explain to you how it made us feel inside. I loved the singing. Lily was a good singer. You could hear her voice singin' out high above the others. All those people are gone now. I suppose Arthur and Daisy are dead, too?'

'Arthur is, but my mother is still alive,' replied Mum.

Jack was very moved. 'Why didn't you bring her with you?'

'We tried,' I replied, 'but she reckoned she was too old to come North. Said her legs wouldn't hold her up.'

Jack laughed. 'That's one thing about Mulbas,' he said, 'they can find an excuse for anything! She's one of the last old ones, you know … Gee, I'd like to meet her!'

'Maybe she'll come next time,' I said hopefully. 'Did Lily have any children, Jack?'

'No. She wanted to. She was good with kids. Looked after plenty of kids in her time. She could turn her hand to anything, that woman. How many kids did Daisy have?'

'Only me,' Mum said sadly, 'I'd love to have come from a big family.'

'Ooh, you ask around,' Jack laughed. 'You'll soon have so many relatives, you won't know what to do with them. You'd be related to a lot up here.'

'Really?'

'Too right. You might be sorry you come!'

'There was another sister,' I said. 'I think she was full blood, but died young. Her name was Rosie.'

'That'd be right. A lot of full bloods died young in those days.'

'I can't believe we've met you,' I sighed. 'All these people have just been names to us. Talking to you makes them real. We didn't think anyone would remember.'

'Aah, mulbas have got long memories. Most around here remember the kids that were taken away. I should have been taken myself, only a policeman took me in after my mother died. Then he farmed me out to other people so I was able to stay in the area. I was one of the lucky ones.'

'Did you know a bloke called Maltese Sam?' Mum asked.

'Oh yeah, he's dead now.'

'Could he have been my mother's father?'

'No, no, not him. I couldn't tell you who her father was. Maybe the station-owner. There's plenty of pastoralists got black kids runnin' around.'

I asked Jack if there was anyone else we should talk to.

'You fellas go and see Elsie Brockman. She's your relation, Albert's wife.'

'Are you sure?' Mum asked in astonishment, 'I thought

they'd all be dead by now.'

'Oh, Albert's been gone a while, but Elsie's still here. Only be as young as you,' he said to Mum. 'Then there's a big mob in Marble Bar you should see, and Tommy Stream in Nullagine. Any of you fellas speak the language?'

'No,' I replied, 'but Arthur could and Daisy can. They wouldn't teach us.'

'Shame! There's mulbas here know their language and won't speak it. I'm not ashamed of my language. I speak it anywhere, even in front of white people.'

'Do you speak the same language as my mother?' Mum asked.

'I speak four languages. Light and heavy Naml, Balgoo and Nungamarda and Nybali. Your mother's language would be Balgoo, but she would speak Naml too. All those old ones from Corunna spoke both. Those two languages are very similar.'

Mum and I exchanged glances. We were going to tackle Nan about that when we got home.

'You mob sure your granny never came back?'

'Not that we know of, why?'

'Well, I recall meeting a Daisy in '23. I was workin' between Hillside and Corunna at the time. Never seen her before. It was like she appeared outa nowhere. Took her from Hillside to stay at Corunna. She had family there she wanted to visit. Half-caste she was, pretty, too. She was pregnant; baby must have been near due.'

'I don't think it'd be her,' I replied.

'Well, I just wondered.'

I was wondering, too.

Over lunch, we talked about Elsie Brockman. Mum and I both felt it was probably a different person. We reasoned that, as Uncle Albert had been the oldest and quite a bit older than Nan, it would be unlikely for his wife to be only in her fifties. It would have made her, at the very least, thirty years younger than Albert. We decided to go to Marble Bar, instead.

Fortunately for us, we arrived in Marble Bar on pension day. This meant that most of the people were around town somewhere.

A group of old men were sitting patiently under a tall, shady tree in the main street, waiting for the mail to arrive. We parked nearby and walked over and introduced ourselves. Jack had told us to ask for Roy.

'I'm him,' replied an elderly man with a snow-white beard, 'what do you want?'

'Gidday,' I smiled and held out my hand. 'I'm Sally and this is Paul and my mother, Gladys.' We shook hands all round. 'We're trying to trace our relatives,' I explained. 'They came from Corunna, and went by the names of Brockman or Corunna. We heard you worked on Corunna.'

'Not me! I worked on Roy Hill and Hillside, but you'd be related to Jiggawarra, wouldn't you? I worked with him on Hillside. He built the homestead there. A good carpenter. A good man.'

'You lookin' for your mob now?' another old man asked kindly.

'Yes,' I replied. 'My grandmother was taken from here many years ago.'

'That's right,' he agreed, 'hundreds of kids gone from here.

Most never came back. Some of those light ones, they don't want to own us dark ones.'

'I saw a picture about you lot on TV,' chipped in another. 'It was real sad. People like you wanderin' around, not knowin' where you come from. Light-coloured ones wanderin' around, not knowin' they black underneath. Good on you for comin' back. I wish you the best.'

'Thank you,' I smiled, 'we are like those people on TV. We're up here trying to sort ourselves out.' Then, turning back to Roy, I said, 'Did you know Lily, Roy?'

'What do you want to know for?'

'She's my aunty,' Mum said proudly.

'Go on, Roy, tell them about Lily,' the others teased.

Roy shook his head. 'I'm not sayin' nothin'. I'm not sayin' a word about Lily.' The other men chuckled. Lily was now a closed topic of conversation.

'What about Maltese Sam?' I asked.

'Maltese? He's finished with this world now.'

'I was told he was my grandmother's father — you know, the father of Jiggawara's sister.'

'No, no, that's not right,' said Roy.

'You got that wrong,' others chorused. 'Who told you that?'

'Oh, just someone I know in Perth.'

'How would they know, they not livin' here,' replied another. 'We all knew Maltese. It's not him, be the wrong age.'

'Do any of you know who her father might have been?' I asked quietly.

There was silence while they all thought, then Roy said, 'Well, she was half-caste, wasn't she?'

'Yes.'

'Then it must have been a white man. Could have been the station-owner. Plenty of black kids belong to them, but they don't own them.'

Just then, we were interrupted by a lady in her fifties. 'Who are you people?' she asked as she walked up to our group.

'Brockman people,' Roy said.

'I knew it,' she replied excitedly, 'I knew it in my heart. I was walkin' down the street when I saw you people here and I said to myself, Doris, they your people. Now, what Brockman mob do they come from?'

'My mother is sister to Albert Brockman,' explained Mum.

'Oh, no! I can't believe it. You're my relations. My aunty is married to Albert Brockman.'

'She's not still alive, is she?' I asked quickly.

'Yes, she's livin' in Hedland. She was a lot younger than him.' Mum and I looked at each other. We were stupid. We should have believed what Jack told us.

'Come home and have a cup of tea with me,' urged Doris, 'I'll ring Elsie and tell her about you. She won't believe it!'

We thanked the men for their help and said goodbye.

Doris made us a cup of tea when we got to her place and we encouraged her to talk about the old days. She said she could remember Annie, Nan's mother, from when she was a small child, and that she thought she'd died somewhere in the thirties at Shaw River.

'All the old people had a little camp out there,' she explained to us. 'There was nowhere else for them to go. All the old Corunna mob died out there.'

'Did Lily die out there, too?' Mum asked.

'Yes, she did.'

'Roy wouldn't tell us anything about Lily.'

Doris chuckled. 'That's because she was one of his old girlfriends. He doesn't like to talk about his old girlfriends.' We all laughed.

Just then, another lady popped in. She was introduced to us as Aunty Katy. She was Elsie's sister. 'Lily was very popular around here,' Aunty Katy told us. 'She could do anything. Everyone liked her, even the white people. She never said no to work.'

'How did she die?' Mum asked.

'Now, that's a funny thing,' replied Aunty Katy. 'She came back from work one day and was doing something for one of the old people, when she dropped down dead. Just like that! It was a big funeral; even some white people came. Poor old darling, we thought so much of her.'

'She married Big Eadie from Corunna Downs, but there were no children,' added Doris.

'You know, if your grandmother was Daisy, then her grand-mother must have been Old Fanny,' said Aunty Katy. 'I'm in my seventies somewhere, but I can remember her, just faintly. She was short, with a very round face, and had a habit of wearing a large handkerchief on her head with knots tied all the way around.'

I smiled. Mum just sat there. It was all too much.

Just then, the rest of the family arrived. Trixie, Amy and May. We shook hands, then sat around and had a good yarn. In the process, we learnt that Nan's Aboriginal stepfather had been called Old Chinaman, and that he had indeed been a tribal elder on Corunna and had maintained this position of power until the day he died. Also, Annie had had a sister called Dodger, who had married, but never had any children. We also learnt that Albert had been a real trickster, even in his old age.

We all laughed and laughed as funny stories about Albert's pranks kept coming, one after the other. By the end of the afternoon, we felt we knew Albert nearly as well as them.

Just as the sun was setting, Doris said, 'You fellas should go and see Happy Jack. He knew Lily well. She worked for his family for many years. He lives down near Marble Bar pool.'

We were anxious to learn as much as we could, so we took Doris' advice and headed off in search of Happy Jack.

One look at Jack's place and it was obvious that he was an excellent mechanic. His block was strewn with many mechanical bits and pieces, as well as half-a-dozen landrovers that he was in the process of fixing.

We explained who we were and showed him some old photos Arthur had given us of the early days. When it finally dawned on him who we were, he was very moved.

'I just can't believe it,' he exclaimed. 'After all these years ...'

'I know you don't know us, Jack,' I said, 'but it would mean so much to us if you could tell us about Lily. We know very little and we would like to be able to tell Daisy about her when we go home.'

'I'm happy to tell you anything I know,' he said as we settled ourselves around his kitchen table. 'She was a wonderful,

wonderful woman. She worked for my family for many years. You know, she's only been dead the better part of fifteen years. What a pity she couldn't have met you all.'

'We wish we'd come sooner,' I replied. 'Doris told us so many of the old ones have died in recent years.'

'That's right. And that Corunna mob. They were all good people and what you'd call strong characters, and that's by anyone's standard, white or black. Now, my family, we started off most of the tin mining in this area. We would go through and strip the country, and all that old Corunna mob would come behind and yandy off the leftovers. We were happy for them to have whatever they found, because they were the people tribally belonging to that area. Now and then, others would try and muscle in, but we wouldn't have any of that — it belonged to that mob only. We let them come in straight behind the bulldozers. It gave them a living. We were very careful about sacred sites and burial grounds too, not like some others I could mention. The old men knew this. Sometimes, they would walk up to us and say, 'One of our people is buried there.' So we would bulldoze around it and leave the area intact.

'Now Lilla — that's what a lot of us called her, not Lily, Lilla — she was a great friend of my mother's. She worked in the house and was a wonderful cook. Later, when I married, she helped look after my kids too. She had a fantastic sense of humour. What's Daisy like, is she fairly short?'

'Yes.'

'Yes, Lilla was like that. Though mind you, in her later years, she became a fairly heavy woman. She was wonderful to the old people, even though she was old herself. She worked really hard looking after them. We used to call her The Angel. She was a beautiful, gentle old woman, and when she died, I felt very sad, because I felt a thing was lost from amongst the people then.'

'Is there anyone else we could talk to who might help us?' I asked after a few minutes' silence. All I wanted to do was cry, but my voice sounded firm and steady, like it belonged to someone else.

'Yes,' replied Jack thoughtfully. 'You should go to the Reserve and see Topsy and Old Nancy. Nancy is well into her nineties and Topsy well into her eighties. I think I remember them saying they were on Corunna very early in the piece. They might know your grandmother — they were great friends of Lilla's. The only thing is, they only speak the language. You'd have to get someone to interpret.'

'Thanks very much,' I said. 'You don't know what this means to us.' We all had tears in our eyes then. It was as though we'd all been transported back into the past. As though we'd seen her and talked to her. Lily was a real person to us now. Just like Albert was.

'Jack,' I said as we left, 'would you mind if I put what you told me in a book?'

'You put in what you like. I'm extremely proud to have known that woman. The way she conducted herself, the way she looked after her own people was wonderful. Your family has missed knowing a wonderful woman.'

'Thanks,' I whispered.

We drove back to the caravan park in silence. Even the children were quiet. We unpacked the van and set up our things for tea.

Mum and I couldn't help thinking of all the things we'd learnt about our family. Our family was something to feel proud of. It made us feel good inside, and sad. Later that night, Mum and I sat under the stars, talking.

'I wish I'd known them,' Mum sighed.

'Me too.'

'You seem a bit depressed.'

'I am ... It's Lilla. I feel very close to her in the spirit. I feel deprived.'

'How do you mean?'

'Deprived of being able to help her. We could have helped her with those old people. I feel all churned up that she did all that on her own. She never had children. We could have been her children. I mean, she was obviously working hard all day and then going out to camp and looking after the old ones, feeding them ...' My voice trailed off. Mum never said anything.

I tossed and turned that night. The feelings I had about Lilla ran very deep, like someone had scored my soul with a knife. Too deep to cry. Finally, I turned to my old standby. 'Where is she now?' I asked. 'Where are Lilla and Annie and Rosie and Old Fanny? Where are the women in my family, are they all right? I wish I'd been able to help.' Suddenly, it was as if a window in heaven had opened and I saw a group of Aboriginal women standing together. They were all looking at me. I knew instinctively it was them. Three adults and a child. Why, that's Rosie, I thought. And then the tears came. As I cried, a voice gently said, 'Stop worrying, they're with me now.' Within minutes, I was asleep.

The following morning, I awoke refreshed and eager to tackle the Reserve. The deep pain inside of me was slowly fading. I never told Mum what I'd seen. I couldn't.

I was, therefore, rather surprised when she took me aside and said quietly, 'What happened to you last night?'

'I don't know what you're talking about.'

'Last night, something important happened to you. You were asleep, or at least I thought you were, then suddenly, I saw you standing with a group of Aboriginal women. I think there were three of them and a child. I knew you were trying to tell me something, something important, but I didn't know what.'

'Oh Mum,' I sobbed, 'it was them!' Her face crumpled. She knew who I meant.

'They're all right, Mum, they're happy.' She just nodded her head. Then she covered her face with her hands and walked silently away.

By lunchtime, we'd pulled ourselves together sufficiently to be able to tackle the Reserve. We'd asked an Aboriginal woman called Gladys Lee if she would come and interpret for us. Jack had recommended her, and she was very happy to help us.

Armed with our old photos, we went from house to house on the Reserve, asking about Lilla. We drew a blank every time.

Finally, we reached the last house. We stepped up onto the small verandah and Gladys showed the photos to two old ladies. No, they didn't know Lilla. Suddenly, I twigged from Gladys speaking that these two ladies were Topsy and Old Nancy. I asked Gladys to show them the photos again.

Topsy took a closer look. Suddenly, she smiled, pointed to a figure in the photos and said, 'Topsy Denmark.' Old Nancy took more of an interest then. After a few minutes, she pointed to the middle figure and said, 'Dr Gillespie.'

'That's right!' I said excitedly to Gladys. I pointed to the photo featuring Nanna as a young girl and got them to look at it carefully. Suddenly, there was rapid talking in Balgoo. I couldn't understand a word, but I knew there was excitement in the air.

Finally, Gladys turned to me with tears in her eyes and said, 'If I had known Daisy's sister was Wonguynon, there would have been no problem.'

'Who's Wonguynon?' I asked.

'That's Lilla's Aboriginal name. We only know her by Wonguynon. I loved her. She looked after me when I was very small. I used to run away to her and she'd give me lollies and look after me until my parents came. She was related to my father. I am your relation, too.'

Topsy and Nancy began to cry. Soon, we were all hugging. Gladys and I had tears in our eyes, but we managed not to break down. Topsy and Nancy pored over all the photos I had, chuckling and laughing and shaking their heads. They explained, through Gladys, that they had been on Corunna when Nan had been taken. They'd all cried then, because they were all very close.

'They lived as one family unit in those days,' Gladys explained. 'They lived with Daisy and Lily and Annie. This makes them very close to you. They are your family. Daisy was sister to them. They call her sister, and they loved her as a sister.'

I tried not to look at Gladys as she explained things because I was trying to keep a tight lid on my emotions. I knew if I began crying, I wouldn't be able to stop.

Later, we retraced our steps back down through the Reserve, stopping at each house in turn and asking about Wonguynon. It was totally different now — open arms and open hearts. By the time we reached the other end of the Reserve, we'd been hugged and patted and cried over, and told not to forget and to come back.

An old full-blood lady whispered to me, 'No one comes back. You don't know what it means that you, with light skin, want to own us.'

We had lumps in our throats the size of tomatoes. I wanted desperately to tell her how much it meant to us that they would own us. My mouth wouldn't open. I just hugged her and tried not to sob.

We were all so grateful to Gladys for the kind way she helped us through. Without her, we wouldn't have been able to understand a word.

Our lives had been enriched in the past few days. We wondered if we could contain any more.

The following day, we decided to go to Corunna Downs station. Doris offered to come with us, as she knew the manager out there.

The track to Corunna was very rough. Apparently, it was the worst it had been for years. After an hour of violent jerking up and down, we rounded a bend and Doris said, 'There's the homestead.'

When we reached the main house, Trevor, the manager, welcomed us with a nice hot cup of tea and some biscuits. We explained why we were there and he happily showed us over the house. To our surprise and delight, it was the same one Nan and Arthur had known in their day. We saw where the old kitchen had been, a date palm Nan had talked about, and, further over in one of the back sheds, the tank machine in which Albert had lost his fingers. I suppose these would be items of no interest to most people, but to us, they were terribly important. It was concrete evidence that what Arthur had told us and what Nan had mentioned were all true.

There were no Aboriginal people on Corunna now. It seemed sad, somehow. Mum and I sat down on part of the old fence and looked across to the distant horizon. We were both trying to imagine what it would have been like for the people in the old days. Soft, blue hills completely surrounded the station. They seemed to us mystical and magical. We easily imagined Nan, Arthur, Rosie, Lily and Albert, sitting exactly as we were now, looking off into the horizon at the end of the day. Dreaming, thinking.

'This is a beautiful place,' Mum sighed. 'Why did she tell me it was an ugly place? She didn't want me to come. She just doesn't want to be Aboriginal.' We both sat in silence.

We stayed on Corunna until late in the afternoon, then reluctantly drove back to Marble Bar. We wanted to stay longer, but our time was so limited and we now had many other leads to follow.

We all felt very emotional when we left from Doris' house. She looked sad. She'd rung Aunty Elsie and told her we were coming to see her before we returned to Perth. Doris had also suggested that we see Tommy Stream in Nullagine, and Dolly and Billy in Yandeearra.

We kissed everyone goodbye and headed off towards Nullagine. Mum and I were both a bit teary. Nothing was said, but I knew she felt like I did. Like we'd suddenly come home and now we were leaving again. But we had a sense of place now.

Tommy Stream was a lovely old man. He told us that he was Nanna's cousin and had been on Corunna Downs when she had been taken away.

'I remember,' he said softly. 'I was younger than her, so when she left, I was only a little fella, but all the people cried when she left. They knew she wasn't coming back. My kids would be related to you,' he told Mum, 'they'd be like your cousins.'

Mum asked again about Maltese Sam. It was a ghost from the past she wanted very definitely settled.

'That's not right,' replied Tommy after she suggested that Maltese might be Nan's father. 'I knew Maltese; he wasn't her father. I don't know who her father was, but it wasn't him.'

We talked a little more about the old days, and when it began to grow dark, we decided to head back to the Nullagine caravan park. The children were tired and hungry. We thanked Tommy for talking to us. Like Doris, he suggested that we visit Billy and Dolly Swan at Yandeearra, so we decided to head that way the following morning.

Yandeearra was a long drive away, so we set out as early as we could. We telephoned ahead to ask permission to come; we didn't want to intrude. Peter Coppin, the manager, was pleased for us to visit and welcomed us all on our arrival.

Before we had met anyone else, an older lady came striding towards us.

'Who are you people?' she asked.

Mum explained who we were. The older lady suddenly broke into a big smile and hugged Mum.

'You're my relations,' she cried. 'Lily was my aunty, dear old thing. When I saw your car, I just knew I was going to see some of my old people today. No one said anything to me, I just knew in my heart.' We were amazed. Dolly then pointed to Amber and Blaze and said, 'You see those kids, they got the Corunna stamp on them. Even if you hadn't told me, I could tell just by looking at those kids that you lot belong to that old mob on Corunna.'

Dolly introduced us to Billy and we sat and talked about the early days and who was related to whom. He was very pleased that we'd been to see Tommy Stream as well as the Marble Bar people. He explained that others had come through, trying to find out who they belonged to.

'We try to work it out,' he told us kindly. We tell them best we can, but some of them we just can't place. And that makes us feel bad, because we think they could belong to us, but we don't know how. Now, I know exactly who you are so there's no trouble there. I can tell you straight: you belong to a lot of the people here. My children would be your relations. Tommy, he's close, and others, too; then there's some that you're related to but not close, if you get what I mean. You still related to them, though ...'

We stayed the night at Yandeearra. The following morning, Billy and Dolly said, 'We couldn't sleep. We tossed and turned all night, trying to work out which group you belong to. Tell us about where you from again.'

We went through all that we knew again, very slowly. Then

Peter Coppin came over and joined in the discussion. They worked out that Dolly was aunty to Mum, so the groups could be worked out from there.

'There are four groups,' explained Peter, 'Panaka, Burungu, Carriema and Malinga. Now, these groups extend right through. I can go down as far as Wiluna and know who I am related to just by saying what group I'm from. We hear that further up north, they got eight groups. We don't know how they work it out — four is bad enough!' We all laughed.

Then Billy said, 'I think we got it now. You,' he said, pointing to me, 'must be Burungu, your mother is Panaka, and Paul, we would make him Malinga. Now, this is very important, you don't want to go forgetting this.'

Dolly and Peter agreed that those groups were the ones we belonged to.

'You got it straight?' Billy asked.

'I think so,' I laughed, as I repeated the names.

'Well, I'm glad we got that sorted out,' added Peter, 'now you can come here whenever you like. We know who you belong to now. If you ever come and I'm not here and they tell you to go away, you hold your ground. You just tell them your group and who you're related to. You got a right to be here same as the others.'

'That's right,' agreed Billy strongly. 'You got your place now.'

We all felt very moved and honoured that we'd been given our groups. There was no worry about us forgetting — we kept repeating them over and over. It was one more precious thing that added to our sense of belonging.

We were all sad when we left Yandeearra the following day. We'd been very impressed with Yandeearra and the way Peter managed the community. It was a lovely place.

Our next stop was Aunty Elsie's place in Hedland. She had a lovely home overlooking the ocean.

I don't think she could take in who we were at first. She had had little contact with Arthur and Nan, though Albert had talked about them a lot, she told us. As we talked, things began to fall into place. We were surprised at the likeness of some of Aunty Elsie's grandchildren to our own family. We explained how we thought everyone we were related to must be dead and how we couldn't believe she was really Uncle Albert's wife. Aunty told us that she'd been many years younger than Albert when they'd married. There were four children: Brian, William, Claude and Margaret. Aunty was, in fact, roughly the same age as Mum, so they had a lot in common. We showed her photos of the family and laughed once again about all the tricks Uncle Albert played on everyone. Aunty also told us how Uncle Albert had owned his own truck and what a hard worker he'd been. It was a trait that seemed to run in the family.

By the time we finally left, we'd gotten to know her really well. Aunty gave us a big fish for our tea. We promised we would come to Hedland again and asked her to visit Perth so she could meet the rest of the family. We felt very full inside when we left. It was like all the little pieces of a huge jigsaw were finally fitting together.

The following day, it was time to head back to Perth, but there was one last stop to make. Billy and Dolly had told us to call in on Billy Moses at Twelve-mile, just out of Hedland.

When we arrived, we were told that Billy and Alma had gone shopping and no one knew when they'd be back, but we could wait near his house if we wanted to. Only five minutes had passed when a taxi pulled in, bearing Billy and Alma.

I walked forward and held out my hand.After introducing myself, I explained who we were and why we had come. He listened seriously, trying to take in everything I said. Suddenly, his face lit up with a heart-warming smile and he said, 'You my relations! Yes, you've come to the right place. You my people. I am your Nanna's cousin.' There were tears in his eyes. I held his hand warmly, and Alma smiled.

We walked back to his house and sat down for a chat. Billy said, 'I can't believe it. Some of my people coming all the way from Perth just to visit me. You always come here. I'm the boss; you can come and live here. This is your place too, remember that.' We began to talk about the old times and Billy explained how he, too, was taken away at a young age.

'I was very lucky,' he told us, 'I made it my business to come back and find out who I belonged to. It was funny, you know, when I first came back, no one round here would talk to me. You see, they weren't sure who I was. I'd walk down the street and they'd just stare at me. Then one day, an old fella came into town, he saw me and recognised me. He spoke up for me and said, "That fella belong to us. I know who he is; I know his mother." After that, I never had any trouble. They all talk to me now. I belong here. It's good to be with my people. I'm glad you've come back.'

We were glad, too. And overwhelmed at the thought that we

nearly hadn't come. How deprived we would have been if we had been willing to let things stay as they were. We would have survived, but not as whole people. We would never have known our place.

That afternoon, we reluctantly left for Perth. None of us wanted to go, Paul included. We were reluctant to return and pick up the threads of our old lives. We were different people now. What had begun as a tentative search for knowledge had grown into a spiritual and emotional pilgrimage. We had an Aboriginal consciousness now, and were proud of it.

Mum, in particular, had been very deeply affected by the whole trip. 'To think I nearly missed all this. All my life, I've only been half a person. I don't think I really realised how much of me was missing until I came North. Thank God you're stubborn, Sally.'

We all laughed and then, settling back, retreated into our own thoughts. I knew Mum, like me, was thinking about Nan. We viewed her differently now. We had more insight into her bitterness. And more than anything, we wanted her to change, to be proud of what she was. We'd seen so much of her and ourselves in the people we'd met. We belonged, now. We wanted her to belong, too.

Someone like me

When we arrived back in Perth, Nan was really pleased to see us, and so was Beryl. Nan had gone through all the money Mum had left her and had had Beryl on the go nonstop, running up to the shop for chocolate biscuits and putting bets on the TAB.

'I knew you'd all be safe,' Nan said when she saw us. 'I been praying the cyclones wouldn't get you.'

We rounded up the rest of the family the following day and insisted on showing the video we had made of our trip. Much to our dismay, the film turned out to be pretty mediocre. It suffered from the faults common to most home movies: lack of focus, zooming too quickly and panning too slowly.

Throughout the filming of Corunna, I watched Nan. She was taking a keen interest in the old buildings.

'There's the old date palm,' she said. 'That used to be the garden down there. That's the old homestead. And that's where they had the kitchen.'

When it was all over, Nan said, 'Fancy, all those old buildings and the tank machine still being there — I didn't think there'd be anything left.'

Mum told Nan what all the old boys had said about Lily. Nan laughed and laughed. 'Ooh yes,' she chuckled, 'that was Lily, all right. She was the sort of person you couldn't help liking. She had a good heart, did Lily.' I was amazed, Nan had never talked about Lily like that before.

Over the next few days, Mum talked at length with Nan about the different people we had met. Nan feigned disinterest, but we knew it was just a bluff. She was desperately interested in everything we had to say, but she didn't want to let her feelings show.

One night when they were alone, Mum told Nan how Annie and a lot of the other older ones from Corunna Downs had died at Shaw River. 'She had Lily,' Mum said. 'Lily had devoted herself to the old ones. Annie wasn't alone when she died; she had some of her people with her.' Nan nodded. There were tears in her eyes.

'Do any of them remember me?' she asked wistfully.

'They all do,' Mum said. 'Do you remember Topsy and another woman called Nancy? They said they lived with you and Annie on Corunna.'

Nan looked shocked. 'They still alive?' she asked in disbelief.

'Yes.'

Nan just shook her head. 'I'm going to bed,' she muttered. Mum lay down and cried herself to sleep.

A few weeks later, I tackled Nan about being able to speak two languages; she was unwilling to discuss the subject. When I told her about the different skin groups, she said crossly, 'I know all that, I'm not stupid.' She wouldn't be drawn further. There'd been a slight change, a softening, but she was still unwilling to share the personal details of her life with us.

When Mum and I got together, we couldn't help reminiscing about our trip.

'Well, we found out one thing,' said Mum, 'Maltese Sam definitely wasn't Nan's father.'

'That's right. Though it doesn't necessarily mean Howden was either.'

'No, I know. Probably, we'll never really know who fathered her.'

'Do you reckon Jack Grime really is your father?'

'Oh, I don't know, Sally,' Mum sighed. 'When I was little, I always thought Howden was my father, isn't that silly?'

'Howden? Why did you think that?'

'I suppose because he was Judy and June and Dick's father. I guess because I was little and didn't understand, I assumed he was my father too.'

'Yeah, I could see how you might think that. You were all living there at Ivanhoe.'

'Yes.'

'Aunty Judy said you're the image of Jack Grime, though. That'd be some sort of proof, wouldn't it?'

'Oh, I don't know. People can look like one another, but it doesn't mean they're related.'

'Yeah. Hey, I know. I've got a big photo of Jack. Why don't we hold it up to the big mirror in my room? You can put your head next to it and we'll see if you do look like him.'

'Oh, all right,' Mum giggled, 'why not?'

Within minutes, Mum and I and the photo were all facing the large mirrors in the doors of my wardrobe.

'Well, that was a dead loss. You don't look anything like him, even taking into account the fact that you've put on weight.'

'He doesn't look like any of you kids, either, does he?'

'Naah,' I agreed. 'Hang on a tick and I'll get another picture.' I returned quickly. 'Okay,' I said, 'face the mirror.'

Mum fronted up to the mirror and tried not to laugh. I held up a photograph of Howden as a young man next to her face. We both fell into silence.

'My God,' I whispered. 'Give him black, curly hair and a big bust and he's the spitting image of you!'

Mum was shocked. 'I can't believe it,' she said. 'Why haven't I ever noticed this before? I've seen that picture hundreds of times. You don't think it's possible he was my father?'

'Anything's possible. But he couldn't be yours as well as Nan's. You know, features can skip a generation.'

'Oh, I don't know, Sally,' Mum sighed. 'It's such a puzzle. You know, for nearly all my life, I've desperately wanted to know who my father was — now, I couldn't care less. Why should I bother with whoever it was? They never bothered with me.'

'But that's been the recent history of Aboriginal people all along, Mum. Kids running around, not knowing who fathered them. Those early pioneers, they've got a lot to answer for.'

'Yes, I know, I know, but I think now I'm better off without all that business. All those wonderful people up North, they all claimed me. Well, that's all I want. That's enough, you see. I don't want to belong to anyone else.'

'Me neither.'

We walked back to the lounge room. After a few seconds' silence, Mum said, 'Sal …?'

'What?'

'We-ell … You know the Daisy that Jack said he'd met? You don't think that could have been Nanna?'

'Dunno. I asked her the other day if she'd ever been back North, but she just got mad with me.'

'It might have been her,' Mum said tentatively, 'Alice did tell you she'd gone back once.'

'But if it was her, it was in 1923 and she would have been pregnant. Mum … do you think you might have a brother or sister somewhere?'

She nodded.

'But surely Nan would have told you?'

'Not if she wasn't allowed to keep it.'

'This is terrible.' I eyed her keenly. 'There's something you're not telling me, isn't there?'

Mum composed herself, then said, 'The other night when I was in bed, I had this sort of flashback to when I was little. I'd been pestering Nanna, asking her why I didn't have a brother or a sister, when she put her arms around me and whispered quietly, "You have a sister." Then she held me really tight. When she let me go, I saw she was crying.'

I couldn't say anything. We both sat in silence. Finally, Mum said, 'I'm going to ask her.'

A few days later, Mum broached the subject with Nan, only to be met with anger and abuse. Nan locked herself in her room, saying, 'Let the past be.'

'I'll never know now,' Mum told me later.

'You mustn't give up! What does your gut feeling tell you?'

She sighed. 'It tells me I've got a sister. I've had that feeling all my life, from when I was very small, that I had a sister somewhere. If only I could find her.'

'Then I believe what you feel is true.'

Mum laughed. 'You're a romantic.'

'Crap! Be logical, she could still be alive; if she was born in 1923, she'd be in her sixties, now. Also, if Nan had her up North, she could have been brought up by the people round there or a white family could have adopted her.'

'Sally, we don't even have a name. It's impossible! You talk like we'll find her one day, but it's impossible.'

'Nothing's impossible.'

'Could you talk to Nan?'

'Yeah, but she won't tell me anything. I'll let her cool down a bit first.'

'There's been so much sadness in my life,' Mum said, 'I don't think I can take any more.'

'You want to talk about it?'

'You mean for that book?'

'Yes.'

'Well ...' she hesitated for a moment. Then, with sudden determination, she said, 'Why shouldn't I? If I stay silent like Nanna, it's like saying everything's all right. People should know what it's like for someone like me.'

I smiled at her.

'Perhaps my sister will read it.'

Gladys Corunna's Story

I have no memory of being taken from my mother and placed in Parkerville Children's Home, but all my life I've carried a mental picture of a little fat kid about three or four years old. She's sitting on the verandah of Babyland Nursery, her nose is running and she's crying. I think that was me when they first took me to Parkerville.

Parkerville was a beautiful place run by Church of England nuns. Set in the hills of the Darling Ranges, it was surrounded by bush and small streams. In the spring, there were wildflowers of every colour and hundreds of varieties of birds. Each morning I awoke to hear the kookaburras laughing and the maggies warbling. That was the side of Parkerville I loved.

That was my home from 1931 when I was three years old. I was only able to go back to my mother at Ivanhoe three times a year, for the holidays.

There were two sections at the Home. The older children's section, where all the houses were named after people who had donated money, and Babyland Nursery.

Babyland was really just a cottage surrounded by verandahs. Inside was a kitchen with a large wood stove, some small tables and chairs, and highchairs for the really little ones. There was only one dormitory and it was filled with lots of little iron beds that sat close to the floor. They were very neat and tidy in Babyland. You were only allowed to play inside on real wintry days. Normally they made us all sit out on the verandahs, that was so you didn't mess up the rooms once they'd been cleaned.

Every morning the older girls came over to bathe us. We were always cold from the night before because we still all wet our beds. I dreaded bath time because of the carbolic soap and the hard scrubbing-brushes. The House Mother used to stand in the doorway and say, 'Scrub 'em clean, girls!' We'd cry — those brushes really hurt. Our crying always seemed to satisfy her, and she'd leave then. As soon as she left, the girls would throw the brushes away and let us play. Our clothes were kept in a big cupboard and the girls dressed us in whatever fitted.

I guess that was one of the few times when I was lucky to be black, because the older Aboriginal girls always gave us black babies an extra kiss and cuddle. That gave me a wonderful feeling of security. I'll always be grateful for that. You see, even though we weren't related, there were strong ties between black kids. The older white girls never seemed to care about anyone, and our House Mothers weren't like real mothers. They just bossed us around, and they never gave you a kiss or a cuddle.

Every morning I'd sit on the verandah with my friend Iris, who was fat like me. She had very white skin and her freckles stood out like they'd been daubed on with a paintbrush. She always seemed to be unhappy; she had an awful cough and her feet were blue. We didn't have shoes. She loved to sit close to me. We always stuck together. If there were two of you, the others didn't pick on you so much.

After school, the older girls would come back and carry me around. I used to sit on the verandah and press my face against the wooden railing that faced the school oval. It always seemed to be such a long time before they came. When the bell rang, they'd all come running over, fighting over whose turn it was to carry me. I felt sorry for Iris then; no one ever wanted to carry her. I wished the big girls would play with her too, but she was always coughing, and I was so busy enjoying the attention that I soon forgot her.

Every little bed in the dormitory had a grey or dark green blanket on it, and we had to kneel down beside our beds and say our prayers. After that, the lights were turned out and some of the smaller kids had their cots pushed closer to the House Mother's bedroom so she could hear them if they got sick in the night.

I remember one night hearing Iris cough and cough. When I got up in the morning, Iris was gone. I felt very lonely, sitting on the verandah that day. I asked the others if they'd seen her. They said she was sick and had been taken to hospital. I felt very sad.

A few weeks after that, when I was playing on the verandah by myself, she just appeared out of nowhere. She was all dressed up in a white lace dress and she was happy. She wasn't coughing any more. She smiled at me and I smiled at her and then she left. I felt better then. I knew that, wherever she'd gone, she was all right.

When I turned five years old, I was sent to George Turner. It was a house opposite Babyland, across a wide expanse of gravel. I had been told to go and see my new House Mother. There were *no goodbyes to my friends; they just sat playing on the verandah as usual.*

I stumbled down the front steps and began slowly walking across the gravel with my little bundle of clothes. I tried to walk on the clumps of dandelions to keep my feet clean, but they ran out, and after that it was just black sand.

When I finally reached the gate of George Turner, I was too scared to open it. I was worried about my feet. In Babyland, it had been very important that you kept your feet clean — that was why we were never allowed off the verandahs — and now here I was with black, sandy feet. I was sure my new House Mother would be very cross with me.

Suddenly, one of the older girls came up to the gate. I felt relieved when I recognised her; she was one of my friends. She took me by the hand and led me up to Miss Moore, who was waiting on the verandah.

Miss Moore showed me around the house. She said I was one of twenty-five children who would be staying here. She explained to me that the boys slept on one side of the verandah and the girls on the other, with a blind lowered in the middle to make a division. We each had a small cupboard for our own personal things and a small mirror so we could see to comb our hair in the morning. I was amazed that, in all the time she'd been talking to me, she hadn't once mentioned my dirty feet.

I was also surprised to see that all the walls in the dormitories were covered with huge framed pictures of film stars. Of course, I was too young to know then that they were film stars; I just thought they were pictures of mummies and daddies.

After Miss Moore had finished explaining things to me, she told me to put my things away in the cupboard. I never had much, just a few pieces of coloured Easter egg paper and a one-legged teddy that I had hidden in my clothes and stolen from Babyland. I also had a hairbrush that my mother had given me.

My little cupboard wasn't bare for long — I became a hoarder. I loved collecting silver paper from Easter eggs. Sometimes, the big kids would give me some and I would sit for hours, trying to get the creases out. Then I'd stack them gently in an old chocolate box. I collected anything the older children were willing to part with, I wasn't fussy.

I had nightmares at George Turner. I'd never had them in Babyland. Maybe it was the big bed. It was very high off the ground and was the last one on the verandah, next to the blind that divided the girls' section from the boys'. There was a large window just near my bed. I'd look through the window and see only darkness and eerie shadows.

Sometimes, I'd wake in the night with a heavy weight on my chest and my mouth would be all dry inside. I was sure there was someone sitting on the end of my bed. I'd lie under the blankets, too scared to move or breathe. When I awoke in the morning, I'd look straight to the end of my bed to see if anyone was there. There was never anyone.

As I grew older, that fear disappeared. Maybe because I started to learn about Jesus. When I felt really scared, I'd look over the verandah to the tall gum tree nearby, and I'd see him there, watching me. I felt very protected. Sometimes, when I was sad, a light would shine suddenly inside of me and make me happy. I knew it was God.

Apart from these experiences, the thing that helped me most was the music I used to hear at night. As I grew older, I realised it was Aboriginal music, like some blackfellas were having a corroboree just for me. It was very beautiful music. I only heard it at night when I was feeling depressed. After I'd heard it, I knew I could go to sleep. It was that same feeling of protection.

There were many times when I felt very lost. I knew I wasn't a baby any more. I knew I had to look after myself now.

One day, after I'd been at George Turner for about a year, some of the older girls asked me if I'd like to go for a walk. We walked deep into the bush on the far side of the Home. All the kids liked going there. They told me they liked to read the names printed on the crosses.

I gazed at the little graves scattered here and there amongst the low clumps of red and pink bush. Then I followed Enid as she went from grave to grave, reading the names. Suddenly, she grabbed my hand.

'Look,' she said, 'it's that little friend of yours in Babyland: "Iris, three years ten months".'

I gazed in shock at the little mound of earth beneath the small, white cross. Enid moved on, reading out the names of more babies as she went. I stood staring at Iris's grave. I suddenly realised that that was why she hadn't come back to Babyland: she'd died.

I picked up some buttercups and placed them on the top of the grave, like I always did when I found a dead bird in the bush and buried it. I tried to hide my tears from the others, but they noticed. 'It's all right,' Enid said. 'Your friend is happy in heaven.'

***

We had the same routine every morning at Parkerville. They woke us early by ringing a bell. The air was always cold and you never felt like getting up.

You made your bed, got dressed and swept down the verandahs. After that, it was time for breakfast. There was a large table inside the dining room in the house, with long stools that slotted underneath.

During winter, we always had a big open fire going. I remember, at night, we would hate leaving the fire to go out to our beds on the verandahs. They were so cold and draughty.

Every morning the boys got the wood for the stove in the kitchen and the older girls cooked the porridge. I never liked breakfast much. It was the weevils; they'd be staring at me from my bowl of porridge. I covered them as much as I could with milk and sugar. Sometimes, I closed my eyes as they went into my mouth. I hated the thought of them being inside me. I'd love to have been able to forgo the porridge, but I was always too hungry to allow myself that luxury. Apart from a slice of bread and dripping, the porridge was all we got. We all envied Miss Moore, because she had real butter on her toast and plenty of scalded cream.

After breakfast, we cleaned up and then went to morning church before school.

At lunchtime, we all lined up and marched to the big dining hall. Lunch was usually hot, like a stew. The meat sometimes smelt bad, especially in summer.

After school, we were allowed one slice of bread and dripping before going to afternoon church. Tea was usually cold meat and salad, and, if we were lucky, jelly and custard.

Every Friday night we had pictures. They were old silent movies — heart-rending tales about gypsies stealing a child from a family. Of course, by the end of the film, they'd all be reunited. I always thought of myself as the stolen child. In fact, I lived the part so wholeheartedly that it took me ages to come back to reality after the film had finished. We all loved any films about families. Pictures like that touched something deep inside us. It was every kid's secret wish to have a family of their own. But it was never something we talked about openly. During the week, we usually played the movies in our games. One of the most terrible punishments they could inflict on us at the Home was depriving us of our Friday night picture.

The first thing we did on Saturday mornings was line up for a dose of Epsom salts. It was revolting. After that, it was clean-up time. We washed the kitchen floor, wiped down the stove and cleaned out the bath with a mixture of charcoal and cooking salt. The job I hated most was cleaning the table we ate breakfast on. It was covered in white pigskin and it showed every mark. We had to really scrub it to get it clean.

When it came to work, the boys had it real easy. The nuns considered looking after the house women's work. They still had that old-fashioned way of thinking. The boys never even helped with the floors. Though I didn't mind that, I loved polishing the floor.

They gave us large tins of thick yellow polish which was made at the Home. We'd tie old woollen jumpers to our feet, slop huge lumps of wax on the floor, and then zoom all over the place. It was better than roller-skating.

The House Mothers never did any work; their job was to supervise. After we'd finish the house, we'd all march over to the laundry to wash our clothes. They had ladies in to do the linen, but we had to look after our own things.

My favourite time at the Home was Saturday afternoons. Once we'd finished our work, we were allowed to do as we pleased. If it was too cold for swimming, we'd go hunting for food.

I was always hungry. I was like Pooh Bear — I couldn't get enough to eat. My stomach used to rumble all the time. We loved to eat the wild cranberries that grew in the bush; they were sweet and juicy. Trouble was, the goannas liked them, too. You could be eating from one side, and a goanna from the other. You never knew until you met in the middle. I don't know who got the biggest fright.

At the back of the dining room was a shed used for storing apples and root vegetables. The door was always locked, but there was a small window that we could easily climb through. We'd pinch some apples and potatoes and then nick off into the bush to our special tree, where we liked to play Mothers and Fathers.

It was a big, old red gum. It was dead and the trunk was split, so it was like a big room inside. We hid tins and bits of broken china that looked pretty. It was a very happy place. We'd light a fire with a thick piece of glass we kept hidden. We'd shine it onto a dry gum leaf and, before long, the wisp of smoke would start to rise. We'd throw the potatoes on. When we thought they were ready, we'd haul them from the ashes by poking a long stick through them.

The best feed we had was gilgies. They were plentiful in the small pools and creeks around the Home. We caught them with a piece of old meat begged from the kitchen, and tied to a piece of string. It took only a few seconds after you'd dropped the string into the water to catch a gilgie. When we'd caught nine or ten, we'd boil them up in an old tin. They were the best feed of all.

Most of my happiest times were spent alone in the bush, watching the birds and animals. If you sat very quiet, they didn't notice you were there. There were rabbits, wallabies, goannas, lizards, even the tiny insects were interesting. I had such respect for their little lives that I'd feel terrible if I even trod on an ant. We'd come across all sorts of snakes: green ones, brown, black. We used to pick the green ones up, but we never touched the black or brown ones.

One day when I was on my own, I found some fieldmice under a rock near a honeysuckle vine. I often went to that vine, because the flowers were sweet to suck. It was almost as good as having a lolly. I thought the baby fieldmice were wonderful; they were pink and bald and very small.

I had a crying tree in the bush, down near the creek — an old twisted peppermint tree. The limbs curved over to make a seat and its weeping leaves almost covered me completely. You didn't cry in front of anyone at the Home, it wasn't done. A lot of the kids cried in their beds every night, but it wasn't the same as having some place quiet to go where you could make as much noise as you liked.

I'd sit for hours under that peppermint tree, watching the water gurgle over the rocks and listening to the birds. After a while, the peace of that place would reach inside of me and

I wouldn't feel sad any more. Instead, I'd start counting the numerous rainbow-coloured dragonflies that skimmed across the surface of the water. After that, I'd fall asleep. When I finally did walk back to the Home, I felt very content.

Saturday night was spent getting our clothes ready for church on Sunday. We ironed everything with those heavy flatirons you heated up on the stove. It was hard work, especially if you were little. Our clothes were always starched and ironed. We had to iron and iron until not one crease showed. It took ages.

I was lucky that I didn't get seriously ill too often. You didn't get on very well at Parkerville if you had something wrong with you and you couldn't take care of yourself. There were a lot of kids at the Home that were crippled with polio. I felt sorry for them. And you had to be dying not to go to school. If you stopped home, they gave you a dose of salts or castor oil. It cured everything, in those days.

One of the lowest points of my childhood was the time they took me to Princess Margaret Hospital to remove my tonsils. I was so frightened. I was all alone and I thought I was going to die. They put me in a high iron bed and hardly anyone spoke to me. It was like being in a morgue.

I was very sick after the operation. I cried and cried. I couldn't understand why my mother hadn't been to visit me; I thought perhaps they hadn't told her I was sick. She told me later that she couldn't get time off work and she couldn't come at night because of the curfew, which prevented Aboriginal people travelling after dark. I wasn't even allowed to have the comfort of my own mother.

But just after this, something happened that really cheered me up. My Uncle Arthur visited. He'd come to see me once before at Parkerville when I was only very small. The memory I had of him was only dim, but it was important. I did love him and I knew he loved me. I also knew that if he could have taken me from there, he would have. He was very important to me. He reminded me of my mother and home. Sometimes, I used to think that if he and Mum could live together, then I'd have a family. It wasn't to be.

He came and saw me once more after that, then never again. He was too busy trying to make a living for himself and his own family.

On Sunday afternoons, visitors were allowed to come. We never knew whether someone was coming from the station for us or not. That was the worst part. You hoped right up to the very last minute. I used to think, Mum will be here soon, I'll just wait a little bit longer. I remember some years when I only saw her twice at the Home.

If no one came, you put on a brave face and didn't cry. You pretended you didn't care, you just shrugged your shoulders and walked away. If one of your friends got visitors, you'd be so jealous. Of course, if you saw someone coming over the hill for you, you'd get so excited you'd just run.

A lot of kids at Parkerville had parents. Some had mothers, some had fathers. You'd do anything for kids like that, because you always hoped that they might ask you to come along and share their visitors.

It was hardest for the Aboriginal kids. We didn't have anyone. Some of the kids there had been taken from families that lived hundreds of miles away. It was too far for anyone to come and see them. And anyway, Aboriginal people had to get permits to travel. Sometimes, they wouldn't give them a permit. They didn't care that they wanted to see their kids.

Each time Mum came and saw me, she always had a bit of paper with her that said she was allowed to travel. A policeman could stop her any time and ask to look at that paper. If she didn't have it on her, she was in big trouble.

When Mum didn't visit me for a long time, I used to wonder if she'd forgotten me. But the only day she had any time off was on Sunday, and then she had to cook the roast first. She never had any annual holidays, like some of the other servants did. I remember quite a few times when she told me she hadn't come because she couldn't afford the train fare. The only time she had the whole Sunday off was if the Drake-Brockmans went visiting for the day.

When I was still quite young, Sister Kate left Parkerville and took a lot of Aboriginal children with her. I was very sad, because I lost a lot of my friends. There were a few lightly coloured Aboriginal boys left and they kept an eye on me. I don't know why I wasn't sent with Sister Kate. Maybe it was because of the Drake-Brockmans, I don't know.

I think Alice Drake-Brockman thought she was doing a good thing sending me to Parkerville. Sometimes, she'd come up and bring Judy, June and Dick with her for a picnic. That was always in the spring, when the wildflowers were out. Dick and I got on well; we were very close. He treated me like his sister.

I loved it when they all came up, because the other kids were so envious. There was a lot of status in knowing someone who had a car. I thought I'd burst for joy when I saw the black Chev creep up the hill and drive slowly down the road, to halt at George Turner. All the other kids would crowd up close, hoping I'd take one of them with me. It was a feeling of importance that would last me the whole of the following week.

I often prayed for God to give me a family. I used to pretend I had a mother and a father and brothers and sisters. I pretended I lived in a big flash house like Ivanhoe and went to St Hilda's School for Girls, like Judy and June.

It was very important to me to have a father then. Whenever I asked Mum about my father, she'd just say, 'You don't want to know about him. He died when you were very small, but he loved you very much.' She sensed I needed to belong, but she didn't know about all the teasing I used to get because I didn't have a father, nor the comments that I used to hear about bad girls having babies.

I had a large scar on my chest where my mother said my father had dropped his cigar ash. I tried to picture him nursing me, with a large cigar in his mouth.

The scar made me feel I must have had a real father, after all. I'd look at it and feel quite pleased. It wasn't until I was older that I realised it was an initiation scar. My mother had given it to me for protection.

***

We used to have quite a few outings at the Home. We went to the pictures and put on concerts at different places to raise money.

One morning, we were all very excited because we'd been told we were going to the zoo. After breakfast we marched to the *station. When the old steam engine came chugging in, we were all so frightened we'd be left behind that we jumped on while the train was still going.*

The zoo was really exciting, especially the elephants. I'd seen pictures of elephants dressed up in gold, with Indian princes sitting on their backs. I could imagine myself doing that. I felt a lot happier after my day with the animals.

We marched back to the ferry, and were soon chugging back across the Swan River. I had a seat right up near the water and I watched as the ripples came out from under the boat and slowly faded away.

Then I noticed another ferry coming across from the other side, so I leaned over to look to see how close it was going to come to our boat. To my surprise, I saw my mother sitting on the ferry, as pretty as ever in her blue suit. I couldn't believe it. I called out to her and waved my arms. She must have known I was going to the zoo, I thought, but she's got the wrong time, she's going to miss me. She might go to see me at the zoo and I won't be there. I jumped up and down and called and called. My mother never even turned her head in my direction.

Within minutes, our boats had passed. I sat back on the wooden seat and slumped into a corner. The other kids just looked at me, and never said anything. I forgot all about the elephants and bears and lions. All I could think about was my mother. The sadness inside me was so great I couldn't even cry.

***

By the time I'd been in George Turner a couple of years, I began to get as adventurous as the other kids. I became a bit of a leader and had my own little gang.

One day, some kids from a rival gang dared me to go to a cottage where old Sister Fanny lived. All the kids were too scared to go near her because we all thought she was a witch. I wanted to back down, but, being a leader, I couldn't.

I sneaked up very slowly to the cottage until I found myself standing just outside the hessian door that hung from the old tin roof. The flap swayed back and forth in the breeze and I could see inside to the dirt floor. There was a large, black cat lying on the ground asleep — everyone knew witches had black cats.

Suddenly, Sister Fanny pulled the hessian aside, stuck out her old, wrinkled face and said, 'Haaa!' I jumped back in shock. She had lank, uncombed shoulder-length hair and she looked very grubby. As I gazed at her face, I realised that she really did have one blue and one brown eye. The other kids had told me that, but I hadn't believed them.

'I just wanted to pat the cat,' I said quickly.

'Come in, child, come in,' she said in a thin, wobbly voice. I went inside, sat down and patted the cat.

Sister Fanny kept mumbling and walking around the room. It was so shabby, I began to feel sorry for her. I realised then she wasn't a witch, just a frail old lady.

After a few minutes I got up, said goodbye and rejoined the other kids. They couldn't believe I'd actually gone inside. They all thought I was really tough.

'You saw the witch,' they said. 'Is she a real witch?'

'No,' I replied, 'and don't go throwing any more stones at her place. She's just an old lady.'

'Yeah, but she's got one brown eye and one blue,' said Tommy. 'Only witches have eyes like that!'

I couldn't deny that, but I knew in my heart she was just an old lady.

Also, it was around this time that I stopped being scared at night. I actually came to love that part of the night when all the wild horses raced through. There were a lot of them in the hills in those days. When we heard them coming, we'd lean over the verandah and call out. They were so beautiful; some silver, some white, some black and brown. They were going down to the grassy paddocks on the other side of the hill. I suppose they were a bit like us kids in a way, they didn't belong to anyone.

There were a number of adults who I became quite attached to, and used to visit regularly. I found I got on well with older people, perhaps because they often had food, usually biscuits or cakes.

I regularly visited the office lady, Miss Button, who had a little room behind the office, to ask if she had any jobs she needed doing. She was a particular friend of mine. She would get me to dust down her mantelpiece and then she'd make me a cup of tea and give me a biscuit.

At the opposite end of the Home to where Sister Fanny lived was the farm. Mr Pratt lived there, another of my favourite old people, not because of food though, but because he had a horse and buggy. The horse was called Timmy, and he was big and black and beautiful. When he was attached to the buggy, he'd strut like a rooster, waiting to be admired and stroked.

Whenever Mr Pratt did the garden at George Turner, I'd

follow him around, continually chatting about this and that. I liked talking to grown-ups, and he was a darling old fellow.

One day, I was playing chasey with the others on the road, when someone yelled that I was wanted. I walked up the wooden steps and onto the verandah. Little Faye was there, looking scared. 'Moore's in an awful temper,' she said. 'What have you done?'

'I'll be all right,' I replied. I patted her head and walked inside.

'Where's that bloody kid?' I could hear Miss Moore screaming from the kitchen. When I saw her, her face was contorted with rage.

She grabbed me by the arm and started belting me across the head. It was nothing new; she'd given me beltings before. Sometimes, she hit me so much I'd go deaf for a couple of days.

She dragged me towards the large clothes cupboard. I started to cry; I didn't know what I'd done wrong. 'Get your clothes, you stupid girl,' she screamed. I was so upset, my eyes were too full of tears to see my clothes. I grabbed at a dress and she hit me again and shouted, 'Your good clothes.' Then she started shaking me and screaming that I had to be ready in fifteen minutes to go in the car. Where was I going? I felt very frightened — were they sending me away? What about my mother, would I ever see her again? I started to tremble all over and began sobbing.

'Stop crying,' she shouted, 'I didn't hurt you!'

She sent me to the bathroom to dress and wash my face. I managed to get my clothes on, then I splashed my face with cold water, but I still couldn't stop crying. Everything had happened so suddenly, I didn't know what I'd done wrong. I wanted to vomit. I heard the car toot loudly out the front. Miss Moore hauled me out, picked up my bag of clothes and took me to the car, 'Stop snivelling,' she said. 'You didn't do anything wrong.'

I hopped in the front next to Willie, the driver, Sister Dora sat in the back. Willie started up the engine, then glanced down to me and said kindly, 'Don't cry any more. Your mother will be all right.' I was really frightened then.

When we arrived at Ivanhoe, Alice Drake-Brockman took me to where my mother was lying in bed on the balcony. She looked terrible; her eyes were closed, and I thought she was dead. I went to race towards her, but Alice restrained me and said, 'Shhhh, she's asleep.' I tiptoed over and touched my mother's hand, which was resting on the white coverlet. She opened her eyes. Tears trickled down her face, and she squeezed my hand.

The following day, she told me what had happened. They'd taken my Aunty, Helen Bunda, to hospital, but her appendix had burst and there was nothing they could do. They'd asked my mother to give blood. They'd taken the first lot, but it had jelled through carelessness, so they'd taken some more. 'They nearly killed me,' she whispered. 'I'll never go to hospital again.'

I asked her about Aunty Helen and she said, 'Aunty Helen died. The doctor didn't care. You see, Gladdie, we're nothing, just nothing.' I felt very sad, and sort of hopeless. I didn't want to be just nothing.

I stayed at Ivanhoe a week. When the others were asleep, I would sneak into bed with my mother. She'd cuddle me, with silent tears wet on her cheeks. She seemed so unhappy that I'd cry too, loving the comfort of her arms, yet sad at her tears.

I was upset that Aunty was dead, but I was glad Mum was getting better. Alice was very cross with the hospital. She made my mother eat to get her strength back.

One day, when Mum was lying propped up on the pillows, the men from the Daily News arrived to take her photo. We were all very excited when we got the paper. Judy showed Mum her photo and then read the article out to her. It said how she'd nearly sacrificed her life to save her cousin's and how brave she was. I felt very proud.

Everybody knew what had happened when I went back to Parkerville, as some of the kids had seen my mother's picture in the paper. Miss Moore patted my shoulder and said she was pleased to see me back, but I couldn't look at her after the way she'd treated me. I felt betrayed.

***

I always considered Good Friday the saddest day of the year. I couldn't understand how anyone could do such a horrible thing as to kill Jesus.

We'd attend church in the morning and it'd be stripped bare, except for a large cross on which was pinned the brass body of Jesus. After the service, we'd all file out solemnly. Once we were back at the house, we weren't allowed to play or make a noise. It was a day of solemnity.

Easter Sunday would change all that. We'd have a special midday dinner and an Easter egg. Kids who had relatives usually got visitors who brought more Easter eggs. My mother usually came to see me and brought me an egg. It was a really happy day and I'd feel good because Jesus was alive again.

In the May holidays, I usually went to Ivanhoe. Willie would drive me down to Perth and I'd be met by Alice.

I was always pleased to see my mother and really excited that I was going to be with her for two whole weeks. She'd give me a hug and then take me into the kitchen for a glass of milk and a piece of cake.

I loved Ivanhoe and I really loved Judy, who was so beautiful, and she always made a fuss of me. She liked to dress me up, but I'd cry when she insisted on putting big satin bows in my hair. I didn't want to look like Shirley Temple.

I remember one holiday at Ivanhoe when I was in the kitchen with my mother, and Alice came in with June. She had the most beautiful doll in her arms. It had golden hair and blue eyes and was dressed in satin and lace. I was so envious, I wished it was mine. It reminded me of a princess.

June said to me, 'You've got a doll, too. Mummy's got it.' Then, from behind her back, Alice pulled out a black topsy doll dressed like a servant. It had a red-checked dress on and a white apron, just like Mum's. It had what they used to call a slave cap on its head. It was really just a handkerchief knotted at each corner. My mother always wore one on washing days.

I stared at this doll for a minute. I was completely stunned. That's me, I thought. I wanted to be a princess, not a servant. I was so upset that when Alice placed the black doll in my arms, I couldn't help flinging it onto the floor and screaming, 'I don't want a black doll, I don't want a black doll!' Alice just laughed and said to my mother, 'Fancy, her not wanting a black doll.'

I clung to my mother's legs and cried and cried. She growled at me for being silly and bad-mannered in front of Alice, but I knew she didn't really mean it. I could hear the sadness in her voice. She understood why I was upset.

They told the story of this often at Ivanhoe. They thought it was funny. I still can't laugh about it.

It was terrible in the nineteen thirties; the Depression was on and people were so poor, especially Aboriginal people. They would come along the river, selling props. These were long, wooden poles people used to prop up their clothes lines.

I think they liked calling in to Ivanhoe, because Alice had said that my mother was allowed to give them a cup of tea and a piece of cake or bread. Alice was always generous with food.

I used to feel so sorry for these Aboriginal people. I wondered how they could come to be so poor. They had nothing, especially the old ones. A lot of them had had their kids taken off them, and they had no one to look out for them.

My mother loved it when they came. She'd sit on the lawn with them and they'd talk about how it used to be in the old days. My mother always gave them clothes and shoes, whatever she could find. When they left, she'd have tears in her eyes. It hurt her to see her own people living like that.

At Christmas, I also went to Ivanhoe. We'd all sleep out on the balcony at the rear of the house. We had a lovely view over the Swan River from there.

At the top of the house was a large attic which June was allowed to use as a playhouse; it was a lovely room. There were seats under the windows and dolls and a dolls' house. There were teddies and other toys and a china tea set.

It was strange, really, that, at the Home, nobody owned a doll. There were a few broken ones kept in the cupboard, but you were never allowed to take one to bed. I was lucky because I had a rag doll my mother had given me called Sally Jane. I loved her very much. She was kept at Ivanhoe for me and Mum let me take her to bed every night.

On Christmas morning, we'd wake up early and check the pillowslips we'd hung on the ends of our beds the night before. Alice always gave me a new dress, with hair ribbons to match. Mother always made me doll's clothes and I would dress Sally Jane in one of her new dresses. We were very happy together, Judy, June, Dick and I. It was like having a family.

Every year after each of the holidays, I found it harder and harder to leave my mother and return to Parkerville. I couldn't understand why I couldn't live at Ivanhoe and go to school with Judy and June. You see, I hadn't really worked out how things were when your mother was a servant. I knew the family liked me, so I couldn't understand why they didn't want me living there.

***

I can't say I was really rapt in school, and I used to gaze out the window a lot. And I was always getting into trouble. Usually, I managed to get out of trouble by making up a good story. I think one of the reasons I survived was because I learnt to lie so well.

You see, if there was an argument or if something had been damaged, and it was your word against a white kid's, you were never believed. They expected us black kids to be in the wrong. We learnt it was better not to tell the truth, as it only led to more trouble.

The Home also taught us never to talk openly about being Aboriginal. It was something we were made to feel ashamed of.

When I was about eleven, we got a new headmaster at Parkerville, Mr Edwards. He was different to the old headmaster; he didn't yell so much. He encouraged my interest in poetry and introduced me to algebra — I loved both those things. When he realised that I'd read all the poetry books in the library and knew many poems off by heart, he lent me some of his own books, including a set of Shakespeare's plays. I read all of them and loved every one. I suddenly found that school didn't have to be dull after all. I was no longer a middle-of-the-class student, but progressed to the top.

Towards the end of the school year, we'd have our annual trip to the pictures. We went by train to Perth, then marched up Plaza Arcade to the Royal Theatre in Hay Street. As we moved through the theatre doors, we were handed a paper bag containing sandwiches, a cake and lollies. It was such a treat.

All the other Homes would be there too, Sister Kate's and Swanleigh. Some of the kids would be very excited because they had brothers and sisters in the other Homes and it was the only time of the year they saw them. I used to feel glad then that I was an only child. It always upset me to think that all they saw of the rest of their family was just a glimpse and a wave before we were all ushered into the theatre.

***

I didn't go to Ivanhoe that Christmas. I was called into the office and told I wouldn't be going because they had other people staying there. I couldn't understand this, as I didn't take up much room. Sister Rosemary had tears in her eyes because I was so upset. 'Never mind, dear,' she said. 'You'll be going to the beach.' It was no consolation. I felt really hurt, like no one wanted me.

The Home had a house in Cottesloe. It was a large, rambling one and was used mainly for holidays for children who had nowhere else to go. Each child was allowed to stay for two weeks. We went by train to Perth and then changed trains for Cottesloe; it was the longest train ride I'd ever had.

The house at Cottesloe was so close to the beach it took only a few minutes to walk down. Every room was filled with beds so as many children as possible could fit in. The dining room was packed with wooden tables and benches. We had plenty of food, and the kitchen staff let us help ourselves whenever we felt hungry.

By this time, I had made friends with a girl called Margot, who was a few years older than me and very pretty. One day, we were racing into the waves and laughing, when two boys came and joined us. I was completely tongue-tied, I couldn't think of a thing to say. Margot was full of confidence and spun them a story about us being on holiday from the country. You never told anyone you were from a Home because they looked upon you as some kind of criminal.

When the other girls found out that we were seeing two boys, they looked at me through new eyes. I wasn't just a kid any more.

That night I spent ages admiring myself in the bathroom mirror. I could see only my head and shoulders in my mirror at George Turner, so it was really wonderful to be able to look into this full-length one and see the whole of me. I was really surprised, because my figure had changed. I was taller and my stomach had almost disappeared. My hair was a bit longer and it was black and curly. I realised suddenly that I really was pretty; people weren't just being polite saying that. I felt more confident, seeing myself in this new light.

After coming back from Cottesloe in the new year, even Miss Moore treated me as an older girl now. I was allowed to stay up for an extra half an hour after the little ones had gone to bed. Miss Moore let me read some of her magazines and she'd bring in her wireless and we'd listen to the news.

When I went out to bed, I'd tuck little Faye in. I felt really sorry for the little ones at George Turner; I had never forgotten how sad I'd been when I left Babyland. They often needed comforting at night. They'd turn their faces into the pillow and cry, because they knew if Miss Moore heard them, she'd give them a smack. She hated being disturbed at night.

I couldn't stand it if they cried too long, I'd take them into bed with me. Sometimes when they cried, they wet their beds, and they'd be terrified of getting into trouble about it. I'd get up and change their beds and hide their wet sheets and pyjamas in the bottom of the laundry basket. They always wanted me to be their mother. I felt guilty because, sometimes, I used to get sick of them. They wanted to be babies all the time, but they didn't realise that I was only a kid too.

Even though I was twelve now, no one had told me the facts of life. We were totally ignorant about the things that were happening to our bodies. The older girls never told you anything.

I was also aware that I was changing, growing up, because boys who I had previously fought with now seemed embarrassed in my company. The old easygoing atmosphere had gone. I guess they were changing too.

One Sunday, my mother visited. I could tell she was upset as soon as I saw her.

We went for a walk and she told me that Alice had asked her to leave Ivanhoe. 'She said she can't afford to keep me any more,' she said bitterly. 'How many years have I been working for that family and they can't afford to keep me?!'

She was very hurt. I was cross and confused. I, too, had felt like part of the family and now Mum was no longer going to have anything to do with them. I felt very unsure of myself.

It was well known around Claremont what a good worker my mother was. A Mrs Morgan offered Mum a job as a live-in housekeeper and she said that I would be allowed to go and stay there on holidays. Mum was only too pleased to accept this offer. It was the first time she'd been out on her own in the world. She had always told me that she'd be at Ivanhoe for ever, that it was her home.

The Morgans were good to Mum. They gave her an increase in pay, a nice room and, for the first time in her life, annual holidays.

Going to the Morgans was the best thing that could have

happened to her; she developed a new independence. It was a different atmosphere; they didn't have Victorian attitudes towards her. Also, this new job was like a proper business arrangement; it wasn't like being one of the family and not getting any time off.

I loved it when she was there. It meant she could come to the Home and spend her annual holidays with me. The nuns let her sleep in a room just off one of the school buildings and they let me sleep there too. A couple of times, she brought the two Morgan girls, June and Dianna, up with her. They were nice girls and enjoyed all the bush around the Home.

In the morning, we'd walk down to the grocer's at the bottom of the hill. I could never take my eyes off the jars of lollies. There were jars and jars, all containing lollies of all sizes and colours. Hard-boiled striped candy-sticks stood on the front counter and, next to them, large tins of mixed loose biscuits. Mum would buy me a bag of chocolate biscuits that were my favourites.

I was very popular with the other children at this time. They'd rush over when we were sitting on the lawn and would want to sit near Mum and touch her, especially the little ones. She always gave them a lolly, but I think it was when she spoke to them or kissed them that they were really happy. She was a very kind person and tried to make a fuss of everyone.

At Christmas I went and stayed at the Morgans. Although I missed Ivanhoe, I liked June and Dianna, and Mum now had more time for me because there was less work to do. I was pleased for her because I was sick of seeing her work so hard.

After tea she would take me visiting to see Eileen and Nellie, two of her friends who were also servants. They were always happy and laughing and had nice bedrooms too. They always made a fuss of me, giving me clothes and biscuits and milk.

But after Mum had been at the Morgans about two years, Alice asked her if she would come back to Ivanhoe to work. I wanted her to stay at the Morgans, because it was easier for her, but I think Mum still felt a loyalty to the family. It was easy for people to make her feel sorry for them. She was too kind-hearted.

Alice's mother had come to live with them and she was very difficult to look after. I think that's why they wanted Mum back. She had to accept a cut in wages and no annual holidays, but she went anyway. She told me that it was to be permanent and she'd never be leaving there again.

I went to Ivanhoe for Christmas that year. I was about fourteen by then. Judy, June and Dick suddenly seemed a lot older than me. It wasn't the same as our carefree childhood days. Even though we had all loved each other as children, something had changed. Judy, June and Dick had become more like their mother. They treated Mum like a servant now — she wasn't their beloved nanny any more.

June had a friend who was a bit of a snob and this girl was always putting me in my place because I was only the maid's daughter. I was suddenly very unsure of my place in the world. I still ate with the family in the dining room, but I felt like an outsider, especially when Alice would ring a little brass bell and my mother would come in and wait on us.

I suddenly realised that there hadn't been one Christmas dinner when Mum had eaten her meal with us. She'd had hers alone in the kitchen all these years. I never wanted to be in the

*dining room again after that. I wanted to be in the kitchen with
my mother.*

*After the summer holidays Mum took me back to Parkerville,
but when I got there, I discovered that Miss Moore had left and
I was to have a new House Mother. I had been living with Miss
Moore for nine years and I hadn't even had the opportunity to
say goodbye to her.*

*Why was everything changing? I was really frightened,
because my new House Mother had been an enemy of Miss
Moore's and I knew she'd take it out on me. Even though Miss
Moore had belted me a lot, I was considered one of her pets. I
just knew I'd have a bad time.*

*Also, I was worried that I'd get sent out to work as a domestic
and never see my mother again. All the Aboriginal girls were
sent out as domestics once they reached fourteen. Only the white
kids were trained for anything.*

*I cried and cried and begged Mum not to leave me there. I
was so upset I went to the office with Mum to see Sister Dora.
Miss Button said, 'Do you want to leave here, Gladys? Your
mother has said she wants to take you with her.' She smiled
kindly at me.*

*'Oh yes,' I replied, 'yes please!' I couldn't believe it. To
be with my mother for always — it was too good to be true. I
walked over to George Turner to pack.*

*Pretty soon, the news spread that I was leaving and all the
kids crowded round. I handed out keepsakes from my locker.*

*As we set off down the hill, I waved goodbye. I was very
excited to think that, at last, Mum and I were going to live at*

Ivanhoe together. Maybe my childhood dream would come true and I'd be the same as Judy and June. Maybe we'd be one big, happy family, after all. That was what I wanted more than anything.

***

It wasn't long before my dreams came crashing around my feet. Alice was very cross with Mum for bringing me back. She said I couldn't live at Ivanhoe. I wasn't wanted.

It took a week for Mum to find a family who would take me in. The Hewitts had three boys of their own and often took in older girls. I got on well with the boys and enrolled in Claremont High School. I tried not to think about Ivanhoe. I wasn't allowed to stay there weekends, either. If Mum wanted to see me, she had to visit me at the Hewitts. I felt very hurt by it all.

The Hewitts were very religious, but they had a different kind of religion to me. I'll never forget the first Sunday morning they took us all down to Fremantle. I thought we were going to church; I never realised they intended holding a revivalist meeting on a street corner.

We all stood around in a circle and everyone started singing loudly and raising their hands and shouting, 'Praise the Lord!' A lot of people started gathering round and I slowly moved backwards into the crowd, pretending I was one of the onlookers.

The meeting got more and more frenzied and the minister started shouting out to the onlookers, 'Repent before it's too late!' I suddenly felt a dig in my back and a voice said, 'Now!' I found myself suddenly yanked from the circle and pulled away.

I was amazed when I saw that my rescuer was Warren, the Hewitts' eldest son.

'I saw you trying to hide before,' said Warren. 'Isn't it embarrassing?'

'Yes,' I groaned. 'I had no idea it would be like this. I thought we were going to church.'

'We do this every Sunday, you have to be dying to get out of it.'

'Oh no,' I sighed. 'I hope no one I know ever sees me!'

I had been worrying about starting Claremont High School. I didn't want anybody to find out I'd been in a Home and I was concerned that I wouldn't be able to make friends.

As it turned out, I got along with all the other kids really well, especially Noreen and Doreen, who became my very best friends. Noreen was Scottish and was only in Australia because of the war. It was 1940, and she had been sent out with a lot of other children for safekeeping. She had a terrific sense of humour. I spent a lot of time at her house.

Every lunch hour at school, we had air-raid drill. There was a park nearby, with trenches dug in case we were ever bombed. At lunchtime, they'd blow the siren and we all had to run as fast as we could and jump in the trenches.

It was during that year in high school that Mum left Ivanhoe again. I was really angry about that. She'd given up a good job to go back to Alice and now they'd turned around and said that they didn't need her any more and she'd have to find somewhere else to live.

Mum was very hurt. She also had pay owing to her, which I don't think she ever got. They'd treated me like one of the family in the past, but I was glad now that I didn't belong to them.

One of Mum's friends told her about a job that was going for a cook in the Colourpatch restaurant. It was a little place just opposite the Ocean Beach Hotel, which was an R and R place for American sailors. Mum applied for the job and got it. It was well known around the area what a good cook she was.

Molly Skinner, the author, owned a house just behind the hotel and she said Mum could pay rent and live with her if she wanted to.

Molly was very sympathetic to Aboriginal people and treated them kindly. Mum moved in with her, and Molly also said that I could come and stay on weekends. I was very pleased about that, because I had hardly seen Mum for the past few months.

I think Mum would have liked me to live with her full time, but she was reluctant to move me away from the Hewitts. She knew Aboriginal people like her weren't allowed to have families, and she was frightened that something might go wrong and I'd be taken away.

I loved spending weekends with her; she'd spoil me, and Molly was always pleased to see me.

Every Saturday afternoon, Mum would give me threepence to go to the pictures with Noreen and Doreen. We had great fun. All the kids from school would be there and we'd yell and scream.

The Colourpatch was really busy on Sundays, so Mum often got me to help out with the waitressing. The Americans were lovely. They'd leave large tips for me under their plates. All the other waitresses had to hand their tips in, but I was told I was allowed to keep mine. I think it was because Mum was such a good cook. She always gave everyone double helpings and nothing was too much for her. It was a really happy time for me.

One Sunday night I arrived back at the Hewitts to be met with serious faces from the whole family. Mrs Hewitt took Mum into the lounge and I had to sit out in the hall.

'You're in big trouble,' Warren whispered. I didn't know what I'd done wrong. Then the youngest Hewitt boy came out and said, 'Gladys, you've sinned!'

A few minutes later, Mrs Hewitt came out and said, 'Will you please come in, Gladys?'

I looked at Mum. She looked completely dumbfounded.

'Now, Gladys,' said Mrs Hewitt, 'I am going to ask you a question and I want you to answer truthfully. Did you go to the pictures and enter that house of sin on Saturday afternoon?'

I couldn't think of what to say.

'It's no use trying to deny it,' she said. 'One of the ladies from the church saw you.'

That was when I hung my head in shame. Except I didn't feel sinful — I'd had a great time. Mrs Hewitt turned to Mum and said, 'I don't think it will be suitable for Gladys to stay here any longer. I'm trying to turn her into a good Christian and you're letting her sin on Saturday afternoons!'

Mum just looked at me. She'd never heard of pictures being sinful before.

Mrs Hewitt pointed to the corner of the room and said, 'Gladys, I've taken the liberty of packing your suitcases. I think you'd better go now.'

Mum and I went back to Cottesloe. We didn't know what to say to each other. For the first time in our lives, we were together. I don't think Mum knew how to handle it. I think she was afraid that I would be taken off her again.

Molly was very happy to have me there.

***

I finished school at the end of 1943. I was sixteen. All my friends were going on to business college, but I knew that wasn't possible for me.

I spent my time helping Mum in the restaurant. I was put in charge of making up milkshakes in the lolly shop attached to the Colourpatch. I took great pride in my work and people would come from miles to buy a milkshake off me. I experimented with the contents all the time and would put in great dollops of ice-cream. Sometimes, I put in so much the mixer wouldn't turn.

After a while, Alice got me a job on trial with a florist in Claremont at six shillings a week. In those days, if you were monied people or if you had a name, like Drake-Brockman, it was like 'Open Sesame'. People ran after you, and rushed to serve you.

I was very excited about my job. I used to ride from Cottesloe to Claremont on an old bike.

The other junior who worked there was great. She was as fair as I was dark. She warned me about my new boss. 'She's a bit of an old cow,' she said. 'She'll leave money on the floor just to see if you'll pinch it, so watch out.'

Sure enough, I was told to sweep the shop and there, on the black oiled floor, was a two-shilling piece. I gave it to the boss, who feigned surprise and put it in the till. A week later, there was another two-shilling piece on the floor. I handed that in, too. That was when I was told that, from then on, I was on staff and would get ten shillings a week.

Kathy, Violet and I were all about the same age. We got plenty of attention from the Americans, because they were always going into florist shops to order corsages for their girlfriends. They were very different to Australian men, much more polite.

About a year later, Kathy became engaged to an American sailor, so we'd often go out to the pictures with his friends. For the first time in my life, I felt free. I didn't have to answer for everything I did. Of course, Mum tried to be very strict with me. It was all very innocent, but she kept saying I didn't know what the world was like or what men were like. I realise now that she was right. I had had a very protected life. I stopped telling her when I was going out and who I was going out with, as it only made her worry.

I remember one Sunday, waiting at a bus stop for a bus to my girlfriend's house, when a lady came along. She was catching the same bus as me, so we started to chat.

'You're very beautiful, dear,' she said, 'What nationality are you, Indian?'

'No,' I smiled, 'I'm Aboriginal.'

She looked at me in shock. 'Oh, you poor thing,' she said, putting her arm around me. 'What on earth are you going to do?'

I didn't know what to say. She looked at me with such pity, I felt really embarrassed. I wondered what was wrong with being

Aboriginal. I wondered what she expected me to do about it.

I talked to Mum about it and she told me I must never tell anyone what I was. She made me really frightened. I think that was when I started wishing I were something different.

It was harder for Mum than me; because she was so broad featured she couldn't pass for anything else. I started noticing that, when she went out, people stared at her, and I hadn't realised that before.

The conversation with that lady at the bus stop really confused me, and made me feel terrible. Looking back now, I suppose she knew more about how Aboriginal people were treated than I did. She probably knew I had no future, that I'd never be accepted, never be allowed to achieve anything.

I tried for a while after that to talk to Mum and get her to explain things to me, especially about the past and where she'd come from. It was hopeless; we'd been apart too long to get really close. I knew she loved me and I loved her, but, for all my childhood, she had been just a person I saw on holidays. I couldn't confide my worries to her. She just kept saying, 'Terrible things will happen to you if you tell people what you are.' I felt, for her sake as well as my own, I'd better keep quiet. Molly Skinner sold her house, so we had to find somewhere else to live. We managed to rent another place near the Ocean Beach Hotel. It was a nice little weatherboard house.

Mum and I began to disagree a lot more. I had bought myself a few things from my wages and she would give them away to her friends without even asking me. If they said they liked something, she'd say, 'Oh, Glad doesn't want that; she can buy another one. *You take it.' People would come and deliberately point out something of mine and she would give it to them, especially if they were white people. I used to think she was trying to impress them, trying to buy white friends. There were so many things that I didn't understand, then.*

Another lady came to help cook at the Colourpatch and I became very good friends with one of her daughters. We went many places together and I often stayed overnight at her house. She had brothers and sisters; I really envied that. One of her sisters became engaged and I was invited to the engagement party. That was where I met Bill.

As soon as I was introduced to Bill, I knew my carefree days were over. I wasn't ready to settle down and get married, but I knew I didn't have any choice. This was meant to be.

Bill was different from other men I'd gone out with. He was older, more worldly. I knew he'd been a POW in Germany, but I didn't realise then what a terrible time he'd had.

None of my friends liked Bill and Mum disapproved of him, too. 'He drinks too much,' she told me. 'You don't want to marry a drinker.' My friends tried to warn me about him. They said he was wild, sometimes crazy, but I didn't listen.

The day after I'd met Bill, he said, 'You're going to marry me.'

'No, I'm not,' I said.

'Yes, you are.'

I was going with someone else at the time, so I thought, well, I might be able to hold him off for a while. But it wasn't to be. We went out for a year before we married. Mum never changed her mind about him. I told him I was Aboriginal, but he said he didn't care. And I don't think he did then; it was later that he changed.

His parents disapproved of me. They didn't want their son marrying a coloured person. At the same time, they were glad to get him off their hands, because they hadn't been able to control him. They were sick of him wrapping trucks around telephone poles.

I managed to get Bill to cut down on his drinking; I hoped it was a change for the better that would last. Mum didn't want to come to the wedding and neither did Bill's family, so we went and got married in a registry office. I was twenty-one. Mum and I had talked about it before and it had only led to arguments. She had always been very jealous of anyone who took my attention away from her. She wanted me to stay home for the rest of my life and look after her.

***

After we were married, we lived with Mum. I was very happy. I continued to work at the florist shop. Things didn't improve with Bill's family. They were very disappointed that he had actually gone ahead and married me. Bill's mother was very narrow-minded, and used to say things to Bill behind my back. I knew she would never accept me as an equal. I don't know how much Bill's father worried about me being coloured. He was always under the weather. Sometimes, he'd make a big fuss of me because I'd slip him a bit of money. I think he liked anybody who'd give him a few bob.

Grandpa Milroy used to travel around putting in petrol

bowsers for the Shell Oil Company, and Bill's mother was always sending Bill off to the Goldfields to haul his father out of the pubs and bring him home. Bill's father gambled away a fortune, and had Bill drinking beer from his early teenage years.

When Bill was fourteen, he had run away from home and got a job up North as a stockman. He told everyone he was sixteen; he could pass for that because he was tall. He loved the life up there and was very upset when his father found him and made him return to Perth.

I found it difficult mixing with Bill's brothers and their friends. I'd been brought up strictly, whereas they lived in a brave new world. It was becoming a permissive society, even then.

Bill was different to his brothers. He had strong ideas and a kind heart. His mother was a strict Catholic, and when Bill was younger, he had wanted to become a priest. Bill never talked about his religious beliefs, but I knew they were there, deep inside him. Sometimes, when he talked about the war, I felt that there was a spiritual force that helped him get through. There were many times when he should have died, but didn't. He was meant to come back.

When I found out I was pregnant, I was really excited. Bill was overjoyed, expecting it to be a son, but it was Sally. I couldn't believe that I finally had a family of my own. Mum was really pleased, too. In a strange way, I think it made her feel more secure; she was a grandmother now.

It wasn't long after that that Bill applied for a tradesman's flat down at Beaconsfield, where he was working as a plumber.

We were pleased to be moving into our own place. The

surroundings were very pretty; it had originally been a farm and everyone still called it *Mulberry Farm*. There was a huge mulberry tree opposite our flat and olive trees dotted all over the place.

When we first moved in, we were always broke; it made a difference, having to pay rent. I had to give up work when I became pregnant. Also, people were always coming around, wanting to borrow money. I felt sorry for them and would give them what I had, but they never paid any of it back. Apparently, this was the norm, but I didn't know. I had to cut down on my lending.

There was plenty of action at Mulberry Farm, domestic fights all the time and some funny things going on. It always gave me a good laugh.

Sally was very sick when she was small, and we nearly lost her a couple of times. Sometimes during the night, I'd awake to see the figure of a nun standing next to her cot. It didn't frighten me. I knew she was being watched over, the way I had been when I was a child. I knew that she would never be a strong person, but she wouldn't die young.

Bill began having nightmares again. He'd suffered from them ever since he'd come back from the war. He'd scream and scream at night. I used to feel so sorry for him. Before we married, I had thought that the idea of being a POW was something very heroic and romantic, but now I thought differently.

I used to try and get him to talk about his nightmares — it helped him a little — but he'd never go really deeply into what had happened to him. I knew there had been one German commandant that had treated him really badly. Bill absolutely *hated him. I think if he'd had the opportunity, he would have killed him. Bill would never tell me what had happened. A lot of his nightmares were about this chap. He would dream he couldn't get away from him.*

One time, Bill's mother came around, and told Bill that a tall man with an accent had come up to her at the trots and said, 'Did you have a son who was a POW during the war in Germany?'

'Yes,' she said, 'how did you know?'

'It's the eyes,' he said, 'you have the same eyes. I would recognise those eyes anywhere.' Then, apparently, he disappeared into the crowd.

I'll never forget the look on Bill's face when she asked him who the chap could be. He went as white as a sheet. He knew who it was, but he wouldn't tell us. He just locked himself in his room and wouldn't come out.

After the war, a lot of Germans came out to Australia, passing themselves off as different nationalities. This chap was German. I think he was the man Bill hated, I'm sure of it.

It was that episode that precipitated Bill's drinking again. He'd been good since he'd married me, but now, all he was interested in was forgetting the past in a bottle. He hardly ate; he just drank. Mum had to bring me food from the restaurant because I never had any money. Sometimes, he'd disappear for days and I wouldn't see him. I was worried sick.

It got so bad that, in the end, I couldn't stand it, and I took Sally and moved back in with Mum. She was pleased to have me there. I think she'd been worried about what Bill might do.

I'd been at Mum's about ten days and I still hadn't seen him.

I couldn't help thinking about all the things he'd told me about the war. I started to feel so sad about what they'd done to him. I still loved him. I've never told anyone Bill's war experiences, but perhaps it will help you to understand if I write it down.

Bill fought in the desert with the 2/16th Battalion.

He said he found it so hard to kill other people. I remember him telling me about one time when there were Germans in the sandhills and he could see them, they were outlined like sitting ducks in a shooting gallery. Bill was on the machine-gun and the others called to him, 'Shoot, you bastard, while you've got the chance!' He said he couldn't, it was too easy. Someone shoved him aside, grabbed the gun and mowed them down. It made him feel sick.

Bill was wounded during a battle for a town and he was placed in the army hospital. That was how he got left behind in the Middle East, because the rest of his battalion was shipped back to fight in New Guinea.

After he recovered, he was placed in the 2/28th and continued to fight in the desert. I thought it would be like the beach, but Bill said that the ground was so hard you could only dig shallow trenches.

Bill was captured at El Alamein and, along with two thousand other Allied prisoners, was crammed into the hold of the Nino Bixio, an Italian freighter. It was very crowded, and they were only allowed to have the hatch cover open a little bit to allow access to the latrines. A lot of the men had dysentery, so you can imagine what it was like.

On the second day out at sea, they were torpedoed by an

Allied submarine. Bill said he'd been having a joke with the bloke next to him, when a torpedo whizzed straight through, hit the other side of the hold, exploded and flung everyone back onto him.

When he came to, he was covered in blood and bodies, arms and legs, guts, fingers blown off. He didn't know what belonged to him and what didn't. The whole hold was covered with bits and pieces of human beings. He thought he'd had it. The ship started taking water. Some of the men tried to get out through the hole in the side that the torpedo had made, but the swell washed them back in and they were cut to pieces on the torn edges. The steel ladders leading to the top part of the hold had been destroyed, so there was no way out.

Survivors from the top part of the hold threw down ropes and the Captain shouted, 'If anyone's alive down there, climb up!'

By the time Bill got himself out from underneath all the bodies, he realised he was actually still in one piece. He had bits of shrapnel embedded in his arms, legs and chest, but apart from that, he was all right. He picked up the nearest bloke to him who looked like he might be in one piece and climbed the rope. That turned out to be Frank Potter.

The next day, an Italian destroyer took them in tow. They beached on the Greek coast and the wounded were taken to shore and laid out along the beach. Bill said there'd been over five hundred men in their hold when they were hit, but only seventy survived the torpedo and then a lot of them died on the beach.

Some of the men were terribly wounded. To make matters worse, there was no food or medical supplies. Orderlies were going along the beach, hacking off arms and legs that were only just hanging on. They were using tomahawks, and digging out shrapnel with daggers.

Those who could walk were marched through the nearest town and put on show like some great prize. The men spat on them and the women threw their kitchen slops and pots full of excrement onto them.

They stayed in Corinth for a while, and then they were shipped back to Italy and sent to Campo 57.

Bill said the commandant there was a real Fascist. He was very hard and liked to see them suffer. He had a sign up which read, "The English are cursed, but more cursed are those Italians who treat them well!"

When the Allies began bombing the area near the camp, that's when Bill escaped. The guards were so frightened they ran off leaving the gates wide open. All the prisoners followed. Bill said to Abercrombe, the bloke that was with him, 'Not down the middle of the road. The Germans will realise we're being bombed and come to round us up. Down in the ditch.'

Sure enough, a few minutes later, along came the Germans and herded everyone back inside, Bill and Abercrombe hid in the ditch till nightfall.

Abercrombe wanted to head south in the hope of meeting up with the Yanks, but Bill talked him into going north to Switzerland. They travelled mainly at night, stealing food and sleeping in the fields. They knew the Germans were around, but, so far, they hadn't seen any.

They kept travelling north, afraid to enter any town. Eventually, they were worn out, desperate. They watched one small town for a few days, and it seemed all right. They entered and hung around the well. When a woman came for water, Bill asked her if she could take them to the head man. It turned out it was her husband.

They were lucky. These Italians hated the war and the Germans. They took Bill and Abercrombe to a safe farm run by Guiseppe and Maria Bosso and their fourteen-year-old daughter, Edmea. Bill said they were wonderful people, full of guts. They treated him like a son. He learnt to speak Italian fluently and, because he looked like a northern Italian, he sometimes passed himself off as one, drinking vino and singing songs with the Germans in the tavern, just like other Italians did, who tried to stay friendly with the Germans to keep them on side.

During the day, Bill worked in the fields with the other labourers. When they heard that the farms nearby were being searched for escaped POWs, Bill and Abercrombe would hide out down near a small creek. Sometimes, it was days before it was safe; during this time, they lived on frogs, green snakes and berries. It was far too dangerous for even the Italians to sneak food to them.

Eventually, they'd get word that the coast was clear and the whole village would have a big dance in one of the barns to celebrate the fact that they'd outwitted the Germans again.

It was too cold to hide down the creek in winter, so Guiseppe built a big haystack with a room inside. The Germans always stuck their bayonets into every haystack and, if they hit a post, or if there was blood on the end of the bayonet, they'd set fire to the haystack and burn whoever was inside.

One morning, the Bosso family were very upset because they'd had word that the SS had burnt and slaughtered a whole village for sheltering POWs. The town had a meeting to decide what they were going to do. They all agreed to continue hiding Allied prisoners, even if it meant losing the whole village. Bill told Guiseppe it was a risk he wouldn't let them take. All the POWs in the village felt the same. They all decided to take their chances and move on.

Guiseppe got in touch with the Underground, and they sent two members of the Resistance to guide Bill and Abercrombe over the Swiss Alps. Bill had his twenty-first birthday in the mountains. When they reached the border, the Swiss guards told them if they crossed into Switzerland, they'd be there for the duration of the war, which could be years, but if they went back and joined up with the Yanks, it might only be a few months, because the Americans were making rapid progress at that stage.

Bill didn't fancy sitting in Switzerland, so he asked the guides to take him and Abercrombe back to Italy. They then headed off in the direction where the Yanks were supposed to be advancing.

That night, they came to a road and were about to cross, when Bill said, 'Don't, there's something wrong.' Bill had a premonition it was dangerous, so he hid down in the ditch and told Abercrombe to do the same.

Abercrombe said, 'Listen, ya stupid bastard, there's nothing there, I'm going.' He ran onto the road, but halfway across, a searchlight spotted him and he was gunned down by a machine-gun. Bill said he was so shocked he just froze. He knew that he had to move, but he couldn't.

Finally, he forced himself to get going. He walked all night until he came to a large river. He lay down and was half asleep when he heard the sound of barking dogs coming closer and closer. Germans, he thought. He started to run. A bullet whizzed past his head. He stopped and turned with his hands in the air.

To his relief, it was only the Italian police. He told them he was a labourer on his way to work at a nearby farm. They said, 'You're no labourer, you're a rapist and a murderer. You're wanted in Rome for killing many women.' They showed him a poster with the rapist's picture. Bill said he couldn't believe it — it was his double. He was forced, then, to tell them who he really was, and he showed them his dog tags.

'You shouldn't have run,' they said. 'We would have let you go. We can't now, because we have to account to the Germans for every bullet we use. If we let you go, they'll know. We have to think of our families — we're sorry.'

Bill was taken and handed over to the SS. They questioned and tortured him for days, asking where he had been, who had helped him, where he had hidden. Bill said he would rather have died than tell them a bloody thing.

Every day he heard the firing squad in operation, and every day he wondered if he would be next. One morning, they came for him. He thought, this is it, I'm going to die.

When Bill went to get up, the guard butted him with his rifle, knocking him to the floor. He kicked him hard in the ribs with army boots. Bill rose and felt the guard's rifle hard in his back. 'You are being transferred to Germany.'

He was taken to the office, where he was handed over to another guard.

On the way to the train, the guard said, 'Don't try to escape and we'll get along fine.' Bill was surprised that this chap spoke in English. He boarded the train in the company of this guard and two SS officers.

The German guard gave him a cigarette and said quietly, 'Speak in English. The SS can't understand.' He confided to Bill that he had been educated in England and had fought in the First World War as well. He said he hated the SS, and called them animals. This guard was the one who accompanied Bill to the POW camp. Before he handed him over, he gave Bill a heavy overcoat and some good boots. 'Never barter these,' he said, 'you won't survive without them.'

Bill was taken to several different camps on and off. One of them was near a Jewish concentration camp. He said it was terrible, because of the smell and the sounds that could be heard day and night; they sounded like tortured animals. He said even though conditions were bad in the POW camps, he hated to think what they were doing to the Jews.

Bill palled up with another bloke who was half-Jewish. The Germans whipped him all the time. Bill tried to stick up for him and they said, 'You want to stick up for a Jew, we'll treat you like a Jew.' It was really bad for him after that.

In the Sagan camp he was in, he had to work in the local coalmines. It was long hours and damp, dangerous work. He developed a bad chest infection, so they sent him to dig potatoes out of the frozen fields. Bill said it was easier down the mines. The only advantage to working in the fields was if you could pinch a potato and use it in camp for bargaining. Bill said they were fed on vegetable soup which was just water. Once a month, the soup had meat in it: a horse's head. The big thing was to get *the eyes, otherwise you ended up with a bowl full of wet hair.*

Some of the guards at Sagan were really brutal. They loved to burst in in the middle of the night, tell the men to strip and then stand them at attention in the snow. The worse the war went for them, the meaner they became.

One day, towards the end of the war in Europe, they informed the prisoners that they were going to march to another camp. There had been rumours in the camp that the Russians were advancing. They were marched three hundred and fifty miles to Duderstadt. It was very cold and they had to sleep out in the open snow. There was no food; they had to find what they could by the side of the road. Bill said even the German people were starving by then. They stopped near one village and an old German peasant woman ran up to him and shoved a stale piece of black bread into his hand. A guard shot her in the back.

On that march a lot of prisoners died of cold and were just left by the side of the road. I think Bill was really glad that he hadn't traded his heavy overcoat, because he'd really needed it.

When they reached Duderstadt, the conditions were terrible. The camp was infested with lice and there was excrement everywhere. There was only one rough latrine for over a thousand men. Prisoners were dying like flies from dysentery and pneumonia. There was nowhere to put the dead, so they just piled them on top of one another near the gate.

After he'd been there another few days, there was another rumour that the Yanks were close. That scared the Germans and they cut down the torture a bit.

Early one morning, a tank broke down the gates of the camp and a sandy-headed Yank popped up and said, 'Any of you guys want some ginger cake and ice-cream?!'

Bill said the men that had any energy left just cried and cried. The Yanks gave out food, but some of the prisoners had been without for so long that it made them violently ill and they died.

The Yank in charge couldn't believe the state they were all in. He said, 'Is there any one of these German bastards you'd like to kill?' An English soldier lying on a mat raised his hand. He was so weak he couldn't stand, so two of the Yanks supported him as they held the gun in his hand and helped him point it at the German guard who'd given him a really bad time. 'Help me,' the Englishman whispered, and the Yanks pulled the trigger for him. Later that day, the Englishman died.

They were all taken by trucks to American transport planes and airlifted to France, where they were given medical treatment before being transferred to England. Bill spent six months in hospital in England before he was fit to sail home.

I thought about everything Bill told me after I had returned to live with my mother. I knew that was just the tip of the iceberg, and that he hadn't told me the full story.

By the time I'd been with Mum three weeks, he'd sobered himself up and come around to beg me to come back. I knew then that if I did, it was for ever. I couldn't leave him again. He had no one. I still loved him. I thought maybe I could help make up for what he'd been through.

It turned out I was wrong. I couldn't heal his mind. They hadn't broken his spirit or his will to live, but they'd broken his mind. He couldn't get away from what was inside of him. He couldn't escape from his own memories.

***

In no time at all, I was pregnant with my second child. They put me into hospital to bring her on, because they said she was going to be too big. They fed me some pills and gave me over thirty injections. A week later, I still hadn't had her. Finally, the doctor strapped me up, ruptured the membrane and left me with the nurses.

By the time labour started, I was exhausted. I went into some kind of trance and began speaking in an unknown language. They called the doctor in, and when Jilly was finally born she shot out and covered him in a gallon of green water. I was advised not to have any more children, or at least to wait three years before having another one.

Bill was trying hard to hold himself together, but there were still times when he'd go off on a binge and I wouldn't see him for a few days. On these occasions, Mum would come and stay just to keep me company.

She was doing housework now, and could work when she pleased. She was always buying clothes for the kids and dropping in groceries — she knew I had no money.

Bill had a nervous breakdown and they put him in Hollywood Hospital. He couldn't cope with any pressure or responsibility. Bill was sent home eventually, with a couple of bottles of drugs that were supposed to keep him calm.

By the time Jill was four months old, I was pregnant again. I went to the doctor and he told me I couldn't have the baby, that I had to get rid of it. He sent me home with some tablets to take.

I told Mum what he said and she agreed with me that I shouldn't take them. I threw them into the bin.

An epidemic of polio hit Mulberry Farm, and I caught it. I couldn't move, so Mum moved in with us. Bill was working at the time and I needed someone to look after Sally and Jilly. By some miracle, I recovered from the polio.

I went back to the doctor when I was seven months pregnant. He was very cross that I had let the pregnancy continue. I never told him I'd had polio as well.

I gave birth to a son that November, and it was an easy birth. Bill was overjoyed that he had a son at last.

Bill applied for a State Housing home in Manning. Mum was living with us permanently now. I really needed her help with three little ones so close together and Bill the way he was. When Billy was six months old, we moved to Manning. It was nothing but bush then.

There was a large swamp at the back of us, which was alive with wildlife, turtles, frogs, gilgies, grey cranes. It reminded me of the bush from my own childhood days. It was good for the children to learn about nature and how important it is to our lives.

We'd only been in Manning a month, when Mum began to complain about all the Aborigines living in the swamp. 'Did you hear that music last night?' she said. 'They been having corroborees every night. I think I'll go down there and tell them all off.'

I often sat and listened to it with her after that. I've never been to a corroboree, but that music had always been inside of me. When I was little, I was told Aboriginal music was heathen music. I thought it was beautiful music; whenever I heard it, it was like a message, like I was being supported, protected.

One night I told Mum that there were no Aborigines in the swamp. 'You heard the music, Glad,' she said. 'There's a big mob of them down there.'

'There's no one down there,' I told her, 'it's a spiritual thing.' After that, we just accepted it. She'd sit out and listen to it and then go to bed. We didn't hear it every night, but it was there on and off right up until Bill died. Then it stopped.

Bill seemed to pull himself together when we first went to the Manning house. I began to hope for a better future for us all. He managed to get a good job and cut down on his drinking. His nearest watering hole was the Raffles Hotel; he'd go there for a few beers after work and then come home.

On the weekends he worked for the Italian market gardeners in Spearwood. He loved mixing with them and speaking Italian. He had never forgotten the kindness of the Bossos during the war. He'd come home loaded up with fruit and vegetables and bottles of vino. He often did jobs for them free of charge. I think he felt indebted to all Italian people because they'd been so good to him.

Pretty soon, there were other houses going up around us. A widow with three children moved in at the back of us. Grace was such a nice person and Mum often had a chat and a cup of tea with her.

One morning Bill was sitting on the bus going to work, when the chap next to him said, 'You look a bloody sight better than the last time I saw you!'

Bill said, 'Do I know you?'

'You only saved my life, you bastard,' the man replied. It was Frank Potter, one of the men Bill had dragged up from the hold. It turned out he and his wife lived only a few streets away. They saw a lot of each other after that.

Bill began having nightmares again. It seemed that things would just start going right for us and then the whole circle would start all over again.

Things started getting really bad. We were so desperate, we'd gone through Mum's savings and Bill had hocked everything we had of value and spent the money on drink. The doctors increased his doses of pills and other medicines, but, combined with the alcohol, it only made him worse. There were times he'd mistake me for a German SS officer. One night, he nearly strangled me. He was screaming, 'SS, SS,' and had his hands around my throat.

There were times when he'd yell and scream and tell us all to get out the house or he'd kill us. Mum and I would run with the children to Grace's house. Sometimes, we'd sleep the night there; other times, I'd sneak to the back fence and listen to see if he was still shouting. Generally, once he went to sleep, he was all right. We'd go back home then.

In the morning, Bill would have no idea of what had happened. When I told him, he'd get really scared and commit himself to Hollywood again. He told me he thought, one day, he might really kill us and he couldn't bear that thought, because we loved him and he loved us.

***

By the time Billy was just over two years old, I became pregnant again. It was a really bad time to have another child. I knew I would have to give up my part-time job and I wondered how on earth we'd put food on the table. Bill had been in hospital on and off for months and seemed happy with his weekend passes to come home. He was drifting deeper and deeper into the protection of the hospital. I was too scared to approach anyone for help. I never complained about Bill's drinking. I felt it was a family thing and I shouldn't talk about it to others.

One night, I was at my lowest ebb. I'd been praying and I just fell onto the bed, exhausted. When I opened my eyes some time later, there was a light in the room. At the centre of the light stood three men, behind them, the yellow sands of the desert. The men were dressed in long robes and their heads were covered. The middle one told me that a great leader would be born in my house. I suddenly felt very happy. It was like I had a special secret. I slept soundly after that, and, when I awoke, I felt really alive and well.

I was a changed person after that. I knew I had the strength to face anything.

Bill came out of hospital when I was about seven months pregnant. This time, he really tried to help himself. He started to work again and was looking forward to the baby.

I began having a lot of pain and, eventually, Bill drove me to the maternity hospital and left me there. It was about nine o'clock at night and it was a small private hospital, not like the large ones I'd had the others in. A neighbour had recommended it; she said the Matron had delivered hundreds of babies and *was better than any doctor.*

At the end of the corridor, the door was wide open. It was a bedroom, and there was Matron, lying on a large double bed with her huge Alsatian dog asleep beside her. She had a fag protruding from the corner of her mouth and she was reading the paper. I knocked shyly.

'Who are you?' she said. The dog suddenly leapt up and started growling at me. 'Shut up!' Matron said and whacked him with her paper. She got out of bed and pulled a floral housecoat over her nightie. 'I'm Mrs Milroy,' I gasped; the pain was getting really bad.

She led me to a small room. 'Hoist yourself up there,' she commanded, pointing to a sheet-covered table. She examined me and then said, 'You poor thing. No wonder you're in pain — it's a breech. I'll call your doctor.'

My doctor arrived, but said he could do nothing. It was all up to me.

I didn't know such pain existed. I pushed and groaned, with sweat pouring off me. I lost a lot of blood. I was convinced my whole insides were going to spill out onto the table. I became exhausted and just lay there.

My doctor just stood in the corner and watched me. He never said one word of encouragement or held my hand.

I heard the Matron call him a bastard, then she patted me hard around the face and said, 'Come on, you lazy bitch, don't stop bloody pushing. I'm not going to let you go now!' I was sure I was going to die. She grabbed me and started screaming, trying to get through to me. 'You bloody well start pushing,' she yelled. 'You can do it. Come on, I haven't lost one yet.'

Then, something made me glance to the side of the room. The most beautiful angel I'd ever seen was standing there. The face looked at me with love, smiled and said, 'It's Sally's birthday.' I didn't know I'd been in the room all night and it was now morning.

I felt a renewed strength. I pushed and David was born. 'Thank God,' the Matron said, and I knew that was true.

I'd lost so much blood, I had to have a transfusion.

I was woken late in the afternoon by a lass with a cup of tea. I asked to see my baby. He was beautiful. I nursed him for a couple of days, but then they had to take him to PMH for observation. They were worried about him.

I felt very unhappy. It was awful being separated from him so soon. All the other mothers had their babies. I had nothing to do except be milked like a cow for the baby's food supply, which was taken by taxi to PMH.

After a few days, they brought David back from PMH. It was wonderful to be able to cuddle and feed him like the other mothers. After a couple of days, I was well enough to go home.

***

When David was very small, Mum's brother Arthur and his wife, Adeline, and their children popped in to visit us. It was the first time I had seen Arthur in years and years. Mum and I were terribly excited.

Bill was in bed and I asked him to come out and meet them. 'I don't want to meet them,' he said. 'I don't want to know them.'

I was really hurt. I knew if they had been white, he would have come out straightaway. Bill was a strange man. He wasn't prejudiced against other racial groups, just Aboriginals. Bill had spent a lot of his childhood in country towns, and his experiences moulded his attitudes to Aboriginal people. Down South, Aboriginals were really looked down on, and Bill had been brought up in that environment.

Bill went back into hospital and I began my regular visits to him again. He had shock treatment and all sorts of other things done to him, but nothing helped.

I suppose many people must wonder why on earth I didn't just take the kids and leave. Well, I nearly did, on several occasions, but Bill always threatened me. He said if I left him, he'd make sure the children were taken off me. He said, 'Nobody will let someone like you bring up kids and you know it. I'm the one that'll get custody. I'll give them to my parents.'

It was true. Single Aboriginal mothers weren't allowed to keep children fathered by a white man. I couldn't take the chance of losing them, so I had to stay and try to cope somehow. They were all I had.

In April 1959, my daughter Helen was born.

Even though he was sick at the time, Bill had managed to drive me to the hospital. He looked so ill, it made me sad. I knew Helen would be my last child.

One night in October 1961, Bill came into the lounge room, where I was sitting by myself after I'd put the children to sleep.

'I feel odd, Glad,' he said. 'I can't get warm. I feel as though I'm not really here — it's like I'm fading away.' I jumped up and

felt him; he was cold. I felt his spirit had left his body.

I knew then he was going to die. God was preparing me by giving us this time alone together.

Bill sat down and we talked into the early hours of the morning. It was strange; it was suddenly as though he was his old self, as though he'd been released from something. We talked about the children and we laughed. Bill said he hadn't felt so good in a long time. He said he knew tomorrow would be a new beginning for all of us.

Bill was in such a good mood at breakfast that he kept Billy home from school, so he and David and Billy could all have a game of footy together. I left for work.

A neighbour rang me at twelve that day to tell me Bill had died. I was shocked. I went home immediately, but couldn't pull myself together. I walked around in a daze. Mrs Mainwaring, a neighbour, told the children about their father.

Later that night I went out to Bill's room. I noticed that his bottle of medicine was empty. I felt sick. I knew deep down he'd never take his own life, but it still worried me. I'd had it drummed into me at Parkerville that such people went straight to hell. I started to cry, I felt so depressed.

I begged God to tell me where he'd gone — I had to know. I closed my eyes. When I opened them again, I was surrounded by light. I could see Bill standing in a garden near a tree, looking confused. Then I saw Jesus, in a long, white robe, beckon to him. He spoke to Bill and suddenly Bill looked happy. When that vision finished, I was surrounded by a glow of pure love and was so happy. I knew Bill was all right.

***

A fortnight after Bill's death, I went back to work. I had a lot of bills to pay.

We were given a Legatee who was a real godsend. He was able to get my insurance policy paid out and that covered a lot of our debts. He applied for a war pension and was granted it.

Although I still grieved for Bill, I felt as though a load had been lifted from my shoulders. I was much more relaxed. I didn't have to worry about money and the children could make as much noise as they liked. I often had them all in bed with me, poor little kids — they needed all the love they could get.

Bill had only been dead a short time when a Welfare lady came out to visit us. I was really frightened because I thought she might have the children taken away. We only had two bedrooms and a sleepout and there were five children, as well as Mum and me.

This woman turned out to be a real bitch. She asked me all sorts of questions and walked through our house with her nose in the air like a snob. She asked where we all slept, and when I told her Helen slept with me, she was absolutely furious. She said, 'You are to get that child out of your bed. We will not stand for that. The children aren't to be in the same room as you. I'll come back and check to make sure you've got another bed.'

I never told her we often all slept together, or that I was still breastfeeding Helen. I just agreed with everything she said. I didn't want her to have any excuse to take the children off me.

It was after the visit from the Welfare lady that Mum and I decided we would definitely never tell the children they were Aboriginal. We were both convinced they would have a bad time otherwise. Also, if word got out, another Welfare person might come and take them away. That would have killed us both.

Mum said she didn't want the children growing up with people looking down on them. When I was little, Mum had always pinched my nose and said, 'Pull your nose hard, Gladdie. You don't want to end up with a big nose like mine.' She was always pulling the kids' noses too. She wanted them to grow up to look like white people. With Bill gone, we now had some hope of a future and I knew he would want the children to get on in the world.

I took on any job that was going. I wasn't afraid to work. Sometimes, I had four jobs on the go. I forced myself to learn how to drive, even though I was petrified of actually going on the road. I knew I would need that independence and it meant I could take the children on outings. They hadn't had much up until then.

After I'd managed to pay off all the extra debts, our lives really began to change. I never had to worry about where the next meal was coming from now, and I could buy the kids lollies and fruit; sometimes, we even went to the pictures.

I also found that, now we were on our own, I worried less about Mum. She would always have a home with me, and there was enough money for all of us to get by on. Best of all, she had her own family now. All her life, she'd had to mother other people's children, now she had her own flesh and blood. I hoped that would make up for some of her past.

When the opportunity to buy my own florist business came up, I grabbed it. I had always wanted to be my own boss. My old friend Lois gave me a loan. I soon had that shop on its feet and doing twice as well as when the previous owners had it. It gave me a new independence and something to be proud of. Also, it gave us the extra money we needed to get us through the children's teenage years.

I'm very proud of my children and the way they turned out.

I feel embarrassed now to think that, once, I wanted to be white. As a child I even hoped a white family would adopt me — a rich one, of course. I've changed since those days.

I'm still a coward. When a stranger asks me what nationality I am, I sometimes say a Heinz variety. I feel bad when I do that. It's because there are still times when I'm scared inside, scared to say who I really am.

But, at least I've made a start. And I hope my children will feel proud of the spiritual background from which they've sprung. If we all keep saying we're proud to be Aboriginal, then maybe other Australians will see that we are a people to be proud of. All I want my children to do is pass their Aboriginal heritage on.

I suppose, in hundreds of years' time, there won't be any black Aboriginals left. Our colour dies out; as we mix with other races we'll lose some of the physical characteristics that distinguish us now. I like to think that, no matter what we become, our spiritual tie with the land and the other unique qualities we possess will somehow weave their way through to future generations of Australians. I mean, this is our land, after all, surely we've got something to offer.

It hasn't been an easy task, baring my soul. But, like everything else in my life, I knew I had to do it.

The only way I can explain it is by one of my favourite rules, which I haven't always followed. 'Let me pass this way but once and do what good I can. I shall not pass this way again.' Maybe someone else is walking a road that's like mine.

Something serious

It took several months to work through Mum's story and, during that time, many tears were shed. We became very close.

Although she'd finally shared her story with me, she still couldn't bring herself to tell my brothers and sisters. Consequently, I found myself communicating it to them in bits and pieces as it seemed appropriate. It was, and still is, upsetting for us all. We'd lived in a cocoon of sorts for so long that we all found it difficult to come to terms with the experiences Mum had been through.

By the beginning of June 1983, Nan's health wasn't too good.

'You've got to take her to the doctor,' I told Mum one day.

'You know how she hates doctors.'

'But what if it's something serious? You'll just have to force her to go.'

Mum took Nan to see our local doctor a few days later. They sent Nan for a chest X-ray, which revealed that one of her lungs had collapsed.

The night before Nan was due to go into hospital for tests, she stayed at my place. Mum had arranged weeks before to baby-sit some of her other grandchildren. I made Nan a cup of tea and we sat in the lounge room to talk.

'I'd like you to listen to a story, Nan. It's only a couple of pages. Is it okay if I read it to you?'

'Oooh, yes. I like a good story.'

'You tell me if you like it.'

'All right.'

I read her the section on Arthur's boxing days. When I stopped, she said, 'That's a wonderful story. I did enjoy it. Where did you get such a story from?'

'This is what I've been writing, Nan,' I grinned. 'That's Arthur's story.'

'No! I can't believe it! That's Arthur's story?'

'Yep!'

'I didn't know he had a good story like that. You got to keep that story safe. Read me some more.'

I read a little more, and then we began to talk about the old days and life on Corunna Downs Station. For some reason, Nan was keen to talk. As she went on and on, her breath began to come in shorter and shorter gasps. Her words tumbled out one over the other, as if her tongue couldn't say them quickly enough.

When I could see that she was very tired, I said, 'Would you like to lie down for a while now?'

'Yes, I think I will,' she sighed. 'I feel tired now.'

After I'd settled the children down, I walked quietly past Nan's bedroom door. I expected her to be asleep, but she wasn't.

'Sally,' she called, 'come here.'

'What is it?

'I want to tell you more about the station,' she smiled. I nearly stopped her, as she could hardly breathe, but how could

I tell her not to talk when it had taken a lifetime for her to get to this point?

I listened quietly as she spoke about wild ducks and birds, the blue hills and all the fruit that grew along the creek. Her eyes had a faraway look and her face was very soft. I kept smiling at her but, inside, I wanted to cry. I'd seen that look before: on Arthur's face. I knew she was going to die. Nan finally settled down and closed her eyes. I tucked her in again.

I walked back into the kitchen. 'She's going to die, Paul,' I said sadly. 'I saw that look on Arthur's face. They become all soft. They start to talk about things they've hidden for years.'

When I visited Nan in hospital the following evening, she was very bright. Mum had been there on and off all day.

'Hi, Nan,' I said as I walked up to her bed. 'How are they treating you?'

'The nurses are lovely. And that old lady next to me ordered my tea and showed me where the toilet was.'

'Aah, you've been spoilt! How's the tucker?'

'Very good,' she replied, as if surprised.

'Well, I'm glad they're treating you right, Nan. I brought some more of Arthur's story to read, or are you too tired?'

'Read it!' She folded her hands in her lap and leaned back against the pillows, waiting for me to begin. As I read, Nan oohed and aahed in the appropriate places.

'I'll read you the rest tomorrow night,' I said. 'You look tired. Do you want to sleep now?'

'I'd better. They're putting that thing down my throat tomorrow.'

'You won't feel anything,' Mum reassured her. 'They give you some medicine so you don't feel it go down.'

We had to wait a day for the results of the bronchoscopy. I decided to spend the day at Jill's because it was near the hospital, and I wanted to be on the spot when we got the news.

We were fortunate: Mum's dream had been fulfilled and our sister Helen was doing her residency at the hospital, so she was able to get the results for us straightaway — we had a doctor in the family at last.

Mum and I were sitting at the kitchen table having some lunch when Jill came back from answering the front door. 'I think you should prepare yourself,' she said to Mum. 'Helen's just come home in tears. She's in her room.'

We rushed into Helen's room. Helen sat on the edge of her bed, crying. 'She's got a tumour. I suspected it all along, but I guess I was hoping it was something else.'

'Is it malignant?' Mum asked.

'Well, at her age and with her history of heavy smoking, of course it'll be malignant!' said Helen crossly. She was very upset.

'How long?' I asked.

'They haven't completed the tests yet. We won't know until tomorrow afternoon. Depends on if it's a slow-growing tumour or a fast-growing one, but as she's already symptomatic, it must be pretty large.'

Mum went into Jill's room to cry on her own. I left her for half an hour, then went in to find her still sprawled across the bed, crying her heart out.

'She's expecting me this afternoon,' Mum sobbed.

'Would you like me to go instead?'

'Are you sure you'll be all right?'

'I'll be all right. I'll take Helen with me.'

It took us only five minutes to reach the hospital. When we got to Nan's bed, she was lying on her back in a short hospital gown. She was very hot, and, under the oxygen mask, her breathing was laboured.

The doctor was there. When he saw Helen, he said, 'We think when we put the bronchoscope down that some of the bacteria may have spilled over into her bloodstream. The danger is septi-caemia.'

We both sat down beside her bed. Nan seemed to be slipping in and out of consciousness. It was too much for Helen; tears began to flow silently down her cheeks. She reached for a tissue, and just as she was wiping her face, Nan opened her eyes and said, 'What's wrong, Helen?'

'Nothing,' she replied, and looked away. Nan looked straight at me. I looked back. I was only confirming what she already knew inside.

We stayed for a few hours and left when Nan was asleep.

The rest of the results came through the following afternoon and Mum was called to the hospital to discuss them. I visited again that night. To my surprise, I found Nan sitting up in bed, eating tea. She looked much better.

'Gosh, that looks like a good meal,' I said as I walked up to her bed. She was dying — oughtn't I have said something more profound?

'It's lovely, Sally,' Nan smiled. 'There's so much here I can't eat it all.'

I glanced at Mum. She looked like she was holding together. Nan ignored both of us and went on eating. I looked from one to the other. Silence.

Something was going on. Finally, I said, 'So, what's happening?'

Nan began to eat a little faster. Mum said defensively, 'She's coming home for the weekend, then she's coming back on Monday to start radiotherapy.'

Mum could tell by the look on my face I didn't approve. She looked down at her feet.

'How do you feel about that, Nan?' I asked.

'Ooh, you know me, Sally. I'm frightened; I'd rather do without it.' She shrugged her shoulders and looked at Mum. It was a gesture of confusion.

'You'll be able to breathe better if you have it,' said Mum firmly. 'The doctors said it will help.'

And people always think doctors know best, I thought angrily. 'What do you think, Nan?' I asked her. 'Do you want to try it?'

'I'm frightened of it, Sally. Helen says I should have it. She's a doctor, I suppose she should know.'

'Well, Nan,' I sighed, 'if that's what you want, then try it once. But if you don't like it, you tell 'em so. If you don't like it, you tell them, no more!'

'I don't think I should try it at all,' she replied.

I agreed with her whole-heartedly, but I could see Mum was under pressure from all sides and I didn't want to make it harder for her, so I said nothing.

That evening, Mum and I had a talk. We were both feeling very emotional. Our main difference of opinion was whether

Nan should have treatment or not. I was totally against it because I felt Nan was more afraid of hospitals than dying. Mum felt it could be a good thing, because the doctors had said it could give Nan another six months, though they couldn't guarantee this.

Nan was due to come out of hospital the following morning. Helen said she would pick up Nan and take her to Jill's house. Mum would then collect her from there and come to my place for lunch.

By one o'clock in the afternoon, they still hadn't arrived. I began to worry, and wondered if Nan had suddenly taken a turn for the worse.

They finally arrived around one-thirty. They both looked upset. Nan came in slowly and quietly. She sat down in the lounge room and just looked at the floor.

'What happened, Nan?' I asked, after we'd all sat in silence for a few seconds.

'It was terrible, Sally,' she said. 'I'm never goin' back there. They treat you like an animal.'

'Didn't Helen pick you up?'

'Oh yes, she came. I wasn't there! I had been there, all dressed, waitin' for her to come and get me, when this man came in. He told me to hop in the wheelchair. "What for?" I asked, "I'm goin' home!" "You have to see the doctor for a minute," he said.'

'Where did he take you?'

'Oh, to some room. I had to take all my clothes off. There wasn't a nurse there, and they didn't even give me one of those hospital dresses to put on. They made me lie down on the bed, and then this man and that man started thumping my chest. It hurt real bad.'

'Was your doctor there?'

'No! They was all strangers, strange men comin' in one after the other, all thumping me round the chest. I had to lie there with nothing to cover me! I felt 'shamed.'

'These weren't medical students, they were registrars!' Mum said.

'The bastards,' I said angrily. 'Why on earth didn't you yell at them to stop, Nan?'

'I did! I begged them to stop, but, even though I was sobbing, they wouldn't leave me alone. They cruel, Sally, real cruel. I said to one of them, "You just doin' this to me cause I'm black, aren't you?" He said, "Oooh, you mustn't think that. We're trying to help you."'

I wanted to cry. She was so hurt. I was so angry I wanted to scream and beat all those doctors up.

'That's why we're so late,' Mum said. 'Poor Nan could hardly walk when Helen brought her down to Jill's.'

'Why did they do it, do you know?'

'Helen said she thinks it was a practice exam for the registrars. Apparently, they give them mock exams and they always choose patients with good medical signs. Doesn't that make you sick?'

'They shouldn't have done that to me, should they, Sally?'

'No, they shouldn't, Nan. They should be ashamed of themselves. No one's going to treat my grandmother like that!'

'What are you doing?' Mum asked as I walked to the phone.

'I'm ringing the bastards up! This is only the beginning. By the time I get through with them, they won't know what hit them!'

'No, you're not!' Mum shouted as she leapt from her chair. She tore the phone from my hands and slammed it back down. 'I've never asked much of you,' she said tearfully, 'but I'm asking this: leave it alone. For your sister's sake, let her finish her course. I will make sure that Helen complains and tells them what we think, but you are not to do it, Sally, I'm frightened of what you might say.'

My blood was boiling. 'But this is so inhumane. It should be on TV and in the papers! How many other old people have had the same experience! No one wants to rock the boat just because they're doctors. They're not God!'

'I agree, Sally, I really do, but I'm thinking of Helen. She was very upset when she brought Nan home. It's her place to complain, not yours!'

I groaned out loud. When it came to issues like this, I was a person of action. Doing nothing was like Mum asking me to cut off my right arm. I glanced down at Nan, who was looking a little better. 'Nan,' I sighed, 'you decide: what do you think I should do?'

She thought seriously for a while and then she said slowly, 'They was wrong in treatin' me like an animal. They was brutes. I feel rotten inside about this, Sal, but I think Glad is right. It's not Helen's fault, and you shouldn't make it hard for her. She's the one workin' there, so let her complain.'

'You sure that's what you want?'

'Yes. I'm not goin' back there, Sal. I'm not havin' that treatment. You don't know what they might do to me.'

'Well praise the Lord for that!' I said. 'You're better off without them, Nan.'

Good news

The following Monday, Mum arrived early with Nan. We had decided that it was best if Nan stayed with us each day during the week while Mum was at work.

Nan brought her black bag laden with biscuits and lollies for the kids.

'I've got a surprise for you, Nan,' I said. 'Paul and I cleaned out the sleep-out.'

'Ooh, doesn't it look nice?' she smiled as she peered through the bedroom doorway.

'You've got the louvres, so you'll get plenty of fresh air if you want.'

'Yes, louvres are good. That's why I like the sleep-out at Glad's place.'

When Mum came to pick Nan up that afternoon, she said to her, 'You ready to go home, then.'

Nan looked from me to Mum. 'I think I'll stay a few more days.'

Mum was aghast. 'You can't be here all the time. Sally's got a baby to look after. She can't have you as well.'

'I don't mind, Mum. She can stay.'

'It's settled, then,' said Nan.

When Mum came back on Wednesday, Nan told her she wasn't going home.

'This isn't your home,' Mum argued, 'this is Sally's house. The dogs are missing you, and the cats.'

'Oh, they'll be all right.'

'Now Nan ...' Mum began.

'Look, Gladdie,' Nan interrupted. 'I wheel the baby when he's crying and I've done a bit of raking in the garden. Sally can't do it all. I'll stay here till the end of the week and then I'll come home for the weekend.'

Nan kept her word and went home for the weekend. On Sunday, Mum rang.

'Hi, Mum, what's up? Nan's not worse, is she?'

'No, she's as bright as a button. Look, she's been on at me all weekend. She wants to know if she can live with you during the week and come home to me on weekends.'

'Yeah, that's fine,' I replied.

Over the next few weeks, our lives fell into a pattern that tended to revolve around Nan and the baby. Amber and Blaze loved having Nan live with us. Not only did they have an unlimited supply of goodies which were doled out generously, but they also had a captive audience before which they could perform all the television advertisements they had learnt by heart.

Every night Amber read Nan a bedtime story. The stories were about Aboriginal children in the Western Desert. Nan loved to listen to them, and when Amber was finished reading, she'd tell about some of the things she'd done as a child.

Blaze was particularly horrified one night when she told him how tasty witchetty grubs were. 'Hmmn,' she said, 'you gobble them up. They good tucker, real good tucker.'

Nan and the children became very close. The three of them spent hours closeted away in her room. Even though Blaze was only five, he treated Nan like a real lady, worrying over where she was going to sit and whether she was warm enough. Whenever I wanted Blaze, I knew where to look: on the end of Nan's bed.

One afternoon, after his usual session with Nan, he strolled into the kitchen and garbled out a set of instructions in what, to me, sounded like a foreign language.

'What was that?'

'That's what Nan taught me,' he said, smiling. He was obviously very proud of himself. 'You know how we speak English, well she doesn't. That's what she speaks.'

'I see …'

'Gotta go now, Mum. That was just a practice. She's gunna teach me more.'

Then, one afternoon, just after we'd finished lunch, Nan said, 'You still doin' that book?'

'Yep.'

'I dunno if it will do any good.'

'Maybe it won't,' I sighed, 'but it's better than nothing.'

'It wouldn't make a difference.'

'That's what everyone says. No one will talk. Don't you see, Nan, someone's got to tell. Otherwise, things will stay the same, they won't get any better.'

Nan paused and looked at me shrewdly. She was quiet for a minute or so, then she added, 'Maybe I will tell you some things.'

'Really?' I couldn't believe it.

'I don't want to tell you everything.'

'You don't have to. I'll settle for anything, Nan, anything.'

'I can keep my secrets?'

'Yeah.'

'All right. I tell you some things, but that's all … I'm tired now. Tomorrow.'

'Okay.'

When Blaze came home from preschool that afternoon, the first thing he said to us was, 'I want to tell you what I said for news. I stood out the front and said, "I've got some good news this morning. I'd like you all to know I got a bit of blackfella in me."'

Nan burst out laughing and so did I.

'Why are you laughing?'

'We're not, darling, we're not,' I smiled. 'That was good news. What did the kids say?'

'Ah, nothing, but later on, Stewart wanted to know which bit, and I didn't know what to say.'

The following morning, I set up my recorder and, after a cup of tea, we sat down to talk.

'What do you want me to say?' Nan asked.

'Anything. Just tell me what you want to. Maybe you could start with Corunna Downs.'

'Righto.' I waited patiently as Nan sat staring at the recorder.

Daisy Corunna's Story

My name is Daisy Corunna, I'm Arthur's sister. My Aboriginal name is Talahue. I can't tell you when I was born, but I feel old. My mother had me on Corunna Downs Station, just out of Marble Bar. She said I was born under a big, old gum tree and the midwife was called Diana. Course, that must have been her whitefella name. All the natives had whitefella and tribal names. I don't know what her tribal name was.

I was happy up North. I had my mother and there was Old Fanny, my grandmother. Gladdie 'minds me of Old Fanny — she's got the same crooked smile. They both got round faces like the moon, too. I 'member Old Fanny always wore a handkerchief on her head with little knots tied all the way around. Sometimes, my grand-daughter Helen 'minds me of her, too. They both short and giggly with skinny legs. Aah, she was good for a laugh, Old Fanny.

She loving panning for tin. All the old people panned for tin. You could see it lyin' in the dirt, heavy and dark, like black marbles. We traded the tin for sugar or flour. They never gave us money.

Old Fanny went pink-eye to Hillside one day. I never saw her again. They tell me she died on Hillside; maybe she knew she was going to die. She was a good old grandmother.

On the station, I went under the name Daisy Brockman. It wasn't till I was older that I took the name Corunna. Now, some people say my father wasn't Howden Drake-Brockman. They say he was this man from Malta. What can I say? I never heard 'bout this man from Malta before. I think that's a big joke.

Aah, you see, that's the trouble with us blackfellas. We don't know who we belong to, no one'll own up. I got to be careful what I say. You can't put no lies in a book.

Course, I had another father. He wasn't my real father, like, but he looked after us just the same. Chinaman was his name. He was very tall and strong. The people respected him. They were scared of him. He was Arthur's Aboriginal father too. He was a powerful man.

My poor mother lost a lot of babies. I had two sisters that lived, Lily and Rosie. They were full blood. I was the light one of the family, the little one with blonde hair. Of course, there was Arthur, but they took him away when I was just a baby.

My mother cried and cried when they took Arthur. She kept callin' to him to come back. The people thought Arthur was gettin' educated so he could run the station some day. They was all wrong. My poor old mother never saw him again.

Rosie and I was close. Lily was older than me. I spent a lot of time with Rosie. I was very sad when she died. She was only young. My mother nursed her, did everything for her, but we lost her. Good old Rosie — you know, I been thinkin' 'bout her lately. She was what you call a good sport.

I'll tell you a story about our white man's names. My mother was in Hedland with the three of us when an English nursing sister saw her near the well. She said, 'Have you got names for your three little girls?'

Mum said, 'No.'

She said, 'Well, I'll give you names, real beautiful ones. We'll call this one Lily, this one Rosie and this little one Daisy.' We didn't mind being called that; we thought we were pretty flowers.

I haven't told you about my brother Albert, yet. He was light too. He used to tease me. He'd chase me, then he'd hide behind a big bush and jump out and pretend he was the devil-devil. Oooh, he was naughty to me. They took Albert when they took Arthur, but Albert got sick and came back to the station. He was a good worker. He liked playing with me. He called me his little sister.

They was a good mob on Corunna. I been thinkin' 'bout all of them lately. There was Fred Stream — by jingoes, there was a few kids that belonged to him. He had Sarah. Her children were really fair, white blackfellas, really.

Aah, that colour business is a funny thing. Our colour goes away. You mix us with the white man, and pretty soon, you got no blackfellas left. Some of these whitefellas you see walkin' around, they really black underneath. You see, you never can tell. I'm old now, and look at me, look at the skin on my arms and legs, just look! It's goin' white. I used to be a lot darker than I am now. Maybe it's the white blood takin' over, or the medicine they gave me in hospital, I don't know.

The big house on Corunna was built by the natives. They all worked together, building this and building that. If it wasn't for the natives, nothing would get done. They made the station; Drake-Brockmans didn't do it on their own.

At the back of the homestead was a big, deep hole with whitewash in it. Us kids used to mix the whitewash with water and make it like a paint. Then we'd put it all over us and play corroborees.

I 'member the kitchen on Corunna. There was a tiny little window where the blackfellas had to line up for tucker. My mother never liked doin' that. We got a bit of tea, flour and meat, that was all. They always rang a bell when they was ready for us to come, and they also woke us up every morning with a bell. Why do white people like ringin' bells so much?

I saw plenty of willy-willies up there and cyclones, too. By jingoes, a cyclone is a terrible thing! There was men's hats, spinifex, empty tanks, everything blowin' everywhere.

There was a food store on Corunna. It had tin walls, tin roof and a tiny window near the top covered with flywire. You wouldn't believe the food they had in there — it makes my mouth water just thinkin' about it. When it was siesta time, the other kids used to lift me up and poke me though the window. I'd drop down inside as quiet as a mouse, then I'd pick up food and throw it out the window. I had a good feed on those days.

The people were really hungry sometimes, poor things. They didn't get enough, you see. And they worked hard. I suppose I should feel bad about stealin' that food, but hunger is a terrible thing. Aah, you see, the native is different to the white man. He wouldn't let a dog go without his tea.

There was a government ration we used to get now and then. It was a blanket with the crown of Queen Victoria on it. Can you imagine that? We used to laugh about that. You see, we was wrappin' ourselves in royalty.

Then there was a mirror and a comb, a cake of soap and a couple of big spotted handkerchiefs. Sometimes, the men were lucky and got a shirt; the women never got anything.

I 'member my mother showin' me a picture of a white woman all fancied up in a long, white dress. 'Ooh, Daisy,' she said, 'if only I could have a dress like that.' All the native women wanted to look like the white women, with fancy hairdos and fancy dresses.

Later, my mother learnt how to sew. She was very clever. She could draw anything. She drew pictures in the sand for me all the time. Beautiful pictures. Maybe that's where you get it from, Sally.

They had a good cook on Corunna for a while, Mrs Quigley. She was a white woman, a good woman. I think Nell and Mrs Stone, the housekeeper, were a bit jealous of her. Nell was Howden's first white wife. They were real fuddy-duddies and didn't like her talkin' to anyone.

The cook had a little girl called Queenie and it was my job to look out for her. We were 'bout the same age — ooh, we had good times! We'd laugh and giggle at anythin'.

I taught Queenie all about the bush. We'd go out after a big rain. Sometimes, the rain was so heavy up North, it hurt when it hit you. One day, the place would be desert; the next day, green everywhere. Green and gold, beautiful, really. We'd watch a little seed grow. 'Look now,' I'd say to Queenie, 'it's getting bigger.' By the time we finished lookin', that seed'd be half an inch long.

In the evenings, I liked to sit and watch the kangaroos and other animals come down and drink at the water trough. The crows and the birds would have a drink, too.

I was a hard worker at Corunna. I been a hard worker all my life. When I was little, I picked the grubs off the caulies and cabbages at the back of the garden. I got a boiled sweet for that. Now the blackfellas weren't allowed to pick any vegetables from the garden. You got a whipping if you were caught.

We all loved the orphaned lambs. We were their mother and their father. We fed them with a bottle with a turkey feather stuck in it.

Aah, we played silly games when we were kids. I always played with Rosie and Topsy. That Topsy, she was one of a kind, I tell you. One day, Mrs Stone gave her a cake of soap and told her to take a bath. You know what she did? She threw the soap back and said, 'I'm not takin' no bath!' Can you 'magine cheekin' a white woman like that? Aah, she was great fun, old Topsy.

There was a creek that cut across Corunna in the wet. We loved swimming in it and catching fish. They were like sardines. We threw them on the hot ashes and then gobbled them up.

All sorts of wild fruit grew along the creek. There was a prickly tree with fruit like an orange, but with lots of big seeds in it. You could suck the seeds. Then there was another one shaped like a banana. You ate the flesh and spat out the seeds. The best one of all was like a gooseberry bush. You could smell those ones a good way away, they smell like a ripe rockmelon. We'd sniff and say, 'Aah, something ripe in there, somewhere.' We'd lift up all the branches looking for them, they were only tiny. When we found them, we'd say, 'Mmmmm, good old mingimullas.' Ooh, they were good to eat.

There was another tree we used to get gum from to chew. It grew on little white sticks. We'd collect it and keep it in a tin. It went hard, like boiled lollies.

Rosie and I were naughty. We'd pinch wild ducks' eggs and break up their nests. And we'd dig holes to get lizards' eggs. We could tell where the lizards had covered up their eggs. We'd dig them all out, get the eggs and bust them. Those poor creatures. They never harmed us and there we were, breakin' up their eggs. We're all God's creatures, after all.

When I got older, my jobs on Corunna changed. They started me working at the main house, sweeping the verandahs, emptying the toilets, scrubbing the tables and pots and pans and the floor. In those days, you scrubbed everything. In the mornings, I had to clean the hurricane lamps, then help in the kitchen.

There were always poisonous snakes hiding in the dark corners of the kitchen. You couldn't see them, but you could hear them. Sssss, sssss, sssss, they went. We cornered them and killed them with sticks. There were a lot of snakes on Corunna.

Once I was working up the main house, I wasn't allowed down in the camp. I couldn't sleep with my mother now and I wasn't allowed to play with all my old friends.

That was the worst thing about working at the main house, not seeing my mother every day. I knew she missed me. She would walk up from the camp and call, 'Daisy, Daisy'. I couldn't talk to her; I had too much work to do. It was hard for me then. I had to sneak away just to see my own family and friends. They were camp natives; I was a house native.

Now, I had to sleep on the homestead verandah. Some nights,

it was real cold, and one blanket was too thin. On nights like that, the natives used to bring wool from the shearing shed and lay that beneath them.

I didn't mind sleeping on the verandah in summer because I slept near the old cooler. It was as big as a fireplace, and they kept butter and milk in it. I'd wait till everyone was asleep, then I'd sneak into the cooler and pinch some butter. I loved it, but I was never allowed to have any.

Seems like I was always getting into trouble over food. I'm like a lamb that's never been fed. I 'member once, Nell asked me to take an apple pie to the house further out on the station. Nell's real name was Eleanor, but everyone called her Nell. Anyway, I kept walkin' and walkin' and smellin' that pie. Ooh, it smelled good. I couldn't stand it any longer. I hid in a gully and dug out a bit of pie with my fingers. It was beautiful. I squashed the pie together and tried to make out like it was all there. Hmmmnnn, that was good tucker, I said to myself as I walked on.

When I gave the pie to Mrs Stone, I had to give her a note that Nell had sent as well. If I'd have known what was in that note, I'd have thrown it away. It said, if any part of this pie is missing, send the note back and I will punish her.

Mrs Stone looked at the note, then she looked at the pie and said, 'Give this note back when you go.' I did. And, sure enough, I got whipped with the bullocks cane again.

Nell was a cruel woman with a hard heart. When she wasn't whippin' us girls with the bullocks cane for not workin' hard enough, she was hittin' us over the head. She didn't like natives. If one of us was in her way and we didn't move real quick, she'd give us a real hard thump over the head, just like that. Ooh, it *hurt! White people are great ones for thumpin' you on the head, aren't they? We was only kids.*

Aah, but they were good old days, then. When they took me from the station, I never seen days like that ever again.

They told my mother I was goin' to get educated. I thought it'd be good, goin' to school. My mother wanted me to learn to read and write like white people. Then she wanted me to come back and teach her. There was a lot of the older people interested in learnin' how to read and write then.

Why did they tell my mother that lie? I got nothin' out of their promises. My mother wouldn't have let me go just to work. God will make them pay for their lies.

When I left, I was cryin', all the people were cryin'. My mother was cryin' and beatin' her head. Lily was cryin'. I called, 'Mum, Mum, Mum!' She said, 'Don't forget me, Talahue!'

I could hear their wailing for miles and miles. 'Talahue! Talahue!' They were singin' out my name, over and over. I couldn't stop cryin'. I kept callin', 'Mum! Mum!'

***

I must have been 'bout fourteen or fifteen when they took me from Corunna. First day in Perth, I had to tidy the garden, pick up leaves and sweep the verandahs. Later on, I used an old scythe to cut the grass. All the time, I kept wonderin' when they were goin' to send me to school. I saw some white kids goin' to school, but not me. I never asked them why they didn't send me, I was too 'shamed.

Funny how I was the only half-caste they took with them from Corunna. Drake-Brockmans left the others and took me. Maybe Howden took me 'cause I was his daughter. I kept thinkin' of my poor old mother and how she thought I was gettin' educated. How could I tell her? I couldn't write. And I had no one to write for me.

It wasn't the first time I'd been in Perth. I'd been there before with Howden's first wife, Nell. Now I was with the second wife, Alice. Nell had died. When I'd been there before, I'd had to look after Jack and Betty, the children. I was only a kid myself. I was 'bout ten and Jack was 'bout six; I can't remember how old Betty was. We was all kids, but I had to do the work.

Aah, Nell was a hard woman. She was hard on her own kids, too. She bossed Howden around. When I was in Perth with her, she didn't even give me a place to sleep. I had to find my own place. There was a big, empty truck on the verandah of the house we were stayin' in, and I climbed in there at night.

You see, I went to Perth with Nell, and I came back. My mother would be thinkin' I'd come back this time too, but I didn't. They just wanted me to work.

We moved into Ivanhoe, a big house on the banks of the Swan River in Claremont. I was lookin' after children again — Jack, Betty, Judy, June and Dick. I was supposed to be their nanny. I had to play with them, dress them, feed and then put them to bed at night. I had other chores to do as well. I never blamed the children; it wasn't their fault I had to work so hard.

At night, I used to lie in bed and think 'bout my people. I really missed them. I cried myself to sleep every night. You see, I needed my people; they made me feel important. I belonged to them.

Alice kept tellin' me, 'We're family now, Daisy.' Thing is, they wasn't my family. Oh, I knew the children loved me, but they wasn't my family. They were white, they'd grow up and go to school one day. I was black, I was a servant. How can they be your family?

The only friend I had then was Queenie's mother, Mrs Quigley. She was housekeeping for the Cruikshanks in Claremont. I used to sneak over and visit her whenever I could. She understood the North, she knew how hard it was for me. She never said much, but I knew she understood. I never stayed with her long. I was worried they'd notice I was missing.

I did all the work at Ivanhoe. The cleaning, the washing, the ironing. There wasn't nothing I didn't do. From when I got up in the morning till when I went to sleep at night, I worked. That's all I did.

By jingoes, washing was hard work in those days. The old laundry was about twenty yards from the house and the troughs were always filled with dirty washing. They'd throw everything down from the balcony onto the grass, then I'd collect it, take it to the laundry and wash it. Sometimes, I thought I'd never finish stokin' up that copper, washin' this and washin' that. Course, everything was starched in those days. Sheets, pillowcases, serviettes, tablecloths, they was all starched. I even had to iron the sheets. Isn't that silly, you only goin' to lay on them?

The house had to be spotless. I scrubbed, dusted and polished. There was the floors, the staircase, the ballroom. It all had to be done. Soon, I was the cook, too. Mind you, I was a good cook.

I had my dinner in the kitchen. I never ate with the family. When they rang the bell, I knew they wanted me. After dinner,

I'd clear up, wash up, dry up and put it all away. Then, next morning, it'd start all over again. You see, it's no use them sayin' I was one of the family, 'cause I wasn't. I was their servant.

I 'member they used to have real fancy morning and afternoon teas. The family would sit on the lawn under big, shady umbrellas. I'd bring out the food and serve them. I 'member the beautiful cups and saucers. Some of them were so fine, they were like a seashell, you could see through them. I only ever had a tin mug. I promised myself one day I would have a nice cup and saucer. That's why, whenever my grandchildren said, 'What do you want for your birthday?' I always told them a cup and saucer.

In those days, the Drake-Brockmans were real upper class. They had money and, aah, the parties they had. I never seen such parties. The ladies' dresses were pretty and fancy. I always thought of my mother when I saw their dresses. How she would have loved one.

***

I never liked Perth much then. People looked at you funny 'cause you were black. I kept my eyes down. 'Cause you're black, they treat you like dirt. You see, in those days, we was owned, like a cow or a horse. I even heard some people say we not the same as whites. That's not true, we all God's children.

Course, when the white people wanted something, they didn't pretend you wasn't there, they 'spected you to come runnin' quick smart. Someone was always ringin' that damn bell.

I'm 'shamed of myself, now. I feel 'shamed for some of the things I done. I wanted to be white, you see. I'd lie in bed at *night and think if God could make me white, it'd be the best thing. Then I could get on in the world, make somethin' of myself. Fancy, me thinkin' that. What was wrong with my own people?*

In those days, it was considered a privilege for a white man to want you, but if you had children, you weren't allowed to keep them. You was only allowed to keep the black ones. They took the white ones off you 'cause you weren't considered fit to raise a child with white blood.

I tell you, it made a wedge between the people. Some of the black men felt real low, and some of the native girls with a bit of white in them wouldn't look at a black man. There I was, stuck in the middle. Too black for the whites and too white for the blacks.

It was a big thing if you could get a white man to marry you. A lot of native people who were light passed themselves off as white then. One of my friends married a foreigner. She'd promised her husband never to talk or mix with any natives again. We didn't blame her, we understood. He wouldn't have married her otherwise.

Nellie was from Lyndon Station. She was the daughter of the station manager, Mr Hack, but he never owned her. The Courthope family got her from Mogumber to be a servant in their house. Nellie was lucky, because she got treated kindly. She worked very hard like me, but they was good to her. She had a lovely room.

Aah, she was a laugh, that Nellie. She always wanted to be white. All those baths in that hydrogen peroxide and dyein' her hair red. Sometimes, she'd forget to take those baths and then she'd go black again.

I 'member the minister at Christ Church started up a sewing circle for all the native servants. We had to go down there and he'd give us a talk, then we'd sew. One time, he went on and on, tellin' us how we must save ourselves for marriage. But most of us had already been taken by white men. We felt really 'shamed.

Now Sal, I don't want Amber hearin' this, she's too young. You watch out for her after I'm gone. She's goin' to be very beautiful. All the men'll want her. Some men can't be trusted. They just mongrels. They get you down on the floor and they won't let you get up. Don't ever let a man do that to you. You watch out for Amber. You don't want her bein' treated like a black woman.

We had no protection when we was in service. I know a lot of native servants had kids to white men because they was forced. Makes you want to cry to think how black women have been treated in this country. It's a terrible thing. They'll pay one day for what they've done.

Aah, white people make you laugh the way they beat the native to teach him not to steal. What about their own kids? I seen white kids do worse than that and no one touches them. They say, he's sowin' his oats or that kid got the devil in him, but they not belted. Poor old blackfella do the same thing, they say you niggers don't know right from wrong and they whip you! I tell you, this is a white man's world.

Now if I had've been livin' with my big brother Arthur, he'd have protected me. He was a strong man. I 'member I was standin' in the kitchen cooking when I heard this knock. I turned around and there's this big native lookin' through the flywire.

'Is that you, Daisy?' he said.

'Who are you?' I asked.

'Aah, you not Daisy,' he said. 'She had real fair hair. Come on Mrs, you tell me where Daisy is.'

'You listen here,' I growled at him. 'We don't like strange blackfellas hangin' round here. You better get goin' before the mistress comes home. She'll take a stick to you.'

'Don't you go gettin' uppity with me, Mrs,' he said. 'I got every right to be lookin' for my little sister Daisy. I want her to know she's got a brother who's gettin' on in the world.'

'You Arthur?'

'Now how did you come by my name, Mrs?'

'You cheeky devil,' I said.

'What did you dye your hair for?' he asked. 'You was the only one of us with blonde hair.'

Cheeky devil pulled my hair. Maybe he 'spected the colour to come off. Maybe he thought I put boot polish on my hair, I don't know. 'By gee, you a devil!' I told him. I should have known he was my brother. I was fightin' with him, wasn't I?

It wasn't so bad after that. Arthur would come and take me out. Sometimes, he even took me in a car. Can you 'magine that? All us natives drivin' round Perth in a real car? Aah, he thought he was somebody, that Arthur. All the girls wanted him, then. He was the only blackfella they knew with a bit of money in his pocket. He was nice to them all.

When he didn't come, I missed him. We always had a good laugh together. When he couldn't come to see me, he'd write. I *felt real important, gettin' a letter with my name on it. Trouble was, I couldn't read. I couldn't have nothin' private 'cause I always had to get someone to read it for me.*

Aah, he was a clever man. We had fights all the time, but I was proud of that man.

***

I hadn't seen Arthur for a long time when I had Gladdie.

Before I had Gladdie, I was carryin' another child, but I wasn't allowed to keep it. That was the way of it, then. They took our children one way or another. I never told anyone that I was carryin' Gladdie.

Now how this all came about, that's my business. I'll only tell a little. Everyone knew who the father was, but they all pretended they didn't know. Aah, they knew, they knew. You didn't talk 'bout things then. You hid the truth.

Alice bought me a cane pram to wheel Gladdie in. She gave Gladdie a doll. I kept Gladdie with me in my room.

Howden died not long after she was born. When I came home from hospital, he said, 'Bring her here, let me hold her.' He wanted to nurse Gladdie before he died.

After he died, I never had time for anything. I had Gladdie and the other children to look after. There were times when Gladdie ate so much she 'minded me of the little baby pigs runnin' round the station.

It was hard for me with her. Sometimes, she'd be cryin', cryin', and I couldn't go to her. I had too much work to do.

When Arthur saw her, he thought she was beautiful. I think he was jealous: he wanted her to belong to him.

Strange, isn't it, that at one time I was goin' to live with Arthur. Before I had Gladdie, they said they didn't want me any more. Then, they changed their minds. Arthur told me he had a real nice whitefella for me to marry. After Gladdie was born, Arthur wanted us both to go with him. I wasn't allowed to go anywhere. I had to have permission and they wouldn't let me go.

When Gladdie was 'bout three years old, they took her from me. I'd been 'spectin' it. Alice told me Gladdie needed an education, so they put her in Parkerville Children's Home. What could I do? I wanted to keep her with me, she was all I had, but they didn't want her there. Alice said she cost too much to feed, said I was ungrateful. She was wantin' me to give up my own flesh and blood and still be grateful. Aren't black people allowed to have feelin's?

I cried and cried when Alice took her away. Gladdie was too young to understand. I ran down to the wild bamboo near the river and I hid and cried and cried and cried. How can a mother lose a child like that? How could she do that to me? I thought of my poor old mother then. They took her Arthur from her, and then they took me. She was broken-hearted, God bless her.

When Gladdie was in Parkerville, I tried to get up there as often as I could, but it was a long way and I had no money. When I did get paid, Alice was always takin' money out that she said I owed her. It was a hard life. I always got Gladdie something nice to eat when I went up. She loved food; I think she gets that from me.

Parkerville wasn't a bad place. There was plenty of kids for her to play with and there was bush everywhere. I knew she'd love the bush. I used to take her for a bit of a walk, show her the birds and animals like. She was always real glad to see me. I knew she didn't want to stay there, but what could I do? It wasn't like I had a place of my own. It wasn't like I had any say over my own life.

It was during the thirties that they told Gladdie I might die. My cousin Helen Bunda was real sick. They asked me to give blood for her. I said yes. She belonged to me, I had to give blood, but I was real scared.

You never know what doctors are goin' to do to you. The silly buggers, they lost the first lot of blood they took, so they took some more. I was so weak I couldn't lift my head. I think I turned white with all the blood they took from me.

Helen died and I heard the doctors say, 'Doesn't matter, she was only a native.' Then, they looked at me and the nurse said, 'I think this one's going, too.' You see, they treat you just like an animal. Alice came and got me. She was very cross. She took me back to Ivanhoe and nursed me. She was a good bush nurse.

They brought Gladdie down from Parkerville to say goodbye to me. She looked real frightened when she saw me. I tricked all of them — I didn't die, after all. Pretty soon, I was up and doin' all the work again. That's the last time I give blood.

Helen had been a good old cousin. When she died, I thought her things would come to me, I was her family. Turned out I got nothin', not a penny. The white family that she was workin' for got it all. They said she made a will leavin' it to them. Bunda didn't know nothin' 'bout will makin'. That family even come and asked me to give back the brooch she'd given me. The cheek *of it. Bunda had given it me before she died and they come and asked for it back. Right inside my heart, I felt very bitter 'bout that.*

Arthur finally got married in the thirties and I lost track of him. The Depression was on and I knew he'd be havin' trouble makin' ends meet. It was just as well Gladdie and I hadn't gone with him. We'd be only two more mouths to feed. He worked real hard, did anythin' to put food on the table. I think he lost his farm in the Depression. Those white people at Mucka, they were always after his farm. Funny, isn't it, the white man's had land rights for years, and we not allowed to have any. Aah, this is a funny world.

Couple of times, Arthur saw Gladdie at Parkerville. He had a real soft spot for her. Then he got too busy with his own family to see her. I think she missed him. She loved visitors.

The thirties were hard for everyone. You never threw anythin' away, there was always someone who could use it. It broke my heart to see men standin' round for food. Not just black men, white ones too. If I knew someone who was hungry, I'd give them food. I gave away some of my clothes and shoes, whatever I could find. You can't be rotten to people when they in trouble, that's not the bluckfella's way.

***

When Gladdie was 'bout fourteen, she left Parkerville. She'd been with me for holidays at Ivanhoe, and when I took her back, she didn't want to stay. You see, she found out she was havin'

342

this new House Mother and she was a cruel woman. Gladdie was real frightened. I said to them, 'Can she come with me, she's almost grown up now.'

I took her back to Ivanhoe with me. I thought she could stay in my room, but, after two days, Alice said, 'Look, Daisy, you can't keep her here. You'll have to find somewhere else for her to go.' I was real upset 'bout that.

They'd told me to leave before, reckoned they couldn't afford me. I had to go and work for Mrs Morgan. Then, a few years later, Alice begged me to come back. She said it was for good. That Ivanhoe was my home. I thought it would be Gladdie's, too. Aah, you see, promises, promises. Howden, he promised Arthur and me money. He said he'd leave us some. Haa, that's how you get treated by rich people, real rotten. The promises of a wealthy family are worth nothin'.

I found a family to take Gladdie in. They was religious people and they often took girls in. I knew they'd be good to her. She was real upset, though; she couldn't understand why they didn't want her at Ivanhoe.

One day, the Hewitts, that was their name, they said they couldn't trust Gladdie no more. 'She's been goin' to the pictures,' they said. 'Pictures are a sin.' They said they didn't want her bein' a bad influence on the other kids. They packed her bags and said I had to take her.

I was livin' in my own place by then. Alice had kicked me out again. Aah, I was silly to believe her. She owed me back wages, got me to work for nothing, then kicked me out. I was just used up. I been workin' for that family all those years, right since I was a little child, and that's how I get treated. I left a good job to *go back to Ivanhoe. I was silly. When they didn't want Gladdie stayin' there, I should have known.*

My new job was a cook in a restaurant. All the soldiers and sailors loved to come in, because we served good tucker and I gave them plenty. I never cook rubbish. By gee, they could eat. They all wanted second helpings. I felt sorry for them. Some of them were only kids. Goin' to war like that, it's not right.

I shared a house with a good woman. She liked Gladdie, and was good to her. Gladdie and I was livin' together for the first time. She was makin' new friends and so was I. Pretty soon, I was goin' to the trots and other places. I really loved the horses. I'm like Arthur, I got a tender spot for all God's creatures.

Gladdie left school and Alice got her a job as a florist. They didn't want to take her, because she was a native. They were pleased they took her in the end, because everyone loved Gladdie.

Now you'd be thinkin' that, after all those years apart, we'd get on real good. Well, we didn't. Gladdie liked to do things her way and I liked to do things my way. We was fightin' and fightin'. By jingoes, we had some rows.

Gladdie was silly in those days, always wantin' to know her future. She had her palm read and tea-leaves read. She didn't know what she was meddlin' with. You leave the spirits alone. You mess with them, you get burnt. Blackfella know all 'bout spirits. We brought up with them. That's where the white man's stupid. He only believes what he can see. He needs to get educated. He's only livin' half a life.

Gladdie didn't like some of my friends and I didn't like some of hers. Gladdie was always tellin' me I was too suspicious. She said I didn't trust her. Maybe it was the men I didn't trust. Gladdie was innocent; she didn't know what could happen.

One day, she just went off and got married. She was only twenty-one. I s'pose she didn't tell me because she knew I didn't like Bill. He was a drinker. I never liked men who were drinkers. What was she goin' and gettin' married for, anyway? She should have been home, lookin' after her mother.

Well, there's no use cryin' over spilt milk. What's done is done. They got a State Housing place in Mulberry Farm near Beaconsfield. It wasn't a bad little place. I used to visit them, take them a bit of meat. There were some poor families there. Sometimes, I gave them meat too. You can't let people go hungry.

Pretty soon, I was havin' grandchildren. I felt real sorry for Gladdie. She didn't realise how bad Bill was when she married him. He kept disappearing. She was worried sick. It was the grog, you see. I'm not sayin' he was a bad man. He had a hard time during the war.

When Gladdie was carrying Billy, she got polio. There wasn't one family in Mulberry Farm that wasn't touched with polio. It was a terrible thing. I was worried you kids might get sick, too. That's when I moved in. Gladdie couldn't walk, she was stuck in bed. There was no one to look after you and Jilly. Bill didn't like me there. He was so jealous. He wanted Gladdie to himself. What could she do? She needed someone to mind the kids. He was no good around the house.

Now, I tell you something, Sal, this is a sacred thing, so I better speak quiet. I helped your mother with that polio. You see, our family's always had powers that way. I don't want to say no more. Some things I'm tellin' you 'cause I won't be here much longer. That's something you should know.

Gladdie and Bill was offered a house in Manning. It was made from bricks and bigger than the one we was livin' in. Billy was a baby then, and Gladdie was over the polio. I liked the new place. There was bush everywhere. You couldn't see nothin' but bush, and it was near the river. Aah, the birds and the wildlife, it was wonderful. Trouble was, it stank at night. We was near the swamp. That night air was bad for you, Sally. It made you sick. You should have been up North, you're no good in the cold.

Now, this is something I've told no one. You mightn't believe me. 'Member when we first moved there? Couple of nights, you came out on the back verandah and found Gladdie and me sittin' there, and we made you go away? You was always in the wrong place at the wrong time. Well, we was listenin' to music. It was the blackfellas playin' their didgeridoos and singin' and laughin' down in the swamp. Your mother could hear it. I said to her one night, 'I'm goin' down there and tell those natives off. Who do they think they are, wakin' all the white people up.' That's when Gladdie told me. She said, 'Don't go down there, Mum, there's no one there, only bush.' You see, we was hearin' the people from long ago. Our people who used to live here before the white man came. Funny, they stopped playin' after your father died. I think now they was protectin' us. Fancy, eh? Those dear, old people. You see, the blackfella knows all 'bout spirits.

It was hard for us with Bill. He couldn't get away from the grog. We had no money. Grog's a curse. I'm glad you didn't marry a drinkin' man. I 'member when Bill used to see all those little red devils sittin' on the end of his bed. He kept beggin' me to take them away. I don't think he should have been takin' that medicine and drinkin' too. It made him worse. Aah, doctors don't know nothin'.

I never told anyone this, but when Gladdie wasn't around, Bill used to call me a bloody nigger. I know he had a bad time in the war, but it hurt me real bad to hear him say that.

He wasn't a bad man, just very sick. Sometimes, he'd put himself in hospital. Sometimes, he'd keep himself awake all night, just pacing up and down, up and down. He really had to fight hard not to kill us. You see, there was part of him that was real good.

I think Bill knew he was goin' to die. He made his peace. He knew where he was goin'. Aah, it was a sad time. If it hadn't been for the grog and the war, he'd have been a different man. A good man.

Bill's parents were mongrels after he died. They didn't help Gladdie. They wasn't interested in you kids. We had no money, nothin' left to sell. We didn't know what we was goin' to do; we was desperate. Gladdie wrote to the Drake-Brockmans in Sydney to see if they could give us a loan. They said they was broke too.

Lois was good to your mother, then. She gave us some money. Frank Potter was good to us. Turned out his heart was as big as his belly.

We was worried 'bout you kids, then. We thought the government might come and get you. They didn't like people like us rearin' kids with white blood in them. Seems like no one took account of the black blood. You belonged to us; Bill's family didn't want you. You kids loved the bush, you got things passed down to you from Gladdie and me. Things that you only got 'cause we was black.

I tried to stay out the way after Bill died. Gladdie could pass for anythin'. You only had to look at me to see I was a native. We had to be careful. 'Tell them they're Indian,' I told her. 'You don't want them havin' a bad time.'

Your mother got work and pretty soon, we had food on the table, good food. Bill drank money and we ate it.

There was men interested in Gladdie — she was a beautiful woman. She didn't want no one. All she wanted was you kids. Good men are rare in this world.

***

Well, Sal, that's all I'm gunna tell ya. My brain's no good, it's gone rotten. I don't want to talk no more. I got my secrets, I'll take them to the grave. Some things, I can't talk 'bout. They not for you or your mother to know.

I'm glad I won't be here in body when you finish that book. I'm glad I'm goin'. You a stirrer, you gunna have a lot of talkin' to do. I think maybe this is a good thing you're doin'. I didn't want you to do it, mind. But I think, now, maybe it's a good thing. Could be it's time to tell. Time to tell what it's been like in this country.

I want you grandchildren to make something of yourselves. You all got brains. One of you could be like Mr Hawke, Prime Minister, one day. I hope you'll never be 'shamed of me. When *you see them old fellas sittin' in the dirt, remember that was me, once.*

Aah, I'm tired of this world now. I want to get on to the next one. I'm afraid I'll go before I'm ready, can you understand that? God's got a spot up there for me. Probably a bit of bush, eh? Old Arthur'll be waitin' for me. I bet he's causin' trouble up there.

I feel real tired now, Sal, the fight's gone out o' me. I got no strength left.

Now you asked me 'bout the future. I got no education, how can I answer a question like that?

But I'll tell you what I'm wonderin'. I'm wonderin' if they'll give the blackfellas land. If it's the one thing I've learnt in this world it's this: you can't trust the government. They'll give the blackfellas the dirt, and the mining companies'll get the gold. That's the way of it.

You know what I think? The government and the white man must own up to their mistakes. There's been a lot of coverin' up.

Well, I'm hopin' things will change one day. At least, we not owned any more. I was owned by the Drake-Brockmans and the government and anyone who wanted to pay five shillings a year to Mr Neville to have me. Not much, is it? I know it's hard for you, Sal, to understand. I been scared all my life, too scared to speak out. Maybe if you'd have had my life, you'd be scared, too.

As for my people, some of them are naughty, they drink too much. Grog's a curse, I've seen what it can do. They got to give it up. They got to show the white man what they made of.

Do you think we'll get some respect? I like to think the black man will get treated same as the white man one day. Be good, wouldn't it? By gee, it'd be good.

The bird call

When Nan finished telling me her story, I was filled with conflicting emotions. I was happy for her because she felt she'd achieved something. It meant so much to be able to talk and to be believed. But I was sad for myself and my mother. Sad for all the things Nan felt she couldn't share.

Although, there was one thing that had quite surprised me. Nan's voice had changed as she reminisced. She could speak perfect English when she wanted to, and usually did, only occasionally dropping the beginning or ending of a word. But in talking about the past, her language had changed. It was like she was back there, reliving everything. It made me realise that, at one stage in her life, it must have been difficult for her to speak English, and therefore to express herself.

But this, too, only made me even more aware of how much we still didn't know. My mind went over and over her story — every word, every look. I knew there were great dark depths there, and I knew I would never plumb them.

I felt, for Mum's sake, I should make one last effort to find out about her sister. So a few nights later, when Nan and I were on our own, I said, 'There's something I want to ask you. I know you won't like it, but I have to ask. It's up to you whether you tell me anything or not.'

Nan grunted. 'Ooh, those questions, eh? Well, ask away.'

'Okay. Has Mum got a sister somewhere?'

She looked away quickly. There was silence, then, after a few seconds, a long, deep sigh.

When she finally turned to face me, her cheeks were wet. 'Don't you understand yet?' she said softly. 'There are some things I just can't talk 'bout.' Her hand touched her chest in that characteristic gesture that meant her heart was hurting. It wasn't her flesh and blood heart. It was the heart of her spirit. With that, she heaved herself up and went out to her room.

I went to bed with a face full of tears and a mind full of guilt. I was so insensitive, sometimes. I should have known better.

The early morning brought some peace. I would never ask her another thing about the past. And I had hope. Why, she'd even admitted that she was pregnant before she had Mum. That was such a big thing. For the moment, it would have to be enough. I stretched and shouted towards the ceiling. 'I'm not giving up, God. Not in a million years. If she's alive, I'll find her, and I expect you to help!'

One night later that week, Nan called me out to her room. 'I'm stuck,' she muttered, 'get me out.'

I laughed when I found her with both arms raised in the air and her head completely covered by the men's singlet she was wearing. I pulled the singlet off and helped her undress. It had become a difficult task for her lately. Her arthritis was worse and cataracts now almost completely obscured her vision.

'Can you give me a rub?' she asked. 'The Vaseline's over there.' I picked up the jar, dobbed a big, greasy lump of it onto her back and began to rub.

'Ooh, that's good, Sally,' she murmured after a while. As I continued to rub, she let out a deep sigh and then said slowly, 'You know, Sal ... all my life, I've been treated real rotten. Just like a beast of the field. And now, here I am ... old. Just a dirty old blackfella.'

My heart felt cut in half. I finally replied in a controlled voice, 'You're my grandmother and I won't have you talk like that. The whole family loves you. We'd do anything for you.'

There was no reply. How hollow my words sounded. How empty and limited. Would anything I said ever help? I hoped that she sensed how deeply I felt. Words were unnecessary for that.

When I finished rubbing, I helped her into her nightclothes. This was no mean feat, as there were so many. It was well into winter now, and Nan was anxious about the cold. I pulled a clean men's singlet over her head, then a fleecy nightgown and a bedjacket. While she pulled a South Fremantle football beanie down over her head, I covered her feet with two pairs of woollen socks. After that, she wound two long scarves around her neck.

'Are you sure you'll be warm enough?' I asked sarcastically.

'I think you better help me into that cardigan,' she answered after a second's thought, 'better safe than sorry.'

Once that was on, I pulled back the rugs and she rolled in on top of her sheepskin. As I passed her a hot-water bottle, she said, 'Aah, Sal, you're too good to me, too good ...'

I went straight to bed myself after that. I curled up and

pretended I was in God's womb. I wanted to contain the deep emotions that were threatening to swamp me. For the first time in my life, the darkness comforted me.

When Nan was getting ready to go home that weekend, she said, 'You'll keep what I told you safe, won't you?'

'Of course I will.'

'You liked it?'

'I thought it was real good.'

'You see, Arthur's not the only one with a good story.'

'He sure isn't!'

'I'll be back on Monday, bring you some goodies. Here,' she squeezed my hand, 'buy the kids something.'

'You've got to stop giving me money,' I protested.

'Come on, Nan,' Mum called from the front porch, 'the dogs'll be hungry for their tea.'

'I'm coming,' Nan replied crossly.

The weekend passed quickly. When Nan hadn't arrived at my place by ten o'clock Monday morning, I began to worry. The phone rang and I rushed to answer it.

'Sally?' It was Mum.

'What's wrong?'

'She's taken a sudden turn for the worse. The doctor says she can't be moved.'

'I'm coming over.'

I hung up. It'd come so suddenly. She'd been living with me for over six weeks. She hadn't seemed like someone who was dying.

From then on, Nan was confined to bed. Jill, Mum and I took four-hourly shifts so she was never alone. Bill and David came when they could. Bill was a great help with the lifting. And when Helen was off duty, she also came and sat with Nan.

One night, Jill and I sat watching Nan sleep. Jill whispered, 'Doesn't seem fair, does it?'

'How do you mean?'

'Well, we're only just coming to terms with everything, finding ourselves, what we really are. And now, she's dying. She's our link with the past and she's going.'

I couldn't look at Jill. She sighed, 'With her gone, we could pass for anything. Greek, Italian, Indian … what a joke. We wouldn't want to, now. It's too important. It'd be like she never existed. Like her life meant nothing, not even to her own family.'

'We're all really changing. I know we don't talk about it, but it's there.'

'When this is over,' Jill said, 'I'm going to stand up and be counted.'

I felt very close to Jill just then. We both stayed there quietly watching as Nan peacefully slept. It was a promise. A promise from our spirits to hers. We would never forget.

Things finally came to a head and Mum asked Ruth, my brother David's wife, if she would mind doing the nightshift. Ruth was a trained nursing aide and had nursed many people with terminal illnesses. She was only too pleased to help. She'd wanted to all along, but knew we were all very sensitive, so had refrained from intruding.

Ruth nursed her so tenderly, and she came to mean a great

deal to Nan. It was lovely to hear Nan say, 'What would I do without her, Sally? She's so good to me.' It made me want to cry when she talked like that. I felt it was a victory that Nan could accept the love that Ruth offered. I felt so proud of Ruth. I hoped that, one day, I could do something special for her.

By the time Nan had been bedridden well over a week, I began to worry she might have a slow, lingering death. I knew she was concerned she might lose her mental faculties before dying. She'd always made me promise that if I noticed she was going a bit funny, I'd tell her.

One night, I confided my fears to Ruth. 'The doctors told us that, in the case of lung cancer, it could go to the brain. I suppose the longer it takes, the more likely it is to happen. Nan would hate that.'

'Do you think we should pray?' Ruth suggested. 'It might help her to let go.'

'It might be a good idea. We'd have to ask her, couldn't force anything on her.'

We moved close to Nan's bedside and clasped her hands. I then said gently, 'Nan, we were wondering if you would like us to pray for you. We would ask God to take you quickly if you like. You know how Ruth's told you you won't go before you're ready? Well, that's true. We won't pray unless you want us to. It's up to you.'

Tears slowly slid from under her closed eyelids. She lay quietly for a few minutes, then squeezed both our hands and said firmly, 'Do it. Please do it.'

I looked at Ruth. 'You do it,' she said.

We bowed our heads. What was I going to say? I tightened

my grip on Nan's hand, cleared my throat and said, 'God …
you know this is about Nan. We really love her and we know
you do too. She's tired of this world now, and she's ready to go.
We know you've got a good place up there. A big, old gum tree
where she can sit and play her mouth organ. Arthur's waiting
for her and the others. Please show your mercy and take Nan
quickly.' When I finished, I couldn't see for tears in my eyes.
Ruth was crying too.

Nan squeezed both our hands and then gently let go. Within a
few minutes, she was asleep.

The following morning, my phone rang very early. 'Hello,' I
said as I lifted the receiver.

'I heard the bird call.' It was Jill's voice.

'What bird call?'

'This morning, about five o'clock. I heard it, Sally. It was a
weird sound, like a bird call, only it wasn't. It was something
spiritual, something out of this world. I think she'll be going
soon.'

After breakfast, I hurried over. There was an air of excitement
about the place. The heaviness that we'd all been living under
seemed to have suddenly lifted.

Mum was mystified about the bird call. I think she felt a little
left out. Jill couldn't understand why Mum hadn't heard it; it'd
been so loud and gone on and on.

When I walked into Nan's room, I couldn't believe my eyes.
She didn't look sick any more. Her face was bright and she was
propped up in bed, smiling. Something had definitely happened,
but none of us knew what. Even Mum and Jill were happier and

bustling around like their old selves.

'Nan, you look really good,' I said in surprise.

'Feel good, Sal.'

I just stood there, smiling. She seemed so contented. Almost like she had a secret. I was so desperate to ask her about the call, but I didn't know where to begin. I sat by the bed and patted her hand.

Just then, Mum popped in. 'Get me some toast, Gladdie,' Nan said cheekily, 'I'm hungry.' Mum rushed out with tears in her eyes.

'Nan,' I said slowly as she looked at me, 'about that call. You weren't frightened when you heard it, were you?'

'Ooh, no,' she scoffed, 'it was the Aboriginal bird, Sally. God sent him to tell me I'm going home soon. Home to my own land and my own people. I got a good spot up there — they all waitin' for me.'

A lump formed in my throat so big I couldn't speak. Finally, I murmured, 'That's great, Nan ...'

Mum popped back in with tea and toast. ''Bout time,' Nan chuckled. She ate a little then lay back. 'Think I'll sleep now,' she sighed. We tiptoed out.

'Tell me about the call again,' I said to Jill.

Jill's face was a mixture of fear, amazement and triumph as she described to Mum and me what happened.

'Wish I'd heard it,' sighed Mum.

'Me too,' I said enviously.

Later, I whispered to Mum, 'You know, Jill must be very special to have heard that call.' Mum agreed. We both wondered what Jill's future held.

Nan had a very peaceful day that day. A happy day. The intense feeling that had surrounded our house for so long was gone, replaced by an overwhelming sense of calm.

At five-thirty the following morning, Ruth rang for an ambulance. Nan had insisted on it.

As they wheeled her out, she grasped Mum's hand one last time. There was an unspoken message in her eyes as she whispered, 'Leave my light burning for a few days.'

They placed her in the ambulance and Ruth climbed in beside her. Mum stood silently watching, accepting Nan's choice, knowing that this was her final sacrifice: she wanted our old family home free of death.

My phone rang at seven that same morning.

'Sally? It's Ruth. Nan died twenty minutes ago. It was very peaceful.'

'Thanks,' I whispered.

I slowly replaced the receiver. I felt stiff. I couldn't move. Tears suddenly flooded my cheeks. For some reason, Jill's words from the previous day began echoing inside of me. I heard the bird call, I heard the bird call. Around and around.

'Oh, Nan,' I cried with sudden certainty, 'I heard it, too. In my heart, I heard it.'

About the author

Sally Morgan is from the Palyku people of the Pilbara region of Western Australia. Born in Perth in 1951, she grew up in suburban Manning. Sally completed a Bachelor of Arts degree at The University of Western Australia in 1974, majoring in Psychology. She also has post-graduate diplomas from The Western Australian Institute of Technology (now Curtin University) in both Counselling Psychology and Computing and Library Studies.

Winner of the 1987 Australian Human Rights Award for Literature and the 1990 Order of Australia Book Prize, Sally's first book, *My Place,* is an Australian classic.

Sally has gone on to write, edit and illustrate many works for both children and adults, including the verse novel *Sister Heart*, winner of the 2016 Prime Minister's Literary Award. She is also a celebrated artist with works in numerous private and public collections in Australia and overseas.